FINDING MY
PACK

LANE WHITT

D1714497

ISBN-13: 978-1530739479
ISBN-10: 1530739470

DEDICATION

For anyone who has ever been told they can't.

TABLE OF CONTENTS

ACKNOWLEDGMENTS

Thank you to all you wonderful people who have supported me through this new adventure. To the new friends I've been privileged to make, I'll never be able to express how grateful I am to you.

CHAPTER ONE

KITTEN

It feels like my heart's gonna beat out of my chest. I try to focus on that feeling instead of the multiple injuries I can feel screaming from my body. I push myself to keep moving forward. Another step, then another... away. Away from the pain, from the fear and the panic. Away from the body of the man who hurt me. The one I left lying on the concrete floor that I called home. He wasn't moving when I left. *I wonder if he...* I stop myself from thinking of that. It won't do any good. What's done is done.

Keep breathing. Keep moving. I see lights up ahead, a few blocks down. That's good, I should be safe there. People are sure to be there. Normal people. People who live in nice houses, sleep in warm beds, go to school and have families. People who don't know what it's like to feel pain like this, who've probably never truly been hurt in their lives. People who don't wonder when the next time they'll eat is, or what they'll have to do to get it. People who are safe, who don't even know what they are safe from. I don't hate them; I just wish I could be one of them.

I feel the scrape of the building next to me on my arm as I make my way down the alley. It hurts, but I need it for support. I feel like lying down and curling into a ball, but that's a dangerous thought. I know the kind of people that lurk here, and nothing good will come from giving in. My legs are moving much slower than I would like, if I fall, I don't think I could get my body moving again. *Just a little further.*

I keep making my way toward the blurry lights. I don't know what I'm going to do once I get there, I just know I have to make it to the lights. My breathing increases. I'm panting now, my chest feeling like it is on fire. My blurred vision is getting worse, my legs feel like lead weights. The helplessness is overwhelming. I can't stop here, I just can't! The thought of moving from the darkness and into the light keeps me moving forward. If I'm going to die, I want to die in the light, not in the shadows I was born in and where I have spent my entire life.

I reach the end of the brick building, feeling desperate now that I won't have it for support. Pushing off from the wall, I will my shaky legs to move. It's rough going, but I finally make it from the crumbling asphalt of the alley to the smooth pavement of a well-maintained street. The lights I have been moving toward are from a tall cement structure surrounded by grass. A small smile forms on my lips as my legs finally give out, and I fall to my knees in front of it. I look up, wanting to say thank you to my beacon. In front of me is an Angel pouring water from a jug into the fountain it rests on. I give a snort of disbelief. *An Angel, really?* The LED lights make the water sparkle as I sag against the side, resting my head against the cool surface.

The adrenaline coursing through my veins makes me shake. At least, that's what I tell myself. Images of tonight flash through my mind. I close my eyes tightly, hoping they will stop. His face greets me in the darkness. A lone tear falls from my lashes as I stare up at the Angel. Why does it have to be like this? Is life truly only about survival? Is this all there is?

I hear movement behind me. I wonder if it's the man from the warehouse, coming to finish me off. Did he follow me? I knew walking in a straight line was a bad move, not that I had much choice. I wish I could have moved farther away. I don't bother looking up. If it's going to happen then, it's going to happen. I'll die here, at the feet of my concrete angel. The angel that guided me to my death. The last image in my head will not be his dead eyes and evil smirk, it will be the shimmering water that looks almost magical. I can't run anymore, my body is too weak to allow it.

A pair of scuffed black boots come into my line of sight. "Are you okay?" A gruff voice asks. I give an un-ladylike snort. What kind of question is that?

"Okay, stupid question. I mean do you need to go to the hospital? We can call an ambulance, or the police if you need."

At the word hospital, my head snaps up, way up. "NO!" I shout. Making the giant take a step back from me. He puts his hands out in front of him, looking to a guy next to him with a "your turn" expression.

"It's okay. We won't do anything you don't want us to. We promise." Says a soft voice, definitely not coming from the giant.

I swing my eyes to the new voice. A guy, maybe my age, maybe a bit older kneels in front of me. I start to scoot away from him, but pain shoots up my side, making me grunt and stop. I almost forgot about my ribs. The sound makes the guy's eyes widen, but he makes no move forward. Good.

"What's your name?" he asks, using that soft voice again. He has a nice voice, as smooth and gentle as still water.

"I'm Kitten." I answer through my teeth, with the adrenaline seeping away, the pain is killing me now. Black is creeping in around the edges of my already compromised vision.

"Interesting name, Kitten. You're hurt; you need a doctor. Let me call an ambulance..."

"No...please, no hospital. I can't go to the hospital. You don't understand." I plead, meeting his concerned eyes. I hope he can see how much I really don't want to go. If I end up at the hospital, they'll call social services. I've worked too hard to stay out of the system for sixteen years. Two more years and I'll be free. Free from the threat of group homes and case workers. Free from hiding in the shadows. I'd rather die right here than lose my freedom.

"Okay. I get it." The guy says. The way he says it, makes me want to believe him. He can't possibly understand though.

He has the prettiest brown eyes I've ever seen; I notice as I'm mentally pleading with him. They look like warm chocolate. Is it possible for someone to have delicious eyes? A sand colored lock of hair falls over one of them. He doesn't even blink. His eyes search mine, searching. My eyelids droop, breaking my contact. I feel the ground rushing up to meet me as my world goes black.

CHAPTER TWO

I wake up feeling as if my head is full of cotton. I blink my eyes a few times, adjusting my blurry eyes. The sun is streaming through a closed window. Bright red curtains are pulled to each side, welcoming in the bright sunshine. I rack my brain trying to figure out where I am and how I got here. I know I've never seen those curtains before. My foggy brain is throwing random thoughts at me, making no sense what-so-ever. Closing my eyes, I focus on putting them in order.

I remember being home, in my corner an abandoned warehouse. It's where I've been staying for the last six months. I remember being tired and reading a book to try and stay awake. I had known going back there was a bad idea. Sleeping when it's dark is always dangerous, and I knew once I was on my make-shift bed I would want to fall asleep. I was staring at the page, feeling myself nodding off. I must have fallen asleep.

I remember waking to hands around my throat. I start to shake, reliving my attack. Even with the warm sun and a blanket around me, I feel cold. The hand on my throat. The dead looking eyes that were right in front of me when my eyes snapped open. The twisted, sick smile on my attacker's face. How he whispered disgusting things in my ear. Telling me what he was going to do to me. I remember prying at his hand. The panic when his hand didn't budge, raking my fingernails down his face to get him to release me. The anger on his face as blood gushed from the wounds. The joy I felt when he let go, and I was able to push him off and run. Despair as he caught up to me. The pain as he grabbed my hair, pushing me down to the ground, his heavy body falling on top of me...

I'm brought out of my thoughts when something blocks the light from the window. Startled, I nearly jump out of my skin letting out a pathetic yelp. Scrambling up the bed, I push my back to the headboard, focusing on the new threat.

Kind, green eyes peer down at me, a worried frown set on a gorgeous pair of pouty, pink lips. The guy is tall, very tall with a slim, athletic build. With the sun shining on him from behind like that, his midnight colored hair has a halo effect.

"Shhh...It's okay. I'm not going to hurt you. I just came to check on you". I don't recognize the man any more than I did the red curtains.

I shove my hair from my face, the action causing a sharp pain in my side. It's then that I remember the rest of last night. The rest of the attack, running away, the fountain, the giant and pretty chocolate eyes.

"Who are you?" I croak, glancing around the room. It doesn't look like a hospital or smell like one for that matter. The carpet is black, the walls white with a red pattern, and everything else in the room is red, a cheery bright red. The lamp shade, the chair, even the entire bed I'm sitting on.

"I'm Kellan. I've been in charge of your care since you were brought here. You're in Tristan's room here in our home." He answers, giving me a small smile.

"In your house, okay. And who is Tristan?" I frown at him. I don't remember coming here or anyone named Tristan. Maybe I didn't escape after all, and this angel is here to welcome me to heaven?

As if he can read my mind Kellan smirks and shakes his head. "Brown eyes, dirty blond hair, about six feet tall? You met him by a fountain."

"You mean the Giant and Chocolate Eyes?" I ask, and then cringe inwardly. I probably should have left that last part out. I didn't mean it the way it sounded, but that's the names I came up with when I picture the two guys from last night.

To my relief Kellan just chuckles. "Yeah, them. The Giant is Ash and um...chocolate eyes is Tristan. Tristan said you didn't want to be taken to the hospital, so he brought you here. I've been looking after you for the past few days." He finishes and shrugs. I blink at him.

"Days? I've been here for days?" What the heck!

Kellan nods his head. "Yeah for a couple of days now. Do you want to call someone? I'm sure people are pretty worried about you by now. If you didn't wake up today, I was going to have to take you to a hospital, no matter what Tristan said." He frowns at that last part, shaking his head a little.

So I guess Chocolate Eyes, or well, Tristan really did get the message and was looking out for me.

"Would you?" Kellan asks again, holding a cell phone out to me. I look down at my lap and shake my head.

"Surely your parents..."

"No," I whisper, cutting him off.

I suck in a breath, attempting to steel myself for what I need to say. I seek out his concerned, green eyes with mine. "Look, I'll be honest with you Kellan because you took care of me when I couldn't. Thanks for that, by the way. I'll find a way to pay you back. I have no one. No one looking for me, no one to call, nobody out there who's worried about me." I say with the blankest face I can manage. Kellan stares back at me, his eyes narrowing and his mouth forming a hard line.

"Please don't call the cops, or social services or whatever. Give me just a few minutes and I'll be out of your way." I say, pushing the soft red blanket from my legs to stand.

Kellan puts a hand on my shoulder, making me pause. "Okay, I get it," he nods once, standing up from his crouched position by the bed, "You no longer have a fever. None of your injuries required stitches, so you should be fine to shower. Just take your time standing up. The bathroom is over there," he points to an open door. "I'll have someone bring you something to wear, towels are already in there."

I blink at him, not understanding. He stands there, towering over me. His black hair is as dark as night, sleek

9

and shiny. He has a tan like he spends a lot of time outdoors. What in the world is this attractive stranger talking about? He wants me to shower here?

"I think I'll just...go now. Thanks."

He huffs. "I'd like it if you stayed. Please?" I search his eyes and find that he's sincere.

"Okay. If you're sure you don't mind. This Tristan guy won't mind if I use his shower?" I ask, biting my lip. I would love a real shower.

"I'm sure, and he won't mind a bit," Kellan answers with a tight smile. "Just...stay. Okay?" I give him a short nod.

He walks to the door, closing it behind him. I stare at the closed door for a minute, wondering why he would ask me to stay. He might call the police when I'm in there. Whatever. I'm sure I look a mess, and I get a real shower for once, it's worth it.

I stand slowly like Kellan said to do, and my body protests the movement. Oh my god, I hurt! Taking deep breaths, I make my way to the bathroom. I'm exhausted by the time I reach the doorway.

Wow...it's the biggest bathroom I have ever seen. In the corner is a walk-in shower with a door made entirely of glass. On the back wall is a tub big enough to house a small family, with three steps leading up to it. The floor is done in a black and red checker pattern with matching, smaller tiles on the walls of the tub and shower.

I step onto the furry-looking black rug in front of the sink and wiggle my toes. It tickles. I check out the double sink set in a long counter. It has tons of bottles of god-knows-what in different colors and sizes. I want to look at each one, but the shower is calling my name. I can smell myself, and it's certainly not roses.

As I'm turning for the shower, I catch a glimpse of myself in the mirror. Oh, Holy Jesus! I must feel better than I look, and that's saying something because I feel like road kill. My long, wavy, almost-white hair is more of a dishwater brown and stuck to my head in clumps and tangles. My bottom lip is busted, and dried blood makes a line down my chin. Nice. A faint bruise on my left eyebrow stands out on my pale, sickly looking skin, a greenish color almost matching my pale green eyes. Cuts and scrapes mar the skin of my arms, elbows, and knees. Bruises are pretty much everywhere, in different shades of healing. I lift my shirt off and look at the deep purple bruise over my ribs.   I don't think any are broken, thankfully.

I can't stand to look at myself anymore, so I finish undressing and start the shower. I make the water as hot as I can stand it. The water stings as it rains down over my battered body, but mostly I feel pure bliss. Cleaning up in a public restroom is no match for this. A few tears slide down my face before I force them to stop. I can't help but think of what happened. I put my face under the spray as if to hide them, although I'm the only one here, and I can't hide from myself.

After a two-minute pity party, I suck it up and begin the task of making myself feel human again. Washing my hair three times with the best smelling shampoo ever, gently scrubbing my skin free of dirt and tiny debris, I feel like I'm coming back to myself. I see a razor on a shelf and decide to use it too, taking care to avoid areas with more scrapes than bare skin. I feel a bit guilty using someone else's razor but who knows when the next time

I'm going to get a shower this nice? After I'm done washing, I stand under the spray for as long as I can stand it. My legs start to shake, and my body is too tired to stay in here, no matter how much I wish I could.

I wrap a fluffy, red towel around myself and peek my head out of the door leading to the bedroom. I spot a bundle of clothes on the bed and make my way to the door leading out of the room. I lock it then grab the clothes and head back into the bathroom, locking that door as well. There are at least two boys that live here; one can never be too careful.

I take inventory of the clothes. I instantly know they are going to be too big for me, but they'll do. I consider wearing my clothes but after seeing the dirty, bloodstained mess, I think better of it. There are a pair of black boxer-briefs that actually don't fit too badly, a pair of soft, gray, drawstring sweats that I could fit two of me in, and a bright red long-sleeved t-shirt that hangs to mid-thigh. I roll the sleeves up and look in the mirror. Good enough. At least I'll be warm when I leave here.

There's a knock on the door, and I jump, turning toward the sound. "Y-Yes?" I call out, cursing my shaky voice.

I roll my eyes at myself, unlock the door and open it. In front of me stands an absolutely devastating boy. Way too pretty to simply be called handsome. He has light brown hair, cut stylishly. Short in the back with chin-length hair in the front with a bright blue streak. The color matches his unnaturally blue eyes perfectly which are framed with thick, dark lashes. His cheek bones would give billboard models a run for their money. He's tall and lean, but I can see the muscles in his chest and arms through the tight, thin t-shirt he's wearing. It's blue of course. I bet I could guess his favorite color. He's wearing light colored denim jeans, and his shoes are bright white. I bet they are brand new like he just walked in here after taking them out of the box.

The boy clears his throat, making me pause in my assessment of him. I look back to his amazing eyes. He blushes a little and looks down, rubbing the back of his neck with one hand. I blush too. I can't believe I just checked him out so thoroughly like that. What's wrong with me? I don't react this way to anybody.

"Thought you might want this," He says while waving around a hairbrush.

"Oh, thanks." I take the brush and move to sit on the bed. The boy takes a seat on a chair in the corner that I noticed earlier. I pull my ratted hair over my shoulder and start brushing out the ends.

"I'm Logan. Feeling better after your shower, Kitten?" He asks as he watches me from across the room.

"I'm okay, just a bit tired. Do you live here too?" I ask.

Logan nods his head. "We all do, although Jace only stays here part-time," He says with a smirk.

I try to think if I've met Jace yet while still trying to de-tangle my hair. I don't think I have. My arms are getting tired already, it hurts to lift them above my head like this.

"I don't think I've met him. How many of you are there? I mean...that live here?" I blush slightly as I wonder if that was rude to ask.

He keeps his eyes on my hands that are now shaking with the effort to keep going. "There are seven of us.

Kellan, Finn, Tristan, Ash, Reed, Jace and me. Eight if you include Remy."

Wow, that's a heck of a lot of boys. They all live in one house together? Why? And what does he mean by if you include Remy?

"Is this a dorm or something? Are you students?" I ask.

I hit another snag in my hair and drop my hand. I give up, setting the brush down. Logan looks fidgety for a moment then sighs and stands, coming over to me. He takes my hand, pulling me up and gently and snags the brush from the bed.

"Come on," he tells me as he pulls me back to the bathroom. I follow along, curious as to what he's doing. He stops me in front of the toilet, putting the lid down.

"Sit," he orders. I do as he says. "Turn for me, just to the side a bit." I do, and he walks to the sink, grabbing one of the mystery bottles. He squirts some white stuff in his hands, rubbing them together. Walking back to me he rubs the stuff over my hair, starting at the top and moving down to the ends.

"What is that stuff?" I ask him.

"Just some leave-in conditioner. I only put a little in, it'll help to untangle your hair and repair some of the damage. I'll add more once I get it brushed out."

At that, he starts brushing my hair. It's weird. I've never had anyone brush my hair for me. He's a lot gentler than I usually am. I like this. Fifteen minutes later he's done, and my hair looks the length it actually is. All ratted out you'd never know it hangs down to my waist.

Logan steps back and holds his hand out to me. I put my hand in his, and he helps me up, pulling me over to the sink with him. He starts humming as he uses more conditioner stuff then opens a drawer, pulling out a hairdryer. I just blink at him through the mirror the whole time. Is this normal? Is this what normal people do? He acts as if it is, so I just go with it. He proceeds to dry and play with my hair for what seems like forever. My legs start shaking again after standing for so long. Logan notices and sighs.

"Well, I guess I'm done playing, for now." He grins at me, and I have to blink several times. God, he's beautiful. He looks like a devilish angel smiling like that. Someone raps on the door with their knuckles and Kellan pokes his head around the door.

"I wondered what took you so long Logan; you were just supposed to drop the brush off. Guess I should have known better." Kellan says with a chuckle. "Bring Kitten downstairs, I need to feed my patient. She hasn't eaten for days." He drawls out dramatically.

Kellan walks out, and my eyes connect with Logan in the mirror. He grins at me. "Time to meet the rest of the crew." He takes my hand, interlocking our fingers, it shocks me, but Logan acts like it's okay, so once again, I just go with it.

Logan leads me down a long hallway with several closed doors on either side. I wonder what's in them. More bedrooms? We come upon a staircase (if you can call it that). It's wide and has an intricate hand-carved banister. There's a loft-like area then, on the other side, is an exact replica of the staircase in front of me. So I guess it's a grand entrance... thing?

We move down the stairs slowly. Logan is looking back every few steps. Probably to make sure I don't fall down since my tired body is still shaking. We finally arrive at the bottom. How many steps do you really need for Christ's sake? Logan tugs me along while I try to look into the rooms we pass. I just catch glimpses here and there. From what that I have seen so far, these people are pretty well off. I feel out of place. Here I am, walking beside the most beautiful creature I have ever seen, barefoot, wearing someone else's clothes, looking every bit the street rat that I am. I have never felt so much like unwanted trash in my life, and that's saying something. I was born trash. Literally, I was found in a dumpster with my umbilical cord still attached.

As we make our way down a hallway, I hear voices. Lots of voices. I stop, making Logan stop too. He looks at me with a curious expression on his face. I bite my lip running my tongue over the split in the middle. I look around, wondering where the front door is. Maybe I should go now?

"Hey, what's wrong?" Logan asks me.

"Um...maybe I should leave," I reply.

He bends down catching my eyes with his amazing blue ones. "It'll be okay, no one is going to hurt you, Kitten, we're just having breakfast."

I nod, and he continues to pull me toward the voices. A little faster now though, like if he doesn't get me there quickly I'm going to turn and run. It's like he knows me because that's exactly what I feel like doing.

We round a corner and enter the kitchen. Or at least, I think it's a kitchen. The space is huge. Stainless steel is everywhere, including both refrigerators and a flat cooktop that rivals the one in the diner I work at. It looks very...clean and clinical. It all seems a bit much to me, but I guess it would have to be big to accommodate the seven or eight people who live here. If it weren't for the mouthwatering smells wafting to my nose, I would never enter.

Once they see us, all eyes turn in our direction, conversations ceasing. I maneuver my way behind Logan to hide, but he tugs my hand, forcing me to stand beside him again. I look up and see him looking down at me in amusement. I glare back at him and pull my hand out of his. The traitor, I thought we were friends now.

He chuckles lightly as he guides me to sit at the end of a long kitchen island surrounded by tall stools in matching stainless steel. Everyone else is already seated there. I keep my eyes focused on Kellan. I already know him and even though he was confusing, he was nice to me. I don't want to look at the rest of the guys; it will only make me nervous.

"I'll make you a plate, just sit tight," Logan tells me while walking over to a long counter where there are several platters piled high with food.

"I already made her a plate, on the end there," Kellan calls out, pointing. I glance up at him and give him a small smile in thanks.

Kellan is seated directly across from me, with the Giant, Ash? Next to him. When my eyes meet his, he gives me a short nod. I nod back and look away quickly. He's even more intimidating in the daylight. His inky black hair hangs in his eyes, but I can still see that they are dark, just like the rest of him. Ash has tanned skin and is wearing a dark gray t-shirt over his massively built frame.

I feel the air shift beside me, and I look over, straight into chocolaty brown eyes. I remember those eyes from before; Kellan had said his name is Tristan. His sand-colored hair is styled in a messy way, kind of shaggy. I want to reach out and brush the strand that falls in his eyes away. What an odd thought. I look at what he's wearing and blush deeply. He has on a red shirt that looks almost exactly like the one I'm wearing. So, I have this guy's shirt, slept in his bed, and showered in his bathroom where I used his razor. Oh God, I'm such a bum. I look down at the table, embarrassment washing over me.

Logan comes back with a large plate in his hand and sets it down in front of me before taking a seat beside Ash. I stare at the plate of food. Is this all for me? There's so much of it. On the plate is a small pancake with a strawberry on top, an egg, sausage links, a couple strips of bacon and a biscuit. Is this what they eat every morning? No wonder they are all so big and built.

Tristan nudges me with his shoulder. "Hey, what's the matter? I can make you something else if you'd like." He says with a frown on his handsome face. He must be crazy or something. Who wouldn't like this?

"Oh. No, that's not it." I shake my head quickly, biting my lip.

"Then what is it?" Tristan replies in a confused tone.

I take in a breath, releasing it quickly. "What exactly do I have to do for you after I eat this?"

I meet his eyes, my stomach in knots. If it's bad, then I'm out of here. People don't just give food away. They obviously want something from me. The taking care of me, the shower and the clothes, now with the food...

Tristan frowns before his eyes widen, and he inhales sharply. I hear a fork clatter against a plate and someone starts choking. I look around and see everyone looking at me. Tristan shifts uncomfortably on his seat.

"Uh, Kitten, you don't have to do anything. You're hungry; we have food. Just eat." He says with a sad look on his face though I don't know why. I don't know if I should trust him but, not being one to talk myself out of a good meal, I look back to the pile of food in front of me.

"Oh shit, I forgot your fork, Sweetie. Hold on a sec," Kellan says, popping up from his seat.

"And a drink, I'll get her some juice," says one of the boys I still don't know with blonde hair and a white shirt.

Ash slides a napkin at me across the table. I nod at him again. I like that he gets my simple form of communication. Tristan scoots the butter and syrup in front of my plate. The way they move together feels a bit odd. I'm starting to feel a tad overwhelmed here, I'm not used to this kind of attention. They are staring again. Do they think I don't know how to use a fork or something?

I pick up the strawberry, take a bite and let the most delicious flavor roam over my tongue. I have no idea what happens after that. One minute there is a plate full of food in front of me, the next, well, there's not. Confused, I glance at Tristan. His face is a mix of shock, amusement, horror and pride all at once. It's then I realize that my cheeks are puffed out, full of food like a chipmunk. I blush and look down, chewing the massive amount of food still in my mouth. I think it's the pancake, but I can't be sure. How embarrassing to have wolfed down my food like a rabid animal in front of these beautiful boys.

"Do you want more?" Tristan asks quietly in that kind voice of his.

"No, thank you." I take a sip of my orange juice to wash the food down.

I keep my eyes on the table in front of me while the guys finish eating their breakfast like civilized people do. I listen as they chat casually with each other, talking about things they did yesterday and plans for today, about nothing and everything really. I don't join in with them even as a few of them try to include me. I don't fit in here with this group of friends; I don't know what I would say to any of them.

I hear a door slam from somewhere in the house before a loud voice calls out. Someone on the other side of Tristan calls back that we're in the kitchen. Conversation halts as we wait for the newcomer.

"What the fuck is going on? Ten messages! Did someone fucking die?" The voice booms as a man, definitely not a boy, walks into the kitchen.

His gray eyes lock onto me instantly. He stops and leans against the frame. He stares at me, and I stare back. I shrink into myself and unknowingly lean towards Tristan. I don't realize I'm shaking until he puts an arm around my waist, so my back is to his front. This guy is scary as all get out, and he looks angry.

I feel Tristan's lips at my ear as he whispers. "It's alright Kitten, I promise that no one here will hurt you." I feel comforted by his words and his voice, but I still won't look away from the man.

He's sizing me up; I can feel it. I feel like he can see right through me, and the thought makes me shiver. Ash stands, making his way over to the man with the piercing eyes and copper-colored hair. He walks out of the kitchen with the man behind him. I can hear their equally gruff voices, but can't make out what they are saying.

I look over my shoulder at Tristan, and he removes his arm, turning to look at the rest of the guys at the table. They meet each other's eyes, communicating without saying a word. Boys are weird. I feel left out of the weird eye talk. I think about crossing mine just to be included, wondering what message I'd be sending.

Kellan catches my eye, and he gives me a reassuring smile. "So Kitten, you've met me, Tristan, Logan, and Ash, and you've just met Remy. This here is Reed," He says, pointing at the lanky blond guy with the white shirt on the other side of Tristan.

Reed grins and waves his fingers in greeting. He has a really nice smile. It looks genuine, not forced. With his blond hair and pale skin he looks more like me and less like the others I've met. I like his eyes too, with flecks of blue, green and gold they might be the most interesting color of hazel I've ever seen.

Kellan points further down the table. "That handsome lad there is Finn, my twin brother." Finn lifts his hand a bit, and his cheeks tint pink as he mouths the word 'hi'. Maybe he said it out loud and I just didn't hear him. He's a carbon copy of Kellan. Jet black hair, high cheekbones, full pouty lips and green eyes. Although Kellan's look like grass and Finn's look more like a mint green. Maybe this is a house for models? I've never really paid attention to guys or dwelled on their attractiveness, but something tells me the guys in this house are above average in that respect.

I frown at that thought. All these beautiful boys live here in this house and I...I just don't belong here. They are all friends, and I'm just some girl they found. They communicate without words and move around each other with ease, and I just sit here awkwardly. I should really leave now, get out of their way so they can go about their day. They've been so nice, and I hate the thought of leaving, but I've done nothing to deserve their kindness, and the guilt of not being able to repay them is eating me up inside.

I stand up, holding my hand out to Tristan to shake. "It was really nice meeting all of you. Thank you so much, for everything. I'll try to return the clothes when I get a chance." Tristan doesn't take my hand, he just stares at me. Alright then. I turn and head for the door.

Long fingers gently encircle my wrist and keep me in place. I look over my shoulder at Tristan. "Where are you going, Kitten?" He questions.

I open my mouth to respond then stop. I don't have an answer. I can't go back home to the warehouse. If the man that attacked me lived then, he could be waiting for me. If he didn't live...well then I guess that would make me a murderer. Oh my God! I'm probably a murderer!

I pull my arm away from Tristan, who now looks very concerned. My breath is coming in short spurts, and my heart rate has accelerated. I don't have a place to go. All my stuff is in the warehouse. It's not much, but it's all I had. I don't know what I'm going to do. I'm a killer. These boys are being nice to a killer. They invited a murderer into their home, and they don't even know it!

I turn and run, making my way down the hall as fast as I can. My focus is on the double doors straight ahead of me. I have to get out of here. The gray-eyed man steps into the hallway from a room on the right. Before I can even think the word stop, I crash into him. Hard. The result is the same as a fly against a windshield. He doesn't move an inch as I go splat. I bounce off of his brick-like chest and land sprawled on the floor at his feet.

Now I don't know if I can't breathe because I'm having a panic attack, because of the pain from my collision and fall, or because I was running. Either way, my lungs feel like someone's squeezing them, and I can't get enough oxygen. As I'm staring at the ceiling, gasping for air, a face looms in front of me. It's Kellan. Or maybe Finn? No, grass green eyes look down at me. It's Kellan. His pouty lips are moving, but I can't hear him over the sound of blood rushing in my ears. My eyes flick back and forth from his mouth to his eyes. He wants me to do something. But what?

I suck in as much air as I can, holding my breath. Kellan shakes his head no. I let the air out of my lungs and start hyperventilating again, the edges of my vision start to go black. I focus on his face, trying to understand what he wants. He looks so calm and collected. I want to be calm and collected too. His nose is flaring out like he is trying to smell something in the air, and then his sweet breath blows in my face from his open lips. He repeats that a few times, I try to mimic him, thinking he is showing me what to do. I inhale through my nose and exhale through my mouth. Kellan smiles and nods his head yes. It takes a few times before I feel like I can get a decent amount of air. Kellan stays with me, and I'm grateful. I focus on him, soaking up his calm.

I don't know how long we stay that way. Looking into each other's eyes, breathing in together, exhaling at the same time, our breath mixing. Eventually, I feel as though I can breathe normally. Kellan runs his fingers through my hair, tucking the long strands behind my ear. I watch as he stands, noticing that all seven of them are standing around us. I put both hands over my face and groan. How many times can a girl embarrass herself in one morning?

Strong hands wrap around my wrists and start to pull me up. Once I'm standing I feel a bit dizzy and start to sway. A large hand cups my head as an arm snakes around my waist and I'm pulled into a hard chest. After the dizzy spell passes, I realize how awkward a position I'm in. My eyes travel up the body that I'm pressed into, and a shocked gasp escapes my lips. It's that man. Remy. He sees my reaction and slowly releases me. I take a step back and look at the floor.

Remy's booming voice instructs everyone into the living room. I contemplate telling him I was just leaving, but one look at his face makes me change my mind. He clearly meant me as well. I see no point in arguing, for now. I follow everyone else since I don't know where I'm supposed to go, feeling the burn of Remy's eyes on my back the whole way there.

CHAPTER THREE

Once they all found seats on the over-stuffed, red u-shaped couch and the chairs on either side of it, Remy stood before us. With his arms crossed over his chest and his feet set apart in a defensive stance, he looked...mad. Scary too.

I walked in last, not knowing where to sit, or even if I wanted to, I chose to stand. I'm not sure why we got called in here or what happens now. Tristan waves his hand to get my attention. I look at him, he smiles, patting the couch between him and Reed. I shake my head, and he rolls his eyes at me in return.

Standing, he walks over to me and grips my fingers with his, pulling me back to the couch with him. I sigh heavily, but Tristan just laughs and pokes me in the ribs. I inhale sharply, feeling slightly sick to my stomach from the pain. I have not been taking it easy on my body today.

Tristan opens his mouth to say something as a hand materializes and pops him on the back of his neck, hard.

"She's hurt, you idiot."

"Ow! Shit...I forgot. I was going to say sorry. Violence is never the answer Kellan." Tristan says, rubbing the sting out of his neck.

Kellan leans forward to look at me and I beam at him. I think Kellan's growing on me. He smiles back just as widely. Dear God, here I thought the boy was attractive before... I gulp and avert my eyes, finding Remy. He's just standing there, watching us. The other boys are talking quietly among themselves. I get the sense that we're waiting, but I don't know what for.

Since I'm still sort of mad at Tristan for poking me, I turn away and watch Reed. He has a notebook and a pencil, drawing some type of intricate flower. There are other drawings on the page too. He's good. Really good, I note.

"What kind of flower is that?" I ask.

Before he has a chance to answer I hear the door slam again. Are they always this loud? We all watch the doorway. A few moments later another good-looking guy comes in and takes a seat on the arm of the couch, tipping his chin to Remy. I roll my eyes. Don't they have any ugly friends? Or at least, an average looking one? I'm not typically one to notice such things buy these guys make it hard not to.

"Right...now that we're all here we can get started. First things first, Kellan switch places with Tristan in case Kitten has another episode." Remy orders.

Episode? I have one panic attack in my whole life and he makes me sound like a nut, ugh! I don't say anything, though, I'm just ready for this to be over. The sooner the better. Tristan pats my knee before standing and Kellan scoots next to me.

"Let's run through the facts. On Tuesday night, at approximately eleven o'clock pm, Tristan and Ash saw Kitten running to the Angel fountain on West Mound Street. After approaching, Kitten stated, in no uncertain terms, that she did not want to be taken to a hospital. After which, she passed out. Tristan made the decision to bring her here. Ash called Kellan on the way. Upon arriving here, Kitten was placed in Tristan's room at his insistence. Kellan, after leaving work early, arrived and took a look at Kitten. What was your initial assessment Kellan?" Remy asks.

Kellan makes eye contact with Tristan and shifts his weight a bit. "Since Kitten was unresponsive and she had multiple contusions on her torso, my recommendation was for her to be taken to a medical facility," Kellan responds just as formally as Remy. I don't have a clue why they're talking like this and talking about ME like this.

"Then why was Kitten not taken right then?" Remy's gray eyes bore into Kellan like a drill.

"Tristan was adamant that I do everything for her that I could. He stressed how panicked she was at the mere thought of a hospital." This time, Kellan is less formal and more defensive. "It was clear to me, Remy, that the girl had been through an ordeal, and I didn't want to force her into something she clearly didn't want. I saw no immediate, life-threatening injury. I was mostly worried about internal bleeding, and that's something I could keep an eye out for and make the call if she got to that point. Which she didn't." He finishes and reaches for my hand. I let him hold it. I'll always be grateful to this green eyed boy for respecting my wishes.

Remy watches our clasped hands for a moment before he continues, "Kellan then stayed with Kitten for approximately four days, keeping us updated on her condition and progress. We won't go over all that, but we know she was showing great improvement. That brings us to today." He states, those blazing eyes falling on me. "Miss Kitten awoke, having a brief conversation with Kellan. Would you like to tell the rest of what was said Kitten, or would you rather Kellan do so?"

My cheeks are flaming red now, I'm sure. I can feel several pairs of eyes on me, but I just stare down at my lap. What the hell is this? What does any of this matter? Kellan squeezes my hand, and I squeeze back. It's nice. A bright spot in what is quickly becoming a torturous situation. Thankfully, Kellan speaks up, so I don't have to.

"I'm fairly certain that she was having a flashback when I approached her this morning. I offered her a phone to use, but she said..." Kellan looks at me, I nod my head once, telling him it's okay. "She said that she has no one. I assume she meant she was homeless with no parental units." He finishes, squeezing my hand again.

"Is that true? Are you homeless and parentless?" Remy says as if that isn't the most painful truth to admit to. I nod again, narrowing my eyes at him. Why is he doing this? Why do they all need to know? It's not their business.

"Kitten was then given clearance to bathe, brought down for breakfast, and which immediately after, Miss Kitten attempted run from the house." At this point,

Remy looks uncomfortable.

The newest guy, I assume Jace, speaks up, "What do you mean tried? If she wanted to leave then why didn't she? Are we holding her hostage now?" That last one is a good question. I didn't even think of it.

Remy stiffens and glares at Jace, "Of course not. I happened to step out of my office just as she came barreling down the hallway. She uh, bounced off me and landed on the floor, where she proceeded to have an anxiety attack of some sort. Following that episode, we came in here, waiting for you." He says, giving Jace a pointed look.

I can't stand his formal tone and how he keeps talking about me like I'm not in the room. This whole thing is stupid. I raise my hand and clear my throat, "If we're stating facts, Sir, I'd like to point out that I was having a *panic* attack *before* I ran into a concrete wall."

He smirks at me. Actually *smirks*! I guess I didn't really prove anything. At least I got to talk back. No, it doesn't change anything, I feel a little better, though.

"Right, I'm glad you spoke up Kitten. Now it's time for you to explain not only what happened to you Tuesday night but also why you chose to flee today." The smirk is gone from Remy's face now and replaced by a blank expression.

Kellan is trying to tug his hand from mine. I wasn't aware I had a death grip on him until now. I let go of him, and he shakes his hand out. I don't want to answer. It's not their business. I don't know why they care. They won't care at all when they learn I may have killed someone. Maybe I owe them an explanation for the hospitality they've shown me. No, I never asked any of them for anything. Saying I didn't want to go to a hospital isn't the same as begging to be taken to someone's house. They could have just left me there. I do owe Kellan at least. He did take care of me for four days. Which is more than anyone else has ever done. Maybe I could just tell them about the attack. But then I'd have to tell them about leaving the guy's body. They might also ask what I was doing there, and that's a longer and more painful story than I'm willing to share.

I open my eyes and see warm chocolate. Tristan is in front of me now. "I promised you'd be okay Kitten, I meant it. We're just trying to help. There are a lot of us, and meetings like these keep us all up to date. I know that was hard for you. You can get up and leave right now if that's what you really want. No one will stop you. I hope you don't though, I hope you stay. Let us help you, we can and we will if you just let us. But for us to help you we have to know what's going on." He's looking at me with those mesmerizing, pleading eyes. That soft voice, telling me everything is going to be okay.

Truth is, I don't have anywhere to go when I leave here. I don't even have shoes since I ran without mine that night. There's something about him that makes me want to trust him. I want to believe him. I want to tell him, I want to tell him everything. I want him to know me. But I don't know if I could stand it when I tell him I'm a killer. Tristan is making it sound like I have options, but I don't. Not really. If I get up and walk out of here right now, I won't make it a week on the street. Not with my injuries, without shoes, and none of my supplies. I suppose the worst that could happen would be that I tell them, and they call the cops. I would eventually get out of prison since that man attacked me first, right? I would, at least, get to keep my life.

I'm still looking into Tristan's eyes, wanting to remember them as they are now. I take a deep breath and whisper, "I killed a man."

CHAPTER FOUR

Tristan's eyes widen, and he moves back, away from me. I look at my lap again. I knew that would happen. It still stings, though. Tears stream down my face. I curse them; I hate crying in front of people.

"I didn't mean to," I whisper. Tristan walks away, I don't watch where he goes. Kellan tries to take my hand again. This time, I don't let him. I don't deserve to have him comfort me.

The room is completely silent. Only my occasional sniffles are providing any sound. After what seems like forever, Remy speaks again. "Start from the beginning Kitten, tell us what happened on Tuesday." I take a breath, pick a spot on the wall beside Remy to focus on and begin.

"Are you familiar with the Crate District off West

Fifth? Where all the abandoned warehouses are?" I ask but continue without waiting for an answer. "Well, I live in the third one right off the main road. I was tired after I worked a double shift. I try to work only at night so I can sleep during the day, but I couldn't pass up the money. It was getting late, but I thought it might be fine if I was there, so long as I stayed awake. I was reading my book, and..." I pause, trying not to let the memories overtake me.

"Go on Kitten," Reed says from next to me. He sounds sad, staring down at his notebook. Picking at the edges.

"I fell asleep. I woke up choking, a hand around my throat. I scratched him and was able to run, but I wasn't fast enough. He got me back to the ground. He kept hold of my hair and started hitting me, punching my thighs to try and open them. When that didn't work, he hit me across the face and punched my chest."

I remember laying there curled up in a ball, thinking I was going to die, hoping I would before he got what he wanted. My breathing picks up, and I'm trying my hardest to hold it together. I close my eyes and breathe deeply like Kellan showed me earlier.

"He started kicking me. In my back and my sides. Yelling at me. Saying that it didn't have to be like this. That if I just laid there he wouldn't have to kill me. He tried to kick me in the face, but I caught his foot and rolled, pulling him down. I saw a brick next to me..." I choke out a sob, covering my face with my hands.

I wipe away more tears and continue, not opening my eyes this time. "I...hit him. He was on his back, and I....I-I hit him as hard as I could. Then I hit him again. I smashed the brick into his forehead the second time. He stopped moving so I got up and ran as fast as I could. I ran to the lights." I finish and double over, crying so hard it hurts my whole body. I know it makes me look weak, but I don't care. I am. I wasn't smart enough or fast enough or strong enough. Sure, I got away, but at what cost?

A hand is on my back now, rubbing up and down. A different hand is massaging my head. Someone pries my hands away from my face and guides me to sit up.

Remy is in front of me. He reaches out and runs his thumb over the crest of my cheek. "Kitten...that wasn't your fault. It was self-defense. You have nothing to feel bad about. I'm so..." His voice cracks and he clears his throat, "I'm so sorry that happened to you."

His words calm me enough to stop my sobbing. I inhale and exhale shakily. Remy stands and gives Kellan a pointed look. The hand massaging my head falls away as Kellan follows Remy out of the room. Logan comes over and pulls me to stand.

"Let's get you some water, okay?" Logan's eyes are shiny, and his amazingly groomed hair from earlier looks disheveled like he's been running his hands through it. The bright blue streak is flipped over onto the other side of his head now.

"Uh...Logan," I whisper, my throat feeling raw.

"Yeah?" He says warily.

"Your hair looks like crap," I say, giving him a smile.

He busts out laughing, wrapping an arm around my back, and pressing his lips into my hair. The tension drains from the room as the other guys laugh too. Logan pulls back, hooking our fingers together and leads me back to the kitchen for a glass of water. Finn sits next to me and presses his side into mine slightly. He doesn't say anything though. Won't even meet my eyes.

"How are you feeling Kitten?" Kellan asks.

"To be honest, I'm pretty tired. How is that possible when I slept for several days?"

Kellan's lips lift a little, "You were severely dehydrated when I first saw you. I gave you fluids through an IV so you should be a bit better. Dehydration makes you tired though. You also had a fever, which can leave you feeling drained. You should probably go rest for a while."

I blink at him. "You guys aren't making me leave now that you know..."

His hand comes up to cup my face with his warm fingers. "No, we'd really like it if you stayed." I'm sure my confusion shows on my face, but I really am tired.

"Would you like me to give you something for the pain?" He offers sweetly.

I shake my head. "No, no drugs. Ever." I don't care how crazy I sound. I've lived on the street; I know how easy addiction can get its claws into you. I've seen the monster it turns people into. I've also always had a secret fear that my mother was an addict. If that's true, then I might already be an addict.

Kellan looks a little surprised, and I don't know how I feel about that. Did he think I was a druggie? "Just some ibuprofen then, hmm?"

"That would be nice," I say gratefully.

"Good," he says, walking to a cabinet and shaking out two pills, bringing them to me. I take a sip of water and swallow them down.

"Thank you," I whisper.

"You can use my room, Kitten," Reed says quietly. He still looks sad but tries to smile at me anyway.

I nod my head, following him down the hallway to the stairs. How in the world did I forget about the stairs? "No wonder you're all so in shape," I mutter to myself.

Reed's lips tilt up at the corners so he must have heard me anyway. Once we reach the top of the never-ending stairs we head in the opposite direction of Tristan's room. Reed opens the door, and it's like walking into a cloud. Everything is white. Like, the cleanest, purest white there ever was. The double bed up against the window, the tall wardrobe closet, the carpet, the nightstand, *everything*. Not a spec of color to be seen.

He walks to the bed, pulling the top blanket back for me. He lets out a long yawn and gives me a sleepy smile. Oh, that was cute.

"Are you tired too?" I ask him.

"A little," he shrugs a lean shoulder.

I think about it for a minute. He's tired, and now I'm taking his room. They've been so nice to me, maybe I should be nice back?

"Um, you could stay. If you wanted to. You don't have to, of course, it's just that if you're tired, well, I'm going to be sleeping too." I rush out, making an idiot out of myself.

"You sure?" Reed asks. I nod quickly. Truth is, I don't really want to be alone.

I make my way over to the bed and crawl in. Mmmm... It feels like a cloud too. Reed sits on the other side of the bed, taking his shoes and socks off. When he's done, he slips under the fluffy comforter. I face away from him and bring the blanket up so I can snuggle my face into it. It smells divine. We lay there for several minutes. I'm sleepy, but one thing is bugging me.

"Reed?" I whisper, hoping he's not asleep yet.

"Yeah?" He replies softly.

"Why are you so sad?" I blurt out.

It's none of my business. He just seemed so happy and friendly when I met him at breakfast, something has changed. I flip over so I can see his face when he answers, "I'm sad because of what happened to you, Kitten. Hearing you say that stuff, I'm sad you're hurt, you could have died, most people would have. Mostly I'm sad that you have nobody to take care of you. I hate that you've been alone." He's looking at me while he speaks. His eyes are shiny. It breaks my heart a little.

"But you don't know me Reed. You shouldn't be sad for me. Please don't let me make you sad. No one should ever be sad in a bed made of clouds." I say, trying to make him smile.

It works, his eyes turn playful, and he laughs. "Bed made of clouds huh?"

"Yeah, your cloud-bed. I think I'm in love with it." I giggle. The sound strange to my own ears.

Reed shifts, turning on his side to face me, his hands snaking under the pillow. I do the same. "Go to sleep silly girl," He says playfully, kissing my forehead before closing his ever-changing eyes. I close mine too. I drift off, dreaming of fluffy clouds snuggling up to me.

I wake with a jolt. My eyes fly open and panic sets in. Where am I? I take in all the white. Oh yes, the cloud. Reed. I'm in Reed's room in a house full of boys that I know nothing about. They have been nothing but kind to me so far, even though I think they are weird.

The door opens after a light knock and Finn cautiously enters. "Hey, sleepyhead," He says.

"Hey. What time is it?" I reply, looking to the window. The sun is in almost the same place it was when I fell asleep.

"It's ten o'clock in the morning...Sunday." Oh great, I slept for another full day. "Kellan wants to see you before you eat, so come on, I'll walk you down there."

I get up and follow Finn out into the hallway. He leads me down the stairs to a closed door. He's about to knock, but the door swings open and Kellan's standing there with a smile. He gestures for us to come in. The room looks just like how I imagine a doctor's office would look like. On one wall are a cabinet and sink. On the opposite side is a high cushioned table with two cots next to it and chairs positioned between them. The back wall is filled with shelves and floor to ceiling cabinets. I stand uncomfortably in the middle of the room, not sure where I'm supposed to go. Finn takes a seat in one of the chairs as Kellan closes the door.

"So Kitten...ever seen a doctor before?" Kellan asks me.

"Um, no. Why? Is one coming here?" Finn and Kellan both laugh at that.

"I'm a doctor sweetie. I'd like to get your vitals and look over your injuries, see how you're healing. Is that okay, Kitten?"

I stand there, unsure. He looks like he's nineteen at the most. Maybe they just look young? Either way, why would he have a room like this in his house if he wasn't a doctor? I shrug. What else was I going to do? Leaving right now still isn't a good option. If he wanted to hurt me, he could have done so already.

"Alright then," Kellan says while taking something out of a cabinet. "We'll step outside while you change into the gown. Take a seat up here on the table and yell when you're ready. We'll be right outside." Both he and Finn head out the door.

I pick up the checkered green fabric. He called it a gown, but it has no back to it. Did he mean robe? I take off my borrowed clothes from yesterday and slip into the robe. I wrap it around me and climb the little steps on the table.

"Ready," I call out. The door opens, and they both return.

Kellan goes to the sink to wash his hands as Finn sits back down in his chair beside me. Once he's done drying his hands, Kellan digs through a few drawers taking things out and setting them on a rolling table. He rolls it over to me.

He uses different items to check in my ears and my mouth, pressing something to my chest and back. He looks at my fingernails and holds my wrist for a few moments. He rolls something over my forehead and it beeps. When that's done, he walks to the counter and writes something down. When he turns back to me, he looks more serious.

"Now I'm going to need you to lay down Kitten. I'm going to open the gown, and I'm going to press on your stomach and other areas, checking for injuries. While I'm doing that, I'm going to speak to Finn, and he's going to write down what I say. Everything I'm doing is strictly professional; I'm not going to hurt you. If, at any moment you want me to stop, just say so, and I'll stop immediately. Okay?"

I nod and lay back. For some reason I trust Kellan. He starts with my face, turning it this way and that, moving to my throat, his fingers gently pushing. My arms are next; he inspects each side, continuing to talk to Finn, who is writing down his every word. When his hands touch my feet, I pull back. It tickles. Kellan doesn't react, moving my toes around and pushing my feet back.

He takes a deep breath in. "I'm going to open the gown now Kitten." I stiffen but nod. No one has ever seen me naked before. But I think because of the situation it's not so bad, he's trying to help me. It's still embarrassing though. I can't help the blush that spreads over my face. I stare at Finn's hand as he holds a pen to the paper.

A white sheet is placed over me before Kellan begins. I asked what it was for, and Finn told me it was to cover up parts of my body that aren't being examined. That helped to make me feel better about this. I can't bring myself to think badly of Kellan.

Kellan presses on my belly like he said he would. He also pushes on my ribs which earns a grunt from me. He says sorry but keeps doing it. I think we're done when I feel his fingers brush over the tops of my thighs. I suck in a breath and clamp them together. Kellan immediately moves his hands back.

He clears his throat and turns his face away. "Severe bruising on her upper thighs," He tells Finn. Looking back to my face, I notice his eyes are bright, and his cheeks are turning a little pink. Not from embarrassment I note, from anger.

"Kitten are you sure...you could have blacked out...he could have..." His voice cracks." I could check real quickly, just take a look? No touching."

As if I wasn't already dying of embarrassment and shame. I nod and look back to Finn. He looks uncomfortable too. Without raising his head from the paper, he reaches up and takes my hand. I squeeze it, and he squeezes back. I'm glad he's here with me. It's nice not having to do things on my own.

Kellan bends my knees and shifts my legs apart. He lifts the sheet off my bottom half. I think I stop breathing. Quickly after, he closes my legs and lays them down again, pulling the sheet down once again. I exhale and release Finn from my death grip.

He looks relieved and tells me all is well. I was pretty sure that nothing happened in that way, still, it's nice to have confirmation. Kellan then takes his gloves off, washing his hands again. I take Finn's hand in mine as Kellan sticks a needle in my arm, filling little tubes with my blood. That doesn't take long, thankfully.

"We'll leave so you can get dressed, Logan gave me some new clothes for you to put on, and they're by the sink."

With that, he leaves the room, Finn following behind him after placing a chaste kiss on my cheek. I get the clothes, putting them on quickly. This time, it's white boxer-briefs, orange night pants with a white, long-sleeved shirt. I get back on the table and yell that I'm dressed.

This time, it's just Kellan. "If you don't mind Kitten, I'd like to wrap your ribs. It might make you a bit more comfortable."

"Okay. Can I have more ibuprofen too?"

"Sure thing, I keep those in the kitchen though, I'll get them before you eat," He says, with a soft smile on his face.

He pulls out a rolled up piece of stretchy fabric and motions for me to lift my shirt up. I sit up straight as he wraps the fabric around my ribs tightly. It hurts but feels much better once he's done. It's more comfortable to breathe. I let go of the shirt, and it falls back into place. Kellan pulls out a rolling stool from under the table and takes a seat in front of me.

"The hard part's over now." He smiles. "But I would like to talk to you about immunizations. You said before that you've never been to the doctor. How is that Kitten? Are you sure you never went as a kid?" He asks.

"I'm positive. There was never anyone to take me. I was thrown in a dumpster as a newborn, and a crazy homeless lady found me. She thought I was a cat, hence the name". I say, watching Kellan flinch. "She never took me to a doctor or a vet for that matter. I got away from her as soon as I could. She was in no condition to care for a kid or even a cat. I've been on my own ever since." I whisper the last part, looking at my knees. Kellan's long fingers cup my chin, lifting my head. My eyes are now looking into his grass green ones.

"It's okay, you're here now. I would like to give you some immunizations, but not right now. Now, my dear girl, you must eat." He smiles sadly. Again, I think of how good-looking this man is. I hate that I make them so sad. I should learn to keep my mouth shut.

He helps me down from the table, and we head for the kitchen.

CHAPTER FIVE

This time I'm taken to a formal dining room. Kellan pulls my chair out for me as I've read in books. I feel like a princess. What a stupid thought. It looks like most of the guys are already seated as well. I'm seated between Ash and Logan, Reed right in front of me flanked by Jace and Finn, Remy sitting at the head of the table of course.

Kellan comes out of a swinging door with a large plate in one hand, and a glass of orange juice in the other. He sets the plate down in front of me. "Tristan made an omelet for you this morning; you could use the protein." He takes a bottle out of his pocket and gives me two pills. I shoot him a thankful smile and swallow them down.

Ash leans into me, looking at my plate longingly. "Is he making us all omelets, Kell?" He asks.

"No worries Ash, he's making them for everyone. He

wouldn't do that to you," Kellan says laughing.

"Good," Ash says in his gruff voice, leaning back and looking at me, "Tristan makes the best omelets."

It certainly smells good. Little do they know that I'm not that picky. Moments later, Tristan starts carrying plates in for the guys, all with omelets on them, and other plates stacked with bacon, sausage, ham, and toast that he places in the middle. Kellan took a seat next to his twin, so Tristan takes the last seat open beside Ash on his other side.

Once he's seated, everyone begins eating or reaching for things. Ash holds out a plate of sausage, raising a brow in question to me. I nod, and he puts several sausage patties on my plate. I pick up my fork, about to start when I remember how I made a fool of myself the day before. I look around me and decide to act civilized in front of these gorgeous boys.

I see Jace across from me, next to Reed. He's already eating, using his fork and knife to cut the egg into small pieces, taking his time. I mimic what he's doing. When he takes a bite, I take a bite. When he takes a sip of coffee, I take a sip of juice. When Jace wipes at the corners of his mouth with his napkin, I do the same. Because this is the first time in a long time I didn't feel the need to eat in a hurry, I actually taste what I'm eating. Ash was right, this is amazing. The egg is fluffy and light with ham, cheese and onions on every forkful. I wonder how I'm ever going to go back to cold cans of soup and off-brand lunch meat packs after tasting Tristan's food.

Now that I think I have Jace's routine down, I look away from him and see Remy watching me. My hand pauses halfway to my mouth. Oh no! He must have been watching me watch Jace. I probably look like a total creeper. I wouldn't blame him for thinking that either. Jace is as attractive as the rest of them. He's the quintessential golden boy. Hair the color of sunlight, eyes as blue as the sky. And the five o'clock shadow he's sporting isn't hurting either. There is something enchanting and refined about Jace. His fluid movements and the way he holds his body. A really, really good looking body...

I shake myself from those thoughts. Now I really am creeping on Jace like Remy probably thought I was. I turn away from them both. Let them think what they want. What does it matter anyway? As I turn, I notice Tristan is watching me too. Well, me and my plate. He has a hopeful look in his chocolate eyes. Oh, I realize I've stopped eating. I probably insulted him. I take another bite and wipe my mouth before speaking.

"This is wonderful Tristan. Might be the best thing I've ever eaten."

Tristan beams at me, using that kind voice of his, "Thank you, Kitten, I'm glad you like it". For the rest of breakfast, a satisfied smile stays on his face.

After I'm stuffed to full capacity, I sit and watch the guys finish eating. As soon as Logan is done he pushes his plate away and jumps up, clapping his hands together.

"Okay, Kitten, time to do something about that hair. To quote you from yesterday, 'your hair looks like crap'". He says, chuckling a little. It makes me laugh too but earns a few frowns from the table. I guess we have an inside joke.

Logan takes my hand in his holding it all way back to Tristan's bathroom. He picks several things from the drawers and directs me to stand in front of him. He lifts me by my hips, placing me on the counter, between the twin sinks. I gasp, looking at him like he's crazy. That seemed so effortless for him.

"Oh come on, stop looking at me like that. You weigh what? Eighty pounds soaking wet? Are you even five foot Kitten?" He says playfully. I mumble, "I'm five foot one thank you very much. A buck seven too." He hears me anyway and cracks up laughing. I have the sudden urge to kick him in his shin. I've earned every pound, I doubt he would understand that though, so I let it go.

Logan takes his time squirting my hair with a spray bottle, brushing, drying, and then braiding my hair in one long French braid that hangs down my back.

"This way your wavy hair will be extra wavy when we take this out tomorrow," He states like he's put a lot of thought into it.

"Um, Logan?"

"Yes, my life size Barbie?" He replies, and this time, I do kick him in the shin. He laughs.

"Are you going to do my hair every day? At least, every day that I'm here?" I ask shyly.

He looks a little hurt when he responds, "Do you not like me doing your hair?"

"OH, no! I uh... I love it. I just...is it normal?" I look to my lap. I just admitted that I don't know what normal is. Which makes me strange. I am strange, but I don't want him to know that.

Logan uses the end of the brush to lift my chin. "Why do you care what normal is Kitten? Is it that important to be like everyone else? You said you loved it, so does it matter?" His voice and his eyes are sincere.

"No, I guess it doesn't," I say with a small smile.

He smiles. "Good, and yes, I will be doing your hair every day. Every day that you are here. Which is as long as you want to be here. We want you to stay with us Kitten. We've already talked about it."

I give him a confused look, "Why? Why would you want me to stay? You don't know me. I have done nothing to deserve any of this".

His gives me a sympathetic look. "Let me guess, you're on your own. Have been for a long time right?" He asks, I nod. "You don't have anyone right? No parents, no family?" I shake my head, this time looking down. Everyone has parents; I just don't know who they are or why they didn't want me. He knows all of this already, what's he getting at? Logan tilts my chin up again.

"Believe it or not, Sweet Girl, most of us were in the same position as you are now. We know what it's like, and we don't want you out there on your own anymore. You're a tiny, young thing and as beautiful as you are, it makes you even more of a target."

I blink at him. This amazing, kind, insanely attractive boy thinks I'm beautiful? I close my eyes, daring the tears pushing against my lids to fall.

Logan must take this the wrong way because he rushes to say, "If you don't want to stay with us permanently, at least stay until we can make sure you will be taken care of. If that means finding you a family until you turn eighteen, or paying for a home for you and getting you a good, reliable job, then that's what we'll do."

I open my eyes to look at him, tears now flowing

LANE WHITT

freely. Logan gently pulls me into a hug, cupping the back of my head in his large hand. With my face pressed up against his chest, I whisper, "Even Remy?"

After having thoroughly laughed at me for my genuine question, Logan helped me from the counter and dragged me behind him to Remy's office. That's where I am now. Seated in a brown leather chair facing his impressive desk. The room's as intimidating as the man who owns it. It's sparsely decorated in different shades of brown and cherry wood. Both walls on either side of the desk are full bookshelves with files, folders, and worn looking books. Papers stick out all over the place like he just shoved them in somewhere. I wonder if he has a system or has to dig through every time he needs something.

I wish he would hurry up. It feels like I've been sitting in here alone for over an hour. When Logan first brought me into the office, Remy had said he needed to talk to the guys, and he'd be back shortly. Apparently we have a difference of opinion on what shortly means.

Finally, a disheveled looking Remy walks in. Wearing a black button up shirt, untucked and the sleeves rolled up, paired with a dark pair of jeans and black boots, he looks the part of an attractive young man relaxing at home. I know better, I doubt Remy is ever relaxed.

"Sorry for your wait, Miss Kitten, that took longer than expected," Remy says, walking around and taking a seat behind his desk.

He sits forward with his fingers steeped together under his chin. I shift uncomfortably under his piercing gray eyes. I wish he didn't have to be so serious all the time.

"So, what did you want to see me about?" I ask, getting this started so that it can end.

"There are several things. I'm just not sure where to start," He replies, sighing and leaning back in his chair. "I want you to understand Kitten, that all of us, even me," he smirks, "would like you to stay with us. Here, in our home, for as long as you would like." I wait for more, but he doesn't continue.

"Uh, listen. I'll start by saying that I would love to stay here. The guys are nice to me, and your house is amazing, better than any place I could have ever dreamed of staying." I pause, trying to get my words right. I take a deep breath. "The thing is...I just don't get why you would want me to. I mean, Tristan and Ash found me bleeding in the street, for Christ's sakes! I understand that some people can't walk away from a person in need, and I appreciate everything you've all done for me, don't get me wrong." I rush to say. God this is coming out wrong.

Remy speaks up then, saving me from bumbling on. "I understand what you're getting at. Truthfully, I don't know why we want you to stay. I can't give you the answers you seek in that department. It could be your youth, for some, your beauty. Perhaps it's how your gratefulness for simple things reminds us of where we came from. All I know is that each of us finds you fascinating and intriguing. We are simply drawn to you and like having you around." He holds his hands out wide in an 'I-don't-know' gesture.

"Kitten," long, uncomfortable pause. "You haven't been shown the kindness in your life that you deserve. Trust doesn't come easily for you, no one understands that more than me. We don't want to hurt you. We won't make you do things you don't want. That's not who we are. I think you feel comfortable around us, maybe even trust us, just a little. If you thought we were bad people, you wouldn't still be here, would you?" Remy gives me a questioning look, eyebrow raised.

"You're right," I whisper. And he is. I haven't felt like I've been in danger at all since I've been here. I don't know why they want me here, but it doesn't matter. I want to be here, and I want to know these remarkable boys. "Okay, I'll stay."

"Good." Remy smiles broadly. His whole face lights up when he smiles. He should smile more.

"I should work though; I don't want to just live off you. That's not right. There are a few places that let me work under the table. I can make my own money. I don't make much, but I'd like to at least contribute". I state firmly, this is a deal breaker for me.

Remy gives me what I think is a pleased smile. "We pool our money in this house, Miss Kitten. We hold a firm belief in 'what's yours is mine and mine yours'. That way everyone is taken care of. I'm glad you're offering to contribute though only do so if you are willing to use our money as well. Everything is equal here."

That makes me a little uncomfortable. No way do I make as much as these guys. My part won't be equal. Although, no way am I staying and NOT throwing in what I make.

"What kind of work do you do Kitten?" He asks,

sounding genuinely curious.

"There's an ice rink that I work at, a restaurant that lets me wash dishes when they are busy, and a hotel that lets me do laundry for them," I reply. I hate admitting that this is the only work I can get to someone who is obviously rich and probably has a great job. I'm not ashamed though, I do what I have to, and it works for me.

"What do you do at the ice rink?" Remy asks.

"Sometimes I work at the snack bar, and sometimes at the skate rental desk, but my favorite job is when I get to work with the kids. The mornings are family time, and there are little kids falling all over the place. When someone takes the time to show them how it's done, it's like...like the whole world just opened up to them, and they own it. It's not a practical skill but once they can stand up on their own or do a few tricks it makes them so happy. That's what I do, teach them to skate." I look back to Remy, and he has a blank look on his face. I look at my knees. I was rambling. I clear my throat.

"Uh, yeahso, the owner tries to pay me in cash, but on occasion she can't, so I get paid in free skate time. I like it there."

He nods his head, drumming his fingers on the desk. "How about this? I'll talk to the owner at the ice rink and see about getting you hired on part-time with a set wage as a trainer. You drop the dishwashing job altogether. And I'll pay you twice what you made doing laundry if you do it for us. That way Finn will have time to catch you up on your studies when you're not working, laundry will actually get done around here, and you'll have a task at home so you won't feel like you are living off us. Sound reasonable?" Remy states matter of factly, but I'm still stuck on the word 'home.'

I stare at him. Is he serious? He doesn't even know how much I make at the hotel, and he's offering to double it? Then again I'm sure he could afford it no matter what it is.

"Uh, yeah, that sounds fine. I should probably work full time. I don't need Finn to catch me up on anything. I've spent most of my life in a library, reading anything I could. Between the books and using the computers there, I met the standards to pass high school when I was twelve."

"There is always more to learn young Kitten, is there not?" He asks, acting like he's more than a few years older than me. I nod anyway though, he's right, there is. Getting to spend more time with Finn sounds like fun anyway.

"Alright, we're agreed," He says, standing. "I'll have Jace show you where the laundry room is. Ash and I have somewhere to be. I'll see you for dinner." He walks to the door and opens it, standing to the side to let me pass. We walk through the house until we come upon a room done in cream and dark blues. A large screen dominates one wall, on it are characters shooting each other. A couple of the boys are playing the game, one of them being Jace.

"Excuse me, Jace, I need you to show Kitten where the laundry room is. She's going to be doing our washing from now on." Remy says in an authoritative voice. I now realize that he hadn't used that voice with me in his office.

The guys pause their game and have a deer in headlights look about them. Ash stands and claps his hands, rubbing them together. "Finally! I hate washing clothes. You know how to keep black from fading Kitten? I swear, I wash something once and it's like half the color leaves it."

That makes me giggle. I still think it's a strange sound. "Yeah, you wash them in cold water. I think they even make special soap just for dark clothes. You also turn dark jeans inside out so they won't fade as fast and you hang dry certain types of fabric." How do I know this simple thing and they don't?

"Oh yeah, this is gonna be great. Logan can stop hassling me about my shit now." Ash says to Remy.

Remy looks back at Ash, "We leave in ten, get ready." The two share a look, and Ash's face becomes hard again. He nods once and follows Remy out into the hallway.

"Let's get you to that laundry room then," Jace says, laughing. "You might become the most loved person in this house, we all hate washing and folding with a passion. Logan loves to buy them so mostly we just get new ones once they're dirty." He shrugs. That has to be the stupidest thing I've ever heard. Wasteful too.

Turns out they call the entire basement the laundry room. Although I don't know why they don't call it 'The Land of Forgotten Clothes. The washer and dryer are state of the art. They even have a folding table, drying racks and an ironing board with the iron sitting on top of it. Clearly, someone tried to keep up with it but gave up. There are piles of clothes everywhere. Some as tall as me. Washing clothes really isn't that difficult for crying out loud.

Jace walks around the piles like they might bite him or something. I can't help but laugh at him. Big, strong guy afraid of socks and t-shirts. I look around for the bleach to start a load of whites, but I don't see it. There's a cabinet next to the dryer, so I poke around a bit. Several different types of soaps, softeners, and dryer sheets take up most of the space. The bleach is on the top row. I stand on my tip-toes, but it's still out of reach.

"Who's laughing now fun size?" He jokes.

"What?" I ask

"Come on, nobody's ever called you that before?" He says with a disbelieving look.

"No, I don't think so, what does that mean?"

"Holy shit, you're serious!" He laughs. "You know, like the fun size candy, it's smaller than the regular size candy?" I just stare at him, I have no idea what he's talking about.

"Basically, I'm calling you short, but in a friendly way. And you girl, just earned yourself a nickname". He winks at me.

"Sorry, I wasn't the type of kid that was given candy." I shrug.

"Hey," Jace nudges me out of the way to grab the bleach, "I'm sorry, I didn't mean anything by it."

"I know, it's okay. And hey, I am short, it doesn't bother me. I have a lesser chance of falling over in the case of an earthquake." I stick my tongue out at him. He laughs.

I start the load of whites and move on to the first pile. I start sorting through it, dark clothes, jeans, things that will need to be dry cleaned, towels. After a while, Jace says he'll see me upstairs. I guess he got bored. A few items have stains on them that have obviously sat here for so long that I doubt they will ever come out. Bunch of crazies. They should have just washed them.

I stay down there for about four loads of laundry and call it quits. I found a bunch of racks filled with hangers, so I just hung everything up. I don't know what belongs to who yet. I decide to go find Logan and ask him. I'm sure if anyone knows he will.

As I'm rounding a corner near a back door I've never seen, I see a sleek black dog sitting on the deck. I open the glass door and whistle for it. It looks ready to bolt.

"Please, don't run away. I won't hurt you." The dog still looks unsure, but I approach it slowly with my hand out. When I get close enough, I kneel next to it and run my fingers through its shiny fur. It looks well-groomed so it must belong to someone. The guys never mentioned having a dog, but clearly it's theirs. It was at their door. They should really get a collar and tags for it.

I scratch behind the dog's ear, and it closes its eyes in contentment. "Oh yes, I'd totally steal you puppy, I'll make sure you get a pretty collar tomorrow."

I stand, calling the dog to come with me. It still looks unsure but comes in anyway. I watch behind me to make sure it follows. I find the living room, but no one else is here. Oh well. Someone left the TV on so I sit on the couch. I figure one of them will eventually come in here. The dog jumps up and sits beside me.

"No! Bad dog, down, get down." I snap my fingers at it. I don't know if they let the dog on the couch or not but it looks pretty expensive.

I feel bad for yelling at it, so I slide to the floor and lean my back against the couch. "Sorry puppy, come here, I'll sit with you." I pat my legs so the dog will come closer. With its ears pulled back, it comes over and lays its head in my lap. I stroke my hand over its head and down its back. I love the feel of the silky fur between my fingers. The dog rolls over, so I scratch it's, his, belly.

"You're such a pretty boy aren't you puppy? I wish I knew your name. You have such pretty puppy eyes, don't you boy?" I say, rubbing under his chin. He leans into my hand, I guess he likes that. I continue to pet him until my arm grows tired.

I look at the dog lying lazily in my lap. He looks up at me with his mint green eyes. If I had to guess, I'd say this was Finn's or Kellan's dog. I've heard that pets tend to look like their owners. Or maybe that was a commercial?

"Well, I'm thirsty, what about you?" The dog just looks at me. I sigh, "I have no idea why I'm waiting for an answer." I stand again, and he follows me to the kitchen. Tristan is in front of the stove, probably preparing dinner.

"Hey Tristan," I wave when he turns around. "Where do you keep your dog bowls? We're thirsty. Although I'd like my water from a cup." I smile at him, but it dims a bit when I notice how he's just staring at the dog, looking mad.

"Umm...he was at the back door, he didn't have a tag, and I just figured he belonged here. Is he yours?"

"Certainly not mine." Tristan mutters.

"Oh, well.....can we keep him? He's so well behaved, and I like him. I'll take care of him, I promise." I beg. I don't want to send him back outside without knowing if he has a place to go. He probably does, I just don't know where.

Tristan looks even angrier now. I walk up to him and wrap both of my arms around one of his. "Please, Tristan?

You took me in when I was alone. I'll try to find his owner. He's been groomed and smells real nice so someone might be looking for him. Don't make me put him back outside." I pout.

I think Tristan knows how hard that would be for me because his whole body deflates. He untangles his arm from mine then brings me in for a hug, kissing the crown of my head.

"Okay, if my Kitten wants a puppy, my Kitten can have a puppy." He says, and I laugh. When you put it that way it just sounds weird. I lean up on my toes and kiss his cheek.

"Thank you, Tristan." He shakes his head and gets me a bowl from the cabinet. I fill it with cold water and grab a few ice cubes out of the freezer, putting them in the bowl and swirling them around. I get my own glass of ice water and sit at the island. I hear Tristan chuckling so I raise an eyebrow in question.

"Why in the world did you give him ice cubes?" He asks.

"Why wouldn't I? I like ice water, he probably does too. Dogs aren't that different from people you know." I state.

He laughs harder. "For one, that isn't a dog, it's a wolf, and I've never seen anybody give a wolf iced water."

I look back to the dog. It sure looks like a dog. "How do you know he's a wolf?" I ask.

"Trust me, that's no dog. It's a wolf. He's probably not even housebroken," He smirks when he says this. The dog or wolf growls at him.

I hop down from my seat and kneel beside the wolf. "It's okay," I tell the wolf, stroking his silky fur again.

"He didn't mean it. I'm new here too. We'll figure it out together." The wolf nuzzles his face into mine, and it makes me giggle. I stand, glaring at Tristan as I leave the room with the wolf on my heels.

We walk around the house, looking into rooms to see what they are. We come across a set of large oak double doors. I open one and peek my head through. It's dark, so I can't see what's in here. The wolf nudges my leg, pushing me into the room. I leave the door open for light.

Finding a table with a lamp, I pull the little cord. The amount of light it gives off is small, but it's enough to spot a light switch beside the door. As soon as the overhead lights come on I let out a shocked gasp. It's a library! I jump up and down, letting out a squeal of delight. "Mr. Wolf, we found a library! Can you believe this?" I hug his neck, and he licks my face.

Rows and rows of books line the walls with shorter shelves in the middle. No way is this normal. I run my fingers over the bindings, walking down the aisles, exploring my new found treasure. There are several seating areas, one with a grouping of big pillows in front of a floor to ceiling window. Looks like the perfect spot for reading.

I search the shelves for a book. I find a nice thick one and call for the wolf to follow me. I sit Indian style, and the wolf props his head up on my thigh. I decide to read aloud so the wolf won't get bored and wander around. We stay that way for hours. With me reading to the wolf, with one hand on the book and one hand petting his head. I eventually shift so I'm laying down propped up on my elbows, the wolf snuggled into my side. I expect him to drift off, but he keeps his eyes on me the whole time.

CHAPTER SIX

The next thing I know, I'm being shaken awake. Remy's gruff voice calls my name. "Kitten, thank God! We've been looking all over the house for you. Why are you sleeping in here?" He asks in an annoyed tone.

I sit up and look around. "Where is my wolf?" I ask.

"Remy looks stunned for a moment. "What wolf? What are you talking about?"

"I found a wolf at your back door. I thought he was a dog, but Tristan said he was a wolf. He said I could keep him. He was right here with me when I dozed off."

Remy bites his bottom lip. He looks just as mad as Tristan did. "Are you sure you didn't dream the whole thing?" He has the nerve to ask.

I huff. "Yes I'm sure, I'm not crazy. Are you sure you

didn't see him?" I ask. I feel like crying. My wolf left me?

He must see the tears that threaten to fall. He reaches out and tucks my hair behind my ear. "I'll help you look for him, come on." He pulls me to standing and walks with his hand at the small of my back to the door. We search every room we come across but still no wolf.

Later, I'm sitting at the dining room table, pushing food around my plate. We couldn't find him, and I'm positive someone must have let him out, and he ran away. I must be the worst pet owner in the world. Less than a day and I lose my dog. Wolf. Maybe he ran away because I didn't feed him? Why didn't I feed him!? I wipe a tear away and give up playing with my food.

"Want me to make you something else Kitten?" Tristan asks me. I shake my head no. I look up and around. The guys are sharing looks between each other and giving me sympathetic looks. Finn, I notice, just stares at his plate, pushing food around like I am. I lost a wolf, what the heck happened to him?

Since I'm not eating, and he's not eating, I ask him, "Hey Finn? Do you want to go for a walk with me?"

He starts to answer when Remy speaks up, "You shouldn't leave the house when it's dark outside, Kitten. Besides, Finn has some things to take care of tonight." He glares in Finn's direction. Finn looks up at me with a guilty look.

"I'm sorry Kitten," Finn says in a voice that would break my heart if it wasn't already broken.

"Fine. I just wanted to look for my wolf." I grit out, trying to keep my tears at bay. I leave the table, stomping off to, well, I don't know. I don't know where to sleep, and I'm not sure if I could anyhow. I'm worried about my wolf. I head back to the basement and do laundry until I fall asleep, exhausted, on one of the piles.

I wake up with a stiff neck, shivering from the lack of heat in the basement. I forget why I am down here. Oh yeah, I lost my puppy and went crying in a corner like a two-year-old. I swear I'm acting so unlike myself lately. The plus side of my temper tantrum is that I got a crap load of laundry done. If this is going to be a continuous thing I might make the suggestion that they all have the same kind of socks. Pairing that many different kinds was ridiculous. I really need to find Logan so I can start sorting where all of this stuff goes. Also, I have a few ideas to run by him.

I make my way up the stairs, trying to work the kink out of my neck. When I open the door, I'm shocked to see a sleeping Ash sitting across from me. I close the door as quietly as I can, but he still stirs awake.

"Hey there," He mumbles.

"Hi. Did you sleep there?" I ask in disbelief.

"Yeah, I know you wanted your space, but I didn't want to leave you completely alone." He gives me a meaningful look. Though I don't know what it means.

"I'm sorry about how I acted. I don't know what came over me. Would you like to get some food with me? I'm no Tristan, but I make a fantastic bowl of cereal."

He snorts out a laugh. "Sure thing, little one."

We walk in comfortable silence to the kitchen. Just

as I'm about to enter, Ash grabs my upper arm, surprisingly gentle for such a huge guy. He lets out a breath. "About yesterday, I get it. You have abandonment issues. I'm not the most talkative of the group, and I know I come off a little... reserved. I just wanted to let you know that the wolf didn't run off because of anything you did." He says.

I look up at his face. His masculine features make him look more scary than some of the other guys, but the thought that comes to mind when I really take in everything about him is ...deadly attractive.

"Ash?" I say quietly.

"Yeah?" He grunts.

"Thank you for saying that. It's because you're the quiet one that makes your words mean more when you do speak up."

Ash looks way for a moment before gesturing with a nod of his head that we should enter the kitchen. I think we might be the first ones up. There's no sign that anyone has been here yet. Ash walks over to a coffee pot, to get it started. I've always liked the smell of coffee, so I stand beside him as it brews.

"Want some?" he asks, once the pot is done filling.

"I've never had it."

He takes down two mugs from a shelf. He pours one to the top and then the other, leaving a few inches of space. He walks to the fridge, so I take the less full one and take a gulp. Burning the ever-living-crap out of my tongue!

"Damn it! Kitten, I was getting you some creamer to cool it off.

Here, put that on it," he hands me an ice cube.

I take the ice but put a hand on Ash's arm. "It's okay, I'm fine."

Ash shakes his head at me. He takes both our cups to the island and motions for me to sit. I do, and he brings me a container of liquid creamer and some sugar. I watch as he drinks his without any of that. I take another sip of mine too. This time slower. I like this how it is. It's bitter, but I don't think I've tasted anything like it before. Not even a little. Maybe that alone is why I like it.

Ash nods and his lips lift at the corners. I think that's approval. I continue to sip on the hot concoction as he gets things out to cook.

"I thought we were having cereal?" I frown.

He snorts again. "As if I'd ever feed you cereal for breakfast. I'm no Tristan either so don't go getting excited. I can make scrambled eggs though."

I really like this side of Ash. I thought he was going to be a mean type of person, but I think that's just a front. Maybe. He starts making eggs, and I seek out the cabinet with the ibuprofen.

When he has finished cooking, he brings over two heaped plates for us. I get the coffee and refill our cups, grabbing forks as well. We eat in the comfortable silence which I'm starting to realize comes with being around Ash. It's nice to be around someone else who doesn't feel the need to fill the silence with empty words. Ash only talks when he has something to say. I like that about him.

We finish, so I pick up the dirty dishes and place them in the dishwasher. I turn back to Ash and pat my stuffed tummy. "That was delicious, thank you. Next time I think we should put bacon in them."

He smiles. "I knew I liked you for a reason." Ha! I

got a full blown smile out of him, and I'll be darned if the giant isn't even more beautiful when he smiles.

He gets up, taking his coffee with him. I grab mine too and follow him. He looks back and raises an eyebrow at me, I just shrug. What else is there to do? We end up in a garage full of vehicles. I'm pretty sure the white SUV is Reed's but beyond that, I don't know.

"So, what are we doing?" I ask.

Ash snorts a laugh out, "We, huh? Do you know how to do an oil change?"

I bite my lip and shake my head no. "I've never even been in a car, only on the city bus."

"I'll teach you to drive sometime. For now just watch. I'm gonna change the oil in a few of these today." He didn't even blink at my confession, and I'm grateful for that. So far, these guys haven't judged me for anything I've told them.

He works quietly, taking the time to explain this and that to me. Pointing out each tool he uses and how you use it. I stand back, watching and listening, just letting him do this thing. After a couple hours pass, I go back to the kitchen, looking for something easy I can take back with me so I can talk Ash into a break. I'm sure he's hungry by now.

Tristan is up, cooking. He's still in his night clothes, a white tank top, and red flannel pants. He smiles at me when I enter.

"Hey there, breakfast will be done shortly. What are you doing up? It's only seven." He says in his kind voice.

"Actually, I already had breakfast, Ash made us scrambled eggs. I was going to make us some sandwiches, but I don't know what he likes. Any ideas?"

"Hmm. I see. I'll fix you up a few BLT's. What are you two up to?" He gives me an odd look.

"Just changing oil and checking things on the cars. Don't worry, I'm not touching anything." I say playfully, earning me another beautiful Tristan smile.

He fries up some bacon and puts the sandwiches together, wrapping each in a paper towel. I grab two water bottles from the fridge. I give Tristan a hug and lean up on my toes to peck him on the cheek.

"You're awesome Tristan. Thank you." He looks a bit shell shocked so I motion for him to bend down to me, "Don't tell Ash, but I'd take your eggs over his any day." I whisper in his ear. He barks out a laugh, very un-Tristan-like. I giggle and make my way back to the garage. The door is tricky with my hands being full, but I finally get it after tucking a bottle of water under my chin.

Ash is bent over the front of an older, shiny black truck. I don't think he notices me so I take the time to check him out. God, the boy is a tower of pure muscle. His rumpled gray shirt is hiked up in the back, showing off a sliver of tanned skin. Is it odd that I want to lick it?

"I thought you got bored," He says. I blush and clear my throat. At least he didn't catch me ogling him.

"Nope, just went to get some food. You boys are spoiling me. I've never had such open access to food before." I hand him two of the three sandwiches.

He takes a big bite, like half of it. "Boys?" He asks in an amused tone after swallowing his food. "Do I look like a *boy* to you, Kitten?"

Oh no, I've insulted him. "No I guess not, but you guys can't be much older than me."

"Looks can be deceiving," He mutters, finishing his

food. I hand him a bottle of water and he nods his thanks.

So he's older than he looks huh? So... what? Twenty-five? I suppose it doesn't matter in the long run. It makes sense though. Kellan is some sort of physician, and they all seem to have skills that exceed what I've seen of normal teenagers. Tristan's cooking, Reed's artistic ability, Ash and his knowledge of cars. Remy has his own office for crying out loud! That's when it hits me. That's why I feel like I fit in so well here, they aren't normal either. I find that comforting and disturbing all at once.

When I'm finished with my sandwich I stand next to Ash, his head still in the truck. Curious, I ask, "So who does this one belong to?"

"Why, do you like it?"

I take a look at all of the vehicles. "Yeah, I think I like this one best. It's pretty."

He smiles, and his chest swells with manly pride. "This truck here is mine, the red car is Tristan's Charger, and the black Escalade is Remy's, the white one Reed's. Over there is Logan's electric blue R8. Kellan drives a Mercedes, Finn a burnt orange Dodge Ram truck that he keeps parked outside, and Jace, has the flashiest car of course, a yellow Corvette."

I look around, I don't see the yellow or blue ones, but I do see a motorcycle that looks like it's made of glass. I walk to it and hover my hand over it. I don't want to smudge it. I briefly wonder what it looks like in the sun.

I look back to find Ash watching me. "I've changed my mind, if I had to choose, I'd want this."

He raises an eyebrow, "What if it rained?"

I shrug, "It's just water."

"What if it was cold?" he asks.

"I'd wear a jacket."

"And what if you fell off it?" I can hear the smile in his voice now.

I turn and look him in the eyes with a smile of my own on my face, "That's why they made helmets."

He laughs under his breath. "This is mine too. I built it from scratch." He wraps a large arm around my shoulder. "Yeah, we're gonna get along just fine Kitten, just fine."

I beam up at him. "If you teach me to drive this then I think you might be my favorite giant ever."

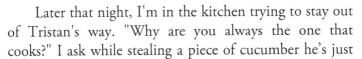

Later that night, I'm in the kitchen trying to stay out of Tristan's way. "Why are you always the one that cooks?" I ask while stealing a piece of cucumber he's just sliced for the salad.

Tristan swats my hand before replying, "Because I like cooking. If I don't want to someone else will and trust me, you do not want that to happen. Or we just eat out." He laughs.

"I can make grilled cheese." I smile up at him. He smiles back.

"God you are adorable, go set the table before I kiss that little heart shaped face off."

I nearly choke on the cherry tomato I just stole. Did he just say that? I shake off my shock at his words. He's just in a good mood. And playful. I grab the plates and silverware and go set the table like he asked. He probably just wanted me out of the kitchen so I didn't devour half the salad before it was brought out.

Once everyone is seated the food dishes get passed around. Tonight Tristan made a three meat lasagna with garlic bread and a house salad. It still amazes me that they get to eat like this every single night. With great food, surrounded by friends. Ash pokes the side of my face before handing me a plate of bread. I take two and pass it to Reed.

Looking down the table, I seek a bright blue streak of hair. "Hey, Logan?"

He looks up, "Yeah Kitten?" He takes a bite and I swear he growls in satisfaction. These guys love food as much as I do.

"I was wondering if you could help me out. I did a bunch of laundry, but I don't know where to take it once it's done. Can you help me with that?"

He smiles and bounces in his chair a bit. "Sure thing, I usually keep most of the clothes down there and only bring up what I want the guys wearing for the next couple of weeks. Most of that stuff can be thrown out. Winter season is around the corner, and I'll be buying new stuff."

I nearly choke for the second time today. Thrown out? They really do throw away once worn clothing? Ash pats me hard on the back to stop my choking.

"How about, once I get everything washed up, you come down a pick out what to keep, and I'll donate the rest? There's no need to be so wasteful, there are plenty of people out there that would love to have your stuff." I barely manage to hold the anger and disbelief out of my voice. I thought they were like me once upon a time? Either it was a really long time ago, or someone was lying. If even one of them was ever homeless, they'd remember what it was like to be cold. To be a have-not in a world full of haves. I'm sure that will stay with me forever.

Remy clears his throat. I didn't realize I was glaring at Logan. I look down at the table. I shouldn't be like this. They've been so nice to me, and here I am lecturing them. I feel like such a horrible person. Remy clears his throat again, so I look up at him, trying to hold back the tears.

"I think that's an excellent idea, Kitten." He must see the tears in my eyes because his commanding voice softens, "I think we forget sometimes how far we've come. Don't feel bad, we deserved that."

They didn't, but I don't contradict him. Something tells me he's not used to being talked back to. Besides, he was trying to make me feel better.

"Tomorrow I want you up bright and early. Logan and I are taking you shopping for something to wear, and then we're heading to the ice rink to talk to the manager." He continues to eat after that statement like its set in stone.

"I haven't done enough laundry yet to afford clothes, Remy," I say quietly. Embarrassed.

His eyes snap to mine. "Did I say that you were paying for it, Kitten?" His powerful voice washes over me, and I gulp.

"No, but..." He cuts me off.

"Then don't worry about it. We discussed this earlier. You'll need something to wear tomorrow, and I said I'd take care of you didn't I?" I nod.

His eyes bore into me even more intensely. "Didn't I Kitten?"

"Yes, Remy." He nods once, returning his attention to his dinner. I look down at my plate, my appetite disappearing. A large hand rubs my back, and I look to Ash. He gives me a small smile and gestures at me to eat. I pick up my fork and push my dinner back and forth until everyone else is finished.

Finn and Reed start to clear the table, and I go to help. Logan snags my hand and pulls me to walk behind him. "Oh, no. It's my time with you Babygirl. I didn't get to dress you or play with your hair today, the least you could do is look at clothes with me." He smirks, making my spirits lift a little. I don't know how anyone could stay mad at Logan for long.

An hour or so later Logan is humming, separating the clothes I put on hangers the day before. We have several full bags of things to be donated. I explained to him that we should drop off certain things to certain places. The coats, hats, gloves and thick sweaters from last year or several years before, we could personally give away at the soup kitchen. The unwanted t-shirts and jeans could be left in a Salvation Army drop box. While the nicer stuff could be given to an organization that specializes in giving clothes to those who are rejoining the workforce. I'd have to look that last one up. I've only heard of it, not dealt with it personally.

I mentioned the idea of buying the same kind of socks for everyone and Logan just laughed at that. He did, however, say he'd donate all the ones down here so it would be easier to match them up in smaller increments. He also took the time to point out each guys' style to me. After that, it was much easier to see what belonged to who. Logan made it fun and turned it into a game. He'd hold up a piece of clothing and have me guess the owner. It may have been stupid, but it made the time fly.

It turned out that Tristan would steal anything red from any of the guys, so they had all stopped wearing that color except Tristan. That made me laugh, he really didn't seem the type. I could've guessed when I was told that Ash tends to stick to blacks and grays, much to Logan's disappointment. He told me that he once took all the black and gray from him, only leaving the colorful clothes. Ash chose to walk around the house naked until Logan gave them back. My face turned beet red at that story.

"I'm done for the night. Want to get a shower and head to bed Kitten?" Logan asks as he staggers over heaps of clothes.

"Sure, although I don't know where I'm supposed to sleep," I reply

"You can sleep with me if you want. I don't have an en-suite bathroom, I took the room with the biggest closet, but there's one down the hall with a huge claw-foot tub. You want a bath?" he asks.

"I'll stick with the shower for tonight, I'm exhausted. I could just sleep on one of the couches. Or in the library room." I suggest.

Logan looks hurt by my words. "I don't mind, you slept in Tristan and Reed's beds, what's wrong with mine?"

"Nothing, I just didn't want you to feel like you had to offer. That's all."

With his smile back in place, he grabs my hand, entwining our fingers, and leads me up to the upstairs bathroom. This one is all white with hints of blue everywhere. I'd say that Reed and Logan share this space. It's not as big as Tristan's, the tub taking up most of the space, but it's freakishly clean and better than good enough for me.

"My bedroom's across the hall from Reed's when you're finished. I'll do your hair for you. Just dry it." Logan states, more than asks.

I don't bother responding. Something tells me he'd brush and blow dry my hair in my sleep if I said no. Not that I want to, I love it when he messes with my hair. I quickly shower and wrap a towel around myself. Stepping out, I look around for the clothes I had on, but they're gone. There's a knock on the door, so I open it.

"That was quick, I thought I'd have time to leave some clean clothes before you got out," Reed says, looking down as he speaks. He holds the clothes out, and I take them from him, my fingers brushing against his. His skin feels hot.

"Thanks, Reed, that was so nice of you." I lean my head out further from the doorway to kiss his cheek, but he turns his head at the last moment, my lips fall on his. I jerk my head back and cover my mouth with my hands.

"Oh my God, I'm so sorry Reed. I didn't... I mean... I was going to..." Reed pulls my hand away from my mouth. He puts his index finger over my lips to stop my babbling. His pretty hazel eyes look into my pale green ones as he rubs his finger slowly back and forth over my lips. His eyes flick down to watch his movements. He removes his hand and leans in, kissing me back softly. I stand there, stunned.

He tucks my hair behind my ear before leaning into

me, his breath fanning my neck. "Good night Kitten," He says softly, walking to his room.

I finally manage to move my legs and shut the door. My body feels like it's been drugged. What the hell was that! Does this mean that Reed likes me? Did he kiss me because he thought that's what I wanted? Did I want him to kiss me? I have no idea but...I liked it. Oh my God! My first kiss! Does a pity kiss count though?

My tired brain doesn't want to process this right now, so I get dressed in a pair of yellow sweats and another white, long sleeved t-shirt. Someone forgot underwear, but beggars can't be choosers and the pants have a tie in the front.

I take one last look at myself in the mirror and shrug. On the counter is a tube of toothpaste. I grab it, thinking I'll use my finger until I can get a toothbrush. I see a bright blue one in a holder. Hmmm... I pick it up and run my finger over the bristles. I decide to use it. I'm sure it's Logan's, maybe he won't mind.

When I'm done brushing, I head to Logan's room. Reed has shut the door to his cloud room, Logan's is open. I kind of expected his room to be loud and crazy. Instead, it's done in black and tan. The only blue in the room is the bedspread and Logan's pajama bottoms, or at least, I think they are as I can't seem to make my eyes leave his bare chest. All that smooth skin! My eyes are drawn lower as he walks toward me. I watch the muscles in his stomach flexing and rippling with each step he makes. I feel an odd pull low in my tummy.

I finally look away when I feel pain in my hands. I'm clenching them so tightly my nails are digging into my skin. I have no idea how long he's been standing in front of me now, no longer moving, but I can't look at him. My face is on fire, and I know he sees it. I shift from one foot to the other and feel a strange, yet pleasurable, tingle in my chest. I look down and can see my nipples poking through my shirt. They've hardened like they tend to when it's cold outside. Oh no, Logan can probably see that too. I want to crawl into a hole and die.

A finger comes up under my chin, forcing my eyes to meet his pools of blue. Logan's face is serious, intense. He uses his finger to tug my bottom lip from my teeth. We stare at each other for seconds or hours, I can't tell. My brain shuts down, and my mouth takes over.

"I used your toothbrush!" I practically yell at him. "I'm sorry, I don't know why I did that. Reed kissed me, and I couldn't think, but actually that was after I kissed him. By accident, I think. I also used Tristan's razor when I showered in there the other day. I didn't know I was going to end up staying here, and now I feel bad about it. And I feel bad about using your toothbrush too I...I just...I have no idea why I did that! Then I stare at you like. Like you..." I can't breathe! I'm getting hysterical, and I'm not even sure why.

Logan looks a mixture of amused, angry, shocked, and confused all at once. It's an interesting look on him. He finally bursts out laughing, and my hands fly to my face to hide the embarrassing tears that choose this moment to fall. He pulls me into a hug. Wrapping his arms around me and rocking us side to side while petting my hair.

"It's okay Kitten. Shhh. You're okay. I don't care that you used my toothbrush or that you looked at me. Tristan won't care that you used his razor either; he probably put it in there for you. Everything is okay." I sob into his chest. It's been forever since I truly cried and now I can't stop it.

Logan scoops me up in his arms and carries me to bed. Tucking me in and climbing behind me. It feels soothing to have his strong form wrapped around me. Natural even. My smaller body fits into his perfectly. With one of his legs thrown over mine, his arm wrapped around my waist, and his lips pressed to the crown of my head, I have never felt safer. He holds me like this while I cry myself to sleep.

CHAPTER SEVEN

My eyes fly open, hearing a deep growl. I move to get up but am trapped by an arm around my waist, holding me tightly to a firm body behind me. My heart rate picks up until I remember that it's Logan. We're still in the same position as we fell asleep. I blush furiously and rock back and forth slightly, trying to wake him.

"Logan...let go," I say in a hoarse whisper.

Remy stomps over to Logan's side of the bed and smacks his bare back. He must have been the one making that noise. The arm around me disappears, and Logan jumps up, looking mad as all get out. His eyes fall on Remy, standing with his massive arms crossed over his chest. Logan visibly deflates and smirks at him. The bigger man rolls his eyes and turns to me.

"Time to get up, we leave in a half hour." With that,

he walks out of the room, leaving the door open.

Logan walks out of the closet, fully clothed and carrying a pair of sneakers. "These should do until we get you some of your own. Hurry up so I can do something with all that hair of yours."

"Can you put it in a ponytail today?" I ask, still rubbing the sleep out of my eyes.

He makes a face. "Sure, why?"

"Because everyone is always tucking my hair behind my ears. I don't think they like it very much." I say, thinking about how much my hair must annoy them.

Logan laughs so hard he doubles over. "Sure Kitten, I'll pull it back for you, but I don't think they do it because of that." He manages to say after his laughing fit.

I reluctantly leave the bed and follow Logan to the bathroom after I've tied the shoes on as tight as I could. I feel like a clown in them, like I'm about to trip and fall. Logan brushes my hair quickly and oddly enough he had a hair-tie. After he's finished spraying my hair with something, he walks to the counter, picking up his toothbrush. I look to the floor, remembering my horrible outburst last night. Logan runs it under the water, squeezing out some toothpaste and hands it to me with a huge smile on his face.

I mumble out a "Thank you." Stepping to the sink and brushing my teeth. He watches me, and it's a little uncomfortable. I spit and rinse, cleaning it off when I'm done. Logan then picks it up and repeats the process of readying it. He locks eyes with me as he puts it in his mouth and starts brushing his own teeth. I can see him smiling around the handle like a kid with a secret. I guess he really didn't mind last night then.

Ten minutes later, Tristan sets an egg and cheese sandwich down in front of me. Remy and Logan are drinking cups of coffee, talking to Tristan as I eat quickly. I overhear Tristan telling Logan to buy me something red. I roll my eyes. I wonder if I did get something red if he would steal it and claim it like Logan said he did with all their stuff. It would be hilarious to see tall, cute as hell, Tristan trying to fit into my clothes.

"Someone's happy this morning. What's the smile about over there?" Tristan asks. I giggle and shake my head at him. No way am I sharing that thought.

"Someone is also done eating, so let's get a move on," Remy says, dumping his leftover coffee in the sink.

Logan takes my hand in his, and the three of us make our way to the door. The black Escalade is already parked in front of the steps leading to the house. I take a look around, this is the first time I've been outside since I was brought here. The wide expanse of green lawn is well manicured, box bushes trimmed to perfection lining the walk. The circular driveway is tan brick, and I can't see where it leads to. There's also a fountain, the center of it is a wolf with its head thrown back in a howl, water shooting in a stream from its mouth. It makes me miss my wolf.

Tristan squeezes my hand, pulling me out of my thoughts and to the back door of the SUV. He opens it and guides me in, pulling the strap to buckle me in. He climbs in the passenger side, Remy already behind the wheel. As we make out way down the drive, I take in all the trees and open space we pass. Do they know how lucky they are to have all this? They must own a lot of acres of land to have a driveway this long. Geez!

I remained quiet on the drive to town until we pulled up in front of a small store called *Miss Petite's*. Logan jumps out as soon as Remy stops the car. He opens my door with a gleeful expression on his face. Bouncing around all crazy like. He takes my hand and drags me through the glass door.

Logan pushes me into a dressing room immediately. I thought we were going to look at the clothes but he tells me to stay in there and he'll bring me stuff to put on. I wait, looking myself over in the mirror. I don't know what I'm doing here. Letting people I barely know buy me things I haven't earned. I haven't done anything to deserve any of it.

The door opens, and Logan hangs several items on a hook. "Put the underwear on first, I already took the tags off so you can wear them out of the store. I'm still looking for shoes, you wear what, a size six?"

I blush thinking about this incredibly attractive man picking out panties and a bra for me. How would he know the right size? I don't say anything though, walking to the hook and running my hand over the delicate black lace of the bra. I've never had something so nice. I usually get my clothes from second-hand stores and I tend to pick out things that I'll think will last longer. Not really paying attention to style, more warmth and practicality.

"A five and half, actually. I usually have to look in the kid's section." That makes him laugh, and he exits the small dressing room, closing the door behind him.

"Try the blue one on first," He shouts through the door. "Come out here when you have an outfit on, I want to see it."

I take my borrowed clothes off and put the bra on, it

fits perfectly. The panties are made of the same material, they look like really tiny shorts. Once on, the bottom of my cheeks peak out. I tug on them trying to get them to cover everything. It doesn't work.

"Logan?" I call out.

"He's looking for shoes. Is there a problem?" I hear Remy's voice in answer.

"Umm... I think he got the wrong size for me."

The door opens, and Remy stands there, looking me over. I blush and shrink into myself. That gray gaze of his makes me more self-conscious than I have ever felt. He doesn't make a move to leave though. Remy clears his throat.

"What doesn't fit?" His voice sounds deeper than normal.

Oh, Lord! I shouldn't have said anything. I bite my lip, and then suck it up. He's here now so I should just get it over with. "The panties, they...don't cover everything. They're too short in the back. I turn, showing him what I mean.

Remy's eyes fall on my behind, the intensity in his gaze feeling like a caress, heating my skin. I shiver. He blinks as if coming out of a dream and looks back to my face. "That's how they are supposed to fit Kitten." With that, he turns and walks out of the room.

I take a deep breath, getting myself under control. I slip into a white cami-top, pulling the soft blue sweater Logan wanted me to wear on. On the hook are a pair of black shorts, a black skirt, and a silky pair of black dress pants. Behind them are several shirts. Dressing up always makes me feel like an impostor but my legs are in no shape to be seen so pants it is.

There's a tap on the door. "You about ready?" Logan calls.

I open the door, stepping out. Logan frowns and Remy shakes his head. "Well, blue is not your color sweetie, you look as pale as a ghost. Turn around for me," I do as he asks. "Those pants look great on you though. Go back in, I have the perfect thing."

After a few moments, Logan brings in a forest green sweater, the same soft one as the blue. I don't wait for him to leave I take the blue one off and slip the green one over my head. Logan fixes my hair, turning me toward the mirror. He stands behind me with his hands on my hips, satisfied smile on his face.

"Perfect," he whispers in my ear.

I meet his eyes, beaming a smile at him. I know he's probably more excited at his skills for clothing choices than who's wearing them, but still. Hearing him say I look perfect makes me happy. When we walk out Remy gives me a nod of approval. Logan has me sit on a bench and hands me a pair of dress socks to put on. He kneels in front of me and takes my foot in his hands.

"So tiny," He mutters. He opens a box next to me, taking out a velvet-like ankle boot with at least a three-inch heel. He puts it on me and zips the side. He does that for the other one too, pulling me up to stand when he's done. I wobble a little, never having worn anything but sneakers. I walk around, holding onto his arm until I feel steady enough to walk on my own. Remy gathers the clothes and shoes I took off and tucks them under his arm.

As we approach the counter, I notice a small pile of clothes already sitting there. Logan pulls the tags off the pants and shirts I'm wearing, handing them to the lady that works here. Remy takes out his wallet, handing Logan a handful of money. Remy then takes my arm, leading me back to the car while Logan pays. I look up at Remy, wondering why we aren't waiting for Logan. He ignores my look as he leads me to his side of the SUV, opening the door and buckling me in like before. Logan comes out, putting the bag of clothes in next to me and jumps in the front.

"I can't wait to take you shopping for real Kitten," Logan says looking back at me. I don't know what to say to that, so I just look out the window.

"Now, let's get you hired Miss Kitten," Remy says as we drive off.

As we walk into the ice rink, I spot Miss Annie, the owner, behind the skate rental counter. She smiles and waves, I wave back. She hands a pair of skates over to a customer and walks around to greet me.

"Look what the cat done dragged in," She says while giving me a soft hug. She says the same thing each time I see her. With her Texas drawl, it never fails to make me smile. I've always liked Miss Annie. She's a bigger woman, but it just makes for better hugs, as she would say. I've always wished she was my grandmother. She's short like me, so there's a slight resemblance in that way. She'd do anything for anybody. Even give a homeless girl with no address or phone, an illegal under-the-table job.

She looks at the two imposing men who have moved to stand behind me. "And who do we have here?" Miss

Annie asks, wrapping a hand around my wrist and tugging to move me behind her.

Remy lifts an eyebrow at her move but puts on a smile. "I'm Remington Greyson, this here is Logan Miller. I'm Kitten's new guardian. Pleasure to meet you, ma'am." He holds out a hand, and Miss Annie shakes it. She looks back at me for confirmation, and I nod my head slightly.

"Well, that's just great. About time someone looked after my precious girl. What can I do for y'all gentlemen?"

Remy leans forward and pulls me back toward him, throwing an arm around my shoulder. "Kitten here has told us many great things about your establishment and the time she's spent here. We thought we'd take a look around, and I'd like to speak with you about giving her a paying part-time job."

Miss Annie's face falls a little at this, and I know why. She can't afford to pay me any more than she already does. The rink makes good money, but there's a lot of upkeep, and there are repairs that need to be made to the aging building.

Remy must see this because he says, "Logan, why don't you have Kitten show you around while I talk to..." Oh! I forgot to introduce her.

"Miss Annie," I say, cursing my bad manners.

"Yes, Miss Annie." Remy finishes.

Logan shrugs and holds his hand to the side, "Lead the way."

I take his hand and pull him to walk beside me. I point out the snack and rental counters. We walk by the lockers, and I show him the one with my name on it. Miss Annie gave me a pair of the rental skates to call my own and lets me keep a locker here. I'm proud of it, none of the other employees have one, and usually they are for customers only.

I lead him through the swinging doors to the heart of the building, where the stands and the ice itself are located. We take a seat on the first row of the stands and watch the few people out on the ice.

"Have you ever been?" I ask Logan.

He chuckles. "Actually, no. I haven't."

I bounce a little in my seat. "Would you let me teach you?" I ask excitedly. It would be a great way to pay him and the others back for all they've done for me. Funny to think that I may have a skill that they don't.

He barks out a laugh. "Maybe, we'll see." I pout, doing my best impression of puppy eyes at him. He just laughs harder and pokes me in the cheek. We sit together for a while, just watching. There are two little girls out on the ice that I taught to skate. I smile as I think about how far they have come. Their mother is a sweet woman who paid attention and learned to skate too so she could keep up with her kids. Not all of the parents do that.

"Are you thirsty? I'm going to get me a soda." Logan says.

"I'll take some water if you don't mind." I smile up at him.

"Of course I don't," He replies, kissing the crown of my head as he stands to leave. I watch his form as he walks away. He's so graceful like he plans every move each of his muscles makes. I sigh heavily, I can't imagine how amazing that body of his would be on the ice. He goes through the doors and I can't see him anymore, so I turn back to watch the little girls.

"Well, well, well, if it isn't the little runt. I haven't seen you around. Where have you been?" A cold, mocking voice behind me says. I recognize it immediately. It's Adam. The guy most girls drool over, the town hockey star, the bad boy, my tormentor.

"Hello, Adam," I reply, looking straight ahead. Ignoring him won't work. I've tried that before.

"I thought for sure you would have turned hooker by now, I was going to start searching the street corners for you." His comment causes hoots of laughter behind me. I should have guessed he wouldn't be alone. He never is, he always has his pack of hyenas with him, the ones I refer to as his 'yes men'.

"Nope, not yet Adam."

He takes a seat beside me; someone sits on the other side of me as well. I had hoped he'd say his mean comments and just walk away. Looks like that's not happening. Yay, lucky me, I think with sarcasm.

"I don't mean that as an insult Kitty, I think you'd make a great hooker. I'd love to be your first customer. Are going to charge money or just hold a sign that says 'will suck for food'?" More laughter. I don't answer him this time.

"Hey Adam, it looks like someone beat you to it man, check out what she's wearing, she almost looks like a lady. Ya know, if it wasn't for that poor person stench coming off her in waves I might actually believe it." I feel Adam stiffen beside me as the guy high fives the rest of the 'yes men'.

Adam leans down and talks into my ear, his hand grabbing my hair at my neck. "Is that true Kitty? You been spreading those thighs for somebody else? Or did you get on your knees and beg for money? Tell me." he pulls my hair harder. He's never touched me before. I don't know what's changed now.

He pulls his face away and talks to the hyenas more than to me. He still has my hair though. "Did you get all dressed up for me? Think I'd notice you and want you?" He laughs. "I don't have room in my bed for a filthy slut like you, sorry to disappoint."

"*Hey*!" Logan shouts his voice echoing. "Get. Your. Hands. Off. Her." He growls darkly. The 'yes men' back up, seeing the rage on Logan's face. Adam just grips my hair tighter, making me whimper out loud.

"Ah, this must be the unfortunate guy who paid for your....services." Adam sneers at me, keeping his eyes on Logan. He plasters a mean smirk on his face, looking to Logan. "Tell me though, was she nice and tight? Or was she as used up as I thought she was?"

Logan drops the cups he was carrying, taking a step forward, and growling low in his throat, blue eyes shining with fury. "I won't say it again. Get your fucking hands off of her. *Now*!" Adam finally releases me. He stands holding his hands up feigning innocence, smirk still in place.

"No disrespect man, just curious." The yes men flank him as he walks off laughing. Logan is at my side in an instant, a possessive arm around my shoulders. When the others are further away, I hear Adam's voice saying, "I guess a good cocksucker does inspire loyalty."

Logan starts to stomp in his direction, but Remy walks through the swinging door and calls to Logan. Logan is breathing hard, his eyes on Remy. Blue meeting gray in a silent plea. Remy shakes his head, staring back. I put my hand on Logan's arm, running my fingers down to his, locking them together. We move toward Remy. As we go to pass him, Remy puts an arm around my waist. I still don't let go of Logan though. I think he was going to fight Adam, and I'm afraid he still will if I let go.

We walk like that out to the Escalade. Remy gets me seated, closing my door and pulling Logan aside to talk. I can't hear what they're saying, but Logan still seems mad. He's yelling at Remy and waving his arms around. Remy's face is stoic. He says something to Logan that seems to calm him down and Logan looks in my direction, blowing out a huge breath. Remy pats him on the shoulder, and they both get in.

At first, we ride silently. After a short time, Remy breaks the silence. "Who was that boy, Kitten?"

"His name is Adam Vanderson. He's the big shot of the ice rink. Plays hockey." I respond, not really knowing what he wants me to say.

"So he's there all the time then. I won't allow you to work there and deal with him, Kitten. You'll have to choose another place to work." Remy says in that tone that says his word is final.

"Does that mean that Miss Annie said I can work there then? Like really work there?" I ask.

Remy's lips press into a hard line. He nods. "She said she'd hire you on as a trainer four days a week, making fifteen dollars an hour and you'll be given a couple of hours Monday mornings to skate. As I said though, that will not be happening now. I'll not have you exposed to that *boy*, any longer."

I roll my eyes. If he knew how long I've been "exposed" to Adam and his pack of laughing hyenas he'd know that I could handle it by now. He didn't say anything today that I haven't heard a million times. Although he did touch me today, which is new.

"If she said she'll hire me on as a trainer then I won't be there when he is. Hockey practice and games are always after the little kids and open skate." I reply. "I don't know why he was there this early today. School must be on a break or something."

Remy arches an eyebrow but simply states, "We'll see." Logan growls at this. Remy shoots him a look and he quiets.

None of us speak for the rest of the car ride. I'm sorry that Logan had to witness that. I'm used to being treated that way, but maybe he's never seen something like that before. People probably treat him and the rest of the guys like royalty. I've only dealt with a handful of people that have treated me with any kindness. Miss Annie being one, the librarian at my favorite library the other, and the guys themselves. Everyone else has either seen me as trash or a target. Once again I'm reminded how much I don't fit with them. Hopefully I won't bring them down.

"Tristan sent a text, says he's not making dinner tonight. Want to pick something up?" Remy asks Logan.

Logan shrugs, "How about some wings from the bar?"

"Call it in now so we won't have to wait so long this time," Remy says, flipping his turning signal and making a U-turn.

The bar we go to is just starting to fill up with customers. On the phone Logan ordered over two hundred chicken wings, I have no idea how long that will take, but I guess we are going to wait inside until it's done. A very attractive raven-haired waitress greets the guys with a broad smile and a hug for each of them. We're seated at a table right in front of a big screen TV showing a football game. As soon as Logan is sitting, the waitress takes a seat in his lap. I turn my shocked face to Remy. He glares at the dark haired girl, so I look down at my knees. This must be Logan's girlfriend, and Remy must not approve.

"Uh, Angela... won't your boss be angry at you for sitting here?" Logan asks her.

The girl giggles in the highest pitch I've ever heard. "If she knew you boys were here she'd be draped all over Remington right now." I peek up to see her batting her lashes at Logan, sticking her chest out in his face. Her very large chest. But Logan isn't paying attention.

"Why don't you go see if our order is ready Angela?" Remy says, still glaring.

She pouts her bright red lips before kissing Logan's cheek and bouncing away. I can't stand to look at the lipstick print she left on his cheek, so I pretend to watch the game on TV. The guys start talking to each other, but I don't join in. I try to figure out the warring emotions that course through me. I'm hurt by what happened, but I don't know why. I should be happy for Logan. He has a beautiful girlfriend who seems really happy. I wonder if he does her hair like he does mine. I don't like that thought. Maybe I'm angry because she acted like I wasn't even there. Next to Remy and Logan, I guess I would be invisible. They are perfection while I am.....not. Why did he let me sleep in his bed if he had a girlfriend though? I doubt she'd like that. I don't know much about relationships, but if Logan were mine.... well, he's not, so it doesn't matter. Is that why I'm hurt? Did I want Logan? I guess Remy has a girlfriend too, Angela's boss. And he saw me in my underwear today!

Logan nudges me, and I shrink away from him. I suddenly don't want him to touch me. He has a look of hurt on his face, but I don't care. "What's wrong Kitten?" he asks me.

"Nothing, just trying to figure out what's happening in the game," I reply nodding to the screen. That's a lie, I understand football well. I don't know why anyone plays it, but I understand how it's played. Logan then tries to explain in simpleton terms, which normally would make me laugh, but right now I don't feel like laughing.

About twenty minutes later Angela and a tall blond woman bring out our order of chicken wings. I can only guess more kissing will ensue so I stand and walk out to the car calling a "meet you out there" over my shoulder.

I climb in and buckle myself in for the first time today. Now I wonder if they did that because they think I'm helpless. Whatever, it's not like I care what they think. I sigh, yeah right.

The guys come out a few minutes later. Both of them ask me questions, trying to get me to talk. I answer yes or no, and eventually they stop trying. I tune them out, watching the sun set as we drive back to their house. I count the trees as we make our way up the drive. At tree seventeen I see a large dog running away from the house. A black dog.

"*Stop*! Stop the car!" I yell.

CHAPTER EIGHT

emy slams on the brakes and I unbuckle myself and jump from the car. Hearing both of them shouting at me to get back in the car only makes me run faster. The dog, or well, wolf runs for the trees that surround the open lawn, I follow it. A few feet in I hear movement. I slow my pace, a little winded after that sprint. I step around a big evergreen tree and gasp. There are a bunch of wolves! A much bigger, but just as black, wolf pounces on my wolf. It looks like it's going to hurt him, so I shout for it to stop. The three black wolves snap their heads to me then immediately look to the left of me. I peer around the tree and see... I don't even know what.

There's a blond looking wolf, but it's, *doing* something. As I stare, trying to figure out what's happening, I feel my black wolf pushing against my legs, but I can't take my eyes off the blond wolf. Maybe ten seconds go by and then, Reed. Reed is exactly where the wolf was. I didn't blink though; I saw the wolf...turn into Reed? What. The. Hell. I look down at my wolf that is still pushing at me. I see his eyes. They are grass green. I look to the other smaller wolf, mint green. The bigger black one has almost black eyes. Then I get it. Reed *was* the wolf. The wolf was *Reed*. And the others are Kellan, Ash *Finn*. Finn was *my* wolf.

I feel light headed and stumble to my knees. I can't get enough air. This doesn't make sense! Wolves don't turn into people; people don't turn into wolves. It just *does not* happen. My vision goes dark; I fall on my back, still gasping for air. I hear people shouting and wolves barking and whining. Then I hear and see nothing as I pass out.

I come awake to the sound of voices. I strain my ears to hear them. One is Remy, and he's angry. "Make sure Tristan talks to her first, she likes his voice, and she trusts him."

Another voice, Ash. "Did you see her? What did she think she was gonna do? She just walked up to us like she could have pulled me off, Finn. Who walks into a den of wolves and isn't scared?"

"A crazy ass girl is who. She thought you were going to hurt her 'dog.'" Jace says laughing.

"Enough! This isn't funny. What the hell are we going to do? Tell her it was dream?" Kellan.

"She's too smart for that, I saw it in her eyes before

she passed out. She knows." Finn says in a sad voice.

"Well, she can't!" Kellan again.

"How about we tell her the truth? We haven't known her long but you know she likes it here. I don't think she'll run off. It's not like she'd tell anyone, and if she did no one would believe her." Jace says like he doesn't have a care in the world.

"I agree with Jace. Although I don't like how he's saying it. I think we should tell her the truth because she deserves it. We agreed to make her a part of our family and our family doesn't keep secrets. If she wants to leave, we'll make sure she's set up. Taken care of. You still need to tell her about that Charles guy Remy, and soon, she needs to know." That's Tristan speaking now. Always looking out for me.

I open my eyes and see them all standing in front of the couch that I'm lying on. I look to Tristan, searching his chocolate eyes. "I don't want to leave," I say to him.

That gets everyone's attention. The guys start speaking all at once. Some to me, some to each other. I cover my face with my hands, rubbing at my temples. A headache is forming, and it feels like my head is splitting in two. Remy yells for them to shut up. Not helping my poor head, but at least they all quiet down.

I look up at Remy. "This is what's going to happen now. Kellan is going to get me some ibuprofen because I have a headache, Logan is going to sit somewhere out of my sight and not talk because I'm mad at him and don't know why. Reed, the same because I can't stop seeing what happened." I point to Jace, "You're an ass, and I'm not sure I like you after what you just implied. I'm not here to use you. I didn't ask to be here, *you* guys asked *me* to stay."

I point to Finn, "How *dare* you!" I can't believe he acted like my pet then ran away, making me feel awful. I finally point to Tristan and Remy. "You two are going to sit on this couch and are not leaving until you explain what the hell is going on. You, Remy, because you seem to be some type of leader around here, and Tristan because his voice won't hurt my head and so far has done nothing to make me mad at him." I lean my head on the back of the couch and close my eyes after my little rant.

I hear Jace chuckling until someone smacks him. "You heard the girl, the rest of you clear out!" Remy shouts, and I groan.

"Sorry, I forgot," he says.

The three of us wait until Kellan comes back with two pills and a cup of water. I tell him thank you, and he leaves the room as well. I look to Remy.

"To begin with, no you are not crazy. You saw Reed, the wolf, turn into Reed, the man. We're wolves, Kitten. I guess you could call us werewolves, but most of us just prefer to be called wolves." He pauses like I'm going to deny his words. Denial has never been my thing.

Tristan reaches for my hand, but I pull back. "You're still safe with us, we won't hurt you." I think about that. They are part animal, and animals are notoriously unpredictable. But I spent time with Finn when he was a wolf, and he still acted like Finn when he's a person. God this is confusing. I nod my head at Tristan. I believe him. They've shown no sign that they want to hurt me, and they could have. I think they would have done it already if that's what they wanted.

"How...how is it possible?" I ask.

"There's a lot of information and I'm not sure you want it all right now. There have always been werewolves since there was man, there have been werewolves. Lilith was Adam's first wife, Eve his second. Werewolves are the descendants from Lilith and Adam. Humans the descendants from Eve and Adam."

"O....kay, that was a long time ago, would you like to talk about the present? It concerns me a bit more don't you think?" I reply.

Tristan takes over; his blessedly soft voice is as soothing as ever. "Okay, so there are born wolves, and there are changed wolves. There are very few changed wolves, but that's what we are."

"What's the difference? And why aren't there a lot of you?" I ask, I have so many questions.

"I was getting to that," Remy says, giving me a pointed look. He continues. "In the early nineteenth century, a virus broke out in the wolf community. It killed off almost seventy percent of us and left most of our females barren. Before the outbreak, there were millions of us, maybe more. Today there are a lot less of us in the world. Almost all of them are male. With so few females, children are not an option for most. Even if you find your mate, the chances of her being able to bear children are slight."

"So that explains that, but you said you are changed. Why don't you just change more females?"

Tristan gives me a sad smile as Remy answers. "They tried that, right after the outbreak. Few female humans live through the change. The odds are something like one in two thousand. There aren't many changed wolves because we tend to be stronger than born wolves. With so much competition for females, well, they don't want to add to it. The only reason any of us are alive is because we were left for dead and survived."

So werewolves do attack people. I wonder...

"So do you guys...eat people?" I had to ask.

"NO!" Both of them answer at the same time. I giggle, nothing is funny about this, but it's just so crazy that I can't help it. We're sitting here talking seriously about mythical beings after all.

"How is it that you all found each other then? Why do you all live together?" I ask.

"You have to understand Kitten, wolves uh, we tend to live, that is to say that...uh...we don't die unless we are killed. Remy is the oldest of us. He came across Ash, who was left in the same position as him. He took him in, the same with the rest of us. Wolves are happier in packs, we live like humans for the most part, but we like being together. It made sense for us to share a house." Tristan says kindly.

The living together thing makes sense, but my brain can't process the fact that they live forever. How old are they then?

I look to Remy, "Is Angela a wolf then?" I blush, feeling stupid that I asked that when there are better questions.

Remy squints his eyes at me. "No, she's a human. Why do you ask?"

I shift in my seat. "I was just wondering if, you know, since she's Logan's girlfriend if, you know, they could...you know?" Wow, I sound smart. No wonder this guy thinks I need a tutor.

He chuckles under his breath. "They can have sex,

yes. But they can never have children. Humans cannot carry wolf offspring and human males cannot impregnate female wolves."

"Oh," I say, looking at my knees.

"Furthermore, Angela is not Logan's girlfriend," he says. Smirking at me.

"But she kissed him! And the tall blond, she's your..."

He cuts me off. "Kitten we have been around for a very long time, we have, certain needs, if you will, of the female variety. We prepare ourselves for a lifetime of loneliness and meaningless relationships, but that doesn't necessarily mean we have to be alone all of the time. Male wolves can choose to attend the Mating Games and win a mate if they would like. We cannot, as we would most likely be killed for trying.

I nod. "Uh, okay." I have no idea what to say to that. I want to know more about these Mating Games but now doesn't seem like the time. I have so many questions. I don't understand how this all can be real. I know it is. I saw it with my own eyes but...

"We've given you a lot to think about. How about we call it a night?" Tristan says. I nod again. As we get up and start to walk from the room, I pull Tristan aside.

"Do you mind if I stay with you tonight?" I ask, hoping he'll say yes. Maybe it's his voice or his eyes, I don't know, I trust Tristan. Maybe I shouldn't. I think a normal person in my position would run for the hills, but since when have I ever been normal.

Tristan flashes me his charming smile, "I'd be honored Kitten. Are you going to eat though?" He asks.

I shake my head. "No, I think I'd like to lay down now." No way am I going to sit around the table with all of them right now.

"Okay, I'm going to go eat, I'll meet you up there later. Remember the way?"

"Yeah, I remember. Do mind if I use your tub? A bath would be wonderful right about now."

He kisses my cheek "Of course, I'll see you in a bit." If my mind wasn't spinning a mile a minute, I might have taken the time to freak out about Tristan kissing me, as it is though, I just file it for later.

I turn to the stairs as he walks to the kitchen. Logan must have guessed I'd stay in here because the bags from our earlier shopping trip are sitting on Tristan's bed. I dig through them seeing a pair of sleep pants and more panties and bras. There are more cami-tops too. Other stuff is in there as well, I briefly wonder how Logan had the time to get all this, but push that thought away too. I put together an outfit and head to the bathroom.

After I fill the tub with water and bubbles, I use the hair tie from my ponytail and wrap my hair up in a bun. I sink into the hot water, feeling my body relax. I can't believe what a crazy day I've had. Werewolves not only exist, but I'm living with them. I'm in a werewolf's bathtub right now. A werewolf that owns bubble bath. I giggle to myself. I guess I've never been normal, but even here I'm an outcast. I really don't fit in. A Kitten amongst wolves. Ha! I crack myself up sometimes.

CHAPTER NINE

Tristan must have come to bed after I fell asleep. I didn't hear him come in at all. I must be slipping. I turn over, prop my head up in my hand and watch Tristan sleep. His bare back is uncovered with the sheets wrapped around his waist. He's clearly a blanket stealer. His sand-colored hair is a wild mess. I like it that way.

"What are you doing?" I can barely understand him with his face buried in the pillow.

"Oh, nothing. I've decided to become your new creepy stalker, that's all. I buried your old one out back, hope you don't mind." I say, deadpan.

Tristan grumbles something and turns his head toward me. "Someone woke up in weirdo mode," He says.

I widen my eyes and give him the creepiest smile I

can manage without a mirror. "You have a squishy face, and I shall call you squishy face and you shall be *mine*."

Tristan bursts out laughing before he smacks me with a pillow right in my face, causing me to go into a giggle fit. "Oh my God, you are such a strange little thing. I had no idea. You've been walking around here pretending to be a good little girl while hiding all your scary."

I kick him lightly in the leg. "Oh no, no you didn't. You wanna play little one? I guarantee you I'll win." Now Tristan is the one with the creepy smile.

I back off the bed, acting like I'm going to run around it. Tristan follows from the other side. I fake like I'm making a run for it, he takes the bait, and I jump on the bed, bouncing off it and sprint for the door. I throw it open and dash down the hall, Tristan right behind me laughing his head off. I make it to the stairs and slide down the wide banister. I hear him say "Oh shit" somewhere behind me before I hear footfalls on the steps.

I run down the first-floor hallway, not really sure where I'm running to. I come to a connecting hallway and go left, running right into Tristan's waiting arms. He picks me up, and I squeal. He's still laughing, spinning me around when we hear someone clear their throat. We both freeze and look for whoever made the noise.

Turns out we are right in front of the games room. Where everyone is sitting, staring at us like we've lost our minds. I look back at Tristan. When our eyes meet we burst out laughing again. I take advantage of the distraction and smack his arm. "Tag, you're *it*!" I call as I run off again. I've never played this game before but I've watched other kids do it at the park and have always wanted to.

I hear Tristan say the same thing before he's suddenly beside me. I wonder who's *it* now. He leads me to the back door, and we run down the patio steps and into the yard. I hear several of them behind us, and my giggling starts up again. I have no idea why I started this, and I never expected anyone else to join in. This is great. I feel freer than I ever have in my life.

"Shush girl, you're going to lead them straight to us," Tristan says playfully. I turn my head and see Ash coming toward us at a full sprint. I laugh louder. He might have longer legs and be stronger than me, but I'm closer to the ground and can out maneuver him. As he gets closer, I break away from Tristan, circling back, just out of Ash's reach. I run and hide behind Remy. It's obvious that he's not playing. He's standing against the rail of the deck, arms folded over his chest, watching the craziness.

"Are you having fun, Miss Kitten?" He asks. I can hear the smile in his voice.

I lean my head against his back, trying to pull in more air. I can't stop laughing though. I can't remember if I have ever had this much fun. Or laughed so much. "Yes," I manage to giggle out.

"She's behind Remy!" I hear someone call. I peek my head out. It looks like Logan is *it* now.

"Hey, how do you win this game?" I ask Remy.

"Win? You don't really win a game of tag, Kitten. Besides, even if you could, you'd never win against a pack of wolves." He turns to face me, a broad smile on his face. Reed comes up to hide with me, not even out of breath.

"Hey, guess what?" Reed asks me.

"What?"

He reaches out and flicks my arm. "You're *it*!" He shouts, already down the steps. Dang that boy is fast. I step up next to Remy. The guys have lined up in the grass, waiting for me. I take a step forward, they take a step back. I take another step forward and reach back, tagging Remy. I run to stand beside the guys. Turning and waiting for him now.

When I turn around, he's still standing where I left him. I pout at him. "You're *it*, Rem, don't you want to play with me?"

"Yeah, Remy!" Calls Jace, his tone full of humor. Remy takes a step forward, and the guys move back. I stay there, keeping my pale green eyes on Remy's gray ones. A smile creeps up my face. I want to see the strong, grumbly leader play. I turn slowly, picking out my path in a glance. I see Remy take his shirt off out of the corner of my eye. Is he trying to distract me? It's sort of working. I want to stare at him, but I force my eyes away.

"I'm going to give you a ten-second head start Kitten, and then I'm coming for you." His deep voice and heated way he says this sends a thrilling shiver throughout my body. The other guys laugh and start taking off their shirts too, and their shoes. I find this odd, but then Remy starts to count, distracting me. Before he finishes saying 'one,' I'm off and running. I head for the tree line in the distance. I hear the number ten being said before I hear howling. I turn my head to look back and am shocked to see several huge wolves giving chase. How in the heck did I ever mistake one of them for a dog? I increase my speed and almost make it to the tree line before I feel a nudge on my calf.

I stop running and collapse on the ground. Doing a

mixture between panting for breath and laughing my heart out. A huge red wolf nuzzles my neck before licking my face. "You totally cheated." I accuse the wolf. He nods his head up and down. If a wolf could look smug, I'm sure this is what it would look like. I roll my eyes at him.

A golden wolf pokes his nose into my hand, forcing himself under it. I bet this one is Jace. I pet his coat. He's so pretty. Jace is a fine specimen as a man, and it transfers well to his wolf form. I whisper in his ear that I forgive him for yesterday. I don't think he even likes me. Knowing what little of him that I do, he's probably just showing off his breathtakingly beautiful wolf.

A light brown wolf pounces on Jace. Logan. At first, I'm afraid that he'll hurt him but neither one looks aggressive. They roll around, nipping at each other. I realize that this is how they must play. A few of the others start playing too. I sit and watch. I'm happy they are having fun. I know that a serious conversation will take place later, but I'm not yet ready for it.

The mint green eyed wolf that is Finn sits next to me, snuggling into my side. "Hi Finn, I really missed you when you left me, you know?" His response is to lick my hand with his wet tongue. I throw an arm around his big neck and lean back into him. I haven't forgiven him yet. I'm sure I will eventually but he lied to me and left me. I truly did miss him though, and I don't want to let him go just yet. I enjoyed being close to him then, and I still do now.

A lean looking wolf with pretty hazel eyes walks up to me with his head low, ears back. I smile at him, "Hey Reed, come here." I hold my hand out. Reed comes to me, I scratch behind his ear for a moment before he lays his head in my lap. Two shiny black wolves take a seat in front of us. One massive one and a smaller, yet still big one. The grass green eyed one barks at me.

I giggle, "Hi Kellan, hi Ash." Kellan barks again. A wet nose nuzzles my neck from behind. I turn and see the big red wolf. Remy is simply stunning in wolf form. I turn my face and press it back into his neck. If he can do it so can I. His fur tickles my nose, but it feels comforting feeling the coarse hair against my face. It feels *right*.

I don't see Tristan or Logan anywhere; they must have headed back to the house already. We sit around for a while, the guys taking turns having me pet them. Eventually though, Remy barks. Probably saying something I don't understand, and the other wolves get up and trot to the house. He's commanding even when he can't speak. Figures. I get up slowly, stretching and follow.

That was the most fun I have ever had. And I owe it all to a bunch of wild animals. The thought makes me smile.

***

We gather around the kitchen island. The guys are already passing around plates of pancakes and bacon, chatting happily away with each other. I smile to myself, a girl could really get used to this. Reed comes up behind me, placing a plate of strawberry topped pancakes in front of me with one hand. His other hand finds my hip, squeezing it gently. I turn my head to the side and give him a kiss on the cheek.

"Thank you, Reed."

"No problem. I know you like strawberries, I figured I'd just make you a plate." He shrugs. He acts like it's nothing, but to me, it means a lot. He didn't just put food on a plate for me. He chopped up the berries and made a smiley face, a dab of butter for the nose. It's cute, I love it. Who knew someone could be artistic with food?

As I'm smiling at my pancakes like a total freak, a hand shoots out and snatches the strawberry that was an eye. I look up to see a smug looking Ash, happily chewing away at the stolen fruit. I mock glare at him, but I can't keep the smile off my face, so I'm sure it's less than intimidating.

Reed backs away from me, going behind Ash and smacking the back of his head with a loud pop. Ash makes a choking noise. Holy crap! Reed just hit Ash! I start giggling uncontrollably, the others joining in with me. Logan makes a move to grab another piece but is too slow, and I push his hand away. I hear Reed huff behind me before he pulls me out of my seat and sits down. What the heck? Is he mad that I laughed?

"Come here Kitten."

"Uh, where?" I reply brilliantly.

Reed huffs again, both of his hands going to my hips, turning and lifting me onto his lap. I suck in a shocked breath, looking over my shoulder and up into his face. He has a satisfied look on his face but doesn't say anything as he pulls my plate closer to us. He picks up the fork, looking it over, twirling it in his hand. He puts it back down then uses his long fingers to pick up one of the coveted strawberries, bringing it to my mouth. Holy Jesus, Reed's going to feed me!

I open my mouth, more out of reflex than anything

else. The sweet taste spreads over my tongue. My eyes close to half mast as I let out a small moan. God how I love these!

"Shit..." Ash says under his breath, bringing me out of my daze.

Reed shifts underneath me. I feel the heat rise in my cheeks at my reaction. I should really try to control myself one of these days. I notice that it's now quiet throughout the kitchen. Whatever, not my problem they can't appreciate the taste of strawberries the way I do. Reed brings another berry to my lips. I'm still embarrassed from before, so I don't immediately open my mouth. Reed slides the sweet fruit slowly over my bottom lip, my tongue darts out instinctively, lapping up the juice. That makes Reed shift again. He must be uncomfortable with me sitting on him, so I open my mouth, taking the bite. Better to hurry, so his legs don't fall asleep than to draw this out.

Once I'm finished eating, Reed feeding me every bite, I help Jace clear the table. He's been quiet. I wonder if it's because he simply doesn't want to talk to me.

"Did I do something to make you mad at me?" I blurt.

Jace's head snaps up, his sky blue eyes finding mine. "No."

O....kay. One word answer, huh? Guess there will be no small talk then. "Then why don't you like me?"

"Who said I don't like you?" Jace returns his attention to loading the dishwasher.

He so did not answer the question. "Does that mean you do?" I know the answer, but I need him to say it.

Instead of answering he asks his own question. "Why

are you here, Kitten?" I blink at him in surprise. He's as blunt as I am.

"I guess because I was asked to stay." I shrug.

Jace slams the door closed on the dishwasher, causing the dishes to clink around. I hope he didn't break anything. I back away from him, toward the doorway. I don't know why my answer made him angry, but if he tries anything I'm ready to run.

He watches me out of the corner of his eye. He turns, leaning back on the counter, his hands gripping the granite top next to his hips. "By that logic, you'd stay with anyone that invited you to. I don't believe for an instant that no man has ever asked you back to his place. Even for a night," He sneers. "but instead of being at some random guy's house, you're here. In a house full of wolves, wealthy wolves." He finishes.

Even though I'm not surprised by his words they still hurt. He thinks I'm after their money. I could see why he thinks that but...that's just not me. Maybe the others don't think that because they actually took the time to know me. He hasn't. And he's seen them spend money on me.

"Jace I'm not here for money, or the things that you could buy me. I'd rather earn the things I have than have them given to me. Everything the others have given me, or done for me, I'll pay them back. Do you think I don't know every piece of food I've eaten here? That I haven't added up in my head the cost of being under Kellan's care? I have! It might take forever to do it, and it might not always be cash payments, but my debt here will be repaid in full." I'm close to tears, and I hate it. The weight of their hospitality is pressing on me. I know the sooner I leave, the less debt I'll keep racking up here. The thought of leaving breaks my heart though.

"So that's how it is then? You plan on repaying them with kisses and smiles? You planning on spreading your legs and using your body too? I didn't think you were like that. I guess enough money thrown in a girl's face can turn anyone into a whore." My mouth drops open. No. He. Didn't.

"Are you serious?!" I scream at him. I hear footsteps running in the hallway, but I pay them no mind. "I'm a friggin' virgin, Jace! I've never...and I mean *never*, sold my body. Not for food, or a place to sleep or *anything*, for any reason! And I never will. I was asked to stay here. I didn't beg or crawl on my knees for any of you. I want to stay because for once in my life, I felt wanted. Do you have any idea what that means to me? Huh, Jace? Of course you don't!" I walk to him and shove at his chest. He barely moves.

I bring my face as close to his as I can with him being so much taller than me. "I'm sure with your good looks and charming smile and obvious wealth that you have never been denied. Am I right? The whole world just welcomes you with open arms huh, Jace?" I shove him again. His face is a hard mask, the blue of his eyes darkening with anger.

Arms go around my chest, pulling me back. I can tell its Remy. I'm not done though. "Can you understand that I have never had anyone? That I stayed because, for as long as I was wanted here...." I sniffle, the traitorous tears now streaming down my face. "...I didn't have to be alone. For once I was living, not just surviving." I choke on a sob, my voice finally giving out. Remy gets a better grip on me, pulling me from the room.

My head spins as I'm guided down the hallway. Jace called me a whore. Reed kissed me. Did he do that because he thought the same? He did have me on his lap...Oh God! I've slept in their beds. Of course they think that of me, all of them do. I struggle to get away from Remy. He just holds tighter as I fall apart in his arms.

"Get off of me!" I shout at him.

"Calm down, Kitten. Whatever you are thinking, stop. Stop right now." He orders.

He places me on the couch in the living room. I bring my knees up to my chest, wrapping my arms around my legs.

"Wait here," Remy says in his commanding voice. "Do *not* try to leave this house. Not right now. I'll be right back."

I don't answer him. I bury my face in my knees. I've been so stupid. You know what, I don't care. I've enjoyed being here. I liked spending time with these guys, even if they thought I was a whore. I can't stay now, but I won't regret it. I'll walk out of here with only what I had when I came in. I'm sure someone knows where my clothes are.

Several pairs of footsteps walk into the room. I don't know which ones are here or if all of them are. I hope Jace isn't. I'm sure, in his mind, he was just protecting his family, but that doesn't make it hurt any less, or make me less angry with him.

Remy's voice is short and clipped. He's obviously mad. "I called this family meeting because Mr. Rotherstone here, thought it was a great idea to tear Kitten to shreds." I hear several growls at his words.

"What the fuck, Jace?!" Ash roars.

"Quiet," Remy shouts. He's lost his normal control. "You will explain yourself right now, Mr. Rotherstone." I don't look up. These family meetings are so stupid, now I have to listen to this all over again.

"Explain myself? Why don't you explain yourself, Remy? Why is she here? Why are you all acting like it's okay that she knows about us? Don't you see what's happening here? You brought home a stray, a homeless little girl with nothing to lose. She can out us! You're just giving away secrets that we've worked our whole lives to keep hidden. You've given her the power to blackmail us all, and for what? A girl who acts all innocent? Who kisses your cheeks and blushes on cue? Please... It's not like any of us has ever had problems picking up women, we don't need her."

So, it's as I thought. He thinks he's protecting them from me. Normally that thought would be laughable. "Jace, I would never tell anyone about you. I have a natural aversion to padded rooms for one, but also because I wouldn't want anything bad to happen to the rest of the guys." I say the last part pointedly, looking straight at him.

"As I stated earlier, someone like you could never understand someone like me. Tristan cooked for me. Gave me food like it was the most normal thing in the world. To you it probably is, for me, it's the proof that kindness exists in the world. Sure... I've eaten before. I've had food. But it's never been as good as his and I've had to work my ass off for every bit I've ever had. He made it for me and just handed it over. That's no simple thing.

"Logan brushed my hair. To you that's probably

silly, to me, it's someone taking care of me. Did your mother brush your hair as a child, Jace? Well, mine didn't. No one ever has except me. It *means* something to me. Don't you get that? Not only would I never do anything to endanger them, but I'd give my life to protect them. Just for those stupid insignificant things that you probably laugh at." I say, my voice now small and sounding sadder than I'd like it to.

Jace deflates at my words. I think he finally gets it. To me, there are no small acts of kindness. "I'm sorry Kitten, I just thought..." He trails off, running a hand over his golden hair.

"I will make sure that Mr. Rotherstone does more than say sorry. I'm not defending his actions, so please don't think that, but I think he was just looking out for us, no matter how misguided that may have been." Remy tries to explain.

I nod slowly. "I know that."

Remy looks stunned. "You do?"

I sigh. "Yes, and as much as I want to hate him for what he said, I can't. His thinking was wrong, but his heart was in the right place. I don't blame him for trying to eliminate a perceived threat to his family. As I said, I'd want protect you guys too."

"You're such a fucking ass, Jace." Logan huffs.

"I think you can see you were way off track about Little One, right, Jace?" Jace nods his head, his eyes now trained on the floor. I wouldn't want to face Ash and his rage right now either if I was him.

"Now that we're all on the same page here, the meeting's over. Kitten, would you like to follow me please?" Remy says, holding out a hand to me. I don't take it, moving to stand on my own, and follow behind him to his office.

I curl up in the leather chair in front of Remy's desk. Remy surprises me when he moves the matching chair in front of me instead of sitting behind the desk. "Listen, Kitten, I'm sorry for what happened..."

"No," I cut him off. "You didn't do anything Rem, don't apologize. I don't really feel like talking about this again anyway."

He raises his eyebrow, sitting up straight in his chair. "If you had let me finish, I was saying that I'm sorry for what happened, but I think we should move on." Heat colors my cheeks, whoops.

"Sorry," I say sheepishly.

"Jace can be a little *abrasive* at first. In his time as a human, he was the son of a Duke. It's true that he's used to a life of privilege, he was born into it and has continued to live as such. That's not to say that he has not had his own challenges. In his day, women flocked to wealth and power. It's what drove them." I nod. Everyone has bad times, I'm sure being turned into a werewolf isn't a pleasant experience.

"I'm not sure what you want from me here, Rem. You want me to forgive him? I already did. Twice actually." I throw my arms out in an I-give-up gesture.

"I wanted you to come in because I'm worried about you. About what's running around that pretty little head of yours. Jace was wrong to call you a whore or imply that you have ulterior motives for being here. He knows that you are not experienced in that manner. I'm sure he was just picking out a weakness of yours." I don't have a clue what he means by weakness but wait...back up.

"And how would he know that I've never...that I'm *inexperienced*?" I struggle to ask.

Remy's face flushes a little. "We can sense it, Kitten."

"How?"

"To put it mildly, we can smell your innocence. Us wolves have a strong sense of smell."

"Well then." I have no idea what to say to that. It's creepy as all get out but I don't say that out loud.

"I hope you don't see this incident as a reason to leave. We took a vote as a family to ask you to stay. Jace agreed at that time as well. I think he's just worried how quickly his brothers have taken to you." Remy says sympathetically. I wonder if he worries about that as well.

"Remington...I don't get any of this. Friendships, relationships, whatever this is. What's wrong and what's right according to society is something I have little or no knowledge about. Moving too fast or making the wrong move, who decides that? I've read countless books, most of what I know comes from them. Or simply seeing people out in public when I chose to pay attention. I...just don't know what I'm doing anymore." I slouch in my seat.

Remy reaches out, taking my hands in his. "I know Kitten, everything will work out. Jace is sorry. I know that for a fact. You'll get into a routine here with us; it won't be so stressful then. You said you felt wanted here right?"

"I did, yes."

"You are. Don't let this little setback ruin that feeling for you." His eyes are imploring me to believe him. I want to. I do but...

Remy sits back again, blowing out a breath. "Let me ask you something Kitten. Why did you kiss Tristan's cheek in the kitchen the other day?"

"I...I don't know. It just felt right I guess. Like that's what he wanted and would make him happy." Remy runs his hand under his chin, looking thoughtful.

"And when you offered to let Reed sleep in the bed with you? When you used Logan's toothbrush? Or when you pressed your face into my neck earlier today, what about then? Did you do all of those things because they just felt right?"

I looked at my lap. Where's he going with this? "Yeah, it just felt right. I didn't think about what I was doing before I did those things."

Remy's eyes shine a bright silver. "We wolves are a lot like that too. It's a lot less complicated in wolf form. We act on impulse, instinct if you will. We are the same person, we are one with our wolf, but, for the most part, we just do what we feel is right at the time. I don't ever want you to be ashamed of what you do Kitten. As long as it feels right to you, do it. If there was ever anyone that understands that, it's us. Do you hear me?"

My heart feels a bit lighter having Remy tell me that I've done nothing wrong. I nod my head yes, my lips lifting a little in the corners. Remy smiles broadly at me, using our joined hands to pull me up with him.

"Good. Glad that's settled. Will you please join me for bed Kitten? I believe I have not yet had the privilege."

He's asking me to sleep in his room? With him? Jace's words float through my mind, along with Adam's. Calling me a whore, implying that I use my body in gratitude. Long, warm fingers pull my lip from my teeth, tilting my chin up.

"Does it feel right? You coming with me now?

Letting me comfort you, you reassuring me that you're still here, tucked into me, does it feel right to you Kitten?"

Without overthinking my answer, I nod. "Yes, it feels right."

CHAPTER TEN

I follow Remy down a hallway on the first floor that I haven't yet explored. His room has double doors that look like they're made of solid oak. He pushes them open, standing aside to let me pass. His room is as immaculate as he is. Slate gray walls, mostly bare except for the tribal designs spanning from floor to ceiling. His walls have tattoos? Makes more sense than marking your skin I suppose. The floor is made of shiny black stone; I can see my reflection in it. The space itself is smaller than other bedrooms I've been in, but unlike the others, it appears that Remy only sleeps in here. I guess most of his time in the house is probably spent in his office.

Facing the door, in the middle of the room is the biggest four-poster bed I've ever seen. The canopy? Whatever, the top is made of the same black stone as the floor, but it looks like some sort of puzzle with zigzag patterns running throughout the bottom of it. Hanging from the sides are panels of flowy looking silver silk, I can't help but run my fingers over it. It feels as smooth as it looks. On the end of the bed is a fur blanket. I turn, giving Remy a look in question as I run my hand over the black fur.

"It's from a black bear," He answers my unspoken question.

As he shuts the doors I notice that the inside of them are made entirely of mirrors. Weird. I look tiny standing at the foot of this massive bed in the reflection of the mirrors.

Remy brings me a long sleeved button up shirt from his dresser. "Put this on and jump in, I'm going to take a shower. I watch him walk into the attached bathroom, leaving the door cracked open a little ways. I do as he says, quickly changing into the over-large shirt, pulling the blanket back and sliding in.

He only has one pillow, which I think is weird, so I use it to prop my head up as I mentally trace the patterns on the shiny canopy. I wave at my reflection, letting out a small laugh at my own stupidity. I lay there for what seems like forever. I'm not tired, but I am relaxed. Finally, I hear the shower turn off and Remy moving about in the bathroom. I think about pretending to be asleep, but somehow I think he'd know.

"Is the bed to your liking Kitten?" His gruff voice asks.

"I love it, but you're asking the wrong person if you want an unbiased opinion." Remy just smiles slightly, shaking his head. His copper colored hair looks darker when it's wet, taking most of the red out of it. He's dressed in a plain white tee and silky black pants. Pulling the covers back on the other side of the bed, he climbs in next to me, leaning over and flipping a switch to turn the lights off. Well, most of the lights. Several dim ambient lights shine from the bottom of one wall, making his room seem magical.

I expected a guy like Remy to keep his distance, but he surprises me by laying his head right next to mine. I suck in a breath at the closeness.

"You didn't really think I'd let you steal *my* pillow, did you?" I can hear the smile in his voice.

"You'll have to settle for sharing then," I reply playfully.

"I have a much better idea," He says as he yanks the pillow from under my head. I almost laugh, that is, until he tugs on my arm, causing me to roll right into him. I end up splayed over his chest. His very firm chest. I blink at him. What is he doing?

"I use my pillow, and you can lay your pretty head on me." His gray eyes sparkle with something unknown. "Wait," He says, pushing me up gently. I sit on my knees, waiting.

Remy's hand slides up my neck slowly, making me shiver. My eyes close of their own will. That weird feeling in my tummy is back again. He turns my face to the side, his hands now in my hair. I feel a soft tug before my hair falls down my back in waves.

"Much better." His voice is that rumbly tone, which makes that feeling in the pit of tummy flutter. "Kitten, open your eyes," He commands.

I slowly open my eyes, finding his silver pools

swirling in his heated gaze. "Lay down Kitten." I do as I'm told, laying back down on Remy's chest, my face pressed into his shirt, my arm around his stomach, I slide my leg over his for good measure, trying to lay exactly how he had moved me before.

I feel, more than hear, the rumbling growl that comes from him. "Good girl." I think my insides turned to liquid. I practically melt myself into him. He smells wonderful, like spice and cinnamon. "Go to sleep now Kitten, I'll be here when you wake up," He says as he drapes his arm across my back, pulling me even tighter to him.

I wasn't tired before but as I close my eyes, the rise and fall of Remington's chest lulls me to sleep.

Someone is shaking me. Not roughly, but enough to pull me out of a good dream. It starts to slip away from me before I can remember it. How come the nightmares get etched into my brain forever yet the dreams never last? I sigh deeply, taking in the amazing aroma of cinnamon as I do. The smell makes me feel content. Someone tries to move my leg, but I clamp it down. I don't want to move, why can't they just leave me be?

My face vibrates. That's cool; I didn't know it could do that. I snuggle my head into the pillow, and it does it again. I giggle, still keeping my eyes closed. The sleep lifts as time passes and I finally figure out that my face cannot, in fact, vibrate. My eyes fly open, and I push myself up with both hands. My hands vibrate. Because they are pressed into Remington's chest, where my face used to be, and he's laughing at me.

I narrow my eyes at him, and he laughs harder, making us both shake. I feel something pressing against me between my legs. It's a different kind of feeling, pleasant even. It's then that I realize that I'm straddling Remy, my knees on either side of his hips. I scramble to get off him, but his hands clutch at my waist, not allowing me to move. I try to wiggle out of his hold, but it's no use, besides I'm no longer sure I want to move. My brain says I should while my body begs me to stay put. They must have gone to war while I was asleep.

Remy is no longer laughing when I look back up to him. The heated look in his eyes from last night has returned. I know my eyes are the size of saucers.

"Remy..." I whisper. My voice is deeper, it sounds odd to my ears.

Remington doesn't answer me. Not that I know what I was even asking. Instead, he pushes his hips upwards. I gasp at the sensation coursing through my body. That was the most amazing feeling ever. Like lightning shooting through my veins, starting at my core and exploding out toward my limbs. His hips pull back, and I whimper at the loss of pressure. What the hell is going on with me? I grind myself against him instinctively, my hands vibrating again as Remy groans deep in his throat. I bite my lip, willing my body not to move a muscle. Is this okay? What am I even doing?

"Kitten!" Remy commands my attention. His hands on my hips are gripping and loosening.

"Does this feel right?" He moves again, and I moan quietly.

"I have no idea," I answer honestly.

"I'm going to move you, Kitten...God...I need you to move. If you want me to stop just say so."

He doesn't wait for me to say anything else. Remy

tightens his grip with one hand, almost painfully, but I like that too. His other hand slides to my behind, just above where my leg meets my butt. He grips me there, pulling me further into him, using the hand on my hip to push me back. I moan louder this time, feeling his growl before I hear it. Remy moves me faster, and I lose myself in the sensations. My head falls back, my mouth open in a silent plea for something, I don't know what. A minute-hour later I feel myself panting, feeling like I'm about to fall over the edge of something. Confused and a little scared by this feeling, I bring my eyes back to Remy's.

The look on his face almost sends me over that mysterious edge. Remy's intent and blissful look transforms into understanding, he doesn't slow our movements though. "It's okay Kitten, just feel it. Feel me." With his last statement, he pulls me down hard as he pushes himself up, causing me to cry out his name.

"Good girl Kitten. Oh yes....My good... fucking girl." He rumbles out. His voice sends me crashing, or falling or friggin' flying for all I know. My fingernails rake down his t-shirt covered chest, trying to hold onto to something, anything. I feel my hips still moving, but I see nothing and everything at once. Suddenly I stop, at the same time hearing a drawn out growl from Remy.

Releasing his tight hold on me, his hands slide up my back pulling me down to him, my chest to his. The lightning in my body quiets, leaving smaller spasms. My face ended up near Remy's neck, and I inhale deeply. I should probably move, or ask questions or something but I but my body feels heavy, and I don't really want to do either. I might never move again.

All too soon my lethargic state completely fades.

Leaving me confused and scared and embarrassed all at once. With his hands making small circles on my back, under my shirt, I'm certain he feels my body stiffen.

"Don't you dare feel bad about what just happened. You were beautiful Kitten." I relax some, I'm still not sure I can ever look at him again though.

As if reading my mind he says. "Look at me, Kitten." I shake my head, burying my face further into his neck.

Remy smacks my butt. *Hard.* I gasp in shock. Sitting up straight instantly. He looks as smug as ever. "You cheated!" I accuse.

That causes him to laugh. "At what?" Well...I have no idea. He definitely tricked me though. Since I don't have an answer, I clamp my lips shut and glare at him instead. He just smiles.

Bringing a hand up, his thick fingers caress the side of my face, making their way into my hair, smoothing it back. "Do you trust me?" He asks voice low. I nod, chewing on my lip. "Good. I would never force you to do anything you didn't want to do. If you never want to do anything like this again, it changes nothing about your status in this house. Or with me. You understand?" He says firmly.

I move my head yes. He raises an eyebrow. "I understand Rem," I whisper.

"I didn't mean for this to happen. I woke up to you draped over me like the most beautiful blanket, I tried to move you, but you clung to me. I felt your heat and nature took over. I still feel you..." He trails off, closing his eyes. "Are you okay?"

"I think so, that was..." I don't know how to describe what happened, so I don't try to. His fingers press against my lips, and I kiss them on instinct. That makes him smile again. I like seeing him like this.

"Alright, off you go," Remy says, placing me next to him on the bed in a kneeling position. He quickly pulls the blanket over his lap, putting an arm behind his head. "Sorry, if you didn't move soon I don't know if I could have stopped myself." From what? I tilt my head at him.

"You are so adorable. You've never had that feeling before?" I shake my head. "I knew you were untouched, but not to what degree. What you felt is called an orgasm, sweet girl. Or climax, or, my favorite, cumming." He smirks. "It felt right didn't it? Like you should and you wanted to right?" I nod, smiling a little. "No regrets now that your mind has cleared?" I shake my head no. None what-so-ever.

"Okay, but uh...was that... did we have *sex*?" That was a lot harder to ask than it should have been. He looks like he's holding back laughter. Not cool, so not the moment to laugh at me.

He manages to keep it in as he answers. "Not exactly, no. What we did pales in comparison to the real thing."

"Whatever," I mumble under my breath. I can't believe he just insulted me after having the best feeling of my life. He's experienced though, probably has women lined up to do anything he dang well pleases. Women who know things, who are good at this stuff.

"I didn't mean to hurt your feelings. Trust me, I enjoyed myself immensely. I wouldn't change a thing. Watching you fall apart at the seams was an exquisite site." I glance up at him, seeing he's sincere in his words.

As I'm about to ask another question there's a knock on the door. I instantly panic. Oh my God! They're going to know! Jace will know. I just proved him right, didn't I? He'll hate me for sure now. Without my permission tears form and fall from my eyes. I cover my face and start to ugly cry with great, wracking sobs.

Before Remy can get up to get the door, it flies open. I hear someone inhale deeply, so I look up, hoping it's not Jace, here to gloat and call me a whore again. That thought makes me cry harder as I spot Ash, stopped a few feet from the bed. He looks angry, really freaking angry. He reaches out to me as he steps closer. I flinch, naturally scared of angry people.

His eyes flare wide, lips forming a thin line. He snaps his head to Remy, who is ready to stand from the bed. "You're dead motherfucker!!!" Ash says pouncing on Remy.

I let out a scream as the two massive men collide. Ash knocking Remington into one of the posters of the bed. I scramble off the other side, backing myself into a corner of the room. Remy grabs Ash's head with an arm, using his other one to block punches being thrown. Ash sweeps a leg out, robbing Remy of balance, who takes Ash with him to the floor. They roll around, both struggling to get the upper hand. Ash is landing blows to Remy's torso, making sickening crunching sounds. I think I'm in shock. I know I should run, but I can't move. I can only sit and watch as two people I have come to care about hurt each other.

I stare at my knees, counting out loud. Just trying to block out the noise and pretend it's not happening. Maybe denial is more my thing than I knew. Maybe I was in denial about me being in denial? No, that doesn't sound like me. SEE! Denial.

I'm snapped out of my stupid train of thought to nowhere by Ash's booming voice. "What the *fuck* is wrong with you! You hurt her?! My Little One!"

"NO! Just stop for a fucking minute and I'll explain!" Remy says while shoving Ash against a wall. Ash roars, and even though I've only seen it happen once, I know he's shifting.

Remy steps away from the impressive black wolf now in front of him. "Don't do this Aeshlyn. You know where this leads if I shift and you try to fight me..."

Remy doesn't finish his statement as four half-dressed guys come crashing into the room. The door gets knocked back against the wall with enough force to break the mirror. The loud shattering sound causes me to scream again. All eyes snap to me. Movement stops. I stand shakily from my crouched position. A little braver now that backup is here. The huge wolf barks at me. The sound makes me jump, which just makes me mad now. I just collected myself and here he has me all anxious again. I feed on that bit of anger, letting it consume me. I'd rather be angry than crying in a corner.

"Just stop it, Ash!" I yell at him. "Why the hell are you so angry anyway?" I stare him down, waiting for his answer before I mentally slap myself on the forehead, wolves don't talk you idiot. "Change back dang it."

"Yeah dude, we need to talk this out, and we can't do that with you like that," Tristan says in calming voice. All the anger I've mustered up seeps out of me as soon as he speaks. I don't know how he does it, and I'm not sure if I love him for it or want to poke him in the eye. Either way, I make a mad dash to him like the total girl I am. I'd roll my eyes at myself later, right now I want to feel safe again.

I instantly feel at home as Tristan takes me in his arms, his lips going to my head in a soft kiss. Peace fills me as I press my whole body into him. I wish he'd speak again so I could lose myself in his magical calmness. He could read a phone book for all I care. Do they still make those? Or do they just post it online?

I sense a presence behind me, so I turn my head and look. It's Kellan, his deep green eyes telling me everything will be okay without a word. No one has spoken yet, and I wonder if Ash has finished turning. As much as I'd love to hide behind Tristan and Kellan I know I can't. This is about me. I inhale one last breath of Tristan's citrus-like scent and let go of him.

Stepping around Kellan's impossibly tall frame, I see Ash, the man, pulling a shirt over his head, already having put on pants. "Talk to me Ash, why did you attack Remy?"

Ash looks at me with disbelief coloring his face. "Are you serious? I knock on the door to wake Remy up and hear you crying. I thought something was wrong! I see you there" he points to the bed "sobbing your little heart out. This whole room smells like your sex, and his scent is all over you. Did he hurt you, Kitten?" He asks, looking for the world like he wants me to say yes so he can tear Remy apart.

"He didn't hurt me, Ash. I promise. Remy didn't do anything I didn't want him to." I look to Remington, pleading with him to tell them what we did later. After I'm gone. He nods his head once, message received.

Ash deflates a little, still not looking satisfied. "Then why were you upset?"

Dang it! I didn't want to answer that. I have to though if I don't want them fighting. "Because when I heard the knock on the door I thought it was him," I say, pointing to Jace.

Ash turns his glare to Jace. I roll my eyes. "No Ash, not like that. It's just, after what he said yesterday and then I..." my voice trails off in a whisper.

"It's alright Kitten, the rest of us need to have a discussion. Logan, you take her to Tristan's room, get her dressed and ready for the day. Kitten, we'll handle things from here, okay?" Kellan says, sounding more commanding than ever. His whole body is rigid, fists clenched at his sides. When his grassy eyes find mine, he forces a smile. "Go on, I'll find you later."

Logan takes my hand, leading me away from the rest of them.

I sit on the corner of the bed as Logan searches through the clothes he bought for me. I feel like absolute crap. I made them fight. Friends who have been with each other for who knows how long. I didn't want to bring them down, but I think that's exactly what I'm doing.

"Go ahead and jump in the shower, I'll be out here," Logan says. It's the first thing he's said to me all morning, I wonder if he's mad at me too.

I climb in the shower, turning the water to scolding. Bowing my head, I let the water wash over me. I wish it could wash the guilt out of me but no, water can't do that. I use Tristan's body wash, lathering it up hoping the reminder of him will lift my spirits. I know he smells somewhat like the soap, but it's not the same. Tristan's underlying natural scent is what draws me. After washing my hair, I decide that I need to get out. My fingers are pruning and I'm feeling a bit waterlogged.

Logan has set a pile of clothes on the sink for me. I dress mechanically in a pair of light colored jeans, a pink tee, and converse sneakers. I open the door and take a seat on the closed toilet lid. I'm sure that's where he'll want me anyway. He walks in, taking a long look at me and shakes his head. I look down, staring at the tiled floor. Logan brushes my hair, but it doesn't feel the same. As soon as he's done, I hop up on the sink without being asked. I hear Logan sigh as he gets a hairdryer out. Once every last strand is dry and placed like he wants it, he puts the dryer away and stalks from the room. I feel sharp pain in my chest as the door to the bedroom slams shut. I'm pretty sure my heart just shattered into a million pieces.

CHAPTER ELEVEN

LOGAN

My feet can't move fast enough. I've been listening in on the meeting, and I'm ready to say my piece. My fucking brothers have been arguing for over an hour, getting no-fucking-where. I'm done with this. I step into the game room where they've gathered and take in the scene. Remy is standing, as usual, while the rest are seated. Nope, not this time, I think to myself.

I snap my fingers at Remington. "No way dude, take a seat." He looks at me like I'm crazy, which maybe I am, they've made me be crazy though. Remy finds a seat anyway.

"Alright, listen the fuck up, I'm only going to say this once because I need to get back. I could give a shit less what any of your personal opinions are. The fact is, there's a girl upstairs that feels confused, guilty, and flat out fucking depressed. She looks to us for social cues, and you are all fucking it up royally. Jace..." I seek him out, pointing my finger in his face. "...you need to fix shit with her, now! That poor girl will probably have issues with intimacy for rest of her life because of you and that fucker Adam, calling her a whore before she even had her first orgasm. That's fucking low dude, no matter your reasons."

I back away from Jace before he can respond, he looks hurt, but I don't care. He had no right to mess with her like that, trying to run her off when he knew damn well the rest of us love having her with us. I find Ash next, I stand in front of him but don't point at him. He hates that shit and let's face it, Ash is one scary motherfucker when he wants to be.

"You need to control your rage around her man, violence scares her, don't forget for even a moment how you found her. A tiny little thing like that, alone, without protection for sixteen years? Yeah, I'm sure she's seen some shit and been through things none of us can imagine. If you want her around, you better reign it in. If you were worried about her, you should have taken her from the room and *asked* her what was wrong." Ash simply nods his head. That's good enough for me.

Lastly, I look to Remy, I've never yelled at him the entire time I've known him, I've never had to. Remy is the epitome of control and has the patience of a saint. Until now it seems. "I agree with what Kellan said earlier man, way too fucking soon. I get that she's hot as hell and sweet and could make the pope beg for five minutes alone with her, I do, trust me. But she just got here. She doesn't know us, not really. She's still healing from some asshole trying to rape her! Let her settle in before we make her think Jace was right. Which she already does by the way."

I shake my head. Watching Kitten earlier, moving around like a toy robot...it sucks. I want her happy and carefree like she was when we played tag. I'm sure she has no idea how beautiful she is when she smiles. Or how amazing she smells. God that girl drives me nuts. These fuckers are taking away the light from inside her, making her question everything she does. It's not right, it stops here and now.

KELLAN

I don't think I've seen Logan this upset before. I knew he was getting close to Kitten, those two had an almost instant connection. If I didn't know any better, I'd say he's already fallen for her, or in the process of it. Logan is usually cold as stone around females. He only associates with them when the need for sex gets overwhelming, even then he has to consume copious amounts of alcohol and takes a random barfly home for a one night stand.

I'm glad when he agrees with me about Remy moving too fast. Psychologically speaking, I don't think Kitten is ready to experience sexual acts. I know my brothers are feeling the need to claim her, and fast, but none of us know what we're doing here. We'll run her off if we push too hard, I just know it.

"I know I made my point earlier about slowing things down, but do we even know what we're doing with this girl? I mean, who is going to claim her? We all can't have her." I point out.

I regret saying it immediately though. Several growls sound around the room, I don't want there to be a fight over her, we need each other, and I'd hate to see us split over this. I can admit though, at least to myself, that if there *was* a fight to have her, I'd be in it. I want her too.

FINN

My brother has a point. We can't all have Kitten. My heart drops to my stomach at the realization. If she was forced to choose, I'm sure it wouldn't be me. Remington and Ash are the strongest of us, the most dominant. She already clings to Tristan and Logan like life preservers in a storm. I doubt she'd choose Jace, so there's that I suppose. I haven't seen her with my brother or Reed much, so who knows about them.

I was ecstatic when Remy said I was to tutor Kitten. That means I'd have loads of alone time with her, and I could show her that others might have the brawn but I have the brains. Some girls are attracted to intelligence; I was hoping she was one of them. I sigh inwardly, even if I managed to get her, how could I expect to keep her with my twin and brothers around?

REED

This whole morning has been wicked crazy. I figured one of the guys would put the moves on Kitten eventually, but I thought we were bringing her into the group as one of us? Sure, I kissed her, but that was just to make sure she'd never forget me. A girl always remembers her first kiss after all. Now there's talk of mating with her, and Rem apparently did something with her that was like sex, but not. That's funny since we're talking about Remy, the ultimate Dom, and all his crazy sex shit. Ash should just be happy that he stopped at whatever he did.

Hearing the growls from several of my bro's at Kellan's statement surprised the hell out of me. I guess I could picture having Kitten as my own as well. She's the perfect girl really. Smoking hot, but she doesn't know it. Sweetness drips from her every pore, and she wears her heart on her sleeve even after the life she's lived. Oh yeah, I could wake up to that every morning. I imagine painting her, the early morning sun pouring over her naked form on my bed. My cloud-bed, as she called it. I chuckle at that. She says the cutest things.

ASH

I growl at Kellan. Of course we can't all have her! How dare he even imply that shit! As much as I like the thought of always having her around, her being mine to protect, I know she deserves better. Before this morning I thought maybe Remy could claim her, it would still be my job to protect her that way. The alpha's mate always has the pack looking out for her. He can be an asshole at times, but I thought he'd make it his mission to make her happy, and my Little One deserves to be happy. I'm too rough and surly to make a sweet girl like her content. I know that. Even though he didn't hurt her like I thought, I still question his actions this morning. That girl is untouched and frankly pretty un-fucking-prepared to take shit to that level. It's clear as damn day. I doubt she's even held a guy's hand before. Fucking Remy....

JACE

Well, there you go. My worst fear realized. They all thought my outburst at Kitten yesterday was because I thought she was after money. One look at the girl and you know that's not true. If she was after money, she could get it easily. Not by whoring herself out exactly, but by marrying some hideous, rich, old man looking for a trophy. She might be a bit young for that yet, in today's society, but I'm sure most of them would put her up until she turned eighteen, then marry her. Kitten is gorgeous, prettier than me even. My fear was that having her here would tear my family apart. Wars have been fought for her kind of beauty, my brothers don't stand a chance.

I won't deny for an instant that I don't want that tight little package as my own. I'd be an idiot not to, every inch of her is perfection. I've dated models that pale in comparison to her. I hated being so cruel. I knew she'd be hurt by my words, that's why I said them after all. I didn't expect her to forgive me though. That was a real shock. She's beautiful on the inside as well it seems, that's a rare occurrence, one that I haven't seen in a very long time.

What Logan said just now makes me feel guilty. I didn't think about the long term effect my words might have on her. I've already decided to make it up to her. As if I had a choice anyway, my brothers would probably string me up and take turns hitting me with a bat if I didn't. Or worse, scratch my car! If we're going to make her choose one of us soon, I better get myself in the game. No way could she be here without her belonging to me. I'd be lucky to find someone with half her beauty, and that just won't do.

TRISTAN

I watch as every single one of them drift off into their own little worlds. Most likely thinking about Kitten. I had no idea the impact she'd have on us all when I brought her here. I'll never forget the night I found her. She was strong, ready to face death on her own terms even though her body gave up on her. I know the others see her as weak, but they're wrong. Living on the streets for sixteen years does not produce weak beings. She raised herself and I think she did a pretty good job considering. As soon as she was awake she had all of us wrapped around her finger, it's been interesting to watch. I love her reactions to me. I don't know why I have the effect on her that I do, but I love it. She has the same effect on me, but she can't see it. I like that too.

I can't believe what Remy did, but I won't say I don't understand why he did it. Kitten has never been around men, not ones that didn't want to harm her. I'm sure her hormones are all out of whack. It's natural for her age, but it's not like she's been eased into any of this. She didn't get kissed on the playground in primary school, or held hands with a crush in middle school, she's a blank slate, suddenly exposed to eight testosterone filled werewolf males. If she even hinted that she wanted something from Remy, he'd give. I doubt the others have noticed his lack of control when it comes to Kitten. I have.

Since no one has spoken after Kellan's statement of 'we can't all have her,' I take the initiative. "Why not?" I throw out.

"What!" Ash booms.

"I said, why not. Why can't we all have her?" I shrug.

"How about because she's not a whore?" Reed drawls, rolling his eyes at me.

"Now hold on, Tristan may have a point." Remy jumps in, rubbing at his eyebrow with his index finger. I'm happy he found his confidence again. He's not used to being questioned, and the guys have been rough on him today. "Why does she have to be a whore to be shared by us? If it's only us she's with, then what does it matter?"

"Are you saying that you, the Alpha of this pack, would willingly share a female with the rest of us?" Asks Jace incredulously. Interesting, he said 'us,' so he must want her too. He has a disturbing way of showing it, but I see his eagerness now.

"I think I would be willing…yes, Mr. Rotherstone. I admit to feeling a pull towards the girl since the moment I laid eyes on her. You would think I would have felt anger, or even jealousy, at having the rest of you paw at her, but…I haven't." Remy states, confusing us all and looking quite perplexed himself.

"You all are insane. You can't share a tiny girl like that! Who says she even wants to?" Ash seems frustrated.

"I say she does." I meet Ash's eyes, showing I'm serious. "I'm not saying she's ready for a sexual relationship with all eight of us right this minute. I still think Kellan was right about that. I'm saying that I think she's strong enough to handle the lot of us. You all think Kitten is young, naive and weak. You're wrong. I mean, she is, but that's not all she is. I think she has as many personalities as us combined. She's intricate. We haven't given her a chance to shine yet, to show us who she is."

Finn clears his throat, getting all of our attention. Rarely does he speak in family meetings. He must feel whatever he has to say is important. "I would just like to point out that Kitten has yet to show any favoritism to any one of us. Given the differences among the eight of us in personality, size, looks and so on, I think it would be reasonable to state that this is an abnormality. Furthermore, given our lacking knowledge of our kind, unless we have personally dealt with an issue…." He trails off and shifts uncomfortably in his seat.

"Please continue Finn." Kellan gently prods his twin.

Finn glances briefly at each of us before settling his gaze on Remy. "Well… it might not be unreasonable to think that Kitten may be our mate."

"Our? As in all of us? How the fuck do you…did you come to the conclusion that this shit is reasonable?" Ash booms angrily.

"You will watch your tone, Ash!" Remy barks. A glance over at Finn tells me that he's withdrawn back into himself. I shake my head, Ash should know better. I think all this talk about Kitten has him all worked up.

Ash huffs and slouches back into his seat, so Remy continues on. "I believe Finn was just pointing out that Kitten seems to work well with each of us individually, as well as a group. He's right about none of us having any knowledge of mates. In all our time here, we've never encountered a mated couple that wasn't protected by a pack, or ever encountered a mate for ourselves."

"Honestly, it's the most reasonable conclusion. With our instincts to desire and protect what is ours, we should be ripping each other's throats out by now." Kellan nods his head as he speaks.

"So what are you saying? We just pass her around like a football? Dudes, you're forgetting the most important fact here, Kitten is human." Reed chimes in.

Remy huffs out a breath. "Very true Reed, though there has to be some kind of explanation as to why a slip of a girl can have this reaction on eight grown wolves. My suggestion is for you, Finn, to research all that you can on this matter, but do not go so far as to speak to any other wolves about her." Finn nods his head in agreement but doesn't reply.

"To address your other statement Reed, I suggest that we continue on as we have been. We allow Miss Kitten to set the pace romantically and allow her to choose how many of us she is willing to take on if any at all. I also want it stated, that even if Kitten decides none of us are right for her, she will remain with us for as long as she wishes. Understood?" Remy speaks to all of us while sending a pointed look at Jace.

I look to Ash, thinking for sure he'll be against this. He seems calm though. I mentally wipe my brow, thank God. I was sure he'd try to rip us all apart for even suggesting this.

Remy looks to each of us. No one objects. "Good, we're agreed. Logan, Tristan, go cheer our girl up." He smirks.

I look to Logan and smile, he returns it, looking like the cat that swallowed the canary. We race each other down the hall and up the stairs, getting back to our girl.

CHAPTER TWELVE

KITTEN

Tristan bursts through the bedroom, scaring the snot out of me. Logan is right behind him. Both of their faces are a little flushed. "Were you guys running?" I ask.

Tristan smiles wide. "Yeah, we were racing, and I won," He states proudly. I give him a weak smile in return. "That means I get first hug!" He says right before he plucks me off the chair I was sitting on, spinning me around. I feel dizzy by the time stops.

"My turn," Logan whispers in my ear. Instead of spinning me, he wraps his arms around me and carries me princess style out of the room. I laugh at his playfulness. These two are so much fun.

"Where are you going?" Tristan calls after us, giggling himself. What a cute sound.

"We're taking her to have some fun, keep up. My

car's a two-seater so run and get your Charger ready." We're leaving? To go where?

Outside I see the pretty red car that was in the garage when I hung out with Ash. Logan sets me down, helping me into the back seat, buckling me in. I giggle. "You know I can do that right?"

"Of course I know, I just want to do it for you." He winks at me before hopping in the passenger seat. Tristan messes with the radio, flipping through stations.

"Where are we going anyway?" I ask, excitement starting to bubble up.

"It's a surprise. You can't know yet." Logan answers.

"You might want to tell me, dummy since I'm driving," Tristan says playfully. Logan leans over, whispering in Tristan's ear. It's annoying. I don't like surprises.

Tristan stops the car in front a large brick building. I don't see a sign, so even though we're here, I still don't know what we're doing. Logan takes my hand, and we walk to the door, Tristan following behind us. We walk into a small hallway-like space, the lighting is dim, and the carpet is neon pink. Logan and I stand back as Tristan pulls out his wallet and talks to the guy behind the little window. He says something about full rental gear. That's not really a clue.

"Stop biting that lip Baby girl, we're here to have fun, and nothing bad is going to happen," Logan tells me in a low voice. I didn't know I was biting my lip, but I stop. He did ask nicely.

Tristan opens a door leading further into the building. "Let's go." As soon as we enter my eyes widen. What is this place? There's a lit up area with racks of who knows what, I see helmets, so that must be the 'gear' Tristan mentioned. The rest of the space is filled with huge red and black foam shapes. Triangles, squares, circles, rectangles, some of them forming pathways. Paint is splattered all over everything. I see two people carrying guns, dressed in all black with helmets covering their faces. I stand behind Logan, gripping his shirt.

I lean on my toes, whispering in his ear. "Logan, those people have guns, we need to get out of here. If we move slowly, they might not see us." Instead of moving to leave though, Logan bursts out laughing, bending at the waist. The noise draws the attention of the gun holders.

I keep my eyes on them as Logan keeps laughing. I feel like kicking him in the shin. Tristan gets my attention. "We are here for paintball Kitten, those are paintball guns, and they won't shoot at you." My head tilts to the side. Paintball guns? I don't really understand but this is Tristan, I can trust him.

I'm led to the gear area where the two of them work together to get me in all the stuff. I feel smothered with a vest, helmet, gloves, and knee and elbow pads on. When they get themselves suited up, we pick out guns of our own. I'm especially happy about this, if the other people here are armed, I want to be too. Tristan picks out red paintballs, Logan, blue, of course, I can't choose between lime green ones or sparkly pink ones. I end up picking the lime green. Logan shows me how to load them in while he explains how to shoot and where the trigger is.

"Who are we shooting and why?" I ask. I get that it's

pretend shooting, I won't be killing people, but why pretend to do it?

"There's other people here too, we'll find a small group and ask them to play against us. And we're doing it because it's fun Kitten. Just give it a try." Tristan says kindly.

"Okay." I agree warily.

Logan found a group of four guys and two girls. I notice both the girls chose the pink paintballs. There's a countdown after we enter the foam shape area. Tristan told me it's so we have time to take shelter. I guess we need to make our way to our flag quickly so we can defend it against the other team. The object of the game is to shoot all the other players, taking them out of the game, or capture their flag.

"Just stay beside me Kitten, move when I move. Got it?" Tristan says. I can tell he's excited, which makes me excited too. Also kind of scared. I give myself a mental pep talk. It's going to be okay, they don't have real guns, this will be fun, and no matter what, those bastards aren't getting my flag. That's right bitches, *my* flag.

The countdown stops, and a buzzer sounds. Logan takes off immediately, Tristan and me behind him. Dang he's fast! We make it behind a tall rectangle. Tristan signals to Logan to climb the tower that holds our green and white flag. It's kind of ugly, but whatever, I'm protecting it anyway. We wait for Logan to hide behind a triangle before Tristan creeps along the wall, poking his head out. He turns waving me forward, he points to a short square then back at me. I run for it.

A 'pop pop pop' sounds right before three purple splats of paint land right next to my face. I stop and turn, lifting my gun, I pull the trigger, aiming at the person who I think shot at me. I'm tackled to the ground before I see if my shots hit my mark.

"Don't stop and stand there, Silly Girl." Tristan laughs out. "Not if you want to continue to play." We back against the wall huddled together.

We hear a "You're out, Mofo!" Called from somewhere. Tristan turns to me, a brilliant smile on his gorgeous face. I beam back at him.

He sticks his gun above his head, two splats of paint hit it immediately, one light blue, one orange. Tristan makes a signal with his hands telling me where the two shooters are. Holding up three fingers, then two I get that he's counting down and ready myself. When all three fingers are down, I jump up, aiming at the target on my side, pulling the trigger. I let out a war cry as I advance on the guy, hitting him once in the chest and once on his face mask. A popping sound comes from my left, so I dive to the right.

Whoever was shooting sounds close, so I weave through the shapes in the direction I think I heard them. As I move, I hear two more 'you're outs'. I wonder if Tristan hit his mark too. That means three down, three to go. I spot a red and white flag up in a tower. This must be the other teams. The two girls are stationed up there, talking to each other.

I decide to try to get their flag. That's one way to win the game and protect my flag right? How hard can it be? Just as I take a step forward, I spot Tristan on my left, making a run for me. The girls stop their chattering and start shooting at Tristan. Something inside of me snaps. Those bitches are shooting at Tristan? *my* Tristan? How *dare* they!

My battle cry is back- the one I didn't know I had until today- and I run to the tower as fast as I can. Pink splats land to the left and right of me but so far, haven't hit me. I take the steps two at a time. A head pops out, over the railing. My gun was ready for that, and I release a steady stream of lime green paintballs at her face. Gottcha.

I slow as I reach the last step. I doubt the other girl will poke her head out. I remember what Tristan did earlier and lift my gun in the air. She takes the bait and fires. Wrong move honey, now I know you're in the right-hand corner. I pull my gun back and aim it around the corner. I hear a yelp. Yay!

I jump up, letting out the girliest squeal I've ever heard. I cough, trying to act cool as the two girls pass me on the stairs. One has her mask up, probably because it's covered in my paint. I smirk at her. I walk into the tower space and yank their flagpole out of the holder, tossing it to the ground below. I can see our flag tower from here, and I see Logan shoot at their last remaining player.

"Game over!" Is yelled from the announcer person. I hear laughing from below me. I lean out the little window, seeing Tristan looking back at me. I smile and wave.

Tristan and I meet Logan in the middle of the play area. I run and jump at him. He catches me, my legs linking behind his back, my arms around his neck. "We won! We won!" I say to him, giggling in glee. Adrenaline is still pumping through my veins, making me a little loopy.

"You should have seen her man, she took out four of

them. The last two in a complete rage for trying to shoot me. It was awesome!" Tristan says proudly.

Logan kisses my forehead, making a loud smacking sound. "My fierce Sweetheart, I knew you'd have fun." He picks up a strand of my hair. "You have tiny flecks of paint in your hair." He tsks at me. I shrug.

"Come on, let's get out of here," Tristan says. Logan lets me down. They start walking toward the exit sign. I don't follow.

"Hey Logan, did you get the flag?" I call to his back.

He turns around with confusion on his face. "What flag? The other teams? You got that, I saw you."

"No, *my* flag," I explain.

"I don't know what you're talking about Kitten," He answers.

I roll my eyes at him. "*My* flag. You guys told me that the green and white flag was *mine*. That we were protecting it. Did you grab it?"

Both of them look like their holding back smiles. I don't know what's so funny. "No Kitten, I didn't. Let's go get it."

We walk back to our tower, Logan runs up, bringing the flagpole with him. He unties the flag, taking the string out of the loopholes. Tristan takes it and folds it into a smaller square. "Here you go Little Warrior." I take it and clutch it to my chest, a huge smile plastered on my face. I probably look goofy, but I can't make it go away.

Changing out of our gear takes less time than it took to put on. Some guy in a black polo shirt approaches us. His name tag reads, Ted. He smiles at me before reaching for my flag on the bench. I grab it before he can. I growl at him, narrowing my eyes. "Mine," I say simply, hiding behind Tristan with my treasure.

Ted looks shocked for a moment before he turns to a laughing Logan. "I think the Lady means to keep it." Logan states.

"Well…uh…I don't think…" Ted stammers.

"We'll pay for it," Tristan says, reaching back and pulling his wallet out. I use my free hand to stop him.

"No Tristan, I earned it. I defended it. It's mine, I own it." I say pleadingly. Why is this such a problem? They are the ones who said it was mine before the game started. Why would I leave it here?

The guy, Ted, shakes his head. "Whatever." He walks away. I watch him go, making sure he's not coming back. What a weirdo. Tristan turns around, one eyebrow raised, looking to my arms cradling my flag.

"Let's go, we have more fun to do today. Sheath your claws Kitten, no more competition for you." Logan beeps me on the nose.

Why no more competition? That was fun!

I'm sitting in the car as the boys discuss what to do next outside. I think it's funny to watch them scramble for ideas. They really had no idea what they were doing. They wanted fun and set out to simply find it. There's something pretty awesome about that. Tristan is looking at his phone, doing who knows what. Logan must see something he likes because he grabs it out of Tristan's hand, jumping in the air. I hear him say. "Hell *yes*!"

They get in, and we speed off to our next mysterious location. I was worried before, but this time, I'm just excited. I'm starting to like surprises. These two seem to have good tastes in fun if paintball was any indication. I believe they are more than qualified to lead this expedition.

"You know what?" Logan asks Tristan.

"What?" Tristan replies, not taking his eyes off the road.

"We should text Reed and Finn, they'd love this too." I like Logan's suggestion, more of the guys need to have fun. Like us.

"Kellan and Jace would as well." Tristan digs his phone out as he speaks. My heart drops, I don't want Jace to come. He's like a gray cloud, ruining my sunny day.

"Not Jace," I say firmly. I know he's their friend but he doesn't like me, and I'm still mad at him. "If he comes then you can just drop me off somewhere else. I don't want to hang out with him."

"No worries Kitten, Jace is busy anyhow, so is Kellan actually. No problems with Reed and Finn though right?"

"None at all. I…they are nice to me, did you text them? Are they coming?" I hope so, those two are so quiet, and I feel like I know them the least. I know what Reed's lips feel like on mine, but not much else. I'd love to spend some time with them, especially if we're having more fun.

"Calm down, I'm doing it now. Are you anxious to see them or something?" Logan asks, sharing a look with Tristan. I nod excitedly. A chirp comes from his phone. "They'll meet us there." He smiles at me. I pull on the blue streak in his hair.

"How long until we get there?" I ask. Logan slaps my hand away, sending me a mock glare.

"We'll get there when we get there Kitten." Tristan answers. I stick my tongue out at him in the rearview mirror, making him laugh. This fun stuff is addictive, and I want more.

CHAPTER THIRTEEN

As we drive down a crowded street I imagine we are getting closer to where we're going. It's probably been fifteen minutes, but it feels like forever. People are walking everywhere, mostly all in the same direction. Children have balloons and some adults have backpacks on or are pulling wagons with them.

When I was younger, I wanted a wagon desperately. A boy my age at the time, which was maybe six, brought one with him to the park. I never played with the kids there. The parents always took them away, telling their kids that I was dirty, and I'd give them lice. I didn't know what lice was at that moment, but I looked it up at the library later, if that's what they thought of me, then I didn't want to play with their kids anyway. I really wanted to ask that kid where he got the wagon, but I never did.

I'm pulled out of my thoughts when the car shuts off, the rumbly engine giving way to silence. We get out and start walking with the crowd. Logan takes my hand, as usual. I reach out and take Tristan's in my other hand. He looks delighted. I am too. I love holding on to these amazing boys.

As the crowd grows closer together in front of a pair of gates I hear excited screams and clanking noises. There's too many trees in the way for me to be able to see anything. Logan pulls his phone out again. "They're here, walking up now." I search the crowd, going up on my tip toes. When I spot them, I realize I didn't have to do that. They are much taller than most of the people here, especially Finn. His black hair glistens in the sunlight, the bright orange button up he's wearing helps me see him too. And... If I had any doubts, the attractive boy next to him, wearing a piece of his cloud, in a white long sleeved tee, erases them. I wave them to hurry up.

They each give me a hug when they finally reach us. I turn, taking each of their hands and face my two fun boys. Bouncing on my toes, I plead with them. "Can we go in now? Please, please, please!" Tristan nods and I run for the gates where other people are going, dragging Reed and Finn with me.

Finn produces five tickets, handing them to the guy in yellow. I let go of the guys' hands as they are simply not moving fast enough. I run up the path, past the stupid trees. "The fair! You brought me to a fair?!" I squeal in sheer happiness. The guys laugh. I've seen these before, passed them from the outside. It costs money to get in, and if I ever had any, I spent it on what I needed. I never needed a trip to the fair.

I see the big wheel with buckets for seats and the ship that swings back and forth. Those always looked like fun. I don't know where to go first, do you start in the front and make your way back? I'm not sure, I defer to my fun expert, Logan. I wrap both of my arms around one of his, looking up to him with pleading eyes.

"What do you want to do first Kitten?" He asks.

I shrug. "All of it." They all laugh again.

"Do you want to ride the rides? Play games? Eat?" He asks.

Games? They have games here? I wonder what kind. "I like playing, let's play the games. Do they have tag?"

"My sweet, sweet, Kitten. Let's start you off with Ring Toss, I don't want your mind blown before we escalate to cotton candy level."

"That sounds gross, my shirt is made of cotton." Reed gives me a sad smile at that. I don't know why. I pull Logan along until he guides me in the right direction for this Ring Toss game. Maybe some games will make Reed happy again.

I watch other people play, trying to understand the game. It takes all of two seconds. You throw the ring and try to get it to land on a bottle. The colored ones gets you a bigger prize.

"You ready little warrior?" Tristan asks.

"Yeah," I reply, stepping up where the people before us were. Logan hands the guy money, and the guy hands me three of the rings.

"Go for the red bottle. If you get it, you'll get one of the big prizes." Tristan tells me.

"I don't want a big prize, I want a goldfish. If I get any of them, I can get one right?" I ask.

"Those are just going to die," Finn says. I stand up straight, turning to look at him.

"Why are they going to die?" I tilt my head at him.

"Because they keep them in those tiny little cups out here in the hot sun for days on end. If the heat doesn't kill them, then the stress will. Not to mention that when you win them, they get put into little baggies with the end tied off. By the time you're ready to leave, they will have most likely used up all of the oxygen in the water, or the sun will have turned the water stagnant." I'm absolutely appalled at Finn's explanation.

I hand the rings back to the man. I will not aid in his goldfish killing scheme. I turn, walking away, taking Finn with me. "Did you bring a lot of money with you, Finn?" I whisper to him.

"Uh, I guess. These fairs deal mostly in cash, not cards."

"Good, keep it will you? I have plans for when we leave." I say in a secretive voice.

Finn looks confused for a split second before it dawns on him what I have in mind. His smile could rival the sun. He throws his arm around my shoulder, giving me a side hug. "Done." Is all he says. He leaves his arm around me. I love that I have a partner in crime now.

Reed is the one to lead us to the next game. At this one, you aim a spray of water at a hole, and a red thing moves up, showing who's in the lead. I lean over the side, making sure they're not hiding helpless goldfish back there. Nope, none.

I nod to Reed, letting him know he made a good choice. "You want to play with me Reed?" I'll let him win if it will make him smile.

He smiles at me, gesturing for me to choose a seat. Tristan hands the guy in yellow money again as Reed sits next to me. I already got him to smile, that means I don't have to let him win now right? I sigh inwardly, I'm an awful person sometimes. I am what I am though. I like winning.

The hose thing is turned on, and I attempt to aim it at the little target. It's harder than it looks. For me at least. The water is only going in half the time. Reed is aiming it right at the target, getting all of his water in. I guess I won't have to let him win after all. The bell dings and Reed is declared the winner. I stand from my seat, kissing his cheek. "You were awesome," I tell him. He blushes all the way to the tips of his ears. I'll have to do that more often, he looks adorable like that.

"Your turn," I say to Logan. He frowns. I frown back. "If I get to play then so do you. Fair's fair." I shrug. He beeps my nose before sitting beside Reed. Reed starts to stand before Logan pulls him back down.

"Uh uh man, challenger takes on the next person. We all play, Kitten's rules." They ready their hoses. Reed wins again. Then he beats Tristan and Finn too. That makes me feel a little better about losing to him. The man's good. When everyone is done losing to Reed, the guy in yellow tells him to pick a prize, he's earned any one he wants.

"Pick one, Kitten," He says.

"But...you won. You beat us all." I reply, not understanding why he'd give his prize away.

"Yes, I won, so I get to do what I want. And what I want is for you to choose a prize that you would like to have." Can't argue with logic like that. Something tells me he'd be insulted if I didn't. I look around at all the odd things hanging from the ceiling, a monkey in a banana peel with dreadlocks, a stuffed green snake, a blown up plastic hammer. My eyes fall on a perfect white teddy bear with brown eyes, a red ribbon tied around its neck in a bow. As I'm about to point to it, I notice a smaller, raggedy brown bear sitting in the corner on the floor. That bear has obviously been through hell. The blue ribbon is pulled out of its bow, one eye is missing, and stuffing is coming out of its foot a little, and it just looks *dirty*. It's perfect. I love it already.

"That one." I point to the brown bear. The man in yellow follows my finger.

"Are you serious? I took that one down after a storm passed through here and it was left out. Why don't you pick a better one sweet cheeks, a pretty girl like you needs pretty things?" He winks at me.

"It's not the bear's fault you forgot about it, and it had to go through a storm by itself. I want the brown one." I glare at his back as he finally does as I asked.

"Have it your way Princess." He sneers at me, handing me my bear. I couldn't care less what the guy thinks, I clutch my bear to me as gently as I can with the excitement of new treasure coursing through me.

"Ahem...I think we should maybe move on to the rides now." Tristan says. I startle a little. I almost forgot the guys. I make my way back to Reed. I throw my arms around his neck, squeezing him as hard as I can, the bear getting squished between us.

"This is the best present I've ever had. Thank you soooo much, Reed." I say into his neck. He smells like his cloud bed. He's as comfortable as it too. I let go, grabbing my bear before he falls. Reed has the goofiest grin on his face. The other guys share a look between them.

"Which one first?" I ask.

"Let's start with The Scrambler and work our way up." Logan, my personal director of fun.

We stand in a short line for a ride that has silver booths with a bar going across them, they move back and forth and side to side. When it's our turn, the guys act like they don't know where to sit. Other people are filling up the booths fast, so I climb into the closest one, calling to Finn. "Are you coming, Mr. Wolf?"

Finn smirks at me. It's a good look on him. "Only if you don't tell me to get down once I climb in." I blush, remembering how I treated him like an ordinary dog. How was I supposed to know? At least we can laugh about that now. I didn't want to stay mad at him anyway. Besides, technically, he didn't leave me, he was there the whole time.

After The Scrambler, we ride a bunch of different contraptions. One was a big tower with a circle around it that went like, a thousand stories high before it left you up there, sweating it out, not knowing when the heck it was going to plunge you to the earth at breakneck speed. Never. Again! Another ride had egg shaped cages that spun in an oval, Logan and I had a good time seeing how many times we could spin our cage around. I was so dizzy after that. It was okay though, Finn gave me a piggyback ride until my head stopped spinning. I think that was my favorite ride, honestly. I blew in his ears, and he couldn't do a thing about it since his arms were around my legs, helping to hold me up.

We get to the boat ride, and I'm ecstatic. Tristan and Reed sit with me in the front seat, Logan and Finn sitting right behind us. As it gets all the way up, I lift my arms into the air like I saw other people doing. I come up out of my seat, like when you go too high on a swing but much better. A hand clamps down on each of my thighs, bringing me back down as the boat swings back. They leave their hands on me, doing it each time. I feel free like I'm flying. I can't stop the constant giggles streaming from me or the smile that is so wide that it hurts my face.

We attempted to go on the Ferris wheel - that's what the big wheel thing is called, Finn informed me. When we were standing in line to get on, I watched as the people in the silver and red buckets talked and chatted in a relaxed manner. Some people my age rocked them back and forth, but still, it looked tame to the other stuff we went on. I sat with Logan, his arm stretched across the back, me snuggled into his side.

"So, what did you name the bear?" He asks me as the other buckets are being filled.

"I'm supposed to name it?"

Logan chuckles. "Yeah, you have to give it a good name."

I bite my lip, trying to think of a strong name for the strong bear. "I'm going to call him Noah." I smile at my bear. He weathered a storm too.

Logan bursts with laughter. "You can't name a teddy bear Noah, most people name them Teddy or Berry. Who ever heard of a bear named Noah?"

I blink at him. "Who ever heard of a girl named Kitten?" That wipes the smirk off his face. Ha! I win.

The wheel starts to spin now, probably filled with people. I look away from Logan and take in the view. We're at the top, looking over the whole fair and beyond. Then I make a mistake, I look down. I'm not afraid of heights but there is something truly sick and twisted about the ground slowly moving up to meet you. This is soooooo much worse than the tower thing. If I'm going to die from a fall, I'd prefer it to be quick, so I don't have to know about it for that long.

I bring my legs up, scurrying into the corner of the bucket, my hands splayed out to either side of me, holding me in place. My sudden movement makes the bucket rock. My eyes fly to every rivet, making sure they are all there and tightly fitted. Why the hell did I climb in this thing without checking out if it was going to fall apart? That seems like something you should do *before* you're freaking out a thousand stories up in the air.

Logan takes in my panicked state with a look of amusement. "What's wrong Kitten?" He asks.

"Uh... nothing, I would like to get off now please." I say as calmly as I can. I have a strange thought that if I insult the wheel, it will get angry and throw me to the ground. Unreasonable? ...Yes. Do I totally believe it in this moment....Yes. Yes, I do.

"I have to say, you are really looking like your namesake right now Kitten." I would kick him, but the wheel would know. By now we have passed the ground. Oh joy, we get to do it all over again.

"Please Logan, I really want off. I think I'm going to be sick." I plead with him to understand that I'm serious.

My hands start to sweat and I curse them. Don't they know that if all goes to hell, we will have to hold onto something? Think hands, think! Logan must finally see how panicked I am because he starts shouting for Tristan.

"Yeah?" I hear him shout back. Logan explains the situation, telling him, and the wheel, everything.

Tristan calls out to me, but I can't make myself answer him. My throat has gone dry and my heart now resides there. He keeps talking though. "Just close your eyes, Kitten, hear me talking to you. Block out everything else. It's just you and me Kitten. We're running in our back yard. Playing tag. Your long blond hair flowing behind you as I chase you. No shoes on, you feel the soft blades of grass tickle your toes. You're laughing, running for the trees. You feel me getting close to you.

My heart rate lowers the more he talks. With my eyes closed, I can almost picture it. Being with Tristan is soothing. It's safety. We're safe, here together, in the back yard. Just him and me, playing.

Tristan goes on. "I reach for you with my hand, brushing against your soft skin. You stop, turning to me, a happy smile on your beautiful face. My fingertips caress your cheek..."

The wheel grinds to stop, making the bucket rock again. My eyes fly open, my panic back. It soon recedes when I realize that I'm back on the ground. Thank God! I've never been happier to see pavement in my life.

"Aww...it was just getting good." A guy shouts from somewhere. Other people start laughing with him. My face is on fire as the man in the yellow shirt opens the bar on the bucket. I forgot that we were, indeed, in public. Tristan shouting the words loud enough for me and others to hear. Logan holds me until Tristan and Reed get off. I throw myself at Tristan, climbing his body like a tree, burying my face in his neck. I should say thank you but I can't speak yet. Tristan holds me back just as tightly, carrying me away somewhere. I peek over his shoulder, noticing that Noah is in Logan's hand. Good. He's safe now too.

After I'm thoroughly stuffed with weird and delicious fair food, the guys had split up, each bringing back a few different things. Finn encourages me to ride one last ride, so I don't develop a fear of all of them, he said. It's hard to deny my wolf when he throws logic and reason in my face like that. We pile into cars on a wooden roller coaster. It's not that high off the ground, thankfully. Finn sits next to me, his long legs scrunched up.

As the man in the yellow shirt checks the bar on our seat I stop him. "When was the last maintenance check performed for this ride?" I ask. I learned my lesson with the Wheel of Death.

The guy blinks his eyes in surprise. "Um, I guess about two hours ago Miss."

"No problems since then?" I ask sternly. He better not be lying to me. If I die on this ride, I swear I will find him and haunt him for eternity. Or at least until I'm bored.

"No ma'am, everything's been runnin' smoothly." I nod my head, and he continues on down the line. Finn grips my hand, bringing it to his lips, kissing my knuckles. His pouty lips are soft and warm.

"That was smart of you Kitten, we'll do that from now on. I don't know why I didn't think of it." To say I'm surprised would be a major understatement. Maybe

Finn isn't shy after all, maybe he's just a gentlemen. That's what gentlemen do in books.

The car starts forward, up the hill. I hear 'clink, clink' noises as we move up. It sounds ominous. I still have Finn's hand though. I don't think he could fall out if he tried. I know he won't let me fall if I somehow come out of my seat. I trust him. We fall over the crest of the hill, the car gaining speed, racing around turns and dips. All too soon we are back where we started.

That was awesome! The bar on the front rises and people stream out of their seats. I want to go again, so I stay put. Finn is already out, standing on the platform with the rest of the guys. He looks at me questioningly.

"I want to go again," I answer his look.

"Alright, we'll get back in line."

I frown at him. "Why would I do that when I'm already right here?" Silly boy.

Tristan shakes his head. "Because it's someone else's turn now, Kitten."

"That doesn't make any sense. When you're on a swing, you don't get off after one swing backward. The person waiting for the swing has to wait for you to be done with it. I'm not done with this roller-coaster." I know I'm looking at him like he's stupid, which is mean and not true. I can't help it though, even I knew that!

Reed steps forward laughing hysterically. "In a perfect world Kitten, playground rules would apply to everything. Sadly, this is not a perfect world." He offers his hand to me to help me from the car. I take it, stepping beside him. It still doesn't make sense, but I'll take their word for it.

As we make our way to the exit, Reed bends down, placing a kiss on my shoulder where it meets my neck. "You couldn't get any more perfect if you tried, Babe."

I'm sure even my toes flush scarlet at Reed's words. He thinks I'm perfect? Really? I wonder what ever made him think that. Whatever it was, I'd like to know so I can keep doing it. I think that would be strange to ask though. I sigh.

"You ready to go Kitten? I think we've ridden every ride at least once." Logan says from behind me.

"Yeah, I'm getting a little tired. We have to do something first though." I step next to Finn. Grabbing his hand in mine, giving it a little squeeze. I look up at him from under my lashes. I know he's already on board, but I don't know if the others will be. I don't know how to ask them for this.

Finn understands me. "We need to rescue some goldfish for Kitten before we go," Finn states to the others. "You guys up for it?"

I hear some chuckling behind me before hearing the three of them give their consent. Okay, so that wasn't so hard after all. I squeeze Finn's hand again in appreciation. "Thank you, Mr. Wolf," I whisper so only he can hear.

He leans over, kissing the crown of my head. "No problem my Dearest Kitten. All you have to do is ask."

We spend the next hour and a half taking over the Ring Toss. This game looked simple before. Turns out it's quite tricky. The guys are winning goldfish left and right. I have no strategy what so ever. I just toss the rings hoping they will land around something. Sometimes they do, but more often than not they bounce off.

Since we've monopolized all the space available for customers the guy in the yellow shirt stands off to the side, smoking a cigarette. When we first walked up, each of my guys pulled out a stack of money and handed it to Tristan, who then had a short chat with yellow shirt man that I couldn't hear. He's the one retrieving the rings for the rest of us. I accidently hit him with one once. I apologized thoroughly as the others laughed and he rubbed his forehead. Oops.

Just when my arm feels like it's about to fall off and my frustration at not being able to master this game reaches an all-time high, Tristan claps his hands together. "Okay, we've officially won all the goldfish!" He announces.

All of them? Really! This is so much more than I could have ever hoped for. I feel tears sting my eyes, so happy I can barely stand it. The boys go about getting all of the little fish into big white buckets. Finn informs me that Tristan paid extra for them. I'm glad he thought ahead, I don't know what we would've done with so many baggies.

I practically skip to the car with Noah snuggled in my arms as the guys carry the buckets. We load them into the back of Reed's white Escalade. Once they're secured, I start to climb in the back seat. I'm stopped when I catch a conversation between Reed and Logan.

"Remind me never to take Kitten to a pet store. She'd be horrified." Logan laughs.

"I just hope they don't die on the way, I think she had fun today, I'd hate to see her be sad again." Reed replies.

I shut the door after I set Noah on the seat. I walk to

the back, looking at the guys standing around. "I'm not stupid. I've been in a pet store before, you know. They had fish kept in small tanks there too. The difference between those fish and these, are that at least the pet store fish had a chance, people would probably buy them and take them home. Take care of them. And the store doesn't leave them out in the sun to suffocate. Some of the goldfish we rescued may die. I know that. But at least we are giving them a chance. That's all I wanted."

I'm not mad at them. Not at all. I know I must seem strange, and I know I've been getting the social things wrong all day. They don't understand me and that's okay. They helped me anyway. Didn't even question it. I just don't want them to think that I'm stupid.

"I didn't mean it that way, Kitten. Your heart is just so big. I hate the thought of disappointing you. That's all." Logan says sincerely.

"You could never disappoint me, Logan, none of you could. Just don't forget where I came from. I wasn't raised in an ivory tower, my eyes have always been fully opened. Some of our goldfish will die, but that won't break me. It's life. It happens. Okay?" I ask, looking to each one of them. They all nod. Reed's sad smile is back on his face.

"Okay then, can we find a pond to drop them off at on the way home?"

"Already taken care of. There's an apartment complex about five miles from here with a pond out front. We'll stop there." Finn tells me. Good. That's not too far. I hop in the SUV, buckling myself in. And just because I think it's funny, I buckle in Noah next to me. Reed and Finn get into the SUV as well. Tristan and Logan make the short walk to the red Charger. Before Finn's door can close all the way though, I hear Logan's voice.

"Did you hear that man? She said home." He nudges Tristan playfully, and the two of them walk past with goofy grins.

We pull into the apartment complex, each taking a bucket at a time. Some of the fish did die and are floating at the top. I'm sorry to see it, but I leave them there, pouring the water out slowly. At least now they can serve as food for some other fish. It's the cycle of life after all. The guys do the same.

When we're down to the last bucket, we all gather around. "Would you like to keep one Kitten? We could get you a fish bowl." Finn asks.

"Yeah, or a whole fucking tank if you want it, give the little guy some room to roam." Logan throws in. Making me giggle.

I shake my head. "No, that's okay. Thanks though. I wouldn't want to take one of them away from his fish family. These guys have been kept captive long enough. They've earned their chance at freedom."

"That's my girl. Maybe one day we'll get you some fish from the pet store." Logan says, dumping the fish out into the pond.

I smile as I watch them swim away. I bend down to a kneeling Logan, kissing his cheek. "I think I'd like that."

I must have fallen asleep on the way home. I feel myself being lifted into thick arms. I want to open my eyes and state than I can walk, but it doesn't happen. My face is pressed into a warm neck, the amazing smell rousing me enough to lift my lead filled arms around a head with silky hair. I think it's Ash. He smells almost exactly like his name. Like fire and charcoal and burning wood. I don't know what it is, but it's uniquely him. Normally I'd think something like that would be off-putting, but if the word 'strong' had a smell, Ash would have it. I soak it in. Wrapping myself in his protectiveness.

I'm placed on cool sheets, a firm pillow under my head. Someone removes my shoes and socks, running their fingers over my toes once they're bare. It tickles. "Did you get Noah?" I mumble sleepily. I don't hear the answer, if there was one because I drift off to sleep.

CHAPTER FOURTEEN

ASH

As soon as I hear a vehicle rolling up outside, I jump up from my perch on the railing of the porch. When Remy told Logan to 'go cheer up our girl' I doubt he meant steal her for the entire fucking day. That's what happens when you get him and Tristan together. Expect nothing but the unexpected. She better not have gotten so much as a damn paper cut. Whatever injuries my Little One gets I'll make sure those in charge of her care get twice that.

Reed's SUV pulls right in front of me, followed by Tristan's car. I sniff the air, finding Kitten in the white one. I'd know her smell anywhere. A woman has never smelled as good as her. I've been on this earth for centuries, so that's really saying something.

I throw the back door open, impatient to see her smile again. I scared her earlier today, and I'm desperate

166

to make it up to her. The poor thing is slumped over in her seat, asleep. At least she has a seatbelt on. That's a good sign. I'm not even gonna ask about the fucked up bear sitting next to her, buckled in as well.

I gently extract her from the car, trying not to wake her. She's probably worn out. Logan can be tiring on his own, add in Tristan ... She stirs slightly as I cup her tiny head in my palm, bringing her face to my neck. She brings her arms up, her fingers glancing over my hair. It feels amazing to have her in my arms, her hands on me. It takes everything I have not to get hard right now. Kitten inhales deeply, letting out a contented sigh. Did she just sniff me? Maybe she has a little wolf in her too. I snort at the thought. If only.

The others stay silent as we make our way in the house. They know better than to question me as I head directly to my room. I've missed her. I've worried about her. She's mine for the night. Ours forever, but *mine* for tonight.

I lay her down as gently as I'm able. It's not in my skill set, but I'm gonna have to learn with Kitten in my life. I untie her sneakers, slipping them off. She has the tiniest little feet I've ever seen. I have to know what they look like so I take her socks off as well. I'm mesmerized by her little toes. I trace each one, loving the way her smooth skin feels under my rough fingers. I vow to protect each precious little one of them. I can't help but put my hand to the bottom of her foot. I smile, yep my hand is bigger. I shake my head.

"Did you get Noah?" Her soft sleep filled voice reaches my ears. Damn that was sexy. Images of her lying next to me float through my brain. Her sex-mussed hair, my scent all over her bared skin as I watch her wake, morning after morning. I'm stopped in my train of thought by her words. WHO THE FUCK IS NOAH?

I leave my room silently, closing my door behind me. I race down the hall in a rage. No man's name other than mine and my brother's should *ever* cross my Kitten's perfect lips. I sniff out the others. They've gathered in Remington's office. I kick the door the rest of the way open, seeking out Logan. I stomp over to him getting in his face.

"Who the fuck is Noah, and where can I find him?" I growl at him.

LOGAN

Remy was a little ticked at us when we came in, but he called a family meeting. He said it was to catch the rest of them up with what happened today, but I think he just missed having Kitten here and can't stand that he missed out. No way would he ever admit that though. Just as Remy asks me to fetch Ash, the door crashes open, knocking into the wall.

Ash is in my face immediately. I'd be lying if I said I wasn't scared shitless. My wolf tries to rise to the surface, but I tamp him down, I don't want to challenge Ash. His deep voice is deceptively low, his words a growl. Ash yells when he's angry, when he doesn't, shit is about to hit the fan. "Who the fuck is Noah, and where can I find him?"

My eyes widen. Do not laugh, do not laugh, do not laugh. I chant to myself. Thankfully, Tristan explodes in laughter, taking Ash's intense focus off me and onto him. Before Ash can jump him, Reed holds up Kitten's ugly bear.

"Ash, meet Noah. I don't think he's much of a threat dude." I watch as the tension drains from my brother. The guys have a good laugh at his expense. Ash usually hates to be laughed at. I think he's too relieved to care right now though.

REMY

That's the second door of mine that he's kicked in today. It's a damn good thing he's the one who fixes things around here. We're going to have to talk one on one about his rage issues. I thought this was under control. Another time perhaps.

"Now that we have that cleared up take a seat, Ash." I use my most commanding voice on him. I lost a little confidence in myself this morning but I'm still the alpha around here, and I'll not have it forgotten.

"What's with the hideous bear?" Jace asks Reed, who still has the filthy looking thing.

"I won it for Kitten at the fair." He shrugs.

"What happened to it? Car accident?" Jace says laughingly.

Reed stiffens, clearly insulted. "Nothing happened to it, I mean...not recently. I told her to pick whichever one she wanted. She chose this one and named it Noah because it survived a storm. Kitten loves it. She obviously asked for it or else Ash wouldn't have stormed in here."

Jace looks at the stuffed animal again. The disbelief apparent on his face. "She really likes that...*thing*?"

Tristan speaks now. "Yeah, our Kitten is all about saving the unfortunate. I don't think we'll be able to take

her anywhere without her being adorably heartbreaking."
He shakes his head with a small smile on his face.

"Unless you dare to shoot a paintball at Tristan, then
she goes apeshit!" Logan exclaims.

"Start from the beginning, neither of you are making
sense to the rest of us," I say, exasperated. I've grown used
to knowing Kitten's every movement and not having her
here today has worn my patience thin.

Tristan and Logan begin by telling us about their trip
to Splatter Arena. It wouldn't be my first choice for an
outing, but I sent the two of them for a reason. They are
better with this new generation than the rest of us. Logan
mentions how Kitten was initially afraid of the guns,
which makes sense, she's probably seen real ones in
action. I'm insanely proud when Tristan talks about her
not being afraid once she got shot at. In fact, she took out
four players on her own. We all have a good laugh when
he reenacts her battle cry, defending Tristan from pink
paint. She even got the other team's flag. Impressive as
hell for a first timer.

"Then she was like, 'did you get my flag?'". Logan
chimes back in. "I didn't know what she was talking
about. She meant OUR flag. She explained why it was
hers, how she earned it. You should have seen her reaction
when the manager tried to take it back. It was epic man.
She clutched it to chest like she was ready to die for it."

"Where is it now? Did you make sure she got to keep
it?" I ask. They better have.

"It's in my pocket. Like I'd let it out of my sight,
after all, she did to have it. Just FYI to the rest of you,
Kitten takes competition seriously. Very seriously. I don't
think *she* even knew that she was that competitive until

today. And if you offer up a prize, you damn well better be ready to hand it over." I'm a little surprised when he doesn't laugh. Logan tends to be a bit dramatic and finds most things funny. He must be a hundred percent serious. How interesting, our frightened little woman turns into a war goddess when pressed. Good to know. Ash seems to be over the moon at this new information while Jace and Kellan both have frowns on their faces.

Reed takes over, telling us about their time at the fair. About Kitten's initial excitement, about how she walked away from the first game because of how the goldfish were treated.

"Damn Finn, why couldn't you just let the girl win a goldfish? She doesn't need her pretty little brain warped by your freakish knowledge on fish." Jace huffs. I too question whether I would have chosen to tell her that. Anyone who has ever been to a carnival of any type has that information.

Staring Jace down, Finn explains himself. "She would have wanted to know. Kitten likes knowing things, she's not satisfied being coddled and paraded around like an airhead. Besides, what would happen once her prize died? What then? She has abandonment issues, she would have cried and been devastated again." He lowers his eyes.

Ah, I see now. He said 'again.' He's still feeling the guilt of pretending to be her pet. I still don't know what he was thinking doing that. I know he got caught in his wolf form, but he should have ran off. He had said that she looked like she needed a friend and he wanted to be close to her. I can understand that, somewhat. But still, it was wrong.

"Did you manage to redeem yourself to her today,

Finn?" I ask.

"I think so, that incident is more of an inside joke to us now. She was quite *friendly* with me today." I'm a little jealous of that last statement. I'll have to work on that. I'm glad that at least one problem was solved today.

Reed continues on. He explains how Kitten came to have the bear. "As I said, I told her to pick a prize. I thought for sure she was going to choose a pristine white one with a red bow, but she changed her mind at the last minute, choosing that thing instead. The attendant almost didn't give it to her, explaining that it had been left out in a storm and damaged. Her eyes went ice cold man, like, just froze over. She put that guy in his place good, saying it wasn't the bear's fault it was left out. Then she..."

Reed trails off, the sad looking smile I've noticed he gets when he thinks about her. Reed is the most laid back person I know, nothing really brings him down. I know his sadness is because he cares about her. He's going to have to accept her past and move on from it at some point though.

"She what..." Kellan speaks for the first time at this meeting. I know he's like me. He was worried about her and felt left out today. He was invited to the fair but had to miss it because he was needed at the clinic. Jace was livid when Reed and Finn left without him today. He wanted to show off for Kitten, I'm sure. Or have her on his arm, parading her around like Finn suggested. No matter how hard I try, I cannot get that man to realize that he is no longer part of the Ton. Hell, the Ton doesn't even exist anymore. I managed to calm him down, explaining how much fun he would have trying to win her good graces. He'd have the opportunity to woo her like he was expected to back in his time. I truly hope that advice doesn't backfire.

"...she took that bear and acted like her whole world stopped. Like it was the biggest diamond there ever was. She told me it was best present she ever received." Reed takes a seat. I guess he's done talking, off in his own little world now. I catch Jace's smug look and struggle not to roll my eyes. Oh yes, it certainly will backfire.

Logan picks up where Reed left off. "We took her on rides after that. Seriously, that girl had already broken my heart over the games. She had a great time riding. I tell ya, that girl is magnificent when she's carefree and laughing. There was an incident on the Ferris wheel though, I don't really get it since she wasn't afraid of heights before that but she had a freakout, Tristan used his magic Kitten taming voice, and she calmed down until we could get her off."

"Yeah and then we filled her full of fried goodness. She actually got a funnel cake for you Remy, but she was eyeing it with so much lust I told her to ahead and eat it. Powdered sugar is a good look on her." Tristan butts in. She thought about me huh? I can't stop the grin that spreads on my face.

"Tell them about the roller-coaster Finn." Reed comes back from his inner thoughts.

Finn has a broad smile as he obliges. "Kitten wanted to ride the roller-coaster again. I told her we could go wait in line again, but she was having none of that. She told us in the most reasonable voice I've ever heard, that it was still her turn because on swing sets you have to wait for the person on the swing to be done before the next person gets a turn, and she wasn't done with the roller-coaster.

Personally, I've never thought of it that way, but it does make sense. I think she has her own logic, and she isn't eager to budge from it. Just like with the flag, in her mind, she earned it because she defended it, even though the rest of the world would say that it belonged to Splatter Arena."

I see Finn's point. Kitten probably had to develop her own logic because there wasn't anyone around to teach her differently. She's very observant. I remember watching her watch Jace at dinner, seeing how he ate. Mimicking his movements. She must have watched other people interact and decided what their actions meant on her own. What interests me most about this is that fact that her logic seems better than everyone else's. In today's society children have one set of rules and adults another. How that happened, I have no idea. It didn't use to be that way. Used to be, from the time you were born, you were trained to be an adult. You didn't wait to "grow up" to learn a skill. Your parents passed down their skill to you, and as soon as you could do something for yourself, you did. Simple as that. Kitten's simple logic falls in line with a time that proceeds her by centuries. She's just full of surprises isn't she?

Tristan is already speaking when I tune back in. "...wanted to go back and save the goldfish before we left. I paid the attendant off, let her play for a while so she'd feel she earned their freedom instead of buying it. I didn't think she'd like that very much. We dropped them off at an apartment complex with a pond."

"You left out when she put us in our place, dude. Kitten must have thought we thought she was stupid for wanting to save the goldfish, she told us that her eyes have always been open, she knew about fish in pet stores and that she just wanted our fish to have a chance like they did. Or something like that, I don't know, I'm tired." Reed explains. He makes his point by yawning.

I feel a bit like an ass that I dragged everyone in here after their long day, but I'm glad I did. It's been informative.

"Alright men, go about your business." I release them.

As he's making his way to the door, Logan stops in his tracks, forcing the rest to halt behind him. "Oh yeah, she called this home." He continues on his way shouting back. "And we owe her a fish tank!"

The last part needs more explaining, but not tonight. I rock back in my chair. Kitten called this home huh? Good.

KELLAN

I head to my room wondering why we owe Kitten a fish tank. I thought she didn't like captive fish? I hung back at the meeting, listening to the guys talk about my perfect girl. I'll take Finn's advice and have talk with Kitten about her anxiety attacks. Whatever scares her is all in her head, each time she's had one it seems to come from out of nowhere. I still need to sit down with her and discuss what happened this morning with Remy, possibly get her on birth control if she wants.

I'm sorry I missed out on time with her, but I'm happy she had fun. I'm a little upset that I wasn't consulted before she engaged in such strenuous activities. I know it's easy for the rest of them to forget she's injured, since she doesn't act like it, but she is, and she needs to take it easy. I feel like the girl has been on warp speed since she opened her pretty eyes.

I sigh, removing my tie and unbuttoning my shirt. The shower is calling my name. The clinic was filled to the brim today with every known sickness to man it seems. I like what we do there, giving medical attention to those who can't afford insurance, but my mind has been elsewhere lately. It doesn't help that some people get the wrong idea about our facility and fake back injuries and sprains just to get prescriptions, wasting our time, money and patience.

I'm not surprised in the least that Kitten is a humanitarian at heart. She's just never been on this side of the fence before. She's always been the one in need. Not anymore though, she's under my care now. Mine and my brothers'. I'm positive between the eight of us that Kitten will be the most spoiled, pampered, and protected woman this world has ever seen. The great part is that I have no fear she'll turn into a brat because of it.

I step under the warm spray of the shower, thinking back to all the things that jumped out at me from throughout the guys' day. Kitten's possessive streak is quite a shocker. There's no doubt in my mind that's what caused her to fly off the handle when Tristan was shot at with paintballs. Remy told us how upset she was when she thought Logan had a girlfriend. I don't think she's aware of why she has those reactions, at least not fully.

But with the possessiveness, her speed, her ability to heal quickly, the fact that she lived in horrible conditions and didn't catch a virus, even though she had no shots to protect her from falling ill. It really makes me wonder. I'll need to run more tests on her blood.

I really need some personal time with Kitten. Not just to psycho-analyze her or check in on her health, but because I just want to be around her. I truly did miss her today. Those full, bow-shaped lips, her long platinum hair.... I give in to my arousal, bringing my hand down my abs to my hard as steel manhood. I let out a groan, picturing those pink lips stretched around me, her pale green eyes looking up at me while my hand fists her hair, guiding her up and down on me. Shit...this is going to be quick. I feel my testicles drawing up, my climax building. I explode, panting for air, wishing she was really here, swallowing my seed.

I finish up and dry myself off. A pang of guilt shoots through my chest at thinking of my sweet girl that way. If fades quickly as I tell myself she will be ours shortly, if not eventually. Then there will be no reason for guilt. She'll be mine as much as I am hers. Man and woman sharing in the most natural act.

I climb into bed, hoping to fall asleep quickly so I can be up and ready when Kitten comes downstairs. I don't want to miss a moment with her on my day off. Hopefully, I can steal her away from the others for a little while. I smile into my pillow at that thought.

REED

I lay awake in bed, reliving the day. I loved spending time with Kitten and my brothers, but honestly, I don't know if I can take many more heartbreaking scenes with the girl. I don't know why I'm so hung up on what's she been through. All of us have been through rough times.

Myself included, and yet her past haunts me so much more than my own. I've drawn her smiling face countless times. The paintings and sketches hanging up in my studio. Her eyes always come out sad though. Every. Single. Time. It's frustrating.

I just want her to be happy. Truly happy. She has such a pure soul and kind heart that it literally splits me in two to think that she never had a toy as a child, she never had a mother to wash her hair and read her stories at bedtime. She deserved to have that and so much more. I wonder if she even had a hug before she came here. Werewolves need physical contact so much more than humans, I'm so happy that our family were the ones to find her. I'll hug her as much as she wants me to. I'll show her what a real family is like.

JACE

I can't believe they are going to let her keep that nasty bear. If I was the one to win a prize for her, I would have found the most perfect one and insisted she have it. The darling girl came straight from the street. They want to give her broken things? What was going through Reed's head? She needs nice things. Things as pretty and shiny as her. I will show them what she needs. No girl of mine will have less than perfection.

Kitten shut me out today. It hurt me deeply. I'll never admit that, but it's true. Young women have always thrown themselves at me to the point of annoyance. This one is different, and I have to say...I'm at a loss. I'm going to take Remington's advice and charm her. The problem with that is, she likes ragged stuffed animals and saving goldfish. She's quite an outspoken little thing too, isn't she? I chuckle at that. I know she has a love of food, but that's more Tristan's territory. I pull at my hair, wracking my brain for an answer.

I smile at my reflection in the mirror, fixing my hair into place. I know the perfect thing. Something she can't refuse no matter how much I hurt her before. I'm sure she'll forgive me. My smile fades when I think how time-consuming my idea would be. I have no problem with that, but that means I still have to think of ways to woo her in the meantime. It's going to be a long night of fixing my hair.

KITTEN

I groan, I'm burning up; feeling like my skin is going to melt off me at any moment. I wiggle around, trying to get my limbs to move. I'm trapped, wrapped up burrito style in a top sheet and brown comforter. Ash's body is curled around me like a boa constrictor. My face against his chest, his leg locking mine between his, arms holding me in a bear hug. If I didn't know any better, I'd swear he was trying to smother me.

"Ash." I groan out. He doesn't move. "Ash, I need to move."

"Not yet Kitten." His voice doesn't sound sleepy at all.

I stop my squirming. If he doesn't want me to move then I know I won't be going anywhere. "How long have you been awake Ash?" I ask softly.

"I didn't sleep."

"Why not?" Somehow I knew he was going to say

that.

"I'm not sure. At first, I just wanted to watch you sleep. I sat in the chair across the room, watching as your little nose twitched as you slept. Did you know that you talk in your sleep, Kitten?"

No. I didn't know I did that. I wonder what I said. I shake my head in answer. "Why am I wrapped up like a burrito Ash?" I wonder how he managed this without waking me. Maybe I was more tired than I thought.

"You looked cold." Is his simple reply. No one has ever cared if I was cold or not.

"I'm not cold anymore, actually, I'm too hot. Can I please get up now Ash?"

"I don't want to let go of you just yet. If I do, you're going to get up, probably shower, then go down for breakfast and get swept away by everyone else. It's okay, I don't mind that it will happen, just not yet."

I smile. He just wants to spend time with me? "Is Tristan already cooking?"

"Yeah, I think he's about done," He grumbles back at me.

"How about I hop in the shower while you go get breakfast for us? We can eat in here, right? Just you and me."

Ash squeezes me tight, his lips press into my hair in a soft kiss. "You're a genius, you know that, Little One?" I giggle. I'm happy he likes my idea, I wouldn't mind more time with him as well.

Ash jumps from the bed and dashed from the room, so now I'm left struggling to free myself. Did he sew this thing together? I roll around and eventually untangle myself. If there was a ninja level of tucking someone in,

Ash would have mastered it.

I grab one of his big gray t-shirts from the dresser on my way to the shower. I don't bother with my hair, I'll have to ask Logan how to get the paint out. For now, I just braid it back. The lack of products in Ash's bathroom is almost comical in comparison to the other boys'. All I see is one bar of soap that has no smell to it. Yes, it all seems very *him*. After drying off, I use my finger to brush my teeth with the toothpaste left out on his sink.

When I step back into the bedroom, Ash is already there, sitting at a small table with one chair, three plates towering with food on top. Three? Is someone else joining us?

"I didn't know hungry you...." He trails off, looking me up and down from my bare feet up to my face.

"I borrowed your shirt, I hope that was okay, I didn't have anything else to put on, I'm sorry." Crap, I should have waited and asked him.

Ash shifts in the chair, his face looking slightly flushed. "It's no problem." He rasps out. "I was just saying that I didn't know how hungry you'd be so I loaded us up." He gestures at the food.

I contemplate where I'm supposed to sit but shrug and walk to Ash, climbing in his lap, sitting sideways. He doesn't protest so I figure he doesn't mind. He does slide me a little farther toward his knees though. "This okay?" I ask.

One of his big arms curls around my hip, holding me in place. "Yeah, I've been wanting to do this ever since I saw Reed do it." He has? Why? I give him a small smile before I tuck into the food. Tristan made runny eggs and biscuits. Yummy.

Ash occasionally holds a bite of fried ham or sausage to my lips for a bite with his fork. Apparently he wants me to eat meat. Just for fun, I give him bites of my eggs and biscuits. He's feeding me, I can feed him too right? Together we manage to eat all three plates. My belly is so full I could already use a nap. I blame Tristan for making his food taste like heaven.

I lean into Ash and press my face in his neck, closing my eyes and enjoying the smell of him. My whole body shakes with his laughter.

"Did you eat yourself into a coma, Little One?" He asks me.

"Maybe." Can you really do that? I'll have to ask Kellan, he'd know. I feel his large hand skim over my leg, starting at my knee, down my calf, to my toes. My belly does the weird flutter thing like with Remy. Maybe I just ate too much. "I wish I could just go back to sleep."

Ash keeps playing with my toes as he answers. "You can, I'll make sure no one disturbs you."

I shake my head, lifting it so I can look at him. His focus is on my feet. "I have a few things I want to do today, I should probably get started with my day." I feel and hear him growl, which makes me giggle. I guess he's still not ready to let me go. That's okay, I don't want him to.

"You could help me, you know," I say to him, resting my head on him once more.

"How so? What do you have to do?"

"I wanted to go get my own toothbrush. Maybe some dental floss too. I was going to ask Kellan if he knew how to sew, see if he can fix Noah up a little. And talk to Remy about starting my job." The more I think about it, the more I have to do. "I should probably find time for laundry as well."

"My Little One has a big day ahead of her. What is it I could help you with?" I almost forget to answer him. He called me his. I smile dreamily into his neck before I realize I still have yet to say anything.

I clear my throat, willing the tingly feelings to go away. "You could be my shadow," I state simply.

Ash laughs out loud. "I think I'm a tad too big to be your shadow, Kitten."

"Nonsense, shadows are always bigger. If you wear black today, you'll be a perfect fit." I say, smiling at him. He beams back at me.

"Yes, a perfect fit." His face goes serious again, black eyes intense. "Is getting dressed anywhere on your list today? You look good in my shirt and all, but I don't think it would be appropriate if I'm taking you to get a toothbrush."

"See? You're already helping me, what would I do without you, Shadow?" I say playfully.

"You'll never have to find out Sunshine," He replies, stealing my breath when he leans in, pressing his lips to mine softly. It's over way too quickly for my liking. "Let's get you to Logan so we can go."

Ash stands, setting my feet on the floor. He puts a hand at the small of my back guiding me out of the room. I wasn't sure if Reed's kiss counted, but Ash's sure did. Yay! I've officially been kissed! And by the sweetest of guys.

I stop in my tracks, turning to face Ash. I just thought of something. I bite my lip, hoping he goes for it. "Hey, um...you said you were taking me shopping right?

For the uh, toothbrush?"

He raises an eyebrow, nodding his head and waits for me to continue. "Well....do you think we could take the glass bike?" Please say yes, please say yes, please say yes. I mentally beg him.

Ash scoops me up in his arms, kissing me again. When he pulls back, a handsome smile lights up his face. "If that's what Little One wants, that's what Little One will get." He carries me down the hallway as I squeal in delight. *Yes*!!! "It's made of all chrome, by the way, Kitten, not glass. Could you imagine crashing on a glass bike?" He shudders. I shudder too. Ouch.

CHAPTER FIFTEEN

Logan tells me that there's no special way to get paint out my hair, I just have to scrub it really good. Handing me an expensive looking bottle of shampoo he waves me into the shower again, telling me he'll pick out an outfit for me and set it on the sink.

My hands are like raisins by the time I think I've gotten all the paint out. Logan has left a silky short-sleeve shirt, tight fitting dark jeans, socks, underwear, and my converse sneakers. I check myself out in the mirror. I look nice. Normal. I don't resemble the street kid I was when I first came here. I don't notice any bruises either, which is sort of amazing.

Logan says there's no point in doing anything with my hair, as the bike ride will just mess it up. He separates my hair weaving it into two braids that he calls pigtails. I giggle at that.

"Why are hairstyles named after animals? Pigtails and ponytails." I ask.

"You know, I don't honestly know. Humans have an unnatural obsession with the ass end of farm animals?" He jokes.

Ash reaches over and slaps his neck. Logan just winks at me, leaving the room. Ash is taking his job seriously. He stood outside the door as I showered and hasn't left my side yet.

"Are you ready to go, Shadow?"

"Lead the way, Sunshine." I have a better idea though.

"Since I have pigtails do you think you could give me a piggyback ride?" I really liked that yesterday. I plan on getting as much of these as I can get away with.

"I could, but you owe me another kiss." I smile, dashing to the bedroom and stand on the bed. Ash follows, amused. "What are you doing?" He asks.

"How was I supposed to kiss you? Jump?" I don't think he thought this through very well. He walks to me slowly, his dark eyes swirling. His hands go to my hips as he stands in front of me. Bringing his face close to mine, he stops when he's just out of reach. Why did he stop?

We stand like that for what seems like forever. Ash's warm breath fans my face as I stare at his lips. Just a bit closer and I can have them. I lean forward, my lips slowly pressing to his. I couldn't help it, I didn't want to wait anymore. Ash presses back with more force. I like that. When we pull back, my tongue darts out, seeking his taste. Ash growls deep in his throat, leaning forward again, the tip of his tongue licks my bottom lip. I gasp, shocked. Then I return the favor tentatively. His tongue slides over mine and my body lights on fire.

Oh my, that was awesome. Ash pulls back, and my face falls. I wanted to do it again. Is this the weird 'turn' thing like yesterday? Do I have to do that someone else first before he'll do it again? He better not do that with anyone else. My vision turns red at the thought.

"Let's go, Kitten, if I don't stop here, I never will. Don't pout." I don't really need a toothbrush that badly. I'm about to tell him that I'll just use Logan's, when he puts his back to me, his hands grabbing my thighs as he pulls me onto him.

My arms cross his chest as he starts walking. I realize that I'm the perfect height now to press my face in his neck. As I inhale deeply, I think to myself, I really, really like my Shadow.

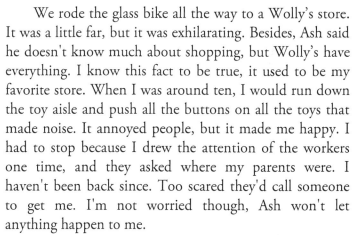

We rode the glass bike all the way to a Wolly's store. It was a little far, but it was exhilarating. Besides, Ash said he doesn't know much about shopping, but Wolly's have everything. I know this fact to be true, it used to be my favorite store. When I was around ten, I would run down the toy aisle and push all the buttons on all the toys that made noise. It annoyed people, but it made me happy. I had to stop because I drew the attention of the workers one time, and they asked where my parents were. I haven't been back since. Too scared they'd call someone to get me. I'm not worried though, Ash won't let anything happen to me.

I climb off the motorcycle on shaky legs, pulling off

Ash's huge leather jacket. I barely felt the wind with it on. He slips it on, placing his hand on my back as we walk in the store. The blow dryer thing at the entrance is still here I see. Even though I'm older, I still don't know what purpose it serves. Do you stand under it and dry your hair? Do you have to have dry hair to enter the store? These Wolly's people sure are picky about their customers.

We walk to the area under the sign that says 'Health and Beauty,' Ash leading the way. I choose a bright purple toothbrush and pick up dental floss in a mint flavor.

"Do you need anything while we're here?" I ask Ash. That really was a long trip for two items. Ash rolls his eyes, taking my stuff and placing it in the cart. I thought it was funny when he refused to push it. He said it's too short, and he looks like a little old lady hunched over. Yeah right, as if he could look anything less than inhumanly attractive.

"Let's get you a bag so we can carry it back," He suggests.

"Can't you just put them in your pocket?" I question. He ignores me, reaching for a tube of mint toothpaste and tossing it in the cart.

I follow him as he walks up and down every single aisle He picks up a pink razor and replacement blades and deodorant too. I should have thought of those. Ash smells each and every shampoo bottle before he finally decides on the Dove one. He throws the matching conditioner and bars of soap in the cart too. I hope he doesn't pick up anything glass, as the stuff tends to bounce around when he does that. My Shadow is no gentle giant.

After finding a set of stretchy black headbands he wants for me, we finally move on from that area. As we pass by the toys, something in the stuffed animals section catches my eye. It's a small black wolf. It can probably fit in my hand, and has dark brown eyes and pointy ears. I reach out to touch it, but before I can, a big hand swipes it. Ash tosses it in the cart. I smile at him, and he smiles back.

"It looks like you."

"I know, that's why I want you to have it. A stuffed Ash is better than a stuffed Noah." I giggle, he doesn't seem to like my bear either. None of the guys do.

"So we're naming it Ash then?"

He nods. "Yep, it's small, so you can call him Little Ash or something."

"What about Ash Jr.?" I ask.

He gets a goofy look on his face like he's stuck in a daydream like Reed gets. When he snaps out of it, his eyes are intense, practically shining. "Yeah Kitten, we'll name him Aeshlyn Jr."

I don't understand why he's being so weird about it now. I walk to the side of the cart and get my new treasure out, sitting him in the front part where small kids go. I buckle him in. "We could call him A.J. for short."

As I'm looking at book bags, Ash is doing something with his phone. I'm not picky about much, but I know the importance of a good backpack. I finally decide on a bright orange one with padding in the straps and a buckle across the chest. It should fit the stuff in the cart. Walking back to Ash, I see he's done pushing buttons.

"You ready little one? Kellan should be home by the time we get back." I nod, following him with the cart. He stops and reaches for something else. I roll my eyes, Ash is just as curious in a store as I am. Maybe he would like to push the buttons in the toy section too? No, I can't picture him doing that. He'd just think I was stupid for asking. I lean around him, wondering what has his attention. They look like socks. He throws a pair of the black ones in.

"You're buying one pair of socks?"

"Yeah they're socks, but they have little holes for your toes. This way you can keep your feet warm, and I can still see your tiny toes." That makes me laugh, he likes my toes? As he starts to walk away, he must think better of it because he turns back to the rack and grabs a pair in every color.

I just laugh harder. "I don't need all of those Ash, we came here for toothpaste remember?"

"Of course you do, gotta protect those things Sunshine, it's my job." He winks at me. Ash winked!

"You know, you're pretty sweet when you want to be," I say to him. He really is, in a gruff sort of way, but sweet nonetheless.

"You make me want to be Kitten, at least to you." He bends down and kisses me. "Only you."

We check out, Ash not allowing me to see how much he spent, and I pack everything up in my bag. I left AJ's head poking out of the top, and he thought that was cute. I climb on the glass bike, my arms wrapping around his tummy as he starts it up. I'm glad I didn't let him let me go this morning.

When we get back to the house, I search out Kellan as Ash takes my bag to his room and grabs Noah. I find him in the kitchen, talking to Tristan. They're sitting at the kitchen island, drinking coffee. I give them each a kiss on the cheek and take a sip of Tristan's coffee. I make a face, handing it back. Yuck, he put stuff in it.

"Well hello to you too Kitten." Tristan laughs. "Have fun shopping with Ash?"

"Yeah, he bought me lots of toe socks."

"What are toe socks?" Asks Kellan.

"Socks with spaces for toes. He said it would protect them." I shrug. I've never had them, and my toes are just fine. But Ash wants me to wear them, so I will.

"Okay, I suppose I'll see them soon enough. Do you think I could talk to you privately sometime today?" Kellan asks me, looking anxious.

"Actually, I was looking for you. Do you know how to sew? I figured since you were a doctor or whatever that you might know how to do stitches."

Kellan's face pales. "Did you get hurt? What's wrong? Did Ash get hurt?" He fires questions at me before I can answer them.

"It's for the bear, calm down," Ash says, walking in with Noah. Kellan looks relieved.

"He needs surgery Doc." I pout my bottom lip.

The three of them chuckle. "No way can you say no to that face Kell," Tristan says, handing me a cup of black coffee. I stop him as he backs away, going on my toes to kiss his cheek.

"I didn't get to say thank you for the wonderful breakfast earlier. I stuffed myself stupid until it was all gone. Your food is truly wonderful Tristan. Thank you." He hugs me close to him, kissing my forehead.

When he pulls back, he tugs on my pigtails. "I like these." His fingers trail over the braids.

"Did you know they're called pigtails?"

He gives me his beautiful Tristan smile. "Yes, I've heard them called that before. Strange right?"

"Very," I answer.

"Alright, Kitten, let's go get your bear fixed up shall we?" Kellan says. "I'll have you know that at one time, I was actually a surgeon." Holy crap, for real? Oh yeah, dummy, he's not really 19.

I'll get Noah from Ash's room. "You coming Shadow?"

"Not, this time, Sunshine. I heard Kellan say he wants to talk alone. You go on, I'll find you later." With that, he kisses me hard on the lips, quickly. My eyes snap to Kellan and Tristan, wondering how they will react. They don't, neither one even batting an eye at Ash's display of affection. Okay then, this must be okay.

Kellan leads me to his doctor's office. "You look nice today," He tells me.

I blush, looking at my clothes. "Thank you, Logan gave me these." That makes him laugh and shake his head.

We each take a chair, facing one another. "Okay Kitten, let's start with what happened between you and Remy yesterday morning." Oh God, I don't know how to talk about that. "I understand this may be difficult for you, but it's important."

"Um...I uh, liked what we did." I whisper.

"Did you initiate it?"

"I think I did, but I was asleep." Kellan makes a note in his folder thing.

When he looks back up to me, he sighs. "I just wanted to check if you were alright Kitten. You were crying when Ash came to the door. Would you care to explain that?"

"It wasn't because of what I and Remy did, not really. He didn't hurt me. It was new, and exciting, and weird and I had no idea what my body was feeling or doing, but I don't regret it if that's what you think. I freaked out when someone knocked on the door because it could have been Jace. And I didn't want him to know." I pick at non-existent lint on my knee. I won't take back my time with Remy.

"It's not bad that you enjoyed yourself, Kitten. The rest of the guys, myself included, just wanted to make sure that nothing was forced on you, that's all. Remy can be a little intense. Persuasive if you will."

He continues. "About Jace..." He sighs heavily. "...You have to know that he didn't mean what he said. No one here thinks that of you." I nod, I already guessed that. "I hope you can get past that with him, but that's between the two of you. I just want you to know that being intimate with someone, or more than one someone, isn't wrong, it isn't dirty, and it doesn't make you a whore. If you have feelings for the person you're with if you want it to happen, and you enjoy yourself, that's all that matters. You don't feel like you have to kiss us or do what you did with Remy as payment of any sort right?"

I shake my head. Kellan nods, writing again. "Kitten, I would like to start you on a series of birth control. Just in case, not because we expect anything to happen. It's for your own protection."

I blink at him in surprise. Birth control? As in babies? I guess I never thought about having any. A family of my own would be nice, not that I know anything about children or can care for one. I'm really starting to feel like I'm a part of this family....wait, hold on. "I thought Remy said that werewolves and humans couldn't have babies? Are you suggesting that I have...sex with other people?"

That hurts a little, ok a lot. I haven't given sex much thought either. Actually not at all before the past two days, Kellan doesn't want me to have sex with them though? Because we can't have babies?

"Kitten, whatever you're thinking, stop. Talk to me. Of course I don't want you with other people, we want you as ours, in every way, when you're ready."

Did he just say..."Ours? Like I'm in a relationship with all seven of you? Eight if you include Jace. Which I'm not sure I do." Kellan doesn't answer, it looks like he's shocked by his own words too.

After clearing his throat, he speaks in a low voice. "Do you think that would be something you could handle Kitten? Have all of us love and care for you? If that scares you...."

"No, it doesn't scare me." I cut him off. "Is that what you guys want? What happens if, you know, things happen?"

Kellan smiles wide. "It is what we want. Something about you draws all of us to you, Kitten. We don't really understand it ourselves. It's not something any of us has tried before. When or if your relationships with us reaches that level, it will all be up to you. You do what feels right to you. My brothers and I will deal with any jealousy that may arise. We're a family, we'll work through everything together."

"You still didn't answer my question Kellan, if we can't have babies then why use birth control?"

"You're right, we can't, it's just a precautionary measure." I shake my head.

"I don't want them Kellan, at least not for now, okay?" He nods, scribbling on the paper.

"That's fine Kitten, it's always up to you. Now, I was informed about your day yesterday, and I'd like to suggest that you join Reed for yoga. He does it every day, and I think it might help you develop coping techniques for your panic attacks. Do you think you'd like to do that?"

"That depends on what yoga is." Is my reply.

"Sometimes I forget how new to this world you are. You can watch him first and decide for yourself if you'd like to try it. It's really just a series of exercises, but there's more to it. I join him myself at times."

"Okay, I like trying things." He smiles at me. I smile back.

"One last thing, then you can get out of here. Would you mind if I took a little more of your blood? I have a few tests that I'd like to run."

After Kellan took my blood and gave me a pink Band-Aid and a sucker, I step out of the room, running right into Ash.

"Did you get your bear all fixed up?" He asks me. Shoot, I forgot all about that. I think I can be let off the guilt hook though. Talking about sex and babies and yoga kind of overrules teddy bear surgery.

Finding Remington is always a simple task, as he spends most of his time in his office. I wonder what he does in there all day. Ash doesn't bother knocking, just opens the door for me. Before he can walk away, I take his arm, pulling him in with me.

Remy looks amazing in his suit coat and white button-up. I'm sure I'm drooling when his gray eyes find mine. Ash reaches over and closes my mouth, snorting out a laugh as he does it.

"Hi." I squeak out.

Remy's famous smirk is in place as he responds. "Hello, Kitten." Mmmm. His deep voice melts my insides. Again. I'm thankful I brought Ash in with me or I might....Something. I'm not sure.

"Kitten wanted to ask you about work, Rem." Ash saves me from having to speak. Good thing too. I can't yet.

"Yes, I've been meaning to speak to about that. You've been a very busy girl." He raises a playful eyebrow at me. I blush in response.

Remy continues. "You start tomorrow Kitten, bright and early. I don't like the thought of you being on your own for so long and you can't drive anyhow. Logan said he could accompany you tomorrow. I'll be making a schedule, you'll always have one of us with you."

I almost roll my eyes. What part about my sixteen years on the street makes him think I can't handle myself for a few hours? I don't though. I don't mind one of the guys tagging along. I just hope they don't get too bored.

"Also, I'll need you to come straight to me when you get off work tomorrow. I know the men like to pull you away for fun and whatnot, but we have business to discuss. Understood?" Remy commands more than asks.

"I understand Remy, I'll find you. If it's about the laundry, I swear, I'm going to catch it up." I know the guys have been spending money on me left and right, and I can only guess how much it cost to free the goldfish. I really have to start earning it.

Ash snorts. "No one cares if you do the laundry Sunshine. That was more for you to feel better about being here than for us." Huh, well I'm going to do it anyway.

"That's all for now unless you have something else?" I shake my head at Remy. Ash stands, opening the door. I start to walk out, and then think better of it.

I sidle up behind Remy, kissing him on the cheek. I put my arms around his broad shoulders and give him a tight hug, bringing my lips to his ear. "I'm sorry you caught so much grief over what we did Remington, but I'm happy we did it. You didn't make me cry, and I'm sorry I did that. By the way, I've missed you." I kiss his cheek again, walking to the door.

"I missed you too, pretty girl." I hear from behind me. I don't look back, not wanting him to see the huge grin on my face. Someone missed me. I can't believe this is my life now.

CHAPTER SIXTEEN

After my talk with Remy, I feel like I'm on cloud nine. My Shadow followed me down to the laundry room and picked out an entire load of clothes that were all his. I had a good a laugh about that, but he just explained that he likes his t-shirts and jeans, and it makes no sense for Logan to buy new stuff for him. That made complete sense to me too so I had him make a pile of just his clothes, that way I can wash them all up first and stop the clothes madness. At least one-eighth of it. To my surprise, Ash didn't mind this task at all. Too late I realized I should have taken a look at laundry products while we were at Wolly's. I'll have to remember to do that soon.

When Tristan yelled down at us that dinner was ready, I had told Ash that I would just skip it and get more work done. He didn't say a word before I was thrown over his shoulder in a fireman's carry and left the basement. I giggled the whole way there, lightheaded as all get out when I was finally plopped in a chair. The food was amazing, as usual, and it was nice to be around all of them at once again. I think if they didn't eat together, they would probably never see each other. They keep pretty busy.

That had got me thinking about what it is that they all do. They must have jobs because they don't even blink when money is spent. Then *that* got me thinking about how much I don't truly know any of them. I know they have pasts, and part of me is dying to know every detail about them. But a bigger part of me wonders if it matters. I decide that at least for now, it doesn't. I'm happy right now. It's not something I've experienced often, and I'll hold onto this for as long as possible. I don't have to know them, not just yet. I know that I trust them, that I want to be around them and that they make me feel safe. It's enough for now.

***

It was decided that I should stay with Logan tonight since he'll insist on dressing me for work and he's the one driving me there. I don't mind a bit. I didn't get much time with him today, and I missed him dearly.

When I got to Ash's room to get my new bag with my toothbrush in it, Ash came in shortly after me, probably ready for bed himself since he didn't sleep the night before. He'd stopped me on my way out though.

"You forgot Aeshlyn Jr." He waved my stuffed wolf in the air.

"No I didn't, I thought he should stay with you, that's why I tucked him into the bed. You'll look after him, right? Make sure nothing happens to him?" He looked at the little wolf intently in his hands. I watched as he placed it reverently back on the bed, covering it up to his head. He had a goofy grin when he looked back to me.

"I promise Kitten, I'll look after him." I smiled at that.

"I knew you would. Good night Aeshlyn."

"Night."

I was going to take my new treasure with me to Logan's room, but something about that didn't feel right. AJ was between Ash and I. I can trust Ash to look after a piece of mine, just like I trust Logan with my flag, and Kellan with Noah, who is spending the night in his doctor room. I know they don't understand why these things mean so much to me, but they don't have to. They get that I want them, and that's enough.

When I showed up in Logan's room, I proudly showed him my toothbrush. He frowned and asked me to use his. At least when I was with him.

"Why?" I asked.

"I don't know, I just like it when you use mine. I like that we get to share something. That's all." He shrugged.

I shrugged too. "Okay." Is all I said. If he wanted me to then that's what I'd do. I put my new one back in my bag and followed him to the bathroom in the hall. He let me use it first again and then he used it, that same kid-like smile in place.

We had crawled into bed, slipping under the

blankets. Logan turned off the lights and snuggled in behind me. "What kind of clothes do you need for tomorrow, Kitten?" He asked me.

"I'm not sure what you mean, I usually just wear what I've got." Before coming here, dressing was simple. I had two sets of clothes. One to wear, one to wash. I liked to keep most of what I owned on me, so if it didn't fit in my bag, I didn't have it.

"Yes, I understand, but you have a new usual now. Do you need dressier clothes? Baggy, tight fitting, shorts, pants, a warm sweater..."

I giggled. How much did he buy when we were shopping? "Logan, I honestly don't know. I've seen other people at the rink wear many different styles. I guess it's about preference, and currently, I don't have one."

"Have you ever seen someone there wear something that you thought you might like to have? Something pretty or something you thought looked more functional than other clothing?" Logan presses. He's not going to let up until I tell him something. Besides, this is a question I can answer.

"There was this one time when a professional couple came in. They were beautiful on the ice. Moved together so effortlessly that it stole my breath away. The lady wore tight exercise pants and a cami with a loose knitted sweater over it. I remember it as my favorite outfit because when they picked up speed, the sweater would billow out and add definition to the clean lines of her movements." I stop, knowing I'm rattling on.

Logan kisses my head. "Sounds beautiful, Kitten. I don't know if I've got anything like that, but I'll try to match it as best I can for tomorrow okay?"

"Okay, and I'd like my hair to be wrapped as tightly as you can get it, too. It gets in my way when I'm skating."

"I'll see what I can do Kitten, get some rest. This job of yours starts way too fucking early in the morning." I snort at that. I've only started sleeping at night since I've been here. I guess if I had such a comfortable bed I wouldn't want to leave it either. With that thought, I snuggle back into him, closing my eyes and thinking, tonight I do have a comfortable bed to sleep in, and a body to keep me warm too.

I found it hilarious watching Logan freak out this morning. At first, I thought he just wasn't a morning person, but I noticed it was because he was frustrated. He didn't have anything like what I had described last night, so he unhappily settled on a pair of skinny leg jeans and a light purple sweater. No matter how much I told him that it didn't matter to me what I wore, he was still upset.

As if that wasn't bad enough, he went into near meltdown mode over my hair. After blow-drying it after my shower, he realized that he didn't own any bobby pins. I managed to calm him down, telling him that he'll be there with me today so if it falls down, he can just put it back up again. That seemed to make him happy.

When we came downstairs, I was surprised to see all of them in the kitchen. What caught my eye first was a very large grouping of flowers in gold vase. As I moved closer, I saw a card with my name on it sticking out of the top.

"These are for me?" I looked at each of them.

"Yeah, they have your name on them, sweetie. When I came down to start breakfast for your big day, they were already here. No one will admit to who got them though." Tristan answered.

How strange. Why would someone get me flowers? "What do I do with them?" I ask more to myself than any of them.

"Just pick a place in the house, where you would like to see them," Remy says, sipping his coffee.

I think about it for a moment before I pick them up and carry them out of the room. When I come back, eight pairs of questioning eyes fall on me. "I put them on the table next to the front door. That way, the first and the last thing we see when entering and exiting the house is something beautiful, and I can share them with everyone." I would have kept them on the table, but they were just too big and blocked my view of some of the guys. The flowers are pretty, but the guys are better.

"Thank you to whoever got them," I added. Still, not one of them owned up to it. I suppose it didn't matter. I shrugged, taking a seat.

Ash placed a mug of black coffee in front of me as Tristan sat three different plates down. I look at him curiously. Surely this isn't all for me. I know I pigged out yesterday, does he think I always need this much food?

"I wanted you to be nice and full on your big day," Tristan answers me with a sheepish smile.

"Why do you keep calling it that? This isn't my first day of work ever. I've even worked at this particular place before." I really don't get it.

"We know that, we just wanted you to feel special. This is your first day of work in your new life. All of us wanted to see you off this morning, and we'll all be here when you return." Says Kellan.

"Thank you," I reply. Stunned by their thoughtfulness. At Ash's prodding, I eat as much as I can without over doing it. A heavy stomach on the ice is no good. By the time I finish off my coffee, it's time to leave.

Standing, I walk to each of the guys, giving them a hug and a peck on the cheek. Not Jace though. To him, I simply say a thank you and head to the door with Logan. He got that much because he came to see me off with the rest of them. I'm sure someone had to drag him from his beauty sleep with threats, but he was there too.

Logan opens the door, and a smile lights my face instantly. I hadn't given thought to what car we would take, but I'm happy I get to ride in a new one. The bright blue R8 looks as fun as the man who drives it.

"Will you teach me to drive this Logan?" I ask excitedly.

Logan throws his head back in laughter. "I would, but then I'd have to kill you, Kitten." He manages to get out, still laughing his butt off.

My eyes go wide, and all the blood drains from my face. Why would he have to kill me? Is this car for werewolves only? I'm glad he told me though. I hope I'm at least allowed in it.

Logan pauses with the driver's side door open. A frown marring his handsome face. "Come on Kitten, get in, you're going to be late if you don't hurry."

"Am I allowed in it?" I bite my lip, waiting for his

answer.

"Of course, silly girl." He answers, and I relax. Good, I'm allowed to ride in it, I just can't drive it.

The engine purrs to life and Logan speeds down the drive, taking me to work.

CHAPTER SEVENTEEN

O h, look what the cat done dragged in. Don't you just look as purdy as a picture?" Miss Annie greets me. I beam at her, giving her a hug.

"Thank you, Miss Annie, you remember Logan right?"

"Don't git many fellas in here with blue zebra stripes in dey hair, course I do. That other'n called to say you'd be stayin' here for the day." Miss Annie's southern drawl seems at an all-time high this morning as she pulls Logan into a bear hug. I guess she likes him too.

"Yes ma'am, I'll stay out of the way though, or you can put me to work as well. I'm just here to look out for Kitten." Logan replies formally. It's odd coming from him, but I'm happy he's showing Miss Annie respect. I just hope he doesn't swear in front of her, she's been known to smack teenagers with a newspaper for that.

"I might just hold y'all ta that boy, got lots a heavy liftin' ta do, for now y'all can just watch Kitten work her magic on the young'uns." Miss Annie waddles away and I head to my locker with Logan in tow.

"Mississippi?" Logan asks.

"Alabama. She moved up here to be closer to her grandbabies." I tell him, figuring he was talking about her accent. I get my locker open and take out my skates and equipment room key. Along with my nametag.

"Are those things safe, Kitten?" Logan is staring at my skates like they might bite him.

"I guess they are a little worn, but they work just fine. The blades are sharpened. I take care of what's mine Logan, don't worry."

After heading to the arena to drop my stuff off, I go to the supply closet and take out the walkers. Essentially they are just pieces of plastic pipe set together in an 'L' shape, but they allow people who don't know how to stand on skates keep their balance. The kids love them because they don't fall on their butts so often. I grab them, the cones, and a rope I use to pull the kids along and help them spin. Logan helps me carry all of it out to the ice.

"Oh crap, I didn't bring any music. The tape I had was at the warehouse." I chew on my lip, wondering what I'll do now.

"Why do you need music?" Logan asks, taking out his phone.

"I use it to warm up and for the free skate at the end of the session."

207

"Where's your sound equipment set up?" He asks. I point to where the booth is that has an old boom box rigged up to the speakers. There's other stuff in there, but I don't know how to use any of it.

As Logan walks off, I change into my skates and begin stretching. After about fifteen minutes he still hasn't returned, so I prepare to take the ice anyway, I'd like to warm up before the kids start showing up. I take a slow lap around the rink, loving once again, how I'm the first person on the new ice. Halfway through my second lap, the speakers blare with a fast pace song. I see Logan walking to where I left my shoes. I give him a big smile before I start showing off for him.

LOGAN

I managed to find an iPod dock in the sound booth, so I scrolled through my playlists on my phone, picking a fun song for Kitten to skate to. *Starset*, *'My Demons'* begins and I nod my head to it. I have to wonder if Miss Annie hooked up the boom box specifically for Kitten. We'll have to do something about that. I don't even know where she would've gotten a tape in the first place.

I stride back to where she left her shoes, thinking that I'd put them in her locker for her. I know how she is about stuff she owns. When the song starts, I look out to the ice to see her reaction to my song. She looks at me like I'm superman, and I just saved the world. Damn, that girl's smile gets me every time. As she passes by me, I catch the mischievous look in her eyes. I stop what I'm doing to watch her as she picks up speed. Kitten's pretty fast on land, but she's a damn rocket on ice. All of a sudden she lifts herself into the air, spinning. My heart drops to my stomach, and my throat tightens. My panic is quick to abate when she comes back down and lands perfectly, her leg swinging out to balance her. She just smiles and continues on. Holy shit! My girl can fucking fly!

Kitten performs a few more tricks before the children arrive. One of which, was when she grabbed the blade of she skate and brought it up behind her, making it touch her head. That was pretty fucking hot, I tried not to get too turned on at the display of her flexibility. The things I can do with that knowledge......Another move she did that completely blew my mind was when she spun in a circle so fast she was just a blur. I expected her to fall over, dizzy as shit, when she stopped, but she just skated on. Why the hell didn't I know of this activity before? I could have been chasing after ice skaters for years! I got me one now though. I can't help but smirk at that thought.

I thought Kitten was amazing when she was alone on the ice, but watching her with those kids was even better. I swear my heart swelled seeing how good she was with them. I shouldn't have expected anything less from her. Her big heart knows no bounds it seems. I could see the hero worship the little girls had for her, how her patience gave them confidence in themselves. I watched as a runt of a boy fell flat on his ass, making the other kids laugh at him, and he shrunk in on himself. Kitten skated toward him and fell down too, telling all the kids that even she falls sometimes, it just happens. The boy gave her a smile that broke my heart. I wish, more than anything, that she could have my pups, I couldn't imagine anyone being a better mother than her.

Just as the free skate part of the session begins, Miss Annie finds me on the bleachers. "A right sight to see ain't it?" She asks me, indicating Kitten.

"Sure is ma'am. She's pretty amazing out there." I say honestly.

"She's a purdy amazin' girl."

"Damn straight," I reply.

I'm shocked as shit when Miss Annie smacks me straight on the nose. "Don't you go a'cussin 'round a lady, boy. I hear any that filth pass that girl's lips, it'll be your butt I'll be a whoopin'. Y'all git me?" I try my damnedest not to laugh at the thought of this old woman beating me up, but one look at her face and I know she's serious. I think her and Remy would get along great.

"Yes, ma'am. Sorry ma'am. It won't happen again." I give her my most contrite look. I've had lots of practice as Remy doesn't approve of my over the top antics at times.

Miss Annie bobs her head once, looking satisfied by my answer. "I got a shipment from the food supplier sitin' out, just ready for some young lad to carry't in. Would y'all mind helpin' an old woman out?" I look out at Kitten, unsure. "I won't keep y'all long from the girl, promise boy." I don't really want to get on this woman's bad side, so I hold my arm out, gentleman style.

"Lead the way ma'am. By the way, you don't look a day over thirty." I smile at her, trying to be the 'boy' she thinks I am.

She snorts but her cheeks color. "Now you save that charmin' smile for my girl over there." She slides her hand on my bicep anyhow, probably out of habit with her Southern manners, and we stroll back to the lobby.

KITTEN

A cheer goes up when I announce it's free skate time. As much as the kids like to learn, they like to play even more. I glance over to Logan and see Miss Annie bop him on the nose, making me giggle. He must have sworn, I guess I should have warned him, but Logan seems like the type that needs to learn the hard way. The two of them talk for a minute before I see Miss Annie blush and Logan smile. It seems like Miss Annie approves of him and that makes me happy. I don't need her approval but I like the both of them, and it's good they're getting along. She doesn't usually like teens in general, not that Logan is really a teen, but she doesn't know that. I watch as they walk off together through the double doors, she probably took him up on his offer to help out.

As I'm collecting the orange cones and other things I used today, I hear hoots of laughter coming from the locker room entrance. I stiffen, already knowing who it is. I keep my back to them all, ignoring them as usual. Maybe they won't see me.

No such luck. "Eww, the hobo's back. Why can't she just starve to death like a good homeless bitch already?" A girl named Kaitlynn sneers. I don't remember doing anything to her, but she always says the nastiest things to me. Her pack of laughing hyenas rivals that of Adam's.

"Now Kat, don't go hating on Kitten." I freeze at the sound of that voice. Oh great, they're all together today.

How fun.

Hooting laughter echo's the whole arena at Adam's lame joke. "Shut it Adam, and don't call me that. My parents actually gave me a name unlike her. She got that name because she eats out of garbage cans like a nasty ass cat."

Ouch. Okay, that hurt a little. Not the trash eating comment, because hey, every street kid has been there. But did she really have to remind me that I have no parents? Can't she see that it's not my fault? To my utter joy, the gaggle of idiots perch themselves on the stands. I hope the kids can't hear their mean words. Children shouldn't know that such mean people exist, not yet anyway, they are too sweet to learn about evil.

I can't avoid them for long though. The supply room is right beside where they are sitting. They probably knew I'd have to go there eventually. I'd wait, but my session is almost over and this stuff needs packed away. I carry as much as I can, hoping I'll only need two trips. As I step off the ice, Kaitlynn grabs a cone from my stack of them under my arm. I stop, keeping my eyes down. I need that back.

Out of the corner of my eye I see her take a marker and write on the cone. When she's finished, she takes a step forward and slams the cone on my head making my neck hurt. "There, much better, now those brats will know to keep their distance."

As she high fives another girl, the cone falls off my head, the hole was too small to keep it there. I see what she wrote and try to keep my face blank. It reads 'CAUTION! Slut approaching'. How very unoriginal. She and her group of friends follow Adam around like he's made of candy or something. I've heard about what she's willing to do to keep his attention. I'm not judging, but it stands to reason that I am not the slut here.

People are who they are. I just wish she'd ignore me like I ignore her. Sighing, I bend down to get the cone, not saying a word to them as I make my way to the supply closet. I'll have to figure out how to get the marker off before tomorrow. She shouldn't damage other people's property. Miss Annie will be mad if she has to buy a new one. I'll be sure to tell her that I'm sorry. If it weren't for me, it wouldn't have happened.

When I walk back out, they all shout things at me in a competition of who can be meaner. I don't listen to them. Instead I replay the song Logan played for me in my head, blocking them out. I grab the rest of the equipment and walk back. I peek up from under my lashes and am brought out of my song when I notice that their attention has shifted behind me. This is out of place as I'm usually their only target. I turn and look, seeing Mikey take another tumble on the ice.

Mikey is my favorite kid ever. My group today was not the usual spoiled kids that get dragged here by their parents, today's class was from a group home of foster kids. Mikey's dad is a drunk and takes all his anger out on the small boy. Mikey is the sweetest kid I've ever met, he has little to no self-esteem and gets picked on for his size. I know what that's like.

I see one of Adam's friends start to call out to Mikey, who is struggling to stand again. This just won't do. "Hey!" I call to Adam. "Aren't you supposed to be in school or something?" I ask, bringing their attention back to me. Good. I don't want them picking on Mikey, he doesn't know any better, and Adam is his hero on the ice. It would crush him for Adam to laugh at him.

"You stupid girl, don't you know anything? School's been out for months, it's just about to start again. God, you are dumb." Adam's 'yes man' replies. I hurry to the supply closet, just dropping the stuff on the floor, I don't want to leave them too long in case they take notice of Mikey again.

As I rush from the room, I run smack dab into Adam. He's by himself, and I don't know if this is a good thing or not. He shoves my shoulders, pushing me into the side of the seating area. "If you wanted to touch me, Kitten, all you had to do was ask." He breathes in my ear, his body flush with mine.

It doesn't feel the same as being close with my guys, Adam pressing against me makes my tummy feel upset. "Go away Adam, I didn't want to touch you then, and I don't want to touch you now."

I shove him back, and he goes willingly. Anger rolls of his stiff form, scaring me a little. I hurry to get away from him, angry people are never a good thing. I make it to the end of the bleachers where the rest of them are leaning over the rails, watching us. I see Mikey look our way and hope he skates away.

Adam grips my arm tightly. "You think you're better than me or something?" He roars in my face. I wish he'd be quieter and not make a scene in front of the kids. "You're just trash, a nobody! A bitch who has to lay on her back for a cheeseburger. Who the fuck are you to say no to me? I was just trying to be nice and offer you five whole dollars for some head. That could feed your ass for a week right?"

"Oh shit!" One of Kaitlynn's hyenas say. Everyone else is silent. I look around, noticing the kids have stopped skating and are staring at us. Mikey is looking at the ground, looking as heartbroken as I knew he'd be when he found out his hero is really a villain. I want to walk away from him like I usually do, but he hurt one of my kids. I can't have that.

"You know what Adam?" I say, making sure the kids can hear me. "I *am* better than you. I'm stronger than you are." His angry face turns to amusement as he laughs. I don't think he's aware of our new audience.

"Are you fucking for real, Kitten? You really think you're stronger than me?" He doubles at the waist cracking up.

I wait for him to quiet before I speak again. "Yes. Yes, I do. Not physically, I've seen what you can do out there..." I point to the ice. "....But I'm stronger because I can deal with people like you and Kaitlynn trying to tear me down, day after day, and I'm still here. I still come back. Every time. Do you know how it is that I can do that, Adam?" I ask, not waiting for his answer before I continue.

"It's because by the time you are out of my sight, I've already forgotten you. I don't think about you, or her. I don't think about your cruel words or how you laugh at me. I may be nobody, but you are nothing to me. You. Mean. Nothing. To. Me. Do you hear me? You can use your words to try to beat me down, and I'll get back up. Every time. You could use your hockey stick and break my bones and split my skin, but I'll get back up. Every time. Because I'm strong Adam, because you are not the biggest bad out there. You're just a spoiled little boy, bored with his station in life."

I'm panting now, anger like I have never felt courses through my veins. I turn and look at the stunned faces of this rotten group of people. "All of you..." I shout at them. ..."can point your fingers and laugh at me all you'd like. Point at the girl with no parents to care for her, it just means I know more than you do. Laugh at the girl with no place to sleep at night, it just means I can withstand more than you can."

I look right at Kaitlynn. "Call the virgin a slut, it just means you have no class. What does it say when young adults like yourself treat people this way when people like me see *you* as trash?"

I look back to Adam. "When I walk out of here today, I will have already forgiven you before I forgot you again. I can do that because I'm strong enough to do it. I have nowhere to go but up, Adam. Where are you heading?" I stare at him, waiting for him to answer me. He doesn't seem to have one.

I turn, going back to my kids. A few of them look scared of me, and I hate it, I shouldn't have raised my voice. I hate that they had to see it, but these kids are alone somewhat themselves. I couldn't let them see me back down. You never stand down to a bully.

Mikey stares at me, but I can't look him in the eye. I crushed his dream of being like Adam when he grows up. At least on the ice. Every kid should have a dream. "Okay, session's over, let's get our shoes back on!" I call out.

The kids rush to the bleachers, some of them falling again. I turn and look where the hyenas are, no one's there anymore. As much as I'd like to think I made my point with them today, I worry about the blowback. Oh well, whatever happens, happens. I'll deal with it like I always do.

LOGAN

After I stacked crate after crate of food supplies for Miss Annie, she asked me to change the light bulbs in the kitchen. I was a bit annoyed, wanting to get back to Kitten but if I didn't do it, Kitten might have to, and I don't want her standing on the rickety ladder. She could fall and hurt herself.

When I'm done screwing in the last bulb, I jump down and dust myself off. "Anything else Miss Annie?" I ask, hoping to God the woman says no.

"That's all for today Dear, I see how anxious y'all are ta get back ta Kitten. She's prolly finishin' up now. C'mon, I'll walk with y'all." I try not to jump for joy in front of her. I don't know when the next time I'll be able to accompany Kitten to work is and I'd like to soak in all I can of her today.

We walk in silence, Miss Annie's hand on my arm again, as we make our way through the doors leading to the ice. I hear shouting and realize I've tuned out my wolf hearing for too long. I got distracted like a fucking idiot.

As I tune back in I hear that dick face, Adam, ranting about someone thinking they are better than him. I snort. Everyone's better than his ass. I walk faster, urging Miss Annie to pick up the pace. I can't react to anything yet as human ears wouldn't be able to hear him at this range.

When we round the corner my vision goes white. My

body on fire as my wolf wants to come out. I start forward, ready to fucking kill his ass. The hand on my arm grips tighter. Miss Annie's voice reaching my ears.

"Now hold on boy, let's see if Kitten can handle herself 'fore you go rushin' right over." I'm about to tell this lady to fuck off, that she shouldn't have to handle herself when Kitten's sweet, but hard voice rings out around the stadium. I've heard her voice like that before. When she told off the carnie at the fair. I stop and watch with Miss Annie as Kitten faces off with no less than a dozen punk kids. Someone's about to be told off, and I get front row seats again. I take my phone out to record this so I can show it to the guys later. You know, for informational purposes. I chuckle to myself, yeah right.

No one can accuse my girl of being short winded but the more she talks, the more I want to kiss the fuck out of her. When she said that she was stronger than the built boy in front of her I thought I'd have to step in and stop her. The kid looks like he'd like to test that theory. The looks on the bitches' faces are priceless as this tiny little girl tells them like it is. Her speech tears at my heart but pride swells within me when she talks about always getting back up. I know she does, my brothers and I have seen it.

Kitten turns to a girl with more makeup on her face than a dead person who's been shot square in the nose. The bitch's eyes narrow at my girl, but she keeps her mouth shut. I think she chose well considering the steel in Kitten's eyes. She looks like she could eat this girl for lunch. As she's wrapping up, I see her turn back to the douchebag. She tells that fucker that she's got nowhere to go but up, and I have to hold back from shouting 'HELL

YEAH BABY!' at her. She then asks where he's heading, and the little fucker stands there with mouth open, unable to answer her. She turns and walks off, looking like she's doing just what she said she did, forgetting about them. I fucking *love* her.

My wolf is purring seeing her display of dominance and begs me to make her mine. Telling me that she'd be a good mate and fierce mother of my pups. I feel a tugging at my arm. I forgot all about Miss Annie being there.

"Stop that growlin' boy, she took care of business jus' like I knew she would." She tuts at me. I didn't know I was.

I turn out of her hold, not wanting anyone's hands on me but Kitten's at the moment. My wolf won't be happy until she's in our arms. "You should do something about that guy," I tell her. "Ban him from here or something."

She heaves a sigh. "I wish I could, fact is, he's ta star player on ta hockey team, him and ta rest them boys are the main income 'round here. I'll talk ta the coach, but seein' as he's his Daddy, I don't reckon he's gonna do much about it." She shakes her head. I can tell she hates the situation, but it's either her place of business or Kitten. Her choice is obvious, even though I hate it.

I watch as the kids race off the ice, readying to leave. The runt that Kitten helped out earlier is looking at her like she holds the moon in her hands. Kitten won't look at him, and I wonder what that's about. The kid finally comes out of his stupor and gets his shoes on as well. Miss Annie approaches her, telling her that she'll collect the skates and clean up here. Kitten looks around, probably for me and I make my way over.

LANE WHITT

"Hey, Logan," She says sadly.

I can't help myself; my wolf won't let me. I grab her waist, pulling her into me. Fuck that feels good. I tilt her chin up and crash my lips down on hers. She gasps in shock, and I use the opportunity to taste her. Fucking shit... this isn't calming my wolf in the slightest. I growl at her taste, savoring every second of it. I hear her whimper, and I'm lost. That's the sexiest sound I've ever heard.

I forgot all about there being children present. Not to mention Miss Annie. "That's enough a that boy, you've made your point. Let ta poor thing breathe."

I pull back, looking down at my girl. Her face is flushed and she's just blinking at me. It's adorable. I smirk down at her. There's more where that came from baby. Out of the corner of my eye, I catch movement. I see that fucker Adam hiding behind the stands like a bitch. The look in his eye says this isn't over. I agree. Kitten may have stood up for herself today, but what that little shit doesn't know and she doesn't seem to remember, is that she has eight terrifying werewolves to back her up now. Oh yes, we'll be meeting again bitch boy, I think at him as I glare in his direction. He takes one last, longing look at my girl and turns away.

CHAPTER EIGHTEEN

KITTEN

The ride home was mostly silent as I stared out the window. When Logan kissed me, my mind had stopped working completely. It was almost scary in its intensity, but the rumble I felt in his chest called out to me, begged me to let go and lose myself. I totally did. Afterward, he backed away from me, his demeanor changing. I wondered briefly if I did it wrong but my embarrassment at doing that in front of so many people, children at that, soon overrode my worry.

Logan tried to put on a happy face when we first got in the car, but it didn't last long. He told me how proud he was for putting those people in their place, and I had told him that people don't have places. That was the whole conversation.

When we pull up to the house, seven gorgeous men are standing on the steps. I can't help the smile that overtakes my face. As soon as Logan stops the car I throw the door open and pounce on Reed, who's the closest.

He chuckles at me. "Hey there, excited much?" I nod my head vigorously. He just laughs harder, his blue, green and gold flecked eyes sparkle as his blond hair blows in the wind. I kiss his cheek quickly and jump down. Seeking my next target.

Finn has turned and started to walk to the door, so I get a running start and jump on his back. It's high, but I managed it. I kiss him quickly too as he stumbles forward.

"Be careful Kitten!" Remy booms at me. I turn and stick my tongue out at him. He smirks and just shakes his head.

"Did you have fun at work Kitten?" Finn asks.

I groan and press my face into his neck. Mmmm Finn even smells sweet. "I don't want to talk about today. How was your day? What did you do?" I ask, trying to change the subject.

Finn brings a hand up, touching my arms where they cross over his chest. It's comforting, and I try to melt myself over him as best as I can as he climbs the steps to the house. "I spent most of it reading actually, but I wanted to be out here when you came home," He answers. Sounds better than my day.

Jace, Tristan, and Kellan rush past us, getting through the door before we can. When Finn stops in the grand entrance room thing, I pull my head up, looking for the reason my ride has stopped. I hear the others shuffle in behind us as I stare at the monstrous sized teddy bear sitting in the middle of the room.

Oh. My. God. It's blonde colored with pretty sky blue eyes and a gold bow around his neck. Around the bear sit's basket after basket of tiny candy bars and packets of different candies. I pat Finn's shoulders, squirming to get down. He releases me.

I pace back and forth in front of the bear from across the room. I look at the guys, hating what I have to do. There's no escaping it though, sometimes things just have to happen. You might not know why it just does.

"Forgive me for what you're about to witness," I say to all of them. I run at the bear that's taller than me, full force, tackling it to the floor. I put my arms around it as far as I can reach and attempt to hug it to death. I giggle uncontrollably as we roll over, the bear's weight pinning me underneath it. It's fluffy, but that's a whole lot of stuffing.

Logan and Tristan are the first to burst out in laughter, but the others soon follow their lead. I'm still trapped under my treasure laughing, struggling to call out for help when I see Kellan's shoes appear. He lifts the bear and helps me to my feet.

"Why on earth did you do that?" He asks.

I wipe tears from my face and calm myself enough to answer him. "It had to be done. Tell me that it didn't cross your mind at some point."

He chuckles. "Actually, that's the same thing Tristan did when he saw it." That doesn't surprise me. Tristan is awesome. "He also said it had to be done.

"Is he the one that got him for me then?" I ask. Kellan looks around, his eyes landing on Remy.

"We're not sure who got it for you, Miss Kitten," Remy says.

"I highly doubt that Rem," I tell him. They know, but just like the flowers, they don't want to say. He smirks, looking pleased about something.

He gets serious. "Follow me to my office now, Miss Kitten? I told you, we have things to discuss." He reminds me. I kiss Kellan on the cheek before bending down and scooping a handful of the candy bars up. I examine one of them. It says fun-size Kit-Kat on it. It rings a bell, but I'm too interested in discovering what's inside of it to care.

"This way." Remy commands.

"Hold your horses, Remington. It's the girl's first candy bar, for crying out loud." Jace pleads with Remy.

I've stuffed three of them in my mouth by this time, and I try not to choke as I hear a 'ding! ding! ding!' in my head. Jace. This is all Jace's doing. The flowers, the candy, the bear. I wish I could say that knowing he was behind all of this makes me unhappy, but it doesn't. I liked the flowers, *I love* the bear, and I might kill anyone who tries to take this chocolate away from me. He even got the fun sized ones. I'm pleased about this, but I'm not going to let him know it. Not yet.

Standing, I pretend like I still don't know who did this. "Well, thank you to whoever got me these things. Again."

Remy clears his throat, so I follow him. When he rounds the corner I rush back and drop my handful of candy, picking up an entire basket instead. Tristan laughs at me, but I just wink at him and take off after Remy.

CHAPTER NINETEEN

When I walk into his office Remy takes one look at my edible treasure and shakes his head. He comes toward me and makes a move to take my basket.

"*Mine*," I growl at him. Turning to the side and placing a protective arm over my candy.

He takes a step back, raising one eyebrow. At first he looked taken aback, now he just looks amused. "Kitten, if I wanted the candy you never would have seen it in the first place. I was merely going to set it aside for now as I have serious things to discuss with you, and I think it will interfere." Remy says slowly.

"Oh," I say lamely. I still don't give him the basket though, I sit on the chair and put the basket on the floor in front of it. He looks down at my basket, for too long, I think! I use my foot to push the treasure under my chair and narrow my eyes at him.

He shakes his head in wonder as he rounds the desk to sit. After putting on his I-mean-business-face he speaks. "First off Kitten, I want to apologize that it took me this long to have this conversation with you. Be honest with me, here. Do you know a man by the name of Charles Daily?"

I shake my head. "I don't think so. Why?"

"Because Kitten, he is very interested in you. Before you came here, did you ever notice anyone following you?"

What kind of question is that? "Uh...no. Who would follow a street kid around?" I ask, confused.

Remy sighs, pinching the bridge of his nose. "When you told us where you resided Kitten, Ash and I went to take a look. We wanted to see if you had, in fact, killed the man who attacked you."

Oh my God! I think I must be brain damaged to have forgotten all about that night. What's wrong with me? Here I am, happy, eating candy, and continuing on like nothing ever happened. I'm a horrible person. The worst kind of person.

"Don't!" Remy barks out. I jump slightly and focus back on him. "Let me finish before you start thinking bad about yourself." The man you hit with a brick didn't die, Kitten, you must have knocked him out. He went through your belongings at the warehouse. They were scattered all over the place. We think he was looking for something. Maybe information on you. Maybe something he thought you had."

I see red as I picture what Remy just said. 'Mine, mine, mine, mine' rings through my skull. That bastard touched MY stuff.

"Focus Kitten," Remy says, the friggin' mind reader. "We brought back everything we could find. I need you to look through it and tell me what's missing. We'll do that when we're done here."

I nod. I'm a little mad that he's had my things, and he's kept them from me. I'll kick him in the shin for that later, hard. Harder than I do Logan. For now, I want to hear what else he has to say.

Remington continues. "We were able to track his scent to a warehouse not far from yours. His blood was all over the place, so it wasn't that hard. The warehouse was empty of people, but we did find evidence that someone has been watching you for quite some time."

What? "What kind of evidence?" I demand.

Remington shifts uncomfortably. "Pictures mostly, notes of your schedule, where you went and when. Who you talked to. Articles of clothing with your scent still on them."

My mind is spinning. Someone has been taking pictures of me? How did I not notice something like that? I did notice when my panties went missing, but I just figured some pervert went through my bag when I was working. Wait...

"He's the one who stole my panties?" I shout at Remy, indignant. Son of a mother-licking-toad! If only I would have hit him again with that brick.

"Yes Kitten, but I think you're missing the biggest point here. Why he took them. Why he was taking pictures of you in the first place." Remy sighs, running his hand down his face. "Wolves had been in that warehouse, Miss Kitten. The man who attacked you was human, but we think he was working for wolves."

I don't know what to say to that. "Do you have any clue why wolves would be interested in you Kitten?" He asks.

I blink at him. "I don't know Remy. You'd know the answer to that more than I would."

He frowns. "What do you mean by that?"

I slouch in my chair, feeling more confused than I ever have. "I mean...that you are wolves too and here I am...sitting in your office with you. Why did you all take me in Remy? You've lived for how long? I couldn't have been the first street kid you ran across, or the first beaten girl either. Why am I here? No other broken girls are here. What made me different?"

"I don't know Kitten, we've been trying to figure that out since you got here. You're here because each of us feels a certain pull toward you like you are our sun and we, your planets. It's never happened before so we don't know the answer to that." He shakes his head sadly.

Minutes or hours pass, I'm not sure. I bite my lip, picking at my jeans. I don't know how to feel about any of this. I was positive that the man who attacked me had been just a random bum who saw me enter the warehouse. I didn't even know werewolves existed until I came here.

"Kitten, talk to me. What are you thinking?" Remy asks, looking a little worried now. I'm worried too.

"Honestly Remington, I'm not sure what to do with this information. Am I endangering you guys being here? Are these people still looking for me? Why were they looking in the first place? Actually, they found me and followed me. But for what reason?" I feel myself tearing up. Why is this happening? What does it mean? I sniffle, bringing my hands to my face.

Remy is on my side of desk in an instant. "Hey, it's going to be okay. You have us. We won't let anything happen to you. Look at me Kitten." I sniffle again but remove my hands, searching Remy's steel eyes, for what? I'm not sure.

"We'll figure all this out together. Do you understand me?" His commanding tone is comforting for once. If Remy wants information, I'm sure he'll get it. I nod my head, leaning into him. I bury my face in his neck, seeking comfort. He must understand because he picks me up and sits in my chair with me in his lap. His strong hand rubs up and down my back.

Minute-hours pass and I finally calm down. I lift my head and look at Remy. His eyes have gone soft now as he brushes loose strands of hair behind my ear. "I need you to go through your things, Kitten. We need to know what he took, if anything. Think you can handle that?"

I nod and push myself off of him. I straighten my clothes and wait for him to lead me to my stuff. Remy takes me one door over from his office to a mostly empty room. There's a coffee table pushed against the wall and a burgundy rug laying in the middle of the room, on it, is my treasure chest. I run to open it, despaired by what I see.

My treasure chest is an old Army footlocker I found at the thrift store one day. I got it, thinking I could drag it around like the boy with the wagon. It was too hard to do that, but I didn't want to give it up. I took it to the woods behind a strip mall that I was certain no one ever entered. Over the years I have collected things, putting them in my treasure chest. Favorite books of mine that the librarian told me I could keep because they were too worn anyway. Pastel drawings I drew once I discovered their magical quality. Other sketches in a sketchbook. A baby blanket that the crazy cat lady said she found with me in the dumpster and the security videos of the market across the street from that dumpster. I had three years' worth of them. The owner of the market was a pack rat, and when the store closed, I offered to buy them. He was nice and traded me a picture for all of them. They were on discs in plastic folders.

But none of those are here. I sob into my hands. I never got around to watching any of them. One of the market's cameras pointed right at the dumpster, I was sure I'd find at least one of my parents with that footage. Or at least, know when I was born. I'm beyond devastated.

Eventually, I hear several pairs of footsteps moving behind me. I cried myself numb, so I sit, staring at the blank wall in front of me. A warm hand lands on my shoulder. "These are pretty good Kitten. Did you do them yourself?" It's Reed, and I know he's just trying to get me to talk. I don't want to, but I don't want to be rude to him either.

I nod my head yes. He makes an 'hmm' sound. Does he not believe me? I look over to see him flipping through the sketchbook, pausing and studying each page. I watch as a tear slides down his cheek. I will admit that some of those drawing are a bit disturbing if you can pick up the meaning behind them. I shouldn't have let him look, Reed's sad enough as it is. And he's artistic enough to read between the lines.

I try to shut the book, hoping he won't ask me about the pictures I drew. No such luck. "This is you isn't it?" He asks. I look at the page he's on. It's me alright. I drew a girl on her knees in front of a mirror. She's smiling at the mirror, looking happy and perfect. The girl in the reflection has one hand beating on the glass, the other clutched to her chest. She's crying, tears streaming down her face, her hair out of place, her dress the exact copy of the other girl's but instead of it being perfect, it's torn and ratty looking. Her mouth is open in a scream, her eyes pointed to the sky, praying to a god that never answers.

"Yes," I whisper to Reed, answering his question.

"And the other one, the woman on the ground?" He asks.

"That was my best friend. She was a hooker. Nicest woman I'd ever met. She'd take me for pie at the diner, and she's also the reason I got the dishwashing job."

"What is this drawing about Kitten?" Reed sniffles but makes no move to wipe away his tears. He's not ashamed of them. I respect that.

I don't want to answer his question but I will, just on my own terms, I don't want him judging her. He needs to know the whole story. "You know, I asked her once why she did what she did. She said it was because it was the life she knew and she was too scared of the possibilities another life could have. She didn't have to be a hooker. She was pretty, and would never tell me what she did with the men that paid her, but she would tell me about how many of them wanted to take her away, to give her a better life where she didn't have to sell her body. But she never went with them. She taught me about hygiene and how to care for myself. Kids used to pick on me and mothers wouldn't let me play with their kids because of how I looked and smelled. She taught me. She said she would have let me stay with her, but her life was too dangerous for me, that I'd get pulled in, and she didn't want that for me."

I hear a couple sniffles behind me and throats clearing. I've gone this far so I might as well explain the picture. He sees it anyhow, right in front of him. "I was walking down this alley one day, there was a bakery that threw out unsold bread and other things daily. I was desperate, so I went to see if they'd thrown anything out recently. A man had followed me, but I was too hungry to notice. The alley was on the edge of where she waited for customers, she saw the man and ran after me. When she called out my name, the man turned and fought with her, he had a gun."

I don't feel like I need to explain more as the picture he's looking at is of a pretty dead woman in short, tight clothing lying on the ground with a bullet wound to the chest. At the bottom of the page is a loaf of French bread that I had dropped. Blood pools around her in a massive puddle, her purse still around her arm but the contents spilled out. There's so much detail because the image is forever etched into my brain. The way her open eyes looked with the life gone out of her. The sound of the shot ringing out.

"Her last words were 'Run Kitten, but don't be afraid like I was.' She's why I'm here now. She was afraid to change her life, afraid of what would happen. When you offered to let me stay here, I agreed because of what she said. She didn't want me afraid like her."

Reed breaks down now. Completely falls apart. It

scares me a little. I've never seen a boy cry before. Not a big one. I do what they do with me. I pull him into me, letting his face press to my chest and stroke his beautiful hair. "It's okay Reed," I whisper to him. I don't know what else to do. I look for Tristan, wondering if his magic voice works on others as well.

I find him with Logan in much the same position as Reed. Holy crap. I made all of them sad. I'll either have to hide that book, or they will have to stop asking me questions. I don't want to be the reason these beautiful boys are broken like me. I just knew I'd bring them down.

Remy clears his throat, getting everyone's attention. He isn't crying, but his eyes are shiny. "Right, everyone out." They all make to leave us, except Reed. He holds onto me tighter.

Before Remy can yell at him for not listening I bring my lips to Reed's ear. "Go on to your room Reed, as soon as I'm done here, I'll come find you, okay?" Reed clears his throat, standing. I yank the sketch book from his hand before he goes. I don't think he can handle what's in there. None of them can. Funny to think that I can do something they can't.

Once they're gone, Remy asks. "So was anything missing?" I nod and tell him about the missing security tapes. "Did you ever watch them? Do you know what's on them?" He asks, looking hopeful.

I shake my head. "I never knew how to look at them. I don't think anyone knew I had them though. Just the guy who gave them to me." I say.

Remy frowns. "What were you hoping to gain from them, Kitten? Just to know what your mother looked like?"

"I'm not sure I ever really cared about her Remy, she threw me away. Mostly I just wanted to know how old I am."

"What do you mean how old you are. You said you were sixteen." He's as white as a ghost. What's wrong with him now, I wonder?

"I am sixteen. At least sixteen. I've counted sixteen summers, I just don't know how old I was when I started counting." I reply, tilting my head at his weird reaction.

He blows out a relieved breath. "Okay then, that's okay. Kellan should be able to help you with that."

"Okay." I get up and make my way to Reed's room.

"Don't ever fucking scare me like that again Kitten."

I keep walking. I don't know what he means. "Okay," I say again anyway.

CHAPTER TWENTY

I run up the stairs to Reed's cloud room and find him looking dejected slumped over on the corner of his bed. I need to make him smile again. I drop to my hands and knees in the doorway and slowly crawl towards him. He meets my eyes on my approach, and my lips lift in the corners. When I make it to him, I nudge my face into the side of his leg, butting my head against his knees so he'll open them. I hear his intake of breath when I perch my head on the inside of his thigh. I blink up at him with half closed lids.

"What are you doing Kitten?" Reed's voice sounds breathy and gruff. Probably from the crying, I think. His ever changing eyes stay on mine the whole time.

"I'm being a wolf," I say simply. Apparently a bad one if he didn't get it.

"Oh." Is all he says. I pout at him, I was trying to be

funny, but I guess it didn't work. He tugs at the band in my hair, making it fall free to the floor. It was starting to give me a headache.

I groan in pleasure at having my scalp set free. "That feels so much better."

"Kitten, you are either the most naive girl in the world or the sneakiest," Reed says, finally giving me a smile. A small one, but it's a start. I, however, frown at him. What does he mean? That gets me a light laugh and a slightly bigger smile.

"I suppose it's the latter then." He pets my hair, and I pretend to wiggle my tail. Not that I have one, I'm just shaking my butt like an idiot. It works this time though, and his head goes back in a big laugh.

I pull back at sit on my knees watching as my sad boy turns happy once more. I smile up at him, wishing he could stay this way. He looks down at me with what I think is an adoring look. Shaking his head slowly, he takes my arms and pulls me to standing.

"Scoot over." I nudge him back to the headboard and climb up beside him. Bouncing a little I tell him "I've missed your cloud bed Reed. Can I stay here with you tonight?"

"Of course you can. Me and my cloud bed have missed you too." I lean in and kiss his cheek. Then decide to just stay there, pressed into his side with my head on his shoulder. It will be easier to talk about what we have to talk about if I don't have to look at him.

"I don't want you to be sad because of me anymore Reed," I say quietly. His response is to kiss the crown of my head.

"I mean it. I want to be around you more, talk to

you and tell you things, do your yoba exercise. But it seems like every time I open my mouth you get sad and pull away from me. Tell me what to do here Reed. Do you want me to fake smiles and only talk about rainbows and puppies?"

He laughs lightly. "First off, it's called yoga, not yoba, and secondly, no, I would never want you to be fake around me Kitten." He sighs heavily. "I just hate so badly what you went through. The kind of life you had to live. It's sad, and it's heartbreaking, and it tears me up inside. When I look at you, I see a beautiful girl with a beautiful heart and the deepest, purest soul. You have deserved so much better than what you have gotten."

I smile, he's sad because he cares. "Kitten, do you know how many people walked by those goldfish at the fair? How many people played that game and took one of them home or threw it in the trash because they got tired of carrying it?" He asks.

"No," I answer.

"Thousands, if not tens of thousands. Your very first time there, you not only refuse to support the game, but you chose to do something about it. Not after you got fed up with it, but immediately. That's such a rare thing Kitten, you have no idea. Then on the roller-coaster, you thought you were right, and you were willing to defend your belief, even though we told you it was wrong. You're just so...." Reed releases a huge breath, obviously not able to think of the right word.

I save him from having to think about it. "Reed, do you think I would be the goldfish rescuing, belief defending person that you seem to admire so much if I didn't live the life that I did?"

He moves me so he's right in front of my face. "Yes, I do Kitten, I think you'd be just the way you are no matter what. You're perfect." I close my eyes against his words. I can't wrap my head around how this attractive, sensitive, and all around good guy thinks I'm perfect. He has a cloud bed in a cloud room for crap's sake. He's the perfect one.

"You're wrong on both counts Reed. Without pain there is no pleasure, without sadness there is no happiness, without knowing what it is like to go without you cannot appreciate when you have enough. I know that you know that Reed. I'm not perfect. I'm not anything. I'm just me."

"And to me, you are perfect," He says. O...kay. We're going in circles here.

"I guess you are entitled to think what you want, and so am I. You don't know everything about me."

Reed leans his head back on the headboard. I guess he's getting frustrated too. We are, after all, arguing about something that doesn't matter. "I know enough," He whispers to the ceiling.

"Enough to what?" I ask.

"Enough to know that I could love you for eternity Kitten Whatever-your-last-name-is."

Holy crap! Did Reed just say he loved me? Well...not technically but yeah...sort of, he did! "Oh, Reed....no, you can't say that. You can't know that." I plead with him.

Reed smiles widely, rocking his head side to side. "See, any other girl would just say it back. Hear me telling her I think she's perfect and agree. But not you. You try to convince me otherwise. Perfection." He says.

I grab a pillow and hit him lightly with it.

"Whatever. You still don't know me." I mumble.

He scoots down on the bed until he's lying on his side, one arm propping up his head. I follow his lead, doing the same. "All you could do is tell me in words about you when you've already shown me in actions. But I still want you to tell me. Tell me about you Kitten, the *real* you."

How does one respond to that? I chew on my bottom lip, thinking hard for the right thing to say. I'm drawing a big fat blank. "Ask me a question, a non-vague one," I tell him.

"Okay, what's your first memory?" Hmm...To tell the truth or not. He told me not to be fake.

"I remember feeling sick. My tummy was upset. The crazy cat lady shushed me and told me to drink my milk. I didn't want the milk. I remember thinking that all I ever had was milk. I tried to tell her that my tummy hurt, and she slapped me and told me that cats don't talk." I answer, hoping he won't be sad.

Reed closes his eyes and shakes his head. "How old were you?"

"I don't know. It was before I started counting my summers."

"Counting your summers?" He questions.

I nod. "Yes, I've counted sixteen summers so far."

His eyebrows lift at this. "So you might be one to three years older?"

"I guess so, I can't remember when I started counting. The librarian told me once that I looked around four years old. I accepted that as my age at the time, but I don't know for sure."

"Is the librarian the one who taught you to read?"

"Yes and no. I had a theory when I was younger. The bigger the building, the less I got noticed. The library downtown is a pretty big building. I stumbled in there one day because it was raining and cold. I loved the smell of it instantly." I smile remembering. "I heard someone reading out loud in a colorful corner, I followed the voice and saw other kids staring at a lady with a book. I had discovered story time. I went every other day and listened to the different people reading. Sometimes they gave the kids their own copies of the books to follow along. I made sure I always got a book and picked up a lot of the words that way."

Reed grins at me. "You were such a smart little girl."

I shrug again. "Maybe, or maybe I just loved the stories so much that I grew impatient."

He laughs heartily at that. "I could see that being true."

"Yeah, so I just consumed book after book after that. I grew tired with the children's books quickly as I never recognized anything in them and it frustrated me." I giggle. "I now realize that children's books are all about imagination. That concept was just too hard for me then. I had asked the librarian for something else to read, and she turned me onto books about States and Countries and Presidents, things like that. I asked her what a word meant once, and she gave me a dictionary. If I didn't understand a concept she'd give me another book, explaining what the other book meant. To me, it was a game. I thought it was fun."

"You have that in common with Finn. He likes to learn everything about everything. Social wise he's a bit of a dummy, but if it's in a book, then he probably knows it." I smile at that. As a wolf, he once pushed me into a library.

"We're talking an awful lot about me, when do I get to hear about you?" I ask hopefully.

Reed shakes his head. "Two more questions then I'll tell you my story. Deal?" I nod my head eagerly. There's so much I want to know. "Tell me how you managed to survive out there Kitten, I know your heart is big but your body is small, and you had no real guidance. It seems impossible that you've made it this far with so little help."

I understand why this is so hard for him to accept. I've seen many a street kid fall from their path. Either from drugs and prostitution to joining gangs and doing bad things out of desperation.

"Well, you know about the crazy cat lady. I left her to escape the milk feedings and punishments. The first place I ended up finding was the hospital. No one really looked at me there. The cat lady had beaten into my brain the fact that social services people were evil and to stay under their radar at all costs. At the hospital, food was easy to come by. There would be trays of it in sleeping people's rooms all the time. I learned quickly when meal times were around there and made sure to be there. If I got caught, the sick people or nurse who caught me just thought I was a kid who wondered off but that I was supposed to be there."

"How long did you do that for? Surely someone noticed that you were there every day." Reed chimes in.

I smirk at him. "The cat lady had me stealing food as soon as I could walk. She wouldn't give me any of it, but still, it was a skill I possessed. Hospitals are big, and people are busy, as long as I moved around, from ward to ward, and didn't get greedy nobody noticed me. They even had toy areas in some of the waiting rooms. I'd sit and play for hours on a rainy day."

"That's where you learned to count isn't it?" It's Reed's turn to smirk now. My eyebrows go up in question. He rolls his eyes. "I've been dragged to a lot of hospitals over the years with Kellan, every single one of them have those rings you slide across the bar in different colors."

I giggle. "You're right. I still count in color to this day. One is green, two is purple and so on. I saw a kid doing it once and then I did it."

"Just once?"

I bite my lip, hating to tell people this about myself. He'd probably learn soon anyways. "Yeah, just once. I found out later, with the help of the librarian, that I have a photographic memory. Images are stored in my head like a real life flip book. I can call on any file in there when I want or need it." I peek up at him, ready for him to say I'm a freak.

He doesn't though, he just has an awestruck look on his face. "That's amazing Kitten. That explains a lot actually."

I'm not sure what he means, but I continue on, not wanting to dwell on this. "So yeah, at the hospital. I stumbled upon a children's burn unit at some point. They had the best toys in the hospital. The other kids in there didn't judge me and I ended up making quite a few friends. They'd give me their Jell-O, which was the best thing ever in the whole world. I spent my time there playing with them and trying to cheer them up. I hated when they were sad too." I pause, giving Reed a meaningful look.

"Things were great then, but of course, it couldn't last. Anywhere else in the hospital, I could fit in, but there I stood out like a sore thumb. A nurse found me once and dragged me into the hallway. She told me that I was dirty and had germs, and I'd get my friends sick if I kept showing up. I didn't want to hurt them, so I never went back.

"After that, I found the library and I already told you about that. It was my go-to place for warmth and when I needed to look something up. The park was another place I often hung out at, I didn't play with the kids much because the mothers thought I'd get their kids sick too. I liked the sandbox, and if other kids would come near it, I'd start pretend coughing or sneezing. I once pretended that I had rabies and chased all the kids off."

I start laughing, and so does Reed. "You were a firecracker even then I see." He jokes.

"Well, I wasn't about to let them run me off. You wouldn't believe how many times I heard the word 'shoo' before I was even ten summers. Like I was a fly or something. I shake my head, remembering. Reed starts to look sad, so I continue on.

"A lot of homeless people hang out in the library in winter, and I learned of the soup kitchen from one of them. A nice guy told me about it, he had been in the Gulf war I think, and I later realized that he had PTSD. He wasn't bad or lazy, he just couldn't function in the real world anymore. I soon learned that if I showed up at the soup kitchen alone that I brought more attention to myself. He often would wait for me there before going in.

His name was Davis. He taught me the importance

of a good backpack and dry socks. He also introduced me to people willing to lie to the food bank people. They won't give out food to homeless people without the proper paperwork, but if you bring a hungry looking kid with you, they usually bend the rules. You just can't keep going back or social services will be there waiting for you."

"Anyway, Davis always came along with us, making sure I got my half of the food. He didn't trust anyone. He always called our trips missions, and would point out potential bad guys and the obstacles we'd face. It was something else I looked at like a game."

"It sounds like he was a great guy that looked out for you Kitten, what happened to him?"

I clear my throat, dislodging the wrecking ball that wants to take up space there. "He jumped from a bridge one day, killing himself," I answer. "He left me a letter, it's in the treasure box in Remy's empty room." Reed looks horrified, so I move on again.

"After he was gone, I quit going to the food bank. It just seemed wrong to go on missions without him to cover me. I had found a nice apartment building by that time. It had a basement that no one ever went into with a storage closet. I also had my treasure box in the woods then, so I only ever needed my pack with me. It made traveling easier, and I could somewhat blend in with school kids in the morning. If a policeman saw me, he'd figure I was just skipping class and threaten to call my parents. I'd give them the library's phone number, but they never called it, just let me go with a warning not to skip school.

By then I was also determined to keep up with what I

would be learning in school, had I been enrolled. The library's educational section was vast, and soon I surpassed where I should've been. With a photographic memory I learned that I didn't actually have to read the pages, just look at them. When the library ran out of material that I wanted, I went to the community college library. I couldn't check anything out, but I could read it there.

"I had no real source of food then, but college kids are wasteful as heck, and they leave stuff everywhere. If you're wondering if I ate trash, then yes, I did. It kept me alive, and I'm not ashamed of it." That's a lie, but I'll never admit it.

Reed's eyes are cloudy as he responds. "It's okay Kitten, I'd never judge you for that. I'm just happy that you stayed alive." I nod my head once.

"I continued on like that until one day a college guy saw me digging through a trash bin. I didn't care that he saw me, but I was worried he'd tell security. I stopped what I was doing and sat by a tree, waiting until he left. Instead of leaving though, he ate his lunch slowly, moaning and groaning about how good it was, making a real show of it. I was drooling at that point, wondering what he had that was so good. When he was finished with it, he didn't take it to the trash bin but threw it on the ground. He had walked over to me, his friend followed him. I don't think he even knew what was going on. He got in my face and told me 'If you want to scavenge like a dog then you can eat it off the ground like a real bitch.' The words hurt, but it wasn't anything I hadn't heard before. What hurt more was look the guy's friend gave me. He pitied me, I saw it in his eyes. He wasn't mean like the other guy, but the look he gave me hit me hard. I didn't want to have someone pity me."

"That was the last day I ever ate trash. I found Marie, the hooker I told you about, after that. I was starving to death by that time, I had no idea how to get money or food. I was getting desperate. She got me the dishwashing job, and when they didn't have work for me there, one of the cooks referred me to the hotel with the laundry job. I had money for the first time in my life. I had moved to the warehouse to be closer to work. After a time, it seemed reasonably safe as long as I didn't go there at night. I even felt good enough about it that I brought my treasure chest, thinking I could make a home of it. I had gotten mugged right before Marie was killed, that's why I needed the bread. The restaurant didn't need me because the owner's nephew was in town and wanted the money and the hotel was cracking down on the illegals working there, which included me, even though I'm a citizen. The night Ash and Tristan found me was just a couple of days after I went back to work at the restaurant. And here I am."

I finish talking, my throat gone dry a long time ago. Reed is just staring at me, not saying a word. I can't tell what he's thinking. When he finally speaks, his voice is rough with unshed tears, he's sadder than ever.

"That's a really messed up story Kitten, a messed up life. So many people could have saved you, could have done something about it, but they chose to look the other way. You didn't have to go through that." A tear falls from his gorgeous eye onto his cheek. I lift my hand up, brushing it away.

"Name one Reed, name one person who you think

did me wrong."

"First off, your parents." I nod, I agree with him there.

"Second, the crazy cat lady."

I smile. Gottcha. "Her name was Patricia Lee Stevens, she was admitted to a long-term mental care facility two years after I ran away from her. She was diagnosed as a bipolar schizophrenic. I tracked her down a couple summers ago in order to find out more about where I came from. She didn't remember me of course, because in her mind, at the time, I was a cat. I managed to get her to tell me what alley and dumpster she found me in by asking her questions like, 'do remember ever having a talking cat? Or a cat who had really long hair and grew bigger than the others?'. That's how I managed to get the security tapes that were going to lead me to my parents and the baby blanket that she found with me. It was still on her person when she was taken in since she believed it made her invisible. You say she wronged me, but I say I wouldn't be laying in front of you right now if she didn't fish me from the trash. Then she aided me once more when she was in the mental facility."

Reeds looks frustrated. "But surely you can see how badly she wronged you, Kitten! What about all of the people you had to have passed on the street? Huh? Did no one care that a mentally unstable woman was in charge of a baby!"

"Yes Reed, she did bad things. But she was confused, she did the best she could under the circumstances. She got me far enough along. Patricia, the person, did no harm to me, the crazy cat lady who looked at a baby and saw a cat did. Her disease made her do those things, it wasn't her fault. I forgave her a long time ago. The dumpster I was in was actually close to a busy street, she's the only one who took the time to stop and hear me. She saved my life."

"Well, when you put it that way..."

"Next person who you think wronged me." I cut him off, in a hurry to be done with this and make him see it my way.

Reed narrows his eyes, he knows what I'm up to. "The nurse in the hospital that told you, you would hurt the other kids and that you were dirty. She had an obligation to report you to social services and instead, she insulted a child and sent you away." He looks so smug. I *almost* hate to wipe that look off his face. Yeah right, I like to win too much, and he already beat me once. I am *so* winning this conversation.

"She had an obligation to her patients first, and I was, in fact, putting them at a higher risk of infection. I can't hate her for not doing something that I didn't want her to do. Which was calling social services. And by her telling me I was dirty, it made me curious enough to look it up and learn to clean myself properly. To this day, I still wash my hands like I saw her do it. Who knows....by washing properly, she could have saved me from getting ill myself. "Next"

Reed frowns but nods. "The librarian. She too could have called social services, but I know you're going to say the same as the nurse. Besides that, instead of telling you the answers to the questions you had, she could have just answered them, or she could have taken you home.

"By her not giving me the answers she taught me to rely on myself. Better than knowing the answers to things, is knowing *how* to find them. Problem-solving skills are a great asset. She had four kids of her own that she struggled to keep fed on a librarian's salary as a single mother."

"The guy with PTSD, Davis. He abandoned you when he committed suicide, I know he broke your heart when he did that, Kitten. You shouldn't have had to learn about that at such a young age."

My throat tightens again, but I swallow it back. This, he really needs to understand. "Before Davis died he taught me a lot. Without the knowledge he gave me, I know I wouldn't still be alive. He taught me how to spot a bad person from a good one before they ever got close. He taught me not to trust the wrong people. I will forever be grateful to him for everything he did for me. It did hurt me when he committed suicide, but that showed me that bad things happen, but you have to move on, push through it and not let it cripple you. Also, that death is a part of life. Everyone learns it, I just learned the hard way. His reasons for doing it are in his letter. I wouldn't have made the same choice, and I only wish I could've helped him. But even with that, it taught me never to wait to help someone, to not be afraid to say what needs to be said, and not to take even one moment for granted with those you care about."

Reed swallows hard. "The college guy," He whispers.

"That experience got me to stop eating trash Reed, that's an obvious one. The look from his friend forced me to take pride in myself."

"Marie, the hooker." He's staring down at his lap now.

"I already explained about her. She couldn't take me

in because she thought it was dangerous. She didn't say it, but the truth was that she had a pimp. What she probably meant by 'dangerous' was that if her pimp knew about me, he'd force me to sell my body to men. I wasn't in a position to defend myself from someone like that Reed, and she wasn't strong enough to leave him. I think some part of her loved him, and he loved her. He buried her at North Lawn Cemetery with a very nice gravestone."

"I'm sorry." Reed whispers.

"For what?" I ask angrily. All of this was for nothing, he's still sad. He still feels sorry for me. That's not what I wanted.

"Because my heart is not as big as yours. Because I can't forgive those people for failing you as easily as you do. Because I still know that you deserved better. And because...." He trails off, taking a deep breath. "... Because I love you more now, then I did an hour ago, and I'm not sure there's anyone alive on this planet that will ever be worthy of you."

My anger disappears. Tears stream down my own face as I study him. He means it, I can tell. I told him everything about myself. The bad things included, and he says he still wants me, that he loves me, that he still thinks I'm a good person.

"Reed..." I sit up, looking down at him. "...I decide who's worthy of me. It's my choice. And you don't have to forgive anyone. Forgiveness is a choice, and I already forgave those people. They were who they were, just trying to make it through this life like everybody else. Sometimes people can't see past today, they can't see that the choices they make now will affect the future. I don't blame anybody else for the life I've had. Whatever happened in the past, set me up for my future. The few people who showed me kindness taught me lessons that can never be forgotten, the mean people made me a stronger person. All of them combined molded and shaped me into the person in front of you who you said you love. Don't you see that Reed?"

For the first time in what seems like forever, Reed smiles. Not just a small one but it finally reaches all the way to his eyes. I blink at him, in absolute awe of the stunning boy in front of me, he's devastating when he smiles like that.

"I understand now, Kitten. I wish you could see yourself like I do."

"I know what you mean Reed." And I do, he can't see what I'm seeing right now.

A cough sounds behind me. I turn and frown at the door. Crossing the room to open it, I'm beyond surprised by what I see, all seven of them line the wall across from Reed's room. They are all staring at me, speechless it seems. I frown at them, my hand going to my hip. "Have you been out here the whole time?" Looks are exchanged between them. That answers my question.

I roll my eyes when nobody answers me. "Well, are you going to explain yourselves or what?" My foot starts tapping.

Remy, of course, is the one to speak. "We just all wanted to hear your story too Kitten, Reed would've told us, we don't keep secrets, and we share information in this house, no way would he have been able to retell all of that, word for word," He explains.

"That's fine, you should have just asked me though. You don't take what I don't give you. Information or otherwise. Understood?" I throw his words back at him. I'm purring inside with his response.

"Yes Kitten, understood." Oh heck yes! I got Remy to say that! My excitement fades though when I see a basket sitting between Logan and Tristan. *My* basket with *my* candy.

My eyes flare wide, and I stand up as tall as I'm able. I point my finger at the basket. "*Mine!*"

CHAPTER TWENTY-ONE

I had attempted to tackle Logan, but Remy had caught me up in his arms before I could. We came to a different agreement.

After having the seven of them stand against the wall, all in a line, I kicked each one of them in the shin, Remy got it twice because I owed him from earlier. Reed laughed at them from the doorway. I will admit that I took it easy on Ash because he's just kind of scary and he takes care of AJ. When I told them what was going to happen, the others all pointed fingers at Logan and Tristan, saying they were the only ones who ate my candy. I explained that those two ate it, but the others allowed it to happen. Finn said that you can't argue with that kind of logic. I agreed, but he got kicked too anyway.

When the kicking was over, everyone piled into Reed's cloud room. Reed, me and Remy took the bed while Logan gathered pillows and blankets from other rooms for the rest of the guys to use on the floor.

When everyone was settled, I went around, handing them each a piece of candy from my basket. "I would have shared had you given me the opportunity. I'm sure I will learn to share better over time, for now, don't tell me it's mine unless you mean it. If you want it to be 'ours' then say so up front."

"Well said Kitten, and thank you," Kellan said from his spot on the floor. I'm not sure why everyone is sleeping in here, but I like it. I want to be close to all of them. I climb back into my spot between Remy and Reed, feeling contentment slide over me. Yes, a girl could really get used to this.

I hear rustling noises coming from somewhere in the room, so I lift my head to see who it is. It's Tristan, stepping over his brothers and heading to the door. He sees me and gives me a cute sleepy smile. "Go back to sleep pretty girl, I'm just going make breakfast, you've still got an hour before you need to be up for work."

I am super comfortable here, laying with Reed tucked up behind me, my body draped over Remy's bare chest on this wonderful cloud bed. But I'm just not tired anymore. I slowly inch myself away from the two guys, trying not to wake them. Once I make it to standing, I hear Reed groan, and he turns his face to me, now lying flat on his stomach.

"Don't go," Reed whispers as I tip-toe to the door.

I stop and smile at him. "I'll see you soon, promise," I whisper. He just smiles back, closing his eyes and drifting off again.

Once I make it to the hallway I try to catch up with

Tristan, but it's no use, and I find him in the kitchen already. I pause in the doorway to watch him, his sleep-mussed sandy hair is all over the place and is cute as heck. I see the lock of hair that seems to always fall into his eyes, and I have to clench my fingers into a fist at the thought of brushing it back. His tall, lean form is covered in red, both top and bottoms and I can his muscles flex under his clothes as he commands this kitchen. I wonder if he can move about in here with his eyes closed.

"Are you going to stand in the doorway all morning, or are you going to actually come in?" I jump a little, forgetting that yes, in fact, the beautiful boy in front of me is real and here and he can speak.

"Sorry," I mumble out, moving to the island and taking a seat.

"For what? Watching me?" I bite my lip and make circles on the countertop. He knew I was staring? I nod. Tristan chuckles. "I like you watching me, Kitten."

My head snaps up. Huh? "You do?"

He walks over to me, bending down and leaning on his elbows, so he's close to my face. "I do. I like feeling your eyes on me from across the room. I like it when your hand twitches when my hair falls in my eyes, I like it when your heartbeat calms when you hear my voice, and I like that you like my chocolaty eyes."

I think I melted to the floor in a puddle. Tristan's voice is low and is doing weird things to my belly. I've never heard him talk with that tone before, but I really, really don't want him to stop. So he notices me and my reactions to him? Wait a minute.

"He *told* you!" I screech. I am so gonna kill Kellan when I see him.

Tristan stands up, laughing. "Yes, he told me. The Giant and Chocolate Eyes. I love the name Kitten, and seeing as how much you love chocolate if yesterday was any indication, I'll take that as a huge compliment." He winks at me, before going to the fridge.

"I do love them," I whisper, not believing that I'm really telling him this. "Not just the color, but how silky they are, smooth. I read your eyes better than I've ever been able to read anyone's. It's how I knew you really wanted to help me the night you found me, how I knew that you understood what I was telling you. You have a gentle soul Tristan, and it shows through your eyes."

Tristan walks back to me slowly, guiding me off my seat, so I stand with my back against the island. "Are my eyes the only thing you like about me, Kitten?" He asks, that low tone back.

"N-no." I stammer.

He lays his forehead on mine. "Tell me, what else you like about me." Part of me thinks I should be embarrassed by what I already said, but the bigger part of me wants Tristan to know just how I feel about him.

"I like your shaggy hair too. I like how you stand up for me. I like how beautiful you are. And I like how you take care of me." I close my eyes, hoping against all hope that he doesn't laugh at me. Which reminds me. "Oh, and I like your laugh. Your food too, your food is magical."

Tristan backs his head away from mine, tilting my chin up. "You think my food is magic huh?" I open my eyes, is that all he heard? I nod, staring into those dang chocolate eyes that started this whole mess. His responding smile is brilliant.

"And your smile," I say.

"Anything else?"

"Your voice, I like your voice too."

"Anything else?"

"I like that you're playful, Like Logan but a little less reckless."

"Anything else?"

Why does he keep asking that? Do all boys need an ego boost in the morning? "Tristan I could stand here all day and list the things I love about you, why don't you just go find a tall mirror to stand in front of. I like everything about you. Now stop trying to kill me of embarrassment." I huff out.

"Can I kiss you, Kitten?" He asks.

"Please." When his soft lips come down on mine, all I can think is, finally! I've felt a connection with Tristan ever since he found me that night. I'm finally able to grab onto him and pull him to me, and it's pure bliss.

When he done kissing me thoroughly, he steps back. "I just wanted to you hear you say you liked everything about me because I like everything about you too Kitten." He kisses the tip of my nose and goes back to the refrigerator. I bring my hand to my lips, feeling that they have swelled. Wow, his kisses are magic too.

"Except your food. I haven't tasted your cooking yet." He says, bringing my thoughts back down to earth.

"Is that a deal breaker?" I ask playfully. I hope not though. It's not like I have any experience with stoves.

Tristan just laughs. "Come here silly girl, you can make the eggs." Yay! Cooking with Tristan!

The rest of the guys slowly trickle to the kitchen after my kiss with Tristan. I try to concentrate on the big pan of eggs, but it's a little hard when adorable sleepy boys are in my line of sight. Each one of them saw me standing at the stove and came over and either hugged or kissed me, telling me good morning. I might have to do this cooking thing more often.

Once we're all seated, we start eating and chatting away. I've learned that most of them only grunt before their first cup of coffee. I start eating my pancakes that Tristan made, with a strawberry syrup he made just for me. I get lost in my own little food haze until I hear Logan shouting.

"Holy shit! What was the recipe for these Tristan? A dash of salt and a barrel of ass?" He spits into a napkin just as I see Jace's mouth open and half chewed food just falls out to his plate. Mr. Manners just did that?

"Fuck, he's right man, gross." Ash chugs his water down like he's been in a desert without for a week.

"Dude, did we do something to piss you off?" Reed chimes in, but it sounds like he thinks it's funny.

Tristan holds his hands out, palms up. "I don't know what you guys are going on about. I made the pancakes just like I always do. I was just eating one, tasted just fine to me." He's defensive, and I can tell a little hurt. My pancake tasted just fine too. It's as yummy as usual.

"No, you idiot, the eggs. Are you trying to kill us off?" Logan says.

I start giggling uncontrollably, laughing so hard that tears are falling down my cheeks, and I almost fall out of my seat. "I...I made...the eggs..." I finally manage to get out through bursts of laughter. The guys start laughing with me.

When I finally calm myself down, I sit up straight again and wipe my face. I see Tristan taking a tentative bite of his eggs and watch as his face turns a little green and gets the I-just-ate-a-lemon look. It takes everything I have not to lose it again.

Tristan sets his fork down slowly and spits out his food into his napkin as well. His face is serious when he looks to me, but his eyes hold humor. "Kitten, I think there should be an award for fucking up eggs that badly."

I giggle again. "Maybe it was my teacher," I tell him.

He smirks. "No way, my food is magical. Remember?" He winks at me, making me blush. The bastard is going to use my words against me.

"So much for being a gentleman and taking the fall for the girl." I mock glare at him.

"Oh I already fell for the girl, but I'm not taking the blame for this atrocity." I stick my tongue out at the cheeky boy. Verbally sparring with him is fun.

"I think I need to add cooking lessons to your schedule Miss Kitten, either that or give the order to shoot to kill if we spot you at the stove." Remy says, and then takes a big gulp of his coffee.

I suck in air feigning shock and bring my hand to my mouth. "Did you just make a joke Remy? Who knew you were capable." He shakes his head at me as the others crack up.

Tristan speaks up again. "I am truly curious as to what you did to those poor eggs. I think you added a pound of salt, half the shells then overcooked them by a whole hour. What happened?"

"It's not my fault you all are so adorable looking

when you wake up. I got distracted." I shrug. Eight glorious smiles light the room, and I think I'm forgiven. These tough men are so not flatter-resistant.

———————— •●• ————————

After breakfast, I got dressed and Logan did my hair for me. I asked him if he was coming with me today but he said he needed to do some fashion research since he'd never had a young woman in his charge and then he was going shopping. I shook my head at him. He takes clothes so seriously. I don't mind though, it means I don't have to be.

After hugging the guys goodbye Finn led me to his truck, and we took off.

"I love the color of this. Is orange your favorite color?" I ask as he's driving.

"Yeah, I like most shades of orange but the burnt orange one, like this truck, is my favorite. It's not an easy color to find in nature, so I make a game of it. It's slow going but fun." He shrugs.

"Like chess then?"

Finn turns his head to me. "You know how to play chess?"

"Does that surprise you?" He shakes his head. "They used to have chessboards at the park. I'd watch people play. Technically, I've never played, but I know the right moves. They took out the chessboards after the city redid the park."

"There's not really 'right' and 'wrong' moves in chess Kitten, the other player is a factor in your decisions and moves. I don't doubt that you'd be good at it. With your photographic memory, you could be the best at anything you wanted." Finn says, matter of factly.

"You make it sound like a good thing, my condition I mean."

His head rocks back in shock. "You don't think it is? Kitten, the type of eidetic memory you talked about last night, has never been demonstrated to exist. Normally only children between the ages of two and six have it, and the percent rate is between two and ten percent for that age group. If it's not found and nurtured, most times it fades completely. Even with all the research that has been done, the ability to glance at something once, say a page in a book, and be able to recall every detail of it, has been ruled a complete myth."

I wonder how Finn knows all of that. I tried to do my own research on my condition but had a hard time finding anything. "So you're saying that I'm a freak then?"

He shakes his head. "No, what I am saying, is that you have been given a truly unique gift and ability Kitten. It's not something to be ashamed of, it's something you should feel honored to have. Scientist and scholars of the world would die to be able to do what you can."

Huh? Smart people envy me, who'd of thunk it? "Does that include you, Finn?" I ask, truly curious.

He turns and smiles at me. "Of course I would love to have your level of eidetic memory Kitten. However, I don't honestly have the need. I can learn anything I'd like, no matter how long it may take me. I've lived for hundreds of years, and I'll continue to live for many more. If I had your ability, I could have already read every book in the world, then what would I do?" He says the last part playfully, and I laugh, making him smile.

"So do you feel the same about your ability to shift into a wolf?"

Enough time passes that I think he isn't going to answer me. Then he does. "I've had many different feelings about being a werewolf at different times. When I was changed, I was afraid. All we had back then were stories that were told at meal times of dangerous beasts of myth. Kellan and I have always been close. As close as twins can be, our father was the doctor of our day for our village, and Kellan was his pupil. When I was bitten, Kellan hid me from everyone else until I was healed and under control. If he'd taken me back to the village, as was custom back then, I would have been put out of my misery, and that was before they even knew I changed form." He shakes his head, and he snorts derisively.

"Even to this day, what people can't understand, scares them and makes them do crazy things. Back then it was worse. So after being afraid I had guilt because Kellan wanted me to change him as well. He said that we did everything together, no matter what. Kellan tried to make me feel better after, saying he liked turning into a wolf. After the guilt, came the grief at having to watch everyone I ever knew die from afar. We didn't age like we should have, and eventually had to leave our family and village, in Ireland. I felt helplessness when Kellan and I had to keep traveling, never being able to get close to anyone or stay too long in one place.

The first time I felt acceptance is when Remington and Ash found us. Then we weren't alone, we weren't the only ones with this curse. Remington is the one who taught me to accept this as a gift, to see that I am special, not a freak. We became a pack, we had family again. Then, and now, I am happy" He finishes, as we pull into the parking lot of the rink.

I take Finn's hand in mine, squeezing. "Thank you for telling me that Finn. I'm sorry for what you went through, but I'm not sorry it happened. I would never of had the chance to know you if it hadn't." I lean over and kiss his lips lightly.

"What was that for?" Finn asks, sounding confused.

"Because I'd think you were special even if you weren't a werewolf." I hop out of the truck and cross the lot, stepping into work.

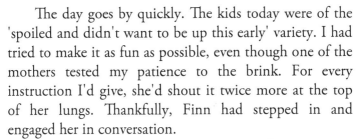

The day goes by quickly. The kids today were of the 'spoiled and didn't want to be up this early' variety. I had tried to make it as fun as possible, even though one of the mothers tested my patience to the brink. For every instruction I'd give, she'd shout it twice more at the top of her lungs. Thankfully, Finn had stepped in and engaged her in conversation.

I didn't see Adam or the rest of them today either, which was a feat itself, considering I saw the hockey team gearing up for practice as we left. I know he was here, but he didn't seek me out like usual. Finn had also helped me with my jumps today, explaining the science behind them, and I went higher than I ever had. My smart boy knows just how to get to me.

When we arrived home, Tristan had made us both snack platters with French bread, fruit, and cheese for us to take with us to the library room. I had eaten most of mine before we even got there. Finn was nice enough to share his with me, and I promised him all the candy bars he wanted for being so sweet. I love watching the crest of his cheeks tint.

"Just one more Kitten." Finn instructs.

"But I don't want to, I've been taking these tests for hours, my braid is short circuiting," I whine, because, yes, I apparently do that now.

He frowns. "You mean brain? You said braid."

"SEE! Short circuiting over here." I wave my hands in the air drastically for effect. I try not to laugh at my own joke, but he must see it anyway.

"Nice try Kitten, just finish this last one. I told you that I need to get a better idea of where you're at, academically speaking. If I'm to teach you, I must know what to teach."

"Fine," I grumble, taking his test.

When I'm finally done, I go the pillow area in the library and fall flat on my face. Finn laughs at me from his spot at the table, grading my work.

"I think we should bring Jace in here," I call to him.

He doesn't look up from my papers. "What do you mean bring him in here? For what?"

Oh, he's making this too easy. "To lay on, he's comfy, you should try laying on him."

Finn's head snaps up, and he looks at me like I'm crazy. I try to keep a blank face, not giving the joke away. His eyes narrow, he's thinking. "You named that mammoth sized bear 'Jace' didn't you?" He asks.

I pout. "You don't let me have any fun. Yes I named him Big Jace that way, the person Jace, is Little Jace, he'll hate that."

Finn throws his head back and laughs. "You're good Kitten. Mean, but good." I thought I was pretty good with that one too.

"So what do you think? He'd be good to lean up against as we read, right?"

"I think that's a grand idea. Would you like to read now?" He asks.

I bite my lip, hoping he won't hate me for what I'm about to ask. "I do but...do you think that you would like to....change into wolf form again?"

Finn sets his pen down, scoots back his chair and kneels next to me. "You want me to? It doesn't make you uncomfortable or feel odd?" He asks.

"Not at all, did you forget about our tag game? I like your wolf, all of them. I know you're not my pet anymore, but I'd still like to see my Mr. Wolf sometimes. Is that okay?" I haven't seen any of the guys in wolf form since we played in the yard, and I don't know why.

Finn reaches out and strokes my hair, freeing it of the tie holding it up. "It's more than okay, we thought you might feel awkward seeing us walking around like that. To be honest, that's how we spent most of our time at home before you came here. Not being able to change has made some of the others a little antsy."

I frown at him. "You guys don't have to stay human for me, I like the wolves. I haven't deluded myself into thinking that you're all just a bunch of teenagers, Finn. Give me more credit than that." I'm a little offended that they didn't think I could handle it.

"I'll let the rest of them know." He smiles at me. "You're a remarkable young woman, you know that?"

"That's what I hear," I say back. I roll to my back and look up at him. He's so sweet and nice and smart. I really like Finn. I like him a lot. "Kiss me, Finn," I say, hoping I'm not being too forward with this shy boy.

He needs no further prodding though, he moves to lay beside me on his side. One of his hands is in my hair as his lips kiss my forehead. He drags his perfect pouty lips down my cheek, to the corner of my mouth, my own lips part at the sensations he's creating. He moves over and nips at my bottom lip dragging it through his teeth. God that felt good. He then does the same to my top one.

"Finn..." I say breathlessly. He finally covers my mouth with his own, pressing firmly. His tongue snakes out and licks my lips, tasting them. He massages my tongue with his, and the rest of the world fades to nothing. I bring both of my hands to his head, running them through his silky black locks. I love his hair.

Finn groans in pleasure when I run my nails over his scalp and his hand goes to my outer thigh, pulling it over his leg. I moan as soon as my center has contact. Our kiss heats up in intensity and soon, Finn has rolled on top of me, giving me the 'more' that I didn't know I needed. I run one hand down his back, determined to find skin. I need to touch his bare skin like my life depends on it. When I reach the end of his shirt, I find...pants. I let out a growl of frustration, my tongue not leaving his mouth, my hand pulling his hair hard as I yank at the shirt that dares to defy me at this moment.

Finn growls loudly, my chest vibrating with the sound, his mouth pressing harder to mine. That only spurs me on more. I have the shirt untucked, but it's not enough. I regretfully let go of his hair, bringing both hands to his chest and shoving. Finn backs off immediately, sitting back on his knees with a confused expression, panting for air. I lean forward and grab where the buttons meet and pull them apart. Buttons fly as the shirt parts down the center.

Skin! Beautiful, glorious, skin. I can't keep my hands off his chest for another moment. My fingers run over his collarbones, down to his lightly defined pecs, circling his tiny excuses for nipples and down to his abs. I see that his pants are tented in the front and something about seeing that, drives me crazy. My fingernails dig into his stomach, and he growls again. I like that sound. Finn throws his head back as I do it again. I bring my hands up to his chest, and his mint green eyes lock on mine as I scratch down his chest to his stomach.

Holy crap! He looks like he wants to eat me. My body melts at his sexy reaction. Finn grabs both of hands and throws them to the side, his chest crashing into mine, pushing me back down. His mouth is hungry and as I let him devour me my hand goes back to his luscious hair. Just as I dig into his back with my other hand and pull his at his hair, causing Finns hips to surge into me, making me cry out...... I hear Tristan.

"Shit...." He whispers. Finn's head comes up and snaps to Tristan.

"What are you doing in here?" He growls, making me moan at his chest vibrating on mine. Thankfully, he backs off and stands. I knew we should have stopped when I first heard Tristan but...I couldn't, I'm happy he still had some control.

"I was just bringing you more snacks. When Remy said to teach her, I don't think this is what he meant." I sit up, composing myself. Tristan has a smirk on his face, but he looks a little flustered himself. What has me blinking at him, is the fact that he's sitting on the table, Indian style, the snacks long forgotten.

"How long have you been there?" I ask.

Tristan looks to me, his chocolate colored eyes swirling. "I got here right before Kitten let her claws out."

I bring both hands to my face, trying to hide. Tristan chuckles and I sense him move closer. "Don't be embarrassed Sweetie, that was hot as hell to watch. I wasn't trying to be a total perv, it's just.....you're my girl too, and I couldn't walk away from seeing you like that."

Tristan turns to Finn, who gives up on trying to button a shirt with no buttons. "Sorry man."

"I don't mind, I only care if you embarrassed Kitten." He raises an eyebrow in question at me.

"I'm fine, as long as he's not laughing at me."

"I would never laugh at what I just saw. My girl was being sexy. I'm jealous that it was Finn on the receiving end of it." Tristan tells me.

I look into his eyes, seeing the truth in them. He's not laughing at me. "You're not mad at him?" I ask Finn.

Finn smirks, making my belly flutter again. Down girl, I tell myself. "No, it's okay. We have to learn to share you, and I'm sure this will be a part of it. If you were a wolf.....Never mind." He turns his attention to Tristan. "We need to go get Big Jace for Kitten and....some water."

Tristan kisses my forehead quickly, and the two of them walk awkwardly out of the room. I hear Tristan ask

Finn. "Are we calling him Big Jace for a reason?" I let out a breath and sprawl out on the pillows.

I stare at the ceiling begging the heat to leave my body. What just happened with Finn was....beyond words. And Tristan watching....My mind thinks up many different scenarios involving the both of them, but I shut them down, I'm trying to cool off, not overheat.

Fifteen minutes later they're back with the bear and snacks. Tristan hands me a water bottle as Finn searches for the book I had started. They place my bear on the pillow section, and I lean against him, getting comfortable. The boys disappear around a bookcase, and I wonder what they're up to. I don't have to wonder for long because minutes later two wolves appear. One sandy colored with chocolate eyes and one silky black with mint eyes.

I smile at them and pat my legs. "Come here, I'll read to you both." They each take a side, laying their heads in my lap. As I read, I alternate which hand holds the book and which pets one of them. As much as I enjoyed myself with Finn earlier, in this moment right here. Just the three of us, I feel whole.

Some time later, after my throat was dry and Tristan had dozed off, Remy had come to find us. He didn't say anything when he first came in, just leaned against the table and looked on. I had kept reading and stroking Finn's head until I came to a natural stopping point in our book.

"I didn't mean to interrupt, I just came to see if Tristan was planning on making dinner. Since he hasn't started anything, I thought you might like it if we went out to dinner." Remy's naturally rough voice is welcoming, I missed it.

"You and me? Or all of us?" I ask.

"Would you like for it to just be the two of us?"

"I like that we always eat dinner together. It's our family time." I shrug. I wouldn't mind spending time with Remy, but I always look forward to seeing them all at the end of the day.

Remy's smile is brilliant when he replies. "Yes it is, family time. You and your wolves should get ready. Kellan has something for you, why don't you drop by his office and tell him our dinner plans?" I nod that I will, and Remy turns to leave.

"I'm going to go get ready then," I say to Finn, my hand running over his shiny coat one more time. Finn nods his big wolf head and barks at Tristan. The sandy wolf's eyes blink open. So cute. I stand and cross to the door as the wolves head to where they left their clothes.

CHAPTER TWENTY-TWO

Kellan was walking out of his doctor room as I rounded the corner. "Hello Kitten, I was just coming to find you," He says with a smile.

I giggle. "I was just coming to find you too. We are going out for dinner, and Rem said you had something for me?" I bite my lip, wondering what it could be.

"Yes, I do." He reopens the door he just closed and holds his arm out for me to enter. "You'll be happy to hear that our patient has pulled through his surgery and is doing better than ever."

I see Noah laying on the high table that I once used. He does look better than ever. His ripped foot is sewn together seamlessly, he has two eyes now, and he looks clean. The funny thing is, he's wearing a shirt with his name on it, written in blue.

"Why does he have a shirt on Kellan? And how did

you find one in his size?" I ask as I pick Noah up and give him a squeeze.

Kellan laughs. "Believe it or not Kitten, there is a whole line of clothing for stuffed animals and dolls. Logan happened by a place called 'Build-A-Bear-Workshop' at the mall, and couldn't help himself I guess. He used an iron to put his name on it himself though."

Seriously? They make clothes for stuffed animals? Weird but...*awesome*! I go to Kellan and hug him around the waist. "Thank you so much, Kellan. I knew you'd take care of him, but you did so much more than you had to. You're my favorite doctor in the whole world." I lean up and kiss his cheek.

Kellan chuckles. "I'm the only doctor you've ever had Kitten. There's not much competition."

"Nope, and there never will be. You're the only doctor I'll ever need." I shrug and take Noah with me to find Logan. I need to thank him for the teddy bear shirt, and he'll probably want to dress me.

I was right. I knew he'd want to dress me, but I had no idea he'd dress me like this. He called it my Grecian goddess gown. It's light blue with only one shoulder strap. The material flows freely from what Logan called a bodice. I thought it was too long at first, but Logan strapped my feet into tall golden shoes. I don't even know why they call them shoes, you can still see my feet, only little scraps of material go from one side to the other. No way do they protect me from anything. Ash might get mad if someone steps on my toes in these.

I don't say anything to Logan about it though, he looks happy and even a little smug as he turns my long white hair into curly cues. It takes forever before he's putting the finishing touches on my hair. The dreaded spray makes an appearance once again after he uses a sparkly gold clip to hold some of my hair back.

"Okay, stand up sexy girl. Take a look at my masterpiece." Logan says, grinning like a crazy person. I do as he says and look in the mirror. I can't believe how pretty I look. I feel like one of those princesses from the fairytale books. I didn't understand them then, but I get it now. Dressing up feels amazing and I want to do it all over again. My crazy boy has taken my breath away.

"Logan...I...I can't believe you made me look so...."

"Stunning," He whispers in my ear, coming to stand behind me at the mirror. "The word you are looking for is absolutely stunning. It's not the dress or the hair though Kitten, it's just you. You look gorgeous in Tristan's shirts. All I did was put you in something a little more deserving of your beauty." He slowly turns me, kissing me lightly.

"But it's time to go now, Kitten," He says when he pulls back. "Time to throw your sexy ass to the wolves." He smacks my butt, making me squeak in shock. He saunters out the door, and I follow him. I'd kick him for that, but I kind of liked it.

As we come down the stairs, I see the guys are already waiting on us. They sing their praises at Logan's work, making me blush seven kinds of red. Jace looked stunned at first, but his face went sad after my boys surrounded me, kissing my temples or giving me hugs.

"We should take pictures," He said in a voice that wasn't his normal haughty tone.

"Right, I'll go get my camera." Reed dashed up the stairs so fast I thought I was seeing things. When he came back down, the guys took turns posing next to me. Reed had to keep reminding me to smile at the camera and *not* at the attractive boy beside me. It was hard though, they all looked so good in their dress pants, button up shirts and suit jackets. They were downright overwhelming to look at.

And even though they all looked similar, I could see little things they did that made them each different. Tristan's bright red tie. Logan's silky blue button up shirt, Finn's orange thing sticking up in his chest pocket, Ash's all black, Reed's white tie and cuffs. Remy had a gray pinstriped suit on while Kellan's was also gray but he had a green shirt underneath his jacket. I thought they went quite well together. I couldn't see Jace's telltale gold anywhere until I noticed his big shiny gold watch and the buttons on his sleeves were gold too. I never took him for subtle. Toned down like that, he's actually quite stunning.

After Reed pushed a magic button to make the camera take its own picture, so we could have one of us all together, we headed out to the black and white SUVs. I sat in the back of the black one between Reed and Ash. Reed had grabbed his camera before we left and was showing me all the pictures he just took.

"I want that one," I said when he reached the group one. I chew on my lip, knowing that you somehow got the pictures off the camera, but not quite sure about the process. "Actually, I want all of them. Can you get them out of there for me Reed?"

"Sure thing Kitten, not a problem. I know I said it before, but you look so beautiful tonight." I blush again.

"You look very nice yourself Reed. All of you do. I think we should do this dressing up thing more often."

"Yes! I finally got you interested in clothes. I think we should too Kitten. Most of them didn't have a reason to get decked out, so I couldn't dress them up. Although Ash is not fucking coming with me next time. The motherfucker had to look at everything we passed. It took forever." Logan goes on from the passenger seat.

I look at the man in black next to me. He really does do that. He snorts out a laugh. "I don't want to go next time. I just needed to get something. That's the only reason I went *this* time." He replies while staring out the window. I spend the rest of the car ride studying the pictures on Reed's camera.

When we get there, I hand the camera back, telling Reed. "It's a very nice camera, maybe one day you can show me how to use it."

Reed puts it in his pocket as he steps out and holds his hand for me to take. "Maybe Kitten," He says with a soft smile. Remy comes around the car and takes my other hand, tucking it into the crook of his arm, and guides me into the restaurant.

The trip to the restaurant was a fun adventure but the French food we had wasn't as good as Tristan's food, and I had told him so. He kissed me in the backseat of the white SUV the whole way home for saying that. His kisses tasted better than the food too.

I ended up going to bed with Logan so he could take my hair down for me and dry it when I got out of the shower. He put me in a pair of comfortable pink shorts and one of his shirts. Logan also gave me a pair of the rainbow striped toe socks Ash had gotten for me. It felt like they were hugging my toes.

Of course I had to go show them to Ash. He played with my sock covered toes for a while as I perched on his lap, snuggling into him and soaking in his scent. We tucked AJ in together, and we kissed goodnight. That was so much fun I decided to do it with each of my guys as well.

Remy was still in his office after having gone back there when we got home. I knocked on his door.

"Come in."

"Hi Remy, I just came to tell you goodnight," I said after entering. I cross the room to stand beside his chair. When he doesn't move, I push at his shoulder so he sits back. "Why aren't you in bed?" I ask as I climb in his lap.

"I have a few things to finish up here, and then I was going to go for a run." Remy smiles down at me with an amused look on his face.

"Anything I can help with?" I ask.

"No, curious girl, I think I can handle it. You get some sleep." He kissed my forehead and pushed away from the desk so I could get up. "Goodnight Kitten."

"Good night Remy, have fun."

I walk around to what I think is Kellan's room. The one across the hall from his doctor room. I knock, and he answers in just a pair of sleep bottoms. After several minutes, my eyes finally find his grass green ones. They are so pretty.

"Need something Kitten?" He asks kindly.

"No, I just want to tell you goodnight is all. Were you asleep already?" I hope I didn't wake him.

"No, no. Just getting ready for bed. I have to be at

the clinic early tomorrow." Kellan says through a yawn.

"Oh, okay. Will I see you at breakfast?" I ask, leaning into him and resting my head on his chest. My hands have a mind of their own as they run over the warm skin of his back. Mmmm...Skin. Reminded of my time with his brother, I can't help but wonder if Kellan's midnight hair is as soft as Finn's. One of my hands slide up....yes, yes it is.

"I'll be gone before then," Kellan responds in a husky whisper.

I pull back and frown at him. "Okay. I'll miss seeing you then. Goodnight Kellan." I lean up to kiss his cheek, but Kellan must have other ideas because his lips find mine for a sweet kiss.

"Goodnight sweet girl." I poke my head in his room, looking for Noah. He's sitting on the bench at the end of his bed. Good, he'll be alright there.

"Do you know where Finn's room is?" I ask him before he closes the door. Kellan smiles and points at the closed door right next to his. Figures. The twin thing is a whole other level of cuteness.

When I go to knock on Finn's door, it swings open before my hand reaches it. "Hey, Kitten."

My head tilts to the side as I ask. "How did you know I was here?"

Finn shakes his head slowly. "Werewolf hearing. I heard you ask where my room was."

I nod. "Well, I just came to..."

"Tell me goodnight. I know."

I stick my tongue out at him. "Know it all," I say playfully.

Finn laughs, bending down and kissing my lips

lightly. "Goodnight."

"Goodnight Finn."

Tristan's room is easy to find since I've been there many times. Instead of knocking on his door, I throw it open quickly and jump on his bed, making him laugh. His arms go around me, and he rolls us around. "You sleeping here cutie?" He asks.

I shake my head, calming my giggles. "No, with Logan. I just wanted to say goodnight."

"Oh really?" He asks with a smirk. His lips crash down on mine, hard. My hands move to his shaggy hair, and I kiss him back, meeting his tongue, stroke for stroke. When he finally pulls back, I'm a little breathless. "Sweet dreams sweet girl," He says as he helps me to the door. My legs like Jell-O.

"See you in the morning Tris."

I make it back to Logan's hallway and knock on Reed's door. He opens it, and I take in his cloud room. Pristine as ever. "Hi, Reed."

"Hey there Kitten." I hug his shoulders telling him goodnight. "You better get to bed now, I'll see you bright and early for our yoga session before breakfast," He says, stressing the 'G' in yoga.

"I can't wait to try yoba," I call back at him from in front of Logan's door. He laughs, shaking his head.

I crawl in next to Logan, laying my head on his chest. "Your lips are nice and swollen, I take it goodnight's went well?" He chuckles. I giggle too.

"Are you going to kiss me too Logan?" He smirks and proceeds to tangle his tongue with mine until my stupid, interfering body makes me yawn. Logan pulls me into him once more, and before I realize it, I'm asleep.

CHAPTER TWENTY-THREE

REMY

I watch from the window in the game room as Reed and Kitten bend this way and that. I find it highly amusing to watch Reed struggle to keep his dick in check. Our little Kitten is one flexible girl. That will come in handy when I step up my personal relations with her. Damn, now it's me who has to readjust himself.

We all know that Reed confessed his love to Kitten, and as far as I know, she hasn't shown any acknowledgment of it. He came to me this morning before he woke Kitten, concerned that he had pushed too far, too fast with his profession. I assured him that she heard him, and when she's ready, she'll say it back. Kitten doesn't seem to lie about anything. Little slips about how certain things in her past affect her now, but those are meaningless lies. I know she won't be pressured into doing anything before she's ready. She's a good girl.

I couldn't help the need to set eyes on her after Jace left my office thirty minutes ago. I pinch the bridge of my nose recalling our conversation. After seeing his reactions last night, before and after dinner, I asked him to see me first thing.

"I know last night was hard on you Jace, and I hope this whole thing has taught you a good lesson." I had said sternly.

"Trust me, it has," He replied. I have to admit, in all of my years with the Duke's son, I've never seen him so worried or stressed. "I should have never said what I said to her. I should have waited to see how everything would play out with her before I did anything. I'm sorry, you know I am Remington."

"I'm aware of that. I believe Miss Kitten is aware of it also. I believe she has also forgiven you to a certain extent, but you need to earn back her trust. She hands out forgiveness like tissues at a funeral, but trust is something very hard for her. Now is not the time to take a step a back Mr. Rotherstone." I raise an eyebrow at him, forcing my point.

"I'm not taking a step back, I've been occupied," He says, using his gift for Kitten as an excuse.

"I see how you are with her. I understand that your pride has taken a hit, and I understand if worry about rejection..."

"I'm not worried about her rejecting me." He cuts me off. I narrow my eyes at him, he knows I hate that. "It's just that...what Reed had said stuck with me. I'm not sure I'm good enough for her. Not after what I did. Not after I hurt her. Not after she told us about her life and I saw just inherently 'good' she is." He runs a hand through his hair. Something I've never seen him do before. The stress really IS getting to him.

"Did you miss out on her reply to that statement, Mr. Rotherstone? She said she, herself, gets to make that decision, not us. I think if you put yourself in her path, she will welcome you."

He nods his head. "You're probably right Remington, I'll try harder. I truly am busy with her gift though. I want it to be just perfect for her. I have to get this right. I *need* to get this right." He blows out a breath.

"How is that all coming along anyhow," I ask.

"Another week should do it, I think. I keep asking the guys about her and the things she likes..."

I cut him off, getting him back for doing it to me earlier. "You should use your time speaking to her directly Jace. Stop backing off. Backing away from her is creating more distance between not only the two of you but your brothers as well. If you want to know her, ask her, talk to her."

"Yes, Sir." He replies, and for once I don't think he means it mockingly.

"I can give you a week to finish your surprise, but no longer. The rest of your brothers have things they want to do as well, but I've held them off, giving you time to do what you need to do. We'd never leave you behind Jace, you're family. But the rest of us still have to prove ourselves to her as well, we're ready to move forward, and you need to move with us. She's with us right now, but we need to make her want to be here forever." It's true, the men have been to my office more than ever lately. They're getting impatient.

"I understand. It'll be done by then, I promise. And

thank you for looking out for me Remington."

"Always," I reply. I'll always look out for my men. That's what I'm here for.

I'm brought out of my thoughts when I see Miss Kitten stand on her hands and walk on them. I let out a chuckle at her antics. I don't think she realizes that her playfulness is perfect for us bunch of wolves. She had told Reed yesterday that she missed seeing our wolf forms. I couldn't be happier about that. I gave the men the go ahead to change at will. She surprises me at every turn, the little thing. As Reed takes advantage of his time alone with her, I turn and head to the kitchen. Maybe Tristan could use some help with breakfast.

KITTEN

I was less than happy when Reed came in to wake me this morning. I grumbled at him, but he had just laughed and kept tickling my feet until I couldn't help but giggle. When I finally unburied my face from the pillow, I looked up to a sleepy but happy looking Reed. I couldn't possibly stay mad at him when he looked like that. Stupid tummy flutters. Logan had muttered that he left me an outfit out on the chair and told me to wear my hair in a ponytail. He must have really been tired if he was letting me do my own hair. I had kissed his bare shoulder telling him, "Thank you squishy face," before getting up and ready. Taking my clothes to the bathroom to change and do my hair while Reed waited outside. I was sure to use Logan's toothbrush like he likes me to.

Reed took my hand and led me out the back door

and into the yard. I guess he was already out here because there were rolled out mats and bottles of water already waiting for us. I was a little chilled in my stretchy black pants and bra top thing, but I'm used to the cold, so I didn't let it bother me.

Reed started us off sitting on the mats, Indian style. He told me to close my eyes and try to forget everything. Or well, he told me to clear my mind. I had closed my eyes, but I couldn't help the giggle that slipped out.

"You do realize that that is an impossibility for someone like me, right?" I ask.

Reed rubs his hands together. "I didn't think of that. Just picture a happy, relaxing moment in your mind then, some time you felt safe and comfortable." He says once I close my eyes again.

I do as he says. Instantly, images of the boys fill my mind. Tristan's eyes, petting Finn's fur coat, Ash's intoxicating smell. It all washes over me, making my lips lift at the corners, peace and tranquility overtaking my body.

"Remember this feeling Kitten, how you feel right now. Keep it with you as you copy my movements. I'm going to position my body in different poses, try to put your body like I have mine. We'll be performing breathing exercises as we go." Reed says in a peaceful tone. He must have found his happy place too.

We move slowly, taking breaths at important times, according to Reed. I forget how many positions we've done so far, but my favorite was the downward dog. Mostly because it's fun to say.

"Okay Kitten, you're shocking the hell out of me here. Let's go back to the 'Locust Scorpion' pose, but after we count to ten, I want you to shift straight into the 'Peacock' pose, hold it and then straight to a 'Headstand Scorpion' okay. Ready?"

I shake my limbs around. Yoba with Reed is proving harder than I thought. I lay flat on my stomach, my head tilted with my chin on the mat. Taking the weight on my arms, I lift my legs and push my torso from the ground, keeping my spine straight as possible as my body turns vertical. I bend my spine backward, bringing my feet down to my head. My muscles burn like crazy, but I manage to hold the pose for ten seconds. Barely. I lift my legs into the air once more, my spine thanking me. Without letting my body fall to the ground again, I push up on my arms, moving my hands around until my fingertips are facing my feet, my elbows forming right angles as I bring my body parallel to the ground. It feels like any minute my wrists are going to snap, but I hold it.

"Beautiful Kitten, just beautiful. God, you are amazing. Last pose Polly Pretzel, 'Headstand Scorpion.'" I move into a handstand, straight up and down and take a moment to breathe, then bend my legs behind me once more, my head tilting up to touch my feet. My arms shake, but I'm determined to hold it for the full ten. Because Reed wants me to, because he's counting on me to do this. He counts it out for me as I struggle for balance. "...ten."

I immediately straighten out my back. Keeping vertical. I briefly wonder if I can walk like this and decide to try it. After I take a few 'steps' with my hands, Reed starts laughing, and I collapse to the ground on my tummy. Friggin' yoba.

"I can't believe you could do those poses. That's pretty advanced stuff, Kitten. Takes some people years to master those poses. Your transitions could use a bit of work, but I'm so completely proud of you right now."

Reed's awestruck voice would usually melt me, but I'm finding it hard to move even the tiniest of muscles right now. "Ugh." Is all I can manage.

Reed looks contrite as he takes a seat next to me, rubbing my back. "I'm sorry sweetie, I might have pushed you a little too far your first time, but I had to see how far you could go. I'm impressed, to say the least. How did you get so flexible?"

Both of his hands move to my back as he sits on my butt. It feels amazing, and I never want him to stop. "I've been skating for years, Reed. It takes balance and muscles and flexibility for that too. I might work some of those poses into my personal routine." I trail off, groaning as his fingers press harder into my shoulders.

"If you can do all that here, on the ground, you must be poetry in motion on ice," He says, moving his magic fingers lower. I groan again.

"I've had lots of practice. I used to get paid in skate time remember? You guys could come watch me on Friday, I get the ice to myself then. Now explain to me why you go through this torture on a daily basis."

He laughs again. "Because I like the challenge of it. Simple as that. I come out here in the mornings, watch the sun rise, and challenge my body to do my mind's bidding. It relieves tension and stress for me. Don't worry if you don't like it, it's not for everyone."

"It's not that I don't like it. Maybe I just need more practice. I definitely liked spending time with you, doing something you liked." I tell him.

Reed flips me over, pressing his fingers into my arms, rubbing in circles. I moan loudly. "I like this too," I tell him.

"Oh, you like this part huh?" He smirks. "I guess you'll have to come back tomorrow so we can do this again." When he's through with my arms, he moves to my calves. My tense muscles turn the consistency of pudding in his hands. Oh yes, it was totally worth it.

When he moves on to my thighs, the tummy flutters return full force. My legs open of their own accord. I tell myself it's so he has more room to work his magic. I know better though, as I'm also silently pleading with him to move his hands higher.

Reed's eyes move from his hands on my legs up to my bare tummy, traveling slowly up, lingering on my heaving chest and up to meet my stare. His nostrils flare as the green, blue and gold fight for dominance in his entrancing eyes. He moves to lay down next to me, the tips of his fingers dragging lightly to my tummy, circling my belly button.

"I love you, Kitten. I know you want something from me right now. I don't think you know what it is though." His lips move to my neck, his warm breath making me shiver. I nod my head, unsure if he even asked me a question. "I'm going to give you what you need Kitten, not just because I'm a man and I can, but because I love you and because I want to." I nod again.

He presses his hand flat on my belly, moving his

fingertips under the band on my pants. His eyes meet mine again. He's asking permission for something. I'm not sure what, but this is Reed, he won't hurt me, I know. Besides, he said he'll give me what I need, something to make this ache go away I hope. I nod again.

Reed's lips find my throat as his hand slides down, into my pants, under my panties. I gasp in shock when his long fingers reach my center. He nibbles on my neck, taking turns sucking, licking and biting. I don't know which feels better, that is, until his fingers part my lower lips, sliding back and forth in my wetness down there. One of his fingers probes into my folds. It feels amazing one second, the next I feel an uncomfortable pressure. My hands fly to his wrists, stopping him. He pulls his hand back immediately.

"It's okay Kitten, you're not ready for that, and I get it. Just let me make you feel good baby." I let go of him, hoping he won't do that again, that hurt. His fingers find a spot above my opening that makes my whole body jerk. Okay, now *that* felt wonderful. He circles that spot with one finger as his teeth clamp down on my earlobe.

"Oh my God, Reed..." I moan out, this isn't making the ache go away, it's catching it on fire. He uses more pressure, and I squirm under him, chasing that magic finger with my hips.

"That's it, baby, it feels good doesn't it?" Reed whisper growls in my ear.

"Yes," I whisper back. The ache builds, making me feel desperate. I remember this feeling from when I was with Remy, but this feels different. His finger flicks back and forth over my spot, making my thighs shake uncontrollably.

"Oh yeah, Kitten, cum for me baby, let me see you cum. " He pinches my spot between two of his fingers, with that, and his words, I fall apart at the seams. Lightning shoots through my veins and black surrounds the edges of my vision. As my body calms down, his fingers slide through my wetness as his palm moves in light circles over my spot.

I'm not sure if I'm supposed to say thank you after that or not, so I say exactly what I feel to be right. "I love you back Reed," I whisper. I heard him when he told me before, I just needed time to process my own feelings for him. I didn't want to say it if I didn't mean it. I never want to do anything to make my sensitive boy sad again.

Reed's eyes snap to mine, his face stuck in a look of shock. I giggle at the funny look. He pulls his hand free of my pants, gripping my butt in his hand, pulling my body into his. "I thought you'd never say it. I love you, Kitten. I love you so much." His lips find mine in a heated kiss, bringing back the tummy flutters. I kiss him back, moving to his neck after a while. I can see the appeal of this. He tastes like Reed and sweat. The mixture is oddly delightful.

"I see the hottest shit when I'm sent after you sexy girl." I hear Tristan say from somewhere close. Reed turns into a blanket, covering my body with his and growling at Tristan, his eyes shining with possessiveness.

"It's okay Reed." I pat his arm, breathing is a little hard with all of his weight on me.

"Yeah, it's okay man, she still has clothes on anyway. I wasn't even perving this time, I just came to tell you breakfast is ready, Kitten needs to eat before work."

Reed rolls off me, letting me breathe. He takes

Tristan's outstretched hand and stands. "Sorry dude, you just caught me off guard. I was a little too lost there." They share a look and goofy smiles.

"Don't worry about it," Tristan says before turning his focus to me. "You might want to catch a quick shower before eating. The scent of you right now will drive the lot of us mad with lust if you don't." He winks at me.

I blush, not sure I'll ever get used to them telling me how I smell. "Okay, I'll go take a shower in your room. Can you tell Logan to bring my stuff in there for me?"

"Sure thing cutie." He kisses my forehead before I jog to the house. I think I'm really going to like this yoba.

JACE

I stood at my bedroom window, watching as my brother thoroughly satisfied the girl that plagues my every thought. My chest tightens with either jealousy or longing, both are new emotions for me, as I'm used to getting my way. I'm still worried how quickly my brothers and I have come to be wrapped up in this tiny girl, but I can now see that she's been good for us. We've been drifting through time, not really paying attention to it or taking pleasure in life the way we should as immortals. Then she came along, and it's like the earth starting spinning again. Things like chocolate and strawberries hold meaning they never had before.

I'm not sure why I saw her as such a threat when I met her. I'll regret the way I treated her for the rest of my life, I'm sure. I've watched her with my brothers, bringing them joy and happiness that I've not seen in them. Even Ash walks around with a smile on his face, the intimidating man cannot seem to help himself. He also has a small stuffed wolf that I catch him speaking to on occasion like it's his own pup. I shake my head at the thought, that girl has turned us all upside down.

I'll admit, at first, I just wanted her for her beauty and to drive the humans mad with envy at my having her. It seems as though Reed's 'karma' does exist and she's a woman with it out for me. I've watched as her face lights up at the sight of the others, I've witnessed her lips swollen from stolen kisses, and I even overheard her telling Tristan all the things she likes about him. It's killing me that I can't be a part of it.

Last night, when she came down those steps, looking like she did....I had nearly fainted. She could have rivaled any princess in my day. It wasn't just the dress, it was also how she blushed so prettily when my brothers complimented her and told them to thank Logan. I chuckle at the thought. She has no idea how beautiful she is, that only endears me to her more. It saddened my heart when the rest of them surrounded her, touching her and showing her their affections. My wolf had begged me to join in, the need for closeness and touch from my pack almost unbearable. But I couldn't, I had hurt her and I wasn't deserving.

We had gathered outside of Reed's suite, seeing if Kitten could heal the wounds inside of him. If she couldn't, we were going to be there for him. It is what we do for each other. Kitten's tale of her friendship with that lady of the night had affected us all, but Reed took it hardest. I suppose it's because he saw her drawing, and we didn't. I had nearly bit my tongue in half when he had told her he loved her. It's just like Reed to jump in head first though. But when she had started telling him about her life before she came here....what she did to survive, the people she met, and what they did to her....anger I have never seen the likes of, shot through me.

The amount of humans that did that child wrong was astronomical. She only mentioned a few that stood out to her, but a child on the street is visible to many. Once she turned into a young woman, I know that her beauty did not go unnoticed, but she didn't mention any of that. Probably best, considering her known audience. When she explained how she forgave those people, how she all but defended them, I thought the girl might be a few crayons short of a box. That is until she explained that each of those people and experiences made her who she is. She was so right about that, and that's true for all of us isn't it? This young woman had a rough start in life, something that can turn the strongest of men into vile creatures, and here she is.... a sweet, caring, forgiving little thing, capable of giving so much love, not hardened by her circumstances one bit. If anything, I think it made her want to save the world, not dream of its destruction like I would have had I lived like her.

I knew then that Reed was right, no one was deserving of her. Least of all me, as hard as that thought was. I know I'm a catch. I have money, good looks, proper manners and all of the best things money can buy. Not to mention my skills at pleasing females. But with all of that...I can't hold a candle to her, a girl with a flag and a torn bear to her name. She said it was her choice who she let in, and I vowed to make her see me. Not the spoiled and condescending man that I have become, but the man that deserves her, the man I want to be.

I was just going through the motions with her gift at that point. I had thought wooing a girl with nothing was going to be a piece of cake. Her reaction to the bear had made that clear to me. Remington had made it clear to get in her good graces, and I said I would, but it was more for my family than for her. After that night though, I knew I had to do something truly special, give her something she deserved, nothing but the best. Not the best in my eyes, but in hers. Putting myself in her shoes has been the hardest damn task there ever was, and I can only hope she likes it.

"Remington, I've been thinking about what you said earlier. I need more time with her, and I'd like to start today. Is there any way that I can escort Kitten to her work?" I all but beg. I know there's a schedule for this, but it's just another thing I have been left out of.

"I think that's an excellent idea Mr. Rotherstone, I'll inform Finn of the change in plans. Go bring your car around for her. I expect you to be on your best behavior with her Jace, another incident between the two of you could put you at odds with her permanently." Remington replies in his commanding tone. Sure, no pressure or anything buddy.

"I will be," I state, making my way to the garage. I didn't know if he'd go for it, but I'm excited at the thought of time with the enchanting Miss Kitten. The idea came to me out of nowhere, and I knew I had to hurry and ask before she left. It was my idea to see her off to work each day and be in the drive when she returned. The suggestion had made my brothers happy with me, and that was my goal at the time. Now, however, it's the only time I get to see her and has become what I look forward to. I need to hurry and get to breakfast, so she knows I care.

I wonder if I am good today if she will come to my suite and kiss me good night as well. Or maybe even spend the night with me?

CHAPTER TWENTY-FOUR

KITTEN

I rush through my breakfast, putting my eggs and a sausage patty between my toasts and forming a sandwich. I took too long in the shower and am pressed for time now. I explained to the boys that it's not my fault that the water pressure in Tristan's shower feels so good.

Kellan laughs. "I'll add that to the list of Kitten logic's." I grunt at him, I don't have time to talk.

"Aww... look at her, she's so cute when she stuffs her face. Isn't she cute Tristan?" Logan teases me. I open my mouth, showing him my half chewed food. See if he thinks that's cute.

"Still adorable sweetie, nice try though," Tristan says.

"Mouth closed, Miss Kitten. I'll let you kick them later for their teasing. Young ladies should not stoop to their level." I really want to do it again, just to see what he says, but he speaks again, making me lose my train of thought. "Or maybe I should just have Mr. Rotherstone, remind you of proper table manners," He adds, making me roll my eyes. I hate that he saw me watching Jace eat that time.

"Have me do what?" Jace says, looking a little out of breath. Did he run here?

"Oh nothing, I was just telling Miss Kitten here, of your impeccable table manners," Remy says.

Jace looks confused as he grabs an apple from the fruit bowl. "Oh, well yes. In my day, proper etiquette was part of the curriculum. More important to the Ton than even arithmetic and literature." Jace states proudly.

I swallow my food down. "That's kind of sad Jace. I'd rather be able to count than to know how to eat soup without slurping." The guys all laugh, including Jace, but his face does tint a nice shade of pink.

"I agree with you there, Kitten. It's just the way things were back then." He says. I nod, I know that. "So...are you about ready to go? I wouldn't want you to be late on my day as your escort."

I blink at him. Seriously? I turn my attention to Remy. "You're not forcing him are you? If everyone else is busy, I can just go by myself." I hear Jace wince, but Remy's gruff voice keeps my focus on him.

"Everyone else is not busy. Mr. Rotherstone asked to go with you, I would not force anyone to do something they did not want to do." Remy's face is as hard as stone, and I realize I said something wrong.

"Okay, I'm sorry," I say to him. Turning my head to look at Jace, I ask. "Why would you ask to come with me?" His face falls, but he recovers quickly.

"Why don't we discuss this on the ride in, hmm?" He walks to the doorway, waiting on me. I wipe my mouth with a napkin, then go around the room, kissing my boys on the cheeks goodbye, and telling Tristan thank you.

When I reach Jace, he takes my hand and places it at the crook of his arm, his hand covering mine. When we get to the front door, he has me pause as he opens it with flourish. He holds my hand down the steps and opens the flashy yellow car door with the same flourish. He's acting so weird.

I watch as he moves with grace and poise around the hood of the car to hop in the driver's seat. Once in, he reaches over and straps me in. Seriously, something is going on, and I don't know what it is. Did he get in trouble with the other guys or something? Is that why he volunteered to take me to work?

"You can just drop me off when we get there. I'm sure you have other things you'd rather do than hang out with me all day." I tell him.

He makes a face. "Is that what you think, Kitten?" He asks.

"Well, it's pretty obvious that you don't like me. I know you got the gifts because the others wanted you to show you were sorry." Does he think I don't know the real reason behind those things?

Jace sighs. "It's true. I did get those things for you because the others wanted me to make it up to you. I also thought it was sad that you never had a candy bar. Chocolate is God's gift to humanity, and everyone should have access to it." I nod again. I feel the same.

"But that doesn't mean I don't like you. I saw you as

a threat to my family at first. I see now that you're not, isn't a man allowed to change his opinion when new facts are brought to light?" He asks.

That sounds reasonable, so I nod again. "So what does that mean exactly?"

"What it means Dearest Kitten, is that I'm sorry. More than I could ever tell you. I would like to start over, you and me. I would like for you to get to know me, and for I, you. Do think that's a possibility?" He sounds sincere, but is he sorry he hurt me, or sorry because of the fallout?

I take a deep breath. "Honestly, Jace, even if I got to know you, and you, me...I'm not sure how well we could understand each other. I've met people like you before, people so wrapped up in their world that they can't see past it. I don't know what I could possibly offer someone like you. Or what you could offer someone like me either. We don't care about the same things. Not at all. I get that you need to be somewhat close to me because of your brothers, but you don't have to try to be as close to me as they are. We can be....whatever we are, and everyone can still be happy."

Jace's whole body is stiff, his face a hard mask. "So that's it then? I make one mistake, and you can't see to forgive me?"

"I've already forgiven you, Jace, I don't hold on to ill feelings. I just don't want you to pretend to care about me if you don't mean it. If I let you in like I've let the others in...and you..." I trail off. It would devastate me. If I come to find out later it was all a lie, it could affect my relationships with the rest of them. I don't know if I could handle that kind of hurt.

Jace relaxes into his seat, a small smile lifting his lips. "So you're saying that you're scared." It's a statement, not a question.

"Yeah, I guess that's what I'm saying."

"Well, it seems we finally found common ground then, Kitten. I'm scared too. In my entire lifetime, I've never had to put myself out there, I've never wanted to. For you, I'm willing to do that. Not because of my brothers, but because I think you're worth it."

Huh, and here I thought he thought of me as worthless. He runs a hand through his hair, messing up his perfectly placed locks. "All I'm asking for Kitten, is a second chance. I don't expect you to trust me at my word, I'll show you that I mean it, that I care for you. I'll earn your trust. I'll prove to you that I'm deserving."

It looks like he's getting frustrated. I am too. I hate the space that's between us, I just don't know how to close the gap without getting hurt in the process. "Alright." I finally say.

Jace's head snaps around, his golden eyes sparkling. "Alright, what?"

I roll my eyes at him. He needs me to say it? "Alright, I agree to give you a chance. We can get to know each other. I'm not making any promises on what the outcome will be, I just agree that we should try to be friends."

His perfect smile is a thing to behold. "That's all I ask. So...where do we start?"

I laugh out loud. "How am I supposed to know?"

He chews his lip in thought. "Right, why don't we start with the 'not understanding each other' part. What don't you understand about me?"

That's a loaded question if I ever heard one. "Okay, here's a question. Do you really like this car, or do you only like it because other people want it and can't afford it?"

He looks appalled. "What? You don't like my car?" He asks, not answering my question.

"I didn't say that. I don't know how I feel about having at least two cars that will I die if I drive, around, but it's a very pretty car, and I like yellow. Now answer my question."

Jace's face looks a mix of shock and confusion. "I'll answer your question but first, tell me what you mean about 'two cars that if you drive, you'll die.'"

Ugh! Fine. "Logan said that if he taught me to drive his car, he'd have to kill me. Your car looks as nice as his so I assumed that it too, was a werewolf only car." I answer.

I can see that he's struggling to hold back laughter. "That's just an expression, Kitten, there is no such thing as 'werewolf only' cars. I just think he meant to stress his love of his vehicle. Logan doesn't let anyone drive his car."

Oh, that makes way more sense. Why didn't he just say that though? "But to answer your question..." Jace continues. "..I would say both. I *do* like this car, it's shapely and fast and has a smooth ride. On the other hand, I do like receiving appreciative looks from others, because of this car."

"Okay, but why is it so important to you what other people think about what you drive?" I ask.

"I don't know why it's important. I like standing out, I like it when people assume I'm doing something better than them or *are* better than them." He replies.

Oh, I see the problem now. This, I can actually relate to. "Who said that you don't stand out without all the shiny stuff Jace? Who says that you need money to be 'better' than other people?"

Jace stares out the windshield, not answering me. I turn my attention out the window, watching the scenery. When he parks the car, I unbuckle myself and go to open the door. "Everyone says that." I hear him whisper behind me.

I shift around until I can see him again. He's slumped in his seat, his eyes cast down to the steering wheel. "Maybe that's true Jace. Maybe most people think that being rich and always getting everything you want makes you better somehow, happier even. But you tell me, Jace, are they right? You have everything you've ever wanted, you can buy anything that catches your eye, but what's the most important thing you've ever had in your life? The one thing you would die to keep?" I'm making assumptions here, but I don't think I'm wrong.

He takes no time to answer. "My family. My family is the only thing I'd die to keep."

I want to smile but keep my face in check. "And how much did it cost you to join them? How much money did Remy charge you for him to take you in, to make you part of his pack?"

"Not a damn cent," He answers, looking at me with a lazy smile. "You're very smart for your age, you know that Kitten?"

I shake my head. "No, not smart, just competitive. I totally won that argument." I wink at him. Jace bursts into laughter, holding his tummy.

"You certainly did Kitten. You certainly did." He mumbles. Getting out of the car, he strides to my door and opens it for me, helping me out. "I'm so happy I got to escort you today pretty girl, you taught me a lesson in thirty minutes that I should have learned decades ago."

I place my hand at the crook of his arm before he can put it there himself. "I didn't teach you anything Jace, the facts were already there. I just helped you come to the correct conclusion. I think if you'd stop worrying about what everyone else thought of you, you'd see that you can be special and stand out, no matter what you did."

"You really think so huh?" He asks.

"I know so Jace. You just have to see it yourself before others will start believing it."

I had a group of foster kids today. They weren't really interested in skating, so I kept the lesson short and let the free skate take over early. Mikey was here with this group of mixed age kids, and I was surprised, to say the least. I guess the state finally took him away from his father. I'm not sure how I feel about that. I guess I'm happy that he's not being hurt anymore, but as a girl with no parents herself, I know what it's like to feel alone in the world. Parents are supposed to look out for you and when they don't, it hurts more than any bruise or broken bone ever could.

I had tried to hide my annoyance when Kaitlynn had walked in, mid-lesson, and I saw her do a double-take at Jace. He was dutifully stationed at the opening to the ice, leaning against the side of the glass. If I didn't know any better, he was taking mental notes on how to skate. As she approached him, she tugged her top down, nearly spilling out of it.

When he turned his head and smiled at her, I felt my heart shatter and my blood burn. I had turned away from the nauseating sight instantly. Of course she would be Jace's type. Jace is just like Adam, willing to look past her blackened soul and mean spirit, concentrating on how her body looks in too tight clothing. To each their own, I try to tell myself. I don't know why it hurts so badly anyway, I already have seven amazing guys who want me, do I really need Jace to want me too? No, I tell myself. I definitely don't need Jace. If he could want someone like her, the complete opposite of me, then I don't want anything to do with him anyway. I could never be like her. I wonder what's wrong with me to make him not want me though.

I shut down those useless thoughts. I don't know what's come over me, making me have such dark thoughts about myself, making me jealous of Kaitlynn. Oh! That's what this feeling is, jealousy. Damn Jace and his bastard self, making me feel things I don't want.

I bring my focus back to the present, back to Mikey. He isn't enjoying the free skate like he usually does. He looks so sad, and it tears me up inside. I skate over to him.

"Hey there Mikey, want to pretend we're at the Olympics, and you're my partner?" I smile at him. Hoping he says yes, I don't want to be rejected by Mikey today too.

"I'm not good enough. I'd just make you fall." He says while looking down at the ground.

"Maybe, but did you see her out there? I think she has enough skill for the both of you. Besides, you should never turn a pretty lady down, young Sir." I stiffen when I realize Jace just spoke from behind me.

"Yeah Mikey, Jace here never says no to anyone. You don't want to be like him though, being picky has its virtues." I instantly regret my snotty tone. Not because of Jace, but because I said that to the little boy.

"I'm sorry Mikey, don't listen to me, I'm just a stupid girl. I have to talk to my friend here, and then I'll come find you. Okay?"

To my utter surprise, Mikey takes a step in front of me, facing off with Jace, who is about four feet taller than him. He squares his little shoulders, and tilts his head back, meeting Jace's eyes. "You better not be mean to Kitten, she's my friend, and she doesn't need any more boys being mean to her. If you say bad things like the other boy, I'll tell on you, and you'll get in trouble."

I feel tears prick my eyes. Little Mikey is standing up for me. I'm glad it's Jace and not Adam though, Jace won't hurt him, I'm not sure what Adam would do. Jace's eyes widen, and he looks taken aback. He eventually comes out of his shock and kneels to Mikey's height.

"I wouldn't dream of being mean to your friend young Sir, in fact, I was hoping she would be my friend too. The thing is, I don't think she wants to be." He says, speaking to Mikey likes he's an adult.

Mikey looks back at me with raised eyebrows, then back to Jace. "Why not? Did you pick on her like Adam did?"

Jace shakes his head. "No, nothing like that. You see, I think your friend here, thinks I thought another girl was prettier than her. Every girl wants to think they are the prettiest, and they get mad at us boys when we give other girls attention." He explains.

My face is on fire, he just called me out, point blank. And he did it in a sneaky way, using my favorite kid against me. He's smarter than I gave him credit for. If I deny it, I will be lying in front of the boy. He knows I won't do that. Sneaky, sneaky, bastard.

Mikey looks back at me once more, stepping to my side, looking for the world like I have two heads. Turning back to Jace he says. "That's stupid. She's the prettiest girl that I ever met." To me he says. "You're pretty Kitten, you should be his friend, and someone not thinking you look nice is not a reason not to be their friend anyway."

I can't help myself, I bear hug him, picking him up off his feet. "You are so sweet Mikey. Thank you for saying that. I told you I was a stupid girl." He squirms, so I put him down, steadying him. He blushes, running his hands over his clothes, probably trying to look cool in front of Jace.

"Girls are weird." He stage whispers. He has to know that I heard him, right? I smirk. I am being weird today.

"Truer words have never been spoken, my friend," Jace says once standing. "What do you say I go get some of those fancy skates like you, and we let the weird girl teach us how not to fall?" Mikey nods his head eagerly. Looks like Jace made a friend after all.

I pull Mikey around the rink until Jace returns. Once he's on the ice, he makes a big show of falling down. Even though he faked it, I still take a small amount of pleasure seeing him on his butt. It only takes me a few minutes of 'teaching' Jace to tell that he's pretty good at this. Either way, he falls every time Mikey does. I let them the two of them have their boy talk as I look on, only interrupting to instruct every now and again. Eventually, Jace says he's tired, on Mikey's behalf, I'm sure. We step off the ice, taking a seat on the closest bench.

"You're a way better skater than me, Big Mike, you'll be as good as Kitten in no time," Jace tells him, removing his skates.

"I don't want to be an ice dancer, I want to play hockey," Mikey replies defensively.

"Oh really, are you in the league here then?"

Mikey shakes his head sadly. "No, I could never get my Dad to sign me up. And my new foster parents don't have the money." He looks down, ashamed for no good friggin' reason.

As I'm about to explain to the boy that not having money is not a big deal in life, Jace beats me to it. Sort of. "But someone brings you here to skate, who does that?"

"I usually come with the rec center, I lucked out today cause Miss Stratford doesn't like to keep an eye on us and this is a cheap way to get us out of her hair."

Jace frowns. 'Who's that?"

"The lady that watches foster kids while the foster parents work." Mikey shrugs.

I see Jace's mind working a mile a minute. What is he up to? "Do you still get to go to the rec center?" He asks the boy. Mikey nods. Jace smiles smugly. "Then don't worry about a thing friend. I'm sure one day you will get to play hockey."

I want to slap the look right off his face. Or maybe just slap his face. He should not be making promises to any of these kids. He doesn't even know what he's talking about. I stand, calling an end to the session. I tell Mikey to go get his shoes on before Jace can open his big mouth again.

"I can tell that I did something else to upset you Kitten, care to explain this one? The jealousy was obvious, but I haven't clue this time." His haughty tone is back, and it only makes me want to slap him harder.

"Why did you say that to Mikey? The rec center doesn't have a league Jace, Mikey will probably end up back with his Dad, it's how that stupid system works. They upset the kid's life as a threat to the parents, the parents say sorry, and they send their kids back to them. Even if you could give money to his new foster parents like I think you want to, there's no telling if they'll use it to let him play. And what if they do? What will happen when he goes back to his father, Jace? Then you've given him something that he gets ripped away from him. How friggin' dare you!"

I'm panting by the time I'm done ranting at him. I'm not only upset because of his small mistake of giving a kid hope for something he can't have, but I'm mad at myself too. I've been admiring Jace for over an hour. The way he was with Mikey tugged at my heartstrings. I had no idea he'd be so great around kids. I even had an unrealistic thought that he'd make a great father one day. Then he says what he did, and it all crashes down. I should have known better.

"If you are quite done verbally assaulting me, both out loud and in your head. I have a question I need you to answer." His smirk is still in place. It's grown if that's even possible.

"What?" I snap.

"Do you know which rec center Big Mike attends?" He asks slowly.

"Uh...yeah. The same one I do. Why?" I ask.

"Well, it seems to me that he attends the rec-center regardless if he's at his foster home or with his father. So if the rec center was to start a hockey program at, let's say, here. Then our little friend would, in fact, get to play hockey. Which would mean that I did not lie to him, or make promises I do not intend to keep. Which, would make your anger at me pointless." He shrugs his shoulders.

I make a face at him. "I told you, they don't have a program."

"That's because they more than likely, don't have the funding. If they received the funding, they'd probably have the program. Don't you think, Miss Kitten?"

I blink at him. Is he saying what I think he's saying? "Do you mean..."

He chuckles. "Yes, my Dearest Kitten, I mean to fund a hockey program at this rec center. If it wouldn't displease you, I'd like you to escort me there one evening. If I'm to stop spending money on myself, I might as well spend it on those kids you feel so protective over."

I'm still blinking. "I-I just assumed..."

"You assumed the worst in me." He runs a hand through his hair again. "I get it, I haven't given you much reason to think differently. I told you I'd prove myself to you, Kitten.

"You shouldn't do it because of me, It'll be something that takes effort, and you can't just drop it once..."

"I'm not doing it for you. It might be your rec

center, but that's the only connection. I know exactly what it will take Kitten, it might surprise you to know that I'm on several committees that reach out and give back, as well as head of my own charity for medical research."

"Oh." Is my brilliant response. How could I have missed all of that about him? I guess it was because I wasn't looking. "I'm sorry. I didn't know."

He shakes his head, taking my hand and leading me out of the arena. "You don't have to be sorry, we got off to a bad start and then avoided each other. That's why we need a fresh start Kitten, no more assuming, from either of us. Deal?"

"Deal," I say. I jumped to conclusions when I shouldn't have. He doesn't fault me for it though. He's definitely a better man than I gave him credit for.

As we reach the doors leading outside, he stops me. "And about that girl earlier..." My face goes hot again. "I am more than flattered that you were jealous, but you have no reason to be. I'm aware of who that girl is to you. I was just....setting her up a little."

The evil looking smirk on his face worries me, but the mischievous glint in his eye just makes me curious. "For what?" I ask as we exit the building.

"This..." He whispers. One second I'm walking, and the next, Jace has me pressed into the brick, his lips on my neck as his hand pulls one of my thighs around his hips.

"Jace..." I say, shocked and a little breathy.

"That's right baby, say my name." Holy crap! What's happening here? Why is he moaning?

"You've *got* to be kidding me? *Her*! The trash?"

Comes a shriek that I know is Kaitlynn.

"Damn straight. This is Kitten, my girlfriend, and she's not trash. She's the hottest fucking girl I've ever had. You could learn a thing or two from her." Jace sneers at her.

I catch the hurt look in Kaitlynn's eyes before Jace pulls me away. I know I should feel bad but, That was *beyond* awesome!! I put my hand around Jace's waist, hugging him to me as we walk to the car.

"I'm sorry I doubted you earlier, thank you for that. It shouldn't, but that felt really, really good." I giggle.

"Not a problem, she deserved it. Don't feel bad baby. And now you get to drive off in my flashy car, with the hottest guy on the planet." He does an impression of a high pitched girl at the end, causing me to laugh heartily. My golden boy came through for me again. I guess he *is* kind of amazing.

CHAPTER TWENTY-FIVE

Before I knew it, it was Friday, the day I had been looking forward to. Reed had mentioned to the others that I invited them to come watch me skate, and they turned it into a huge deal. I explained that I'm not pro level good, but they are acting like it's some big event. I've never been so excited or nervous to skate in my life. Tristan and Remy filled me up on sausage gravy and biscuits this morning that were to die for. They said the rest of the guys were going to meet us there, and they had things to do.

It seems like I rarely see more than two of them at any given time lately. We all eat dinner together, but it's become a rushed affair. I don't know what changed, but something definitely has. I haven't hung out with Jace since he took me to work a few days ago, and I wonder if he changed his mind about being friends. This morning was the first time I've even seen Remy other than at dinner, and even then, he didn't say much. I get time with Reed and Finn though. I've been meeting Reed for yoba sessions and Finn for studying. Sometimes Tristan or Kellan will stop by for story time, so there's that too.

I sigh and let out a breath. Something is up, and I wish they'd just tell me. I finish stretching out my limbs and go warm up on the ice. Remy and Tristan are still waiting for the others in the lobby. I hope Logan gets here soon since he has the music I'll be skating to. I loved the song he played me on my first day back here, and I've been mentally timing my moves to it.

As I take a last lap around the rink, I see the double doors open, and several people walk in. Logan's blue streak shines in the overhead lighting, and I skate over to him. Behind him, I see Remy, Tristan, Kellan and Finn too. They walk over to the bench seats and find a good spot as I meet Logan at the ice entrance.

"Do you think you could play that song for me? The one from the other day?" I ask him.

He flicks his head to the side, shifting his hair, making my eyes follow the blue streak. Does he know how distracting that is? Every time it moves, I want to follow it. "Sure, anything for our big star," He says as he kisses my temple and heads to the music booth.

I watch him mess around in there until I see the doors open again, and Ash and Reed come in. Shortly after they take seats, Miss Annie and another employee here, Rob, I think his name is come in as well. Huh, I didn't know Miss Annie was going to watch me today. She sees me out here enough already, nothing I do will be new to her. A few minutes later Jace strolls in, in all his golden glory. Dang that boy is attractive. It's a real shame he knows it.

I'm brought out of those thoughts as I hear a stampede of footsteps right before Mikey steps around Jace, leading a pack of running kids.

"Mikey!" I shout out to him, meeting him half way. "What are you doing here, kiddo?" I ruffle his hair, and he huffs at me, putting it back in place.

"My friend Jace brought us. He came to the rec center and asked if I wanted to see your big show." He says excitedly.

Now it's my turn to huff. It's not a big show. "That's right, I did, but some of the other kids heard and wanted to come too. You're quite popular over at that place." Jace says, walking up to us.

He kisses my temple, making Mikey make a face and scurry off with the other kids. "How did you get them all here?" I ask. His car only has two seats.

"Turns out, the mere mention of your name in that place turns minds to mush and reservations flee. One of the men who works there gave me the keys to a van, and we loaded them up. Remind me never to do that again, kids are downright rotten in confined spaces." I giggle as I hug him.

"You are all being so silly about this," I tell him.

"Nonsense. Now, I told that man that you'd give him a call, let him know that the kids are, in fact, with you." He takes his phone out, handing it to me. I stare at it for a while before looking back up at him. "Oh, right." He takes it back, pushing at the screen then hands it back. He lifts it up to my ear and tells me that I talk into it.

I laugh as I hear ringing. "I know that much. I've

seen phones and seen people on them. I've even used the ones at the rec center, just not the cordless kinds."

A man's voice comes through on the phone, so I don't hear Jace's reply. "Hi, is this Harold? Yes, it's me, Kitten....Yes, the kids are here at the rink with me....Okay, yes that's fine.... I will. Thank you." I hand it back to Jace since I have no idea how to hang up.

"I still have no idea how you managed this, but thank you, Jace." I hug him again. Even if it isn't as fun as the kids thought it would be, at least Mikey got more time with his new friend.

"Just because you are immune to my charm, does not mean that everyone else is." He winks at me and goes to take a seat. Oh, if only I was Jace, if only I was.

I see Miss Annie and Rob come back in, carrying juice bottles and wrapped up hot dogs. She's so nice to have gotten them for the kids. I'll be sure to thank her later. I laugh when I see Logan take a seat next to the kids and hold his hand out to Miss Annie. She rolls her eyes and hands him a juice and hot dog. Oh, how I love my crazy boy.

The intro to the song starts, and I take my place at the center of the ice. How Logan got it to play when he wasn't over there was interesting, I'll ask him about it another time.

I go through my routine, using as much of the ice as possible. I hear hoots and clapping when I stick my jumps and Ash shouts "Be fucking careful!" when I zip past them, gaining speed for my triple axel. I land it and after another toe-touch, I finish in the center again. My smile can't be contained as the whole group throws roses onto the ice. Or well, most of them, the kids can't seem to make them over the wall. I giggle and take a bow. I can't believe they went through so much trouble for a four and a half minute routine.

I skate to the opening and am greeted with hugs from the kids then a pat on cheek from Miss Annie, followed up by big bear hugs from the guys. Remy is last, and he looks at me proudly.

"You could do this professionally if you wanted to Kitten, you were very good out there," He tells me. I blush and tell him thank you. I know he's only saying that because he's never seen a real pro but still, it's nice to hear.

"Where did all the flowers come from? I didn't see anyone bring them in?" I ask him.

"Logan arranged a delivery last night, and Miss Annie was kind enough to place them behind the benches before we arrived. Nice touch yes?" Remy's eyebrow shift up. Is he seeking approval?

"Oh yes! Very nice touch. You guys always find ways to make me feel special." I say sincerely.

"Kitten! Kitten!" I hear Mikey calling me. I turn to see what he's so excited about. "Here, we made you these. Mine's first since it was *my* idea." He tells me proudly, doing a surprisingly good impression of Jace's smug smile.

I take the folded pieces of construction paper. The first one is blue with 'Happy Birthday' scribbled in white crayon. I unfold it to read what it says. "Don't read that out loud!" Mikey says in a panic.

"Okay, I won't," I tell him. Was I supposed to if he didn't add that? The card reads:

Deer Kitten,

Thank u for beinG my friend. U are a good sKater. I hope I am as good as u one day. u are preTty. i like When u play baskeTball with me eVen though u are not gooD at it. dont tell anyonE but i like your Hugs too. sometimes i wish u were my MOM or my big Sister. HAPPY BIRTHDAY!!!!

love BIG MIKE

P.S. u caN still call me MIKEY just not iN front of JACE

P.P.S U are the prieTtiest girl

At the bottom is a picture of three stick people. One is really tall, and two of them are shorter. I think the one with crazy hair is me. I feel the tears on my face and wipe them away before looking at Mikey. He looks uncomfortable, shifting from foot to foot. A frown on his cute little face.

"You don't like it?" He asks.

I smile widely at him, hugging him hard. "I love it, Mikey. It's my first birthday picture ever. It's perfect."

"You've never had a birthday card?" His horrified expression is priceless. I shake my head at him.

"That's sad Kitten. Here, let me show you." He takes the card back and points at the picture. "That's you with your long hair. There's me in the middle and Jace. I think I made him too tall, though." He frowns at his work.

"No way, it's just perfect. Thank you for the card and the picture Mikey, but who told you it was my birthday?"

"Jace," He answers simply. Like Jace's word is law and that's the way it is.

I seek out Jace, standing behind the group of kids. "Happy birthday Kitten. I explained that it was your birthday today and Big Mike here, ordered everyone to make you a card. That's why we were running a little late. I see that it was worth it though. Good call Big Mike." He says the last part as he high fives Mikey.

I look at the rest of my cards, smiling and shaking my head at the adorable pictures and kind words they gave me. There's one covered in glitter that simply read: Your A, and then there's more glitter in the shape of a star. I look up as Miss Annie makes her way to me.

"Happy birthday Kitten, ma dearest girl, ta think you're all done growed up." She shakes her head. "I gotta git back, but you have fun taday girl." She walks off as Rob gives me an awkward hug, to the sound of many growls. He blushes and trails after Miss Annie.

I look at all of them. "This has been the best birthday ever, thank you guys so much," I say honestly. They said it's my birthday, so I just go with it. I've never had one, and these cards are a great gift.

"You really think it's over?" Logan gasps in mock horror. "With me as the party planner, you think this is the best I've got?" He shakes his head at me. Are there more cards?

"Come on, I think it's time we got these kids back. What do you say, Kitten? You and me ride in the van with Jace and the kids?" I nod my head vigorously. Yes, let's annoy Jace with the kids.

I change out of my skates and take them to my locker as the guys get the kids loaded back up and go to their own vehicles. I pass Adam on the way out, but he doesn't say anything, only stares at me. I rush out of there and hop in the van that is more of a small white bus. Jace is telling the kids to sit down, but no one is listening. I giggle at the sight. They *are* crazy in here.

"*Hey*! Listen up! Sit down or you don't get any cake!" Mikey shouts. The other kids quiet and take their seats. I sit, shocked as he takes his own seat, next to me across the aisle. Commanding little thing isn't he? Maybe he'd get along with Remy too. I never expected that out of the shy boy. Maybe being around Jace really has had a positive effect on him.

The kids teach me a game called 'I spy' on our way to the rec center. You have to say 'I spy something' then you name a color. I'm apparently horrible at this because I keep picking things we've already passed. It's not my fault they didn't specify that the object you named had to be *in* the van.

It's one of the little girls' turn and she says. "I spy something pretty."

"Shhh. There are other girls around, you can't say something is prettier than them, right in front of them." Says the boy sitting next to Mikey, who looks at him for approval.

"No doofus that only applies to us menfolk. And it's 'you can't say a girl is pretty in front of another girl. Right Jace?" He rolls his eyes at his friend as he asks Jace in the driver's chair in front of me.

"Correct, young Sir," Jace says regally.

Logan cracks up laughing next to me. "You taught him that? God that's funny." He leans around me to look at Mikey and his friend. "You should also know that when a girl says something is pretty, you always agree, even if it's butt faced ugly." The three of them roll around laughing as we pull up to the rec center.

After everyone has parked and gotten out, I jump on Kellan's back for a piggyback ride, and we enter the gymnasium part of the rec center. The kids who ran ahead squeal in delight at something, causing my guys to chuckle. When Kellan steps in I can see why. There are three tables set up. One with open pizza boxes and white plates, one with a dozen different buckets of ice cream and bowls, and one with all kinds of candies and cookies and peanuts, other stuff too but I don't know what they are. Yet. The gym is decorated in long strands of paper in neon colors, and there are like...millions of balloons everywhere.

"Kitten...uh...you're kind of choking me here," Kellan says. I release my death grip that I didn't know I had, and hop down to the floor.

My guys surround me as the stupid tears threaten to fall again. "Is this all for me?" I ask in wonder.

Jace starts to answer, but Tristan interrupts him. "Don't tell her anything here is definitely hers. I don't think they'd like if we took the basketball hoop with us on our way out." Tristan winks at me, and I stick my tongue out at him. He does it back.

"As I was saying. Yes, Kitten, this is your party, but, it's for everyone to enjoy." Jace high fives Tristan and I kick him in the shin. Lightly, after all, that was pretty funny.

Remy clears his throat. "I believe the staff here have some gifts for you, Kitten. I hope you don't mind, but we thought it would be best if we told them that it's your eighteenth birthday. The more people who think you're an adult, the better for all of us. No one can take you away if you're of age."

"Who knows, you might actually be eighteen anyway," Reed says, shrugging.

"That's true." Ash chimes in. He tugs at my hair tie, making Logan huff. He just raises a brow at him and turns back to me. "Happy birthday, Sunshine."

I wave him to bend down and I kiss his cheek. "Thank you my Shadow." He smiles at me before heading off to the pizza table.

Tristan fixes me a plate of pizza and sits next to me and Kellan as we lean against the closed bleachers and watch the craziness in front of us. Reed, Jace, Remy, and Logan are playing basketball with a group of boys. Each one of them is totally cheating, giving the boys the ball and lifting them up to the baskets so they can drop it in. It looks like Finn is giving a science lesson on static electricity to a few kids. Taking a balloon and rubbing it on their heads as they watch them stick to the wall. I watch in disbelief as a group of tiny little girls reduce big, strong Ash, to a pony and take turns, two or three at a time, riding his back as he crawls around on his hands and knees.

"I wish Reed had his camera right now," I mutter.

"Already a step ahead of you sweetie." I look over to Tristan, and he has his phone out, pointing it at Ash. I lean back to look at the screen.

"Are you taking pictures with that?" I ask.

"Better, I'm recording a video of him. Blackmail's a bitch." He laughs. While it is funny, I can't help but love Ash for doing this. My insides melt watching him. All the guys seem to be great with kids in their own ways.

After I play a game of basketball with the guys and little boys, and we took turns racing, and we beat up a helpless paper horse filled with candy, we had bubble races. Those were fun. We each got a small can of bubbles, and then we'd blow on the little stick and blow the bubbles over a finish line. I couldn't stop laughing long enough to win, but I had a great time trying.

I got pulled away by the staff, Ash insisting he come with me, to the office where I blew out a candle on a cupcake. Which I shoved in my mouth immediately after I was told to make a wish. It was chocolate, and I couldn't help myself. I was given a t-shirt wrapped in pink paper with the word 'staff' written on the back, the rec's logo on the front. I also got a whistle like the workers here have. I always wanted one these.

"We all pitched in on your real present Kitten." An older woman named Mrs. Smith told me, handing me a small box. I open it, and my hands fly to my mouth as I gasp. It's a gold bracelet with little dangly things. I pick the bracelet up and flick one of them, giggling as it sways back and forth. "Those charms are in the shape of people, and we thought it could represent the kids here. You've been coming here for years Kitten, and we'd love it if you joined the staff as a volunteer. The children just adore you and look up to you. I think I speak for everyone when I say that it has been an honor to watch you grow up into the beautiful young woman you've become."

She gets teary eyed, and so do I. I didn't know they had been paying attention. Technically, I never should have been allowed here. You either have to pay dues or prove that you can't afford it. Maybe it was just obvious that I couldn't afford it?

"Thank you. Thank you all so much. You didn't have to do this, spend money I mean. You already did enough just by letting me come here and not kicking me out." They laugh, some wiping a stray tear.

"Nonsense, Kitten. We were happy to have you. We still are." When they're done, Ash takes my new treasures for me, placing my bracelet on my wrist for me too. He puts his big arm around my shoulders as we walk back to the gym.

The little girls that seem to be entranced with Ash run at us the second we enter. "Mr. Ash, Mr. Ash! Will you help us?" They plead. Ash kneels down in front of them.

"With what?" He asks. The leader of the group whispers something in his ear that makes him smile. He nods and turns to me. "You're supposed to go color with Reed and the other kids, the rest of us have work to do."

"Okay." I smile at him. He picks up the whole group of girls with his long arms, making them giggle in delight and carries them off to a table being set up by one of the staff members. Aww, my sweet, sweet Shadow.

I stretch out on the ground next to Reed, laying on my tummy and propping myself on my elbows like he is. The kids sitting across from us do the same, moving their coloring books to the other side of ours. Reed reaches over and hands me a few crayons from his box.

"I think he likes you." Says the girl, maybe eight years old, laying directly in front of Reed.

"Why do you say that?" I ask while I flip through, looking for what I want to color.

"Because he shared his crayons with you. Boys only

do that if they like you. You should like him back. He must think you're special since he even gave you the blue one, not just the pink one that boys hate. You should probably fall in love with him now." Reed chokes at the last part, probably trying to hold back laughter. The girl never looks up from her coloring.

"Oh, really. And why should I do that?" I ask, playing along.

She drops her crayon, looking up at me like I'm the dumbest person on earth. "You should always love a boy who shares his crayons," She states seriously. I have to laugh at that.

I look to Reed, who seems to be giggling silently to himself as he shades in a purple monkey. "You're right. You gotta love a boy who shares his crayons." Reed looks up at me and smiles brilliantly.

"Just don't start kissing. That's yucky." Says the girl. Reed and I crack up laughing together. I color a red spaceship, two puppies, and a horse with a horn on its head before Ash returns with his troop of little girls.

"They have something for you, Kitten," Ash tells me. I close my book, handing Reed back his crayons, making us both laugh again, and stand to face the tiny girls slightly hiding behind Ash. Oh God, that's cute.

"Here." A shy little girl says as she practically throws what I think is a rubber band at me. I catch it, and she hides behind Ash's leg again. I look at the pink and white rubber band, then up to Ash, the question clear in my eyes. "The girls and I made you friendship bracelets using tiny rubber bands.

Oh, I see it now. I lean around Ash to look at the little girl. I've never seen her before so she must be new.

"You made this all by yourself?" I ask her as I slip it around my wrist.

She shakes her head. "Mr. Ash helped me," She answers.

"What's your name honey?"

"Julie. But my friends call me Jewels." I guess her to be around five.

"Well Jewels, my name is Kitten, and since you came to my birthday party, I think we should be friends. And since you're my friend and Mr. Ash is my friend..." I lean closer, so only she can hear. "...that means that you guys made me a double friendship bracelet, and that is the best kind ever!" She smiles brightly and finally steps from behind Ash.

"You mean it?" She asks shyly. I nod, making my expression as serious as possible. She smiles up at Ash then jumps at me, nearly knocking me off my feet, giving me a hug. The other little girls hand me the bracelets they made explaining exactly why they used each color. Who knew little girls could take rubber band bracelets so seriously? I find it both odd and delightful.

We finally get to eat the ice cream. I think someone put it away while we played, which makes me question why it was out in the first place if we couldn't eat it then. I mentally shrug. The world's a cruel place sometimes. I couldn't decide which toppings I wanted so I let Mikey and his friends choose for me. By the time it was done you couldn't even tell there was ice cream under it all. The boys were very proud of their masterpiece, so I didn't say anything, just thanked them for their expertise and sat next to Kellan.

I shared my ice cream with Kellan, who pointed out

the toppings I didn't recognize. I learned that he loves Oreo cookies, and I like the sprinkles. I ended up with vanilla ice cream because Julie pointed out that it almost matched my hair. I was unsure of the child's reasoning for my ice cream choice, but as I dug to the bottom to try it, I had to applaud her decision. It's good.

"Enjoying day one of your birthday Kitten?" Kellan asks me, taking a big bite of cookie.

I try to answer him, but it feels like something is squeezing my brain. I drop my spoon and hold my head with both hands. "Ouch! What the heck was that?" I look worriedly at Kellan, he's a doctor, he should know.

Kellan laughs, sprawling on his back on the floor. "Oh God, I was hoping that would happen. Just to see your reaction." He manages to get out through his laughter. I frown at him. He was hoping that would happen? "It was just brain freeze Kitten. No reason to panic, it happens when you eat cold things too fast."

"How was I supposed to know there was a correct speed at which to eat ice cream?" I grumble at him.

"I'm sorry. I wasn't laughing at you, Kitten. Okay, I was a little. But it happens to everyone. Don't feel bad." I pick up my spoon and push the melting mess around. I hate being laughed at and he totally set me up. "Will you forgive me if I go get more sprinkles?" He asks.

I nod. I think sprinkles could make anything better. "Maybe some of those peanut butter things too." He kisses the top of my head before he goes. He returns with a handful of each and all is forgotten.

When I'm starting to feel sick to my stomach from too much ice cream, Remy approaches me. "It's almost time to go. Did you enjoy yourself?" I nod. "Did you like the games?" I nod again, I love games. "Did you like your presents?" I nod again, yes I love all my new treasures. "Did you eat too much ice cream and are only capable of nodding?" He asks with a smile in his voice. I look up at him and nod again. "Oh, Kitten. What am I gonna do with you?" He chuckles.

Remy bends down and scoops me up in his arms. I groan, holding my full tummy and resting my head on his shoulder. I feel his laughter rumble through him and groan again.

I hear a smack somewhere before I hear Logan's voice. "Damn Kellan, why'd you let her eat herself into a fucking ice cream coma. We totally broke her on her damn birthday."

"I got her stuff." Says Ash.

"I just finished cleaning up. We should be set to go." Reed says.

"I got her shoes," Kellan says.

"Her shoes? Why did she take her shoes off?" Finn asks him.

"She said to make more room for ice cream. I don't think she was thinking clearly at that point." Kellan responds, making them all laugh as we head to the cars outside. I don't know which one I ended up in because I was dead asleep before we even got to the door. The last thought I had was of Kellan saying this was day one......

CHAPTER TWENTY-SIX

REMY

I stroke Kitten's hair as she sleeps in my lap. I wonder if she knows she talks in her sleep. I'm fairly certain she has whole conversations with herself each time she closes her eyes. The poor girl looks exhausted. I should tell the men to keep the goodnights short from now on, but I'm not sure if they'll listen. I'm not sure I'll listen. Miss Kitten has made a habit of coming to each of us at night. I've never seen my men rush to bed the way they do now.

"We're going to have to start watching what we feed her, she's had quite an unhealthy diet recently," Tristan says from the passenger side of my SUV. I let Ash drive since Kitten passed out in my arms. I didn't want to let her go just yet.

"I think everything is still just so new to her. Give her more time, and I think she'll stop thinking she needs to eat as much of something she likes as fast as she can." Reed states. I think he's right about that. Her street mentality hasn't gone away just because she gets food regularly now. That will come with time. She was used to eating what she could when she could. Besides, even I'm not brave enough to take chocolate away from Kitten. I laugh out loud at the thought.

Ash's eyes meet mine in the rearview mirror. "What are you...?" He trails off and his eyes narrow. "Shit, I think we've got a tail, Rem," He says. What the fuck?

"Make some turns, see if they follow. Reed, get the others on a group call." I hold Kitten a little tighter to me. I don't know if we really are being followed, or Ash just thinks we are. If he's right, I'm sure it's about the girl. No wolf would be stupid enough to attack a pack of changed wolves. Not without an army.

"I got the other cars on speaker Remy," Reed says. I give him a nod of acknowledgment.

"Check in," I order. Five voices fire back at me. Good.

"We need to make some unscheduled turns, get Reed's vehicle behind the tail as soon as possible. Finn, keep your truck one street over at all times. Radio silence until we know for sure. Stay on the line, keep it open."

A few turns and a couple minutes later Ash states. "They've made every turn we have, anyone traveling to a particular place wouldn't have followed us in a circle." I see his knuckles tighten on the wheel. Shit. He was right.

"We need to get her home, but we can't lead them there. Some of us are going to have to fight as the rest get her to safety." I say. Damn it, I won't lose this girl. Not now, not ever.

"Right, Kitten is the priority," Ash adds in. Hell yeah, she is.

I quickly go down the list, assessing my men's strengths and weaknesses. Ash and I are our hardest hitters, Tristan can fight with a clear head, where Ash and I tend to fly off the handle. Logan and Jace are our fastest, Jace making the best distraction if we need it, Logan the best shit talker if we need to buy time. Reed has more stamina for longer fights or running. Finn is good at reading opponents, usually knowing what they are going to do next even before they do. We don't really let Kellan fight unless we absolutely have to. His job is to patch us up when the fight is over, he's too valuable.

I need more information before I can decide on a plan. "I need a head count in that vehicle as soon as possible. No doubt they've figured out we know of them already." They must have been following us since the rec center. I knew we shouldn't have had her party there. If anything happens to those kids, Kitten's liable to kill us all.

"I've got four. One driver, one passenger and two in the back." Jace lists off. Okay, four. We can handle four.

"Wolves?" I ask.

"Windows are up, I can't smell them." Logan states. So it's him and Jace in Reed's SUV, the twins in Finn's truck. Alright, let's do this.

"Finn, find a place to pull over and give us your location. Kellan, stay put. You two will be on the team taking Kitten home, we're going to run her to you, be on the lookout and be ready to take off as soon as she's secured. Understood?" I order.

"Yes, Sir," They reply in unison.

"I could run her," Tristan suggests. I shake my head at him.

"You're needed here. There's only four of them. I'm sending Ash with Kitten. Logan, change in the car, be ready to jump on anyone that tries to exit that vehicle. Jace, stay behind the wheel, you're in charge of recovery. Everyone make it back to the white SUV in case of trouble, got it?" Seven replies of 'Yes Sir' hit my ears.

I turn and look at Reed. "Anyone goes down, I'm counting on you to get them in that SUV." He nods. Alright, I think all bases have been covered here.

"Stopped at the corner of Amberly Way and Donner Street, three possible routes and an apartment complex if we need to hide," Finn calls out. Good, that's a good place. "Ash, if you stop in the middle of..." He trails off just as the small four-door rams into the back of us, jolting us forward.

"*Go*! Move, move, move!" I call out. This messes up the plan a bit, I didn't want them this close to her.

Another crash and another jolt tells me that Jace has effectively blocked them in. Ash is out of the car instantly, pulling my door open. I shove a very confused and frightened Kitten at him as he reaches for her. She's thrown over his shoulder in a flash, and he takes off faster than a big man like him should move.

I hear a howl of pain right before I hear metal crunching. A quick glance shows me that Logan has pounced on the passenger side door, catching the man's arm when he closed it. I sniff the air, wolves alright, born wolves, three here and one managed to follow Ash. Tristan and Reed gets one of them pinned to the ground as I tear the driver's door from its hinges, snatching up the driver and slamming him against the car. Logan, in his wolf form, has the third guy's neck in his mouth, ready for the order to kill. He really should have stayed in the car.

"Why the fuck were you following us?" I growl at the man in my grasp, he's slightly older than me, wearing khakis' and a polo shirt. Not really stake out gear.

"W-we just....s-smelled the girl. We wanted to see who it was. That's all man! I swear!" He's doing a nice job of shaking and acting all innocent, but I think he's lying.

"T, get that one restrained, and come talk to this one." I don't want to use his real name, in case they don't know it yet. Tristan is like a walking, talking lie detector.

"We don't have anything, just knock them out for now, that one just lied his ass off though, I don't even need to see him to know that." I hear a grunt, telling me that either he or Reed did just that.

I roaring growl from Logan breaks my concentration on the man in front of me, he gets a nice hit in to my jaw before I slam his head down to the ground. He's either knocked out or dead. Either way, I don't give a fuck. The guy Logan had shifts into his wolf and takes off after Ash and Kitten, they should be long gone by now, I hope.

Logan's on the ground, wincing in pain, the motherfucker stabbed him. Reed dutifully picks him up, placing him in the back of the white SUV. "What do we do with them?" Tristan asks me, indicating the two unconscious men on the ground. I take the guy at my feet's pulse. Yup, he's dead.

"We take him with us. Tristan, you ride with me in my car, no point in leaving it if we don't have to. This one is dead, leave him. You're in charge of keeping that motherfucker asleep, check him for weapons." I bark at him.

Jace drives away, taking Logan and Reed with him. I know he'll be okay, but I still want him taken to Kellan as soon as possible. He got hurt on my watch, and I fucking hate myself right now for it. I'll hate myself over killing that piece of shit later, for now, it's just payback for my family's blood being spilled.

Tristan and I get the other piece of shit loaded into the back of my car, using our belts, he should be secure enough for the moment. As soon as we hop in, I bark at him. "Get them on the phone." I don't care who, just someone. I drive to the next street over, seeing no cars. Good, they got out of here.

"Ash isn't answering," He says. *Fuck.* "I'm calling Kellan now." I can barely make out what he's saying as he talks to someone. Ash has been by my side for centuries, we've been through everything together. Two of them went after him and Kitten. We should have been more prepared than this. We've been living comfortable for too long. I'm sure other wolves knew where we were, but they either didn't care about us because we have no desire to take over surrounding packs, or they aren't brave or strong enough to take on eight changed wolves. We're stronger than them and older than them. Born wolves age slower than humans, but they still age out and die.

"Kellan said that two of the assailants made it to

them, but no Ash and no Kitten," Tristan tells me.

"How the hell did that happen? They were right behind them!" Are they still out there? They have to be, they aren't in any of the vehicles. "What did they do with the attackers?"

"Killed them," Tristan says. That's fine with me. We only need the one for questioning anyhow.

"Tell them to head home. Now. Logan will need Kellan's help. We'll get this guy secured, then send out a search team." Two of my family members got left behind. It's unacceptable, but it has to be done. One car holds a prisoner, one an injured man, and the other the doctor. This played out in the worst possible fucking way. Ash and Kitten better be okay, or so help me God I'm bringing down this whole fucking city and setting the sky on fire.

KITTEN

My body jerks, bringing me out of my nap. I blink my eyes open, and Remy yells *'Go!* Move, move, move!' two seconds before he pushes me and arms grip me around the waist. I give out an 'oomph' as I'm slammed over a tall person's shoulder. The air gets knocked out of me, and my ribs scream in pain as I'm jostled, the ground in my line of sight a blur as my captor runs. I claw at the person's back until I can finally breathe again. As I take in a much-needed lungful of air, I smell charcoal, fire, and....It's Ash. I'd know that scent anywhere.

I stop attacking Ash once I know it's Ash, and push against his back, lifting myself up to relieve the pressure on my ribs. When I do, I see a man jump into the air, changing to a wolf before he hits the ground. It's scary as heck when it's not one of my wolves. "Ash..." I whisper.

"Shh, Kitten. We're gonna have to hide." How in the world are we going to do that? The guy behind us is gaining ground, he's gonna see where we go.

"Shit, hold on Kitten," Ash mutters out.

The air is knocked out of me again as Ash slams me to the ground. He flips me over, covering me in....mud? Once he's sure no part of me is left clean, he presses me into the ground, flat on my tummy. I take it he means for me to stay. When his hand leaves my back, I panic and look up. He left me? Seriously! It's then that I realize I'm in some kind of ditch, laying in a shallow puddle of water.

I hear grunting above me, but I can't see what's happening. I'm on the verge of one of those panic attack things again. My body is shaking, my lungs burn, probably because I've forgotten how to breathe. I try to imagine that I'm doing a yoba session with Reed, but it isn't working, I'm not calming down. I picture Tristan's chocolate eyes and his calming voice, but that only makes my panic intensify. I don't know where Tristan is or if he's okay, I don't know if any of them are okay. Especially Ash. There was someone chasing us, he could have hurt Ash.

I move to get up, but Finn's voice in my head stills me. Telling me to think rationally. Ash is strong. Nobody is stronger than Ash, right? He wouldn't have just left me here, there must be some kind of plan. He took the time to cover me in mud, he wouldn't do that if he was just leaving me here, would he? Another voice in my head overtakes Finn's, it's Davis', telling me to 'wait right here' as he scouts an area for possible bad guys. Is that what Ash is doing? I thought Davis told me that when he needed to pee. Is the Davis in my head telling me that Ash took a pee break? I lay my forehead in the mud, firmly believing I've lost my damn mind.

ASH

I put Kitten in the deep, but narrow hole someone had in their yard and covered her with mud. That should hide her scent well enough for now. I hate myself for leaving her, but I had to, I smelled two wolves dead ahead of us that weren't my brothers and one behind us. I couldn't fight and protect her too. The fucker that was behind me was waiting and ready for me when I came out of the ditch. If he was smart he would have taken the time to shift, guess he was a stupid fucker. He got me good with a blade, but I was able to snap his neck easily. Catching him before he alerted the others where we were.

I jumped over the ditch, hoping anyone following our scent would continue to follow mine over the ditch now that Kitten's had disappeared. Not the best plan, but it's all I had. I had ran through a few yards, circling back and climbing up on a roof where I can keep watch on Kitten's hole and see any other threats. I hear them, but I can't see them. I hear Logan's howl before I see a wolf below me and another guy running from the side of the house. They meet up and take off together towards where Finn and Kellan are waiting on us. *Shit*! I want to go help my brothers but they stand a better chance than Kitten does, I can't leave her alone. There's still two wolves out here that I know of.

I'm about to say fuck it and head back to Kitten when two men come running from the direction the other guy did on the side of the house. They pause and call out for a 'Paul,' in a whisper. Stupid fucks. They start talking, and I listen in, not daring to breathe.

"This isn't worth it man. The wolves have gone, we can just leave." One of them pleads with the other one.

"No way, they'd find us and kill us if we just ran off. Besides, they promised to turn us, remember that? All we have to do is get the girl." So, someone is changing humans for a price? Fuck, that's not good. What is good though, is that these two are humans, no match for me, and they can't smell me up here either.

"I don't know man, that Daily dude was talking about some pretty weird shit with that girl." The first guy says skeptically.

"Not our problem! Keep looking, that big fucker came through here with her. Shoot *him* and get *her*. Not that fucking hard. Go!" I just stop myself from laughing. This guy has no idea what he's talking about, it's hard as hell to get a kill shot at a wolf, we can hear the bullets coming and move out of the way. Looks like this Daily character either doesn't know that or didn't care to mention it to them.

I wait for the other one to run off before I jump from the roof, pouncing on the dumber of the two. I hear sickening crunching noises as I land, telling me that I already killed him. I shift into my wolf. I'm far stealthier in this form. Sniffing the air tells me that the coward found Kitten's hole, so I run full speed.

When I get there three seconds later, the prick is sliding down the side, going after my Little One. I can hear her heartbeat, and it's going a mile a minute. She's scared to death. When I look over the side, ready to pounce, I'm shocked as shit by what I see. My little Kitten is on top of the guy, attacking his face with elbows, fists, and her nails.

The guy under Kitten, screeches in pain, holding his hand over his eye that's gushing blood, scrambling away from her.

I bark to get her attention, and she jumps. When she looks at me, I see the tears streaming down her face. Oh, Kitten. My poor girl. There's no time to dwell on that though. I jump into the hole and take the fuckers neck in my teeth, ripping his throat out. After, I take advantage of the fact that my sweet girl has turned away and shift back to human, climbing from the hole and shifting back to my wolf. I needed my height to get out.

I bark lowly to get her attention, and she jumps, her head snapping to me. Her eyes are frightened at first, but she must realize it's me because she scrambles to climb up the side. She has to grab at my head to pull herself out.

I know we don't have time for it, but I allow her to throw her arms around my neck and sob her little heart out for a while. Eventually though, I pull away from her. We have to get the hell out of here. I bark again and lower myself to the ground next to her, hoping she catches my meaning. My smart girl does and hops on my back, clinging to me tightly as I take off in the direction we came from in the first place.

When we get to where Remington and Reed's SUV's were, they're already gone. I turn around, hoping to catch Finn and Kellan on the street over, but Kitten has other ideas.

KITTEN

I get off of Ash, wiping away tears that refuse to stop falling. Stupid things, I have no time for you! Ash barks at me again, startling me. "Stop that!" I yell at him. He growls shortly, but I ignore him. I didn't mean to yell, but I'm jumpy enough as it is.

I hurry to the crunched up car that was following us. I need information. If there is anything important in here, someone will be back to get it, and soon. I go the door that has been ripped from its hinges and dive inside. There are papers strewn about, but I don't take the time to look at them. I tuck my shirt into my pants and stuff the papers down the front of my shirt hurriedly. I check under the seats, the pull-down things at the top of the windshield, the lift up thing between the seats and something Finn calls a 'glove box.' Anything I find goes down my shirt. The back seat looks empty of anything.

I jump back out of the car, looking at Ash, making sure he's still okay. I walk to the back of the car, seeing the storage space lid is already partly open. I lift the lid, checking for anything of value. A pack of bottled water, rope, a shovel, black plastic, a tire. Under the tire is a square package, wrapped in cloth, wrapped in plastic. If they took that much care to protect it, it's valuable. It's too big to fit in my shirt though, I'll have to carry it.

As I walk back to Ash, ready to go now, I notice a dead body. I try not to throw up at the sight of his misshapen head. I set the package down and hurry over to him. It, I tell myself, it, the man it was is gone now. I check his coat, finding more papers. In the shirt they go. I check the pockets of his pants, finding a wallet and a set of keys. There's a portable phone too, and I almost leave it, but decide to take it too. Finn knows things I don't, and I don't know if any of this stuff will be useful, but it could be.

I pick up the package and run back to Ash. I climb on his back again and hug him tightly, squishing the package between us as he runs. When we get to a spot between two houses, Ash barks at me, standing in front of shredded clothing that I recognize as his. I go to search it, and he barks again. I look at him, not knowing what he wants. He uses his nose to push the fabric at me. I bundle it all up and take it with us. No more barking, so I guess I did what he wanted.

Ash slows down, watching an intersection and sniffs the air. He whines, making my panic want to burst to the surface. Later, I tell myself, later I will break down, just not now. He seems to come to some decision as he takes off at full speed, crossing a street to a wooded area. I grip him tighter, the mud making me slippery. I don't know where we're going or where the others are, but I have Ash. He killed for me, he protected me. He came back for me. As long as I have him, everything will be okay, he'll get us back to the others.

ASH

This has to be the most uncomfortable run of my life. Not that it matters. Kitten's weight is nothing. It's the stuff she jammed down her shirt poking me in the back with every move that's killing me. That and her hands pulling at my coat. I'm fine with that though, as long as she holds on until I can get her home. I have to stick to the woods, adding another eight miles on. We'll be lucky if no one in that neighborhood saw us and reports it, no way can I take the roads with Kitten clinging onto me. A wolf might be a little out of place, but a girl riding one would do more than raise a few eyebrows.

I can't believe we even have to do this. I can't believe we were left behind. Something really fucking bad must have happened for Remington to leave behind his best friend and the girl he loves. That thought doesn't make me feel any better though. This is the most bat-shit-crazy night of my life. I can't even process what the fuck happened tonight. I shake my head and push myself to run faster. I need to get to my brothers, and I need to get Kitten to safety.

CHAPTER TWENTY-SEVEN

REMY

Just as I turn the ignition in Finn's truck, I see the most beautiful sight I've ever seen. A huge black wolf with a long haired girl clinging to it. I step out of the truck, shouting. "They're here!" With our wolf hearing, I know everyone in the damn house heard me. Logan and Reed get out of the truck as well, Finn and Jace bursting through the front door, proving me right.

Ash stops right in front of us, dropping to the ground. I go to help Kitten up, but she flinches away, standing on her own, although shakily. She walks stiffly to the house, not saying a word, not even looking at us. When she gets just beyond the doorway, she drops a heavy, black square to the ground. Then she untucks her bulging shirt and shakes out all kinds of things. With her back to us, she whispers. "Finn." And points at the ground, before walking away.

Before I can even think about following her, I'm tackled from behind. A blow lands on my ear that hurts like a motherfucker. Only one person I know can hit that hard. I push myself up, flipping over. Another punch hits my jaw, the same fucking spot as earlier tonight. I reign in my wolf that's begging me to be let out. I'm not going to fight Ash, not now.

It takes all of them but they finally manage to restrain Ash enough that he quits fighting back. "YOU! You fucking left us there! What the fuck Remy? How could you do that?" He shouts.

"Logan was hurt, he took priority when we couldn't find you. The way things worked out, we all had to go. We were coming back for you." I explain, even to my own ears, it doesn't sound like enough.

"The way things worked out! The way things worked out Remy was you all left me to defend Kitten alone! And with four of them after us!" He stumbles back, obviously tired.

"Come on Ash, let's get you to Kellan, we'll sort this out later," Reed tells him, tugging him to the door.

I know Ash is pissed at me, and Logan is injured. Hell, Kitten looked pretty broken as well. But we all made it back. We're all here now. We have a ton of shit to do. Things to figure out. But my family is whole in this moment, and I'm grateful for it.

REED

I managed to get Ash settled down enough to walk in the house, and to Kellan. It looked like he got a nasty cut on one of his arms. Kellan got it cleaned out but didn't bother to stitch it up, it'll heal overnight if he rests it. Logan was passed out on one of the cots. His injury was a bit more serious, but he'll make it. That asshole punctured one of his lungs. I'm happy he was given something to knock him out for a while.

Once I'm sure Ash is under control, I seek out Kitten. She didn't look so good when she came in. I don't blame her. She just recently learned that we exist and then finds out some other wolves might be after her, and then tonight she witnesses an attack. I shake my head. Kitten has been through enough already, she doesn't need this.

When I enter Tristan's room, I'm greeted by the sight of several of my brothers. They have expressions of worry and anger as they sit about the room. The door to the bathroom is open, and steam is pouring out of it. I know it's Kitten in there, but why is the door open? Tristan is standing at the doorway, staring inside, looking for the world like someone stole his favorite toy. I walk to him and lean around, peeking inside.

Kitten is on her knees in the shower, fully clothed still. The hot water is streaming down, hitting the top of her head, making her hair fall in her face like a curtain. The bare skin of her arms are a bright shade of pink, no doubt the result of the too hot water. Seeing Kitten like this is breaking my heart. She's so strong, but right now she looks helpless and lost. I watch her for a few minutes, waiting for her to come out of it, but I can't take this any longer.

"Come help me Tris." I tap my shoulder into his as I move past him. I cross straight to the shower, reaching in and adjusting the temperature of the water. I step back and start to undress, looking to Tristan, telling him with my eyes that he should do the same. I leave my boxers on, and so does he.

I stand in front of Kitten, blocking the spray from hitting her any longer, and she still doesn't look up. I gesture with my hand for Tristan to move behind her. When he does, I reach down and lift her stiff body, getting her to her feet. She's completely unresponsive. I don't allow my despair for her to show on face. Kitten is weak right now, and it's my turn to be the strong one.

I turn her and place her in Tristan's arms. He gives me a questioning look, but I don't bother to explain, it'll be clear in a moment. I pick up the bottle of shampoo she uses and squirt some into my palm, rubbing them together. I know she came in here to get clean, and I'm going to help her with that. I massage the shampoo into her scalp slowly, moving my fingers in slow circles. I take my time, making sure I get every inch of her head. I work my way down to the ends of her extremely long hair. When I'm done, I nudge Tristan forward, into the spray. I run my fingers through her hair, making sure it all gets out. The water running to the drain is still brown from the mud, so I do it all again before moving on to conditioner.

Once Kitten's hair is back to its lustrous platinum blond color, I indicate to Tristan to have her stand on her own. I'm unsure about this next part, but worst case scenario, she gets mad at me. She'd have to break out of her spell for that to happen, so either way I feel this is the right move. I take a deep breath before I pull at the hem of her shirt, lifting it up. Kitten doesn't protest, she doesn't even look at me. Tristan lifts her arms up gently, helping me pull the fabric free. Kitten sways a bit, so Tristan takes her back in his arms, her back to his chest. I pick up the washcloth and squeeze out some body wash.

I start with her hand, scrubbing between each tiny finger, up her wrist and forearm, her elbow, her bicep, until I get to her shoulder. I wring the rag out and do her other arm. I leave her bra on, scrubbing her neck and collarbones before moving the rag under the fabric, being as clinical as I can when touching an intimate area of the woman I'm in love with. But now is not the time to take pleasure, I just want to take care of her. I scrub the mud off her ribs and stomach before Tristan turns her so I can do her back. He lifts her hair out of the way for me, and I see an old scar. It runs from one shoulder blade to the other in a straight line. It's faint, but I can make it out. Kitten flinches when I run the rag over it, soaping up her skin.

I hold my breath and turn my head to the side while I peel her out of her leggings. Tristan has to lift each of her legs for me, as Kitten still hasn't responded to us. It looks like the mud from her upper body has ran to her underwear, soiling them. I leave them for now, starting at her hips, working my way down her thighs and calves, to her tiny feet and toes. I whisper to Jace to bring me a towel, knowing he will hear me. He opens the shower door and holds it out, his eyes meeting with Tristan's. He doesn't want to disrespect her either it seems. He steps back and leans against the sink. I wrap the towel around Kitten's hips before reaching under and pulling her panties away, tossing them to the side. I rinse out the rag and stand, getting more soap. I reach my hand under the towel rubbing it back and forth a few times, wishing

Kellan were doing this part. I've never cleaned a girl there before. Well, not when I was actually trying to clean her. I move on to her backside quickly, not letting my mind go there right now.

When Kitten is thoroughly cleaned and rinsed, I take her from Tristan and lead her from the shower. Jace wraps her hair in a towel as Tristan takes another one and dries her body. Remington whispers from the bedroom that he has clothes for her, so I pick her up and carry her to the bed. I stand her in front of it as Tristan slips new underwear up her legs, and then a pair of loose yoga pants. I remove her bra quickly as Remy pulls a red shirt over her head and helps me put her arms through. Tristan puts a pair of footie socks on her feet once I sit her down on the end of the bed, and Jace takes up a spot behind her, drying her hair with the towel and brushing it out as I go talk to Remy in the corner of the room.

"Do we put her to bed like this? Is it shock?" He asks me. Which is so out of place, that at first, I don't know how to respond.

"Kellan's the doctor, but yeah, I'd say she's in shock. She was just mostly naked in a shower with two men and didn't blink an eye." I say, exasperated. Not at him, just at the whole situation.

Remington runs a hand down his face. "I have to go make things right with Ash, check in with Kellan and Logan as well. Can you handle things here?" I can tell that this night is wearing on him too. I see the guilt in his eyes, and it shouldn't be there.

"Sure thing Rem, I know what she needs," I say. He nods and turns to go. I grab his arm. "And Remy, you gotta let this guilt shit go. There was no 'right' call to make. You didn't know what was going on with Ash and Kitten, but you trusted that he would look out for her. He did, he got her back here. What you did know was that Logan was hurt, and he needed Kellan, and you had an unsecured prisoner. Like I said...there wasn't a 'right' call, but you did what you could with the information you had." He nods his head again and leaves the room.

I hope at least some of my words got through to Remy, but for now, I have to concentrate on fixing Kitten. Jace has finished brushing her hair and now they both look lost. I guess they do better when they have a task. I know the feeling. I whisper to Tristan to get dressed and meet the three of us in my studio. He walks to his closet as Jace picks Kitten up in his arms like she's made of glass. We arrive at the door next to my bedroom, and I flip the light on and gesture for him to take her inside. I head to my room to get some dry clothes on.

JACE

I carry my girl into Reed's studio and sit against the wall with her still in my arms. I don't know why we're here right now, but I don't care. Tonight has been one crazy thing after another. Today started out so perfectly, just like Logan and I had planned. He wanted to give her a birthday, and I agreed that she needed one. Things went better than I ever expected. She had fun today and felt special, I know she did. The little thing had worn herself out at her party, which was fine by me, I didn't want her discovering her real gift if she decided to go exploring tonight.

Right now, I would rather her find her gift than be like she is now. After sitting behind the wheel and watching as one of my brothers was stabbed and another had to kill a man, I didn't think it could get worse. When I heard that we had to leave Kitten and Ash behind, I was devastated. I understood the reason but....it was the hardest thing I've ever had to do. I drove as fast as I could make the box-like SUV go, hoping to get Logan to Kellan quickly and go back for them before something bad happened. Ash must have ran his ass off to get here as quick as he did. It makes me wonder if we had stayed just a bit longer....

No. It doesn't matter. It already happened, and there's no changing it now. Obviously, something bad *did* happen though. Or else Kitten wouldn't be in the catatonic state she's in now. I run my fingers through her gorgeous hair as Reed comes back in just a pair of jeans. He walks to one of his easels and sets the canvas aside, putting a blank one up. What is he doing? Now really isn't the time for this. He grabs tubes of paint, paintbrushes, and countless other things, placing them around the easel. He also gets his sketchbook and a pencil.

"Bring her over here, in front of me," he tells me. I'll never understand his artistic strangeness, but it couldn't possibly hurt at this point. I don't know what to do to bring the girl I'm falling for back to me. What's in my arms is just a shell of that girl. I place her on her knees, slumped over, where Reed indicated. He waves me back, and we both take a seat against the wall by the door, on the floor. I shoot him a questioning look, but he just rests his head against the wall.

"Now we wait," He whispers. I thump my head back as well. Yes, now we wait. I just don't know what for.

———————— ● ● ————————

KITTEN

I know I should be uncomfortable right now. Sitting here on my knees awkwardly. But I don't. I don't feel anything. I'm aware of my surroundings, yes. I'm sitting in a room with art supplies spilled around me, staring at a blank thing you paint on. I'm aware, I just don't feel anything about it. I didn't feel the water in the shower, even though I know it should have hurt it was so hot. I didn't feel anything when Tristan and Reed came in there with me. Nothing as they washed and dressed me. Nothing. All I see are the dead bodies from earlier tonight, taking turns flashing in my mind. The one in the hole, the one by the car, the one where Ash's clothes were, the two that were laying near the intersection that I didn't even realize I had seen. My stupid photographic memory won't let me forget every single detail about tonight. But I don't feel anything about that either.

A pencil is placed in my hand, someone pushing my fingers around it. I know if I would shift my eyes, I'd find Reed. But I don't. He and Jace are here, but I don't care, I don't care about anything. A sketchbook is placed on my lap, open to a new page. I stare at it. I don't know for how long, but it doesn't matter. Time doesn't matter anymore. The longer I look at it though, the more I decide I hate it. I resent it. I can't stand to look at it. It's staring back at me, all pure and white and clean. Images of gore and death and mud fill my mind as this piece of paper mocks me from below. How dare this stupid paper do this to me! How dare it have a blank slate while my head is filled with too much! Too much hurt, too much pain, too much sadness and worry and anger! Anger....yes, I like anger. I'll show that condescending paper.

ASH

Remington came back to Kellan's office and spoke to me. At first, I had wanted to hurt him again, but Kellan stopped me, telling me that Logan would wake up if we made too much noise. I didn't want him to be in more pain than he already was, so I had sat and listened. He apologized, saying that he trusted me with Kitten, and he believed I could protect her. That he didn't know about the extra guys waiting. That he got word that all four known assailants were taken care of and he was coming right back for us. That he needed to get Logan help, and he took priority at that point. After hearing him out, I don't know if I would have made a different choice. Tonight has been one big clusterfuck, and I don't really want to stay pissed at my best friend. We need each other, and Kitten needs all of us together if we're to protect her from whoever sent those fucks.

I've been standing here for about an hour now. Watching as Kitten sits like a lifeless doll in the middle of a mess. I had time to get bandaged up, talk to Rem, shower and change before I came here. I'm told that she's been this way ever since she came in. She saw a lot tonight, but I don't know if that's what's wrong with her or not. She handled herself well before. I had stopped and got AJ for her, but I'll wait until she comes out of this to give him to her. I kind of need him right now. I need him as a piece of Kitten in case she never comes back to us.

***

REMINGTON

I find a seat against the wall next to Jace. We're all watching Kitten, waiting for her to either pass out or move or speak, *something*. Ash is starting to worry the fuck out of me, as he keeps petting the stuffed wolf that he shares with Kitten. Seeing a large, full grown man playing with a child's toy is quite disturbing, especially since I know him. Ash doesn't have a soft center to his outer shell. Or at least he didn't until our woman arrived. After some time, Kellan takes a seat next to me. He looks exhausted and worried, we all are. We need to have a meeting, talk about what happened and where we go from here. But I know that that I won't have their full attention until Kitten either falls asleep or comes out of it.

***

KITTEN

I grip the pencil tighter in my hand and bring it to the paper. I begin to draw the scene in the hole. The big black wolf with his gleaming white teeth. Teeth around a man's neck, blood shooting out of the puncture wounds, the man's wide and fearful eyes. Eyes that know what's happening to him knowing that it's too late. One of his eyes is gushing blood, it's streaming down his face. I remember the anger I felt as the man came at me. Anger at being left alone. Anger at thinking that even though I managed to find a family...I was going to die in a ditch anyway. Something I've spent my whole life trying to avoid. As soon as the picture is done, I rip the page away.

On the new blank page, I draw the second man. I don't feel anger when I see him. I feel sadness. Sadness for the choices he made that led him to his death. Sadness that another soul left this earth. A soul that was not meant for evil, not meant to do bad things, but did them anyway and led him here, where he died of a cracked skull. I continue drawing, continue to gain back my feelings, gain control of them, work out the way I feel about each 'photo' in my mind. I finally pick up the paintbrush, deciding that my last drawing needs to be in color. Too many emotions flood me to use just gray. Time passes as I use color after color, stroke after stroke, lines, circles, layers, everything to complete what I see in my mind. I move at a frantic pace, eager to get it out of my head. I need to see this, really see it. *this* is what kept me going, *this* is what I would have regretted leaving if I had been taken from this world tonight.

When I'm done, my body slumps back to the floor. I'm tired. Mentally, emotionally and physically. I look at my painting, happy to have it in front of me. I can hold it now. I made it mine. My eyes flutter closed, and I try to lift them, but it doesn't happen. I don't know what happens after that.

REED

I saw the anger building in Kitten as she sat there. It was slow but unmistakable. I was expecting her to go into a fit at any moment. I had thought that if she got it all out of her system, she would be okay. It works for me. But she's been sitting there for so long that I lost hope of it working. When she grips the pencil, my heart almost leaps from my throat. She moved! A few minutes later the pencil starts flying over the paper, her face set in rage. It's unnerving, seeing her so angry when she's such a gentle person, but at least she's moving. At least she isn't just sitting there.

Hours pass and the sun is peeking over the horizon before she falls back to the floor, her paintbrush in her hand, laying limply to the side. Paint speckles her face and clothing, but the small smile on her face allows me to breathe fully again. She's going to be okay. It worked like I had hoped after all. Ash catches her as she finally passes out, giving into her exhaustion. He places that damn stuffed wolf on her stomach as he picks her up, carrying her to my room next door. We each take turns kissing her forehead, temples, and cheeks and then follow Remy to his office.

Tristan nudges my shoulder. "How did you know that would work?" He asks me.

I shrug. "I didn't. I just hoped."

"Listen up, we're two short right now, so I'm not holding a family meeting just yet. We'll wait for Finn and Logan. Ash and I will patrol the grounds. Kellan, stay with Logan. The rest of you go back to Kitten. Keep her safe. Now..." Remy trails off as Finn rushes in.

"Dump your phones. *Now!*" He says and everyone

pulls out their phones, stomping them to the ground, or crushing them in their hands.

"I take it that you are going to explain that?" Remy asks.

Finn smiles and shakes his head. "Yeah, because our girl's a genius."

CHAPTER TWENTY-EIGHT

FINN

I don't feel guilty for killing two people like I thought I would. I've been waiting for the feelings to come, but they haven't. How interesting. I suppose that killing to protect my brother makes me feel differently on the subject. I feel guilty for leaving Ash and Kitten on their own, but I knew Ash was more than capable, and Kitten is a strong girl. I had to keep reminding Kellan of that on the way here.

When they showed up, covered in mud and blood, I had known something had happened, but they made it back, and that's what matters here. I had watched Kitten pull away from Remy and walk in a trance-like state to the house. The others probably thought she was in shock, but I knew better. Kitten needed time to process. She was stuck in her head. That's to be expected with someone with her mental capabilities after a traumatic event. I saw her drop several items to the floor from out of her shirt and heard her say my name, pointing to them. I'm sure that's all she could manage at the time, and it was okay with me, I'm glad she could do that much.

I'm unaware of what prompted her to retrieve these items, but I could kiss the snot out of her. Most of the papers had mud smeared on them, but I managed to get most of it off without damaging them. She brought home a goldmine of information on our attackers. We knew before that a man named Charles Daily was interested in her, but we didn't know why. The first thing I did was retrieved the cell phones. One, I recognized as Ash's. It was broken, explaining why we couldn't reach him earlier. The second cell phone wasn't any of ours, so I knew she must have taken it from one of the attackers. I ran it to my room instantly. Hooking it up to a USB cord and uploading all the information it held onto my laptop.

While the phone was being taken care of, I returned to gather all the papers. Filling the bathtub with cold water, I slowly dragged each paper through it, removing the mud and leaving the ink. I set them on the floor to dry, reading each one carefully. One was simply a list of names. I don't know how that fits in yet, but I'm sure I will soon. One name stood out though. Adam Vanderson. Considering how he treated kitten previously, I doubt this is a list of people that want to bake Kitten cookies. A couple more were hand written notes on Kitten's activities outside of the house. They never stopped watching her. We would have smelled wolves, so they must have humans working for them. I'll need time to analyze the rest of the information, so I leave them to dry.

Kitten also managed to get the man's wallet, which gives us an ID on him, his address, and a possible lead. There's also a set of keys, so we don't even have to break and enter when and if we go there. How convenient. I set Ash's clothes aside, not needing to check those. I find several hairs and gather them to get to Kellan to run tests later. The last thing I check over is a square that's wrapped in both fabric and plastic. I'm a little wary of it, to be honest. For all I know, it could be a bomb. It doesn't smell like a bomb though. It smells like many, many wolves. Intriguing. I use my pocket knife to carefully cut the plastic away. It's possible that we can retrieve fingerprints or other information from it. I treat the fabric in the same manner, bagging both of them up for later inspection.

Once it's unwrapped, I see that it is a book. Not a square but a rectangle, the fabric just altered its shape. There is a crest on the front of it instead of a title. I recognize it as the symbol of the Mating Games. It's the family crest of the oldest known born werewolf family. How those men came to have anything from them, I'll never know. That family is more secure than the President, Queen, and every dictator out there combined.

I flip through the book, being careful not to tear the pages. I can't believe what I'm seeing. It seems to be a complete history of wolves. Family trees, information on mating and bonding. This is more information than we have *ever* had. A lot of what we know, we figured out ourselves. We were all left for dead, without a mentor to guide us through the werewolf world. Over time, we've picked up little things here and there from encounters we've had but this, this is amazing. I'm simply in awe. I don't have time to read through this properly at the moment, but I will.

As I go to set it down, it slips from my hand, and I catch it awkwardly. Several folded papers slip from the back of it. The first is a short list of female names, most of them crossed off. Kitten's name is on the list. The second paper is a list of female names in one column, the ones that weren't crossed off the first paper, and then a list of male names in another column. The third paper has several lines drawn across it, connecting the names with dollar amounts written above them. Kitten's name has no line or dollar amount, but her name is underlined three times. I don't know what this is, but I know it can't possibly be good. I stuff the papers back into the book and take everything with me to my room.

I check on the cell phone and see that it's done uploading. I scroll through the pictures first, seeing ones of Kitten, ones with us with her, ones of Adam and Kitten that look older, before she came to us. I switch to the text messages and at first, I'm confused. I see a text that I sent to Remington while we were at Kitten's party, telling him I'd like to start a science program for the kids there. It clicks then. They were copying our messages to each other! They have access to our phones!

I shoot up out of my chair, knocking it back as I run to find my brothers. We need to cut them off before we unwittingly give out any other information. What do they know already? How long have they been doing this? *Why* are they doing this? I rush into Remington's office, nearly breathless with my worry. I order them to destroy their phones, and thankfully, they do as I asked before asking questions.

"I take it that you are going to explain that?" Remy asks.

I smile at them. "Yeah, because our girl's a genius," I tell him as I take a seat on his desk. He can yell at me later for that. Right now, I need to catch them up to speed. "That stuff kitten brought in with her? Well, it's all very useful information. Without it, we could have only guessed as to who was behind tonight's attack. She managed to get a cell phone off one of them, and I've determined that they've had access to our phones. I don't know for how long yet because I ran down here to warn you."

"What do you mean they've had access to our phones?" Jace demands.

"Just what I said. I saw a text message that I sent to Remington while we were at Kitten's party. Same time stamp and everything. I can only assume that they were receiving them as we sent them." I explain.

Jace's face pales. "That means they know about Big Mike!"

"That means they know about a hell of a lot," Remy says his expression darkening.

"There's something else you should know. Kitten also returned with a book that looks like it came straight from the Ivaskov family's personal library. There was paperwork with her name all over it tucked inside. I could use some help figuring out what it all means." I tell them, mostly talking to Remy. He nods, running a hand through his hair.

"Go back to the phone, trace what you can. They know we know about the phones now, they'll be dumping everything as soon as possible. Ash and I are going on patrol. As soon as Logan awakes, we'll have a family meeting, sharing everything we know. Reed, you go get Kitten's drawings, maybe they show something we missed, she has a real eye for details." He orders, smiling at his last statement.

Remy continues. "Jace and Tristan, guard Miss Kitten, Kellan you return to Logan, make sure he's still stable. Let's move people, we have work to do." He claps his hands, and we scatter, each going in different directions to our own tasks.

REED

I walk with Tristan and Jace up to my rooms. Neither of them say anything about what Finn just shared, so I don't either. I'll save it for the meeting. They walk into my bedroom, and each take a side of the bed, climbing in with a still sleeping Kitten. I wish I could do the same, but I have other things to do right now.

I back out of the room, entering the door to my studio. The room's a mess, but it usually stays that way. It's the way I like it. I scoop up Kitten's discarded sketches, looking over each one. She is truly talented. It's a shame that she only draws horrible scenes from real life experiences. Poor girl. Remy is right about her attention to detail, they are so life like it's almost like looking at black and white pictures. Her shading is phenomenal. I turn to the easel, thinking I will take that as well, but stop dead in my tracks, the sketches falling to the floor.

Kitten has painted us. All of us. Sitting around the kitchen island, probably at dinner. It's from her viewpoint. I recognize her hands on the outside of the painting, her pointer fingers and thumbs forming a heart around the scene. Remy's sitting at the head of the table, looking stern, Ash looking just as broody as he really is in all black. Jace with a glow of gold around him, Logan looking mischievous, his blue streak in his hair standing out. She painted me bent over a notebook, pencil in my hand. I smile at that. Finn is reading a book that's open in front of him, Kellan has a stethoscope around his neck and a white lab coat on. Tristan is standing behind the lot of us, one hand holding a spatula, the other a plate of something. He wears a smile on his face, looking directly at me. Or well, Kitten, since this is a painting viewed through her eyes.

I can see where she had trouble with the details, our faces being a bit vague, objects blending together. It's an absolutely gorgeous painting. A hell of a thing for a first-timer, but it's obvious that painting frustrated her, she likes the precise lines that you get with a pencil. I remember the small smile she had on her face as she gazed at her work. She was smiling at us. She painted a heart around us, using her hands. Does this mean that she loves us? All of us? I'm usually very good at deciphering hidden meanings behind art, but I see no hidden meaning here. Perhaps I'm just too close to the artist to see it. I love this girl more than life. Seeing her artistic abilities only cements it for me. If she wants to continue to paint, I'd love to give her lessons, teach her everything she wants to know. I can't wait for that. I pick up the drawings once again and head to Finn's room. We have a lot of work to do.

KITTEN

I come awake and am instantly aware that I'm in Reed's cloud bed. It takes too much effort to pry my lids open, so I know I was crying. There's crust ringing my eyes, gross. I rub at them, yawning and stretching my tired muscles. I don't see anyone around and take the time to stare at the ceiling, reliving last night. I know I need to see them. To talk to them. To thank them for all they did for me. I blush from head to toe thinking about just how close I was to Tristan and Reed last night. I want to be mad about it, for the invasion of privacy. But I can't be. They took care of me when I couldn't take care of myself. I wanted desperately to be clean last night, and they knew that and made it happen.

My hand flops down on the bed, landing on something furry. It's AJ. Ash must have brought him for me. I owe Ash my life. I feel instantly guilty that I was mad at him for leaving me when he hadn't. My panic made me doubt my trust in him. I know Remy made the call to leave us behind, and that's why I had to ride Ash as he ran back. I want to be mad about that too, but I've never been in charge of a group of people before. Especially not in a situation like that. I trust him though. Trust him to make the hard calls. He didn't just leave me, he left me with Ash. That makes it different doesn't it?

I run a hand over my face, willing myself to get up. To go see my boys. I drag myself up, giving the cloud bed one last, longing look. I shuffle down the stairs and into the kitchen. Picking your feet up when you walk is overrated. They all stare at me as I walk in, Reed looking at me lovingly. I grunt at them. It's the best 'good morning' I can manage at the moment. I see that someone, probably Ash, has already made coffee, and I grunt again in utter excitement at the sight of the half-filled pot. I think I've developed an unhealthy obsession with the bitter black liquid. Maybe I should look into what makes it so addictive. Eh, another day perhaps.

The guys stay silent as I pour myself a cup, chugging the burning stuff down, and refill the mug. I take the open stool next to Jace and Kellan. Logan is across from me, looking rumpled and tired.

"You okay there Kitten?" Logan asks. His voice is scratchy, and it lacks his usual humor. I nod my head once, and grunt again, tilting my chin up at him. He laughs, then coughs. "Yeah, I'm okay too. Nice cavewoman thing you've got going on this morning." There's my fun boy I know and love. I give him a small grin and his eyes sparkle.

Reed comes over to me with a wet washrag, taking my chin between his fingers and scrubbing at my face. "You got paint splatter and pencil all over your face sweetie." His eyes shine with what I think is adoration. I blush again, I had no idea. I guess I should have looked in the mirror.

"Don't be embarrassed, it's the sexiest I've ever seen you look my little artist." He kisses my lips lightly, washing the gray off my hands before walking back to the sink.

Tristan sits a plate of toast, eggs, and bacon in front of me, kissing the top of my head as he does. No one's really talking as we eat our breakfasts, which is odd, but I don't feel like talking either so I let it go. I notice a book in Finn's hand. He's reading it as he eats. All I see is the cover.

"What book is that?" I ask, taking a bite of toast. "Where did you get it?" I rack my brain, trying to remember if it's something I've read before.

Finn must notice my expression because instead of answering, he asks his own question. "Why do you ask, Kitten?"

I stare at the symbol on the cover. I've seen it before. I know I have. It's very distinctive, two wolves, one small white one and one big gray one, each reared up with their forepaws holding a shield.

The shield has a big letter 'I' in the center of it, crossed with two swords. I chew my lip, flipping through my mental images.

"Oh..." I say, not really speaking to anyone.

"What? What is it, Kitten?" Finn asks frantically. "Have you seen this before?" He points to the symbol. Silverware clatters to plates and I feel all their eyes on me. How can this be? It can't possibly be a coincidence, can it? But if it's not....then what does it mean? Does it mean anything at all?

"*Kitten!*" Remy barks my name. Making me jump, but it brings me out of my thoughts.

"Yes, I've seen that before. It's on my baby blanket. The one the crazy cat lady said she found with me in the dumpster. The one that's still in my treasure box."

I jump in my seat again as eight big males fly out of their seats, all heading for the doorway at once. What the heck is going on?

I run after them, wide awake now. The fast bastards are already in the room, opening my treasure box and digging through it when I enter the room. My hands go to my hips as I call out for them to. "*Stop*! Stop it right now." They freeze, going still as stone.

I exhale harshly. "That's better. I don't care that your paws are all over *my* stuff, but handle it with care or get out of the way." I tell them.

Everyone backs away, sitting on their knees, except for Jace. He turns back to my treasure box and places everything on the floor like it's made of glass. I nod my head and sit as well. Much better. The blanket is in the bottom, wrapped up in a few grocery store plastic bags. It was once white and fluffy, the symbol embroidered into the middle. Even since I've had it in my possession, it's deteriorated. I've never washed it, fearing it would fall apart. I never even knew if it was really mine or just something that was found on me.

"It's the same crest," Finn says to the others. He's right, it's the same symbol as the one on the book.

"What's a crest?" I ask.

"This is a family crest, Kitten. It belongs to the Ivaskov family. They have the longest werewolf lineage known. It dates back to Remington's time. The alpha of that family has always been the one to run the Mating Games as well. They are a powerful family Kitten. The strongest of the born wolves, and have the biggest pack. They are considered Royalty to us." Tristan tells me.

I frown, biting my bottom lip as I take a moment to think about that. "But that doesn't explain how I got their blanket. Or how the blanket got into the trash if it wasn't mine."

Remy shakes his head, looking to each of the others before his steel gray eyes fall on me again. "I'm sure it's yours, Kitten. With all that's happened, it's the only thing that makes sense."

"What does that mean then?"

"It might mean that you belong to the Ivaskov family. It might mean that one of their pack members are your parents. It might mean that the Ivaskov family was responsible for throwing you in the trash. We just don't know. It just means that you have had a connection to werewolves since you were born." Remy explains.

"The guy you had pinned against the car said that they could smell her. That they just wanted to investigate." Jace throws out.

"Yes, but we know he was lying about that." Tristan counters.

"We've never been close to a female wolf before. Maybe that's why we're all so attracted to Kitten. Why we are so enchanted by her scent." Reed says.

"I've done the blood work. She shows no sign of being a wolf. I think you're all overlooking the most obvious thing here, she doesn't change into a wolf." Kellan says. I agree with him. No way am I a wolf, right?

"According to the book that Kitten found, born wolves don't have their first shift until puberty. But that would still mean that Kitten would have shifted by now." Finn informs us.

"She was underfed, in a constant state of worry and panic. It may be possible that she just couldn't." Kellan shrugs. "Maybe it's a learned type of thing. No one taught her so...." He holds his hands out.

"Wouldn't I know if I was a wolf?" I question. "Wouldn't I have recognized you guys as wolves or something? I didn't find out until later."

"Well, when you think about it...you kind of did,

Kitten. I mean, you got comfortable with us pretty quickly. You instinctively push your face into our necks, like wolves do for comfort. Even when we are in wolf form, you do it. The natural reaction for humans is to be afraid of us, you never were. Your first thought was to take care of Finn, when you should have been afraid of him, people just don't do that with wolves Kitten." Tristan tells me.

"You're also possessive as fuck, and protective of those you care about," Ash says. His rumbly voice sounding unhappy at the prospect of me being one of them.

"Those things could be explained away by the way she grew up. She's possessive because she's never had much, protective because no one ever looked out for her." Logan reasons, but he looks excited for some reason.

"Stop. Everybody just stop. This is getting us nowhere, it's all speculation." Remy commands.

"Uh, well...doesn't Finn have a book?" I ask shyly. Finn rolls his eyes and walks over to me, kissing my temple.

"She's right, I'll get the book. Be right back." He says and runs off.

Logan moves to sit next to me. I rest my head on his shoulder, needing to be close to him. "I could have lost you crazy boy, don't get hurt anymore okay?" I say in a low tone, just for him to hear.

He chuckles, his laugh already sounding better. "I wasn't trying to get hurt, silly girl, but I'll make sure it doesn't happen again, just because you said so." I nod my head. "And when are you going to stop referring to us as boys?" He asks, making a face that makes me giggle.

"Probably never. You're all my boys. You're my crazy boy or fun boy." I tell him.

"You have nicknames for us?"

"Well yeah, you all call me many different things. It's only fair. And it's only in my head usually."

"What are the others? I have to know this shit. Mine are cool ones, I get crazy and fun, which is me in a nutshell." Logan's eyes light up. So he likes what I call him in my head huh?

"Well, Ash is My Shadow. He asked me not to call him a boy directly. Remy is My bossy boy, Reed My sensitive boy, Finn, My smart boy, Jace is my Golden boy...." I trail off as Jace and Reed crack up laughing. Obviously they've been listening to our conversation.

I glare at them. They could have had the decency not to laugh at me. "Oh, come on Kitten, you have to finish the list." Jace calls.

I shake my head. "No, it's my names for you guys, I shouldn't have shared them out loud. Sharing only leads to being laughed at." I pick at the pants I'm wearing before bringing my knees up to my chest.

"They didn't mean it like that sweet girl," Tristan says as he sits next to me, pulling me into him with one arm. He's used his kind voice on me, and I melt into his side. I can't stay mad when he fills me with so much warmth.

"You're my sweet boy," I whisper to him.

He smiles his perfect-Tristan-smile and bends to my ear. "Good, because you're my sweet girl." I turn my head and kiss his soft lips. I lose myself in Tristan until someone clears their throat. Oh! I forgot others were here for a moment. I blush eight kinds of red and bury my face into Tristan's neck. Somehow, I ended up on his lap.

Finn returns with the book and we all gather around him. I squirm around, bouncing my leg impatiently as he reads. It's a thick book, lots of information in there. Information that I'd like to know. Like right now. I poke my head around him, glancing at the page he's on. I nudge him with my elbow, trying to hurry him along.

Finn eventually sighs, looking up from the book. "Do you want to..." He doesn't get to finish his thought before I snatch the book into my lap.

I hear several chuckles as I flip back to the front, glancing at each page briefly before flipping it. It takes me less than fifteen minutes to finish 'reading' it. I kiss Finn on the cheek and hand it back over. Standing, I move further away from them so I can process what I just saw, taking the time to read the images in my head now.

I don't know how to read family trees, so I just skip over that part. Finn can explain it to me later. He was wrong about the book being a history of werewolves, it's just the Ivaskov family's history. It seems as though at one point, it was translated into English as some of the sentences didn't make sense. The family started out with a long history in Russia but moved here after what they called 'The Suffering.' Based on what Remy told me, they were talking about the plague that wiped out most female werewolves and left them barren.

The family made it their mission to find a way to procreate. The Ivaskovs' were, and are, the most exclusive family or pack of wolves. Their bloodlines are what they call 'clean,' meaning all born wolves. There is an extensive trial period for you to be able to join their pack, and even if you pass it, if they don't like you, you still don't get in.

They have the largest army of the packs and are fierce in battle.

To me, they sound like a bunch of Adams and Kaitlynns. Not to mention that I think one of them probably wrote this and might be just a teensy weensy bit biased. What interested me more, was the chapters on individual Ivaskovs, especially the more recent ones. There was 'The Grandfather' who has lived longer than any other born wolf. He is said to be kind as well as very harsh in his punishments. Packs from all over the world sought his guidance while he was alpha. He lost his wife in 'The Suffering' but not before she gave birth to two sons and three daughters. Two of his daughters were also lost during that time.

The surviving daughter is known as 'The Beauty' for it's said that no wolf can match her in attractiveness. The eldest son is known as 'The Fair Prince' even though he took over as alpha when his father stepped down. He was dubbed that because he believed in equality amongst wolves. He was a born humanitarian to both wolves and humans. He was also a scientist and found out how to narrow down human women that were capable of surviving the change, thus creating more female Wolves.

The other son was or is, called by his name which is Marcus. Some refer to him as the second son. He was almost as strong as his brother in wolf form and resented him for being named alpha by their father. He isn't very well liked, but he is respected and feared by many. He also tried to marry their sister so that they could have 'pure Ivaskov blood'. Luckily for the sister, his brother shot that down, and it didn't take place. She, instead married an alpha of a rival pack, thus creating an alliance.

Four pages have been ripped from the book in that section from the end.

I skipped over the parts about mating and bonding since that isn't relative to what I need to know. I wish I knew when the book was written, it didn't say, and I'm unaware if any of the people mentioned in the book are still alive or not. I liked reading the short bios of them, imagining what it was like to live in their time. Like Ivan 'The Conqueror' who was the fiercest warrior of his day, who first formed the Ivaskov family, only accepting the best males and females into his pack. Not only the strongest, but the kindest, the most beautiful, the most talented, and the smartest of wolves. He created an entire empire. How cool would that be!

"Earth to Kitten, Kitten are you there?" Logan waves his hand in my face, bringing me back from planning world domination.

"Huh? What?" I reply elegantly.

He laughs. "Have you heard anything we've been saying?" I shake my head. Nope, not a word.

"We were saying, Miss Kitten, that we think we've figured out why wolves, in general, are so attracted to you," Remy says, obviously disapproving of my daydreaming.

"Oh, why?" I ask, tilting my head.

Finn shakes his head. "The research that this 'Fair Prince' did indicates that female humans who can survive being turned to changed wolves smell differently than other humans. Almost like they are calling out to them. Wolves have different reactions to them, ranging from instant connections to recognizing an immediate threat. It depends on the dominance of the wolf and would-be wolf. The closer they are in dominance, the harder to bring the two together, when the wolf's dominance far outranks the would-be wolves, the wolf seeks to protect the would-be wolf, and so on."

I blink at him. What the heck did he just say? "Um... okay, so I smell then. Right. That's why you think.....what exactly?" He could not be any more confusing if he tried.

Ash huffs. "He's saying that you attract wolves with your scent. That you are able to survive being turned. He's saying you're a fucking walking talking target." Ash's voice rises as he continues to speak.

"But you said that human women die once bitten." I state, I know I remember Remy telling me that.

"But some don't," Jace says. "The book says it's in your DNA or something. Very few of you are left, and the ones that are still around, they know what they are and refuse to have children. Were children or human children. They see us as evil."

"Why would they think that?" I ask. My boys aren't evil.

"Because after the plague, wolves descended on human females like flies on shit. This was before the Fair Prince's research. Thousands died, the ones who turned wish they had died because they were either taken forcefully or sold to the highest bidder and forced to bond."

"Do you mean like, uh, rape?" My face is red as I ask, but I have to know.

"Some were, yes." States Remy. "But that's not what bonding means. Mating to us is like marriage is to humans. Bonding is....like becoming one being. Your souls align, your heartbeats synchronize, and it is said that when two perfect mates bond, that they can thought-share."

Okay, I have too much information to process right now. I'd ask another question, but I fear it would only lead to five more questions. There is still one I need to ask though. "So who came after us last night? What did they want? If it was just to turn me like you said, they had the opportunity."

"Shit, she's right," Logan says.

"I have a lot more work to do to get to those answers, Kitten. I promise that I will find them for you." Finn tells me.

"I'm not sure I really want to know. There is so much information, and I'm not sure how it all connects. My last question is what do we do now? I don't want to be taken away, or changed and forced to bond." My body shudders at the thought.

"We will keep you with us, Kitten. I promised you that already, and I meant it." Remington says sternly. "Why don't you come take a nap with me yes?" He does look tired. I still am as well.

"Can Ash come too? I want to make sure he sleeps too." I don't know if I should have asked that, but Remy smiles and nods.

I look to Ash. "Want to come nap with me?" I bite my lip, hoping he says yes. I want him near me right now.

Ash grins broadly. "Only if we can bring AJ with us."

I came to bed with Remy and Ash, but I can't seem to sleep. They were both asleep before their heads hit the pillows. I took turns watching them sleep, memorizing each one of their features, loving how both of my scary boys look so young and peaceful in sleep. They must have stayed up all night to be this tired.

I don't know how I feel about what I've learned today. I think I need more questions answered for that. They say that my baby blanket really is mine, but we still don't know how the Ivaskov crest connects back to me. I think it's a tad farfetched for me to be part of their family. Something tells me a family like that doesn't make a habit of throwing away their babies. With power in the wolf community, it also stands to reason that I wasn't stolen from them.

But if I'm not part of their family, how did I end up with the blanket? If the Ivaskovs' are responsible for throwing me away, then why leave a blanket that leads back to them? What would be the point? The other option was what... one of their pack members did it? Still, why leave the blanket. The thing I really don't understand here is, don't they need females? If I belong to any Werewolf family, wouldn't I have been wanted? Just for being a girl?

I guess I could be one those able-to-be-changed females. I guess I wouldn't know since no one told me. Still, the Ivaskov's are werewolves, and they would have wanted me. But even if you look past that, they said women like that *knew* they were werewolf bait. How did they know? How could they tell the wolves 'No' when they wanted to have children with them? Why are there so many questions? Where do we get the answers?

"The prisoner..." I whisper out loud.

"What?" Ash grumbled.

"Nothing, go back to sleep. I didn't mean to wake you." I whisper back.

"No, it's okay Miss Kitten. I think we've gotten enough sleep for now. Any more and we wouldn't sleep tonight." Remy says from my other side.

"Oh, well I was just thinking that you took a prisoner, right? Why don't we just ask him our questions? He'd know the answers, right?"

Ash snorts. "He's refusing to talk, Kitten. And anything he says could be false." So....they've already tried?

"Maybe you didn't ask the right questions? Can I try?" I ask timidly.

"NO!" They both answer, making me jump. "We're not letting him anywhere near you." Ash grumbles.

"You can tie him up, right? And you guys could come with me, wherever he's at. Make sure he can't hurt me. Please? I need some answers, and he has them. Please, please, please!" I beg.

"It might not be a bad idea, Ash," Remy says, resigned. "However, that will be a last resort. We'll proceed as planned for today. At least as far as you're concerned, Kitten."

I frown. I wasn't aware of any plans. "What are we doing? Don't you think we should try to figure this out?" I ask.

Ash sits up, sliding his legs over the side of the bed. "We'll be working on this Little One, but it will take time. Let's go find Tristan and have him put bacon in our scrambled eggs." I smile at him, he remembered.

"Okay," I say as I get up, kissing AJ's head and waving to Remy.

CHAPTER TWENTY-NINE

I ended up seeking out Logan first. For one, I needed to change clothes and two, I'm still concerned about him. I found him in his room, resting. I stood in his doorway, looking at the gorgeous boy laying on the bed. The longer portions of his light brown hair in the front was pushed to the back of his head where the hair is shorter. The blue streak was laying across his face and my fingers itched to move it for him. He was shirtless, and I couldn't help but admire all of that smooth bare skin. Logan's body was perfection. I sigh, can this boy really be mine?

"Are you going to stare at me all day, or are you going to come in?" His muffled voice sounded amused, and my face lit on fire.

"How did you know I was here?" I ask, hoping he will forget I was admiring him.

Logan huffs a laugh. "Not only did I hear you, but I can smell your delicious smelling self from miles away. Come cuddle with me pretty girl."

I do as he asks, climbing on the bed as carefully as I can. I reach out and brush the blue streak back, sighing on the inside. Logan wraps an arm around me, pulling my body into his. I rub his back, my fingertips memorizing every inch. "Can I ask you a question, Logan?"

"Anything. Always."

"Your bedroom....why isn't it....I don't know, more like you?" I bite my lip, hoping I didn't insult him. It's just that Logan is my crazy boy and is room is just not what I expected.

"I'm horrible at decorating my own room. I love designing the other guys' rooms, most of the house for that matter. But it seems I always have too many ideas for my own, and it turns out strange." He shrugs. I guess that kind of makes sense. "It's like Reed and his bedroom. Reed loves every color under the sun, all that artsy stuff, ya know? But he can never choose which colors or themes he wants. So for this house, I just went with all white, and told him to go crazy with color in his studio."

I pull back so I can look at him. Resting on my elbows. "So I have you to thank for the cloud room?" Logan beams at me. I lean down and kiss his cheek. "I'd like to help you make your room more like you, would you let me?"

"Why would you want to do that?" He asks.

"Because you deserve a space for yourself too. My crazy boy needs a crazy bedroom to match."

Logan grins at me adorably, kissing the end of my

nose. "I'd be honored. We'll do that when we have time."

I crawled up out of the bed, Logan ushering me to shower while he picked an outfit for me. It was a pair of tan cargo pants that fit snugly around my hips and butt and were loose around the legs, paired with a stretchy black halter top and black socks. I thought it was a strange choice on Logan's part, but I liked it a lot. He usually put me in super girly clothes. I liked them too, but these were really comfy, and I knew I wouldn't have to wear the heeled shoes again. I brushed my teeth and hair and went in search of one of them.

When I opened the door, I noticed a piece of paper tapped to Reed's bedroom door. It had my name on the top in pink glitter, with the message, "Welcome to day 2 of your first birthday! When you find one of us, you find your presents. Have fun on your scavenger hunt!"

I bit my lip, staring at the paper. Are there always more than one day of celebrations for a birthday? Yesterday was great, the best birthday ever. Well, except for the end that is, but that wasn't planned, and it wasn't their fault. So I have to find them? Are they going to hide from me? This sounds like a game. I love games. I wonder how you win this one.

———— ◆ ● ◆ ————

I rush down the stairs, heading to the kitchen. Tristan should be easy to find. He's always in the kitchen it seems. I rounded the corner and a pang of disappointment shot through me. Tristan wasn't here, none of them were. On the kitchen island was a plate of scrambled eggs with bacon in them and toast. A glass of apple juice and a mug of coffee were sitting there as well. I sat down in front of it, picking up the folded note sitting under the silverware. It simply read: Follow my kisses, Sweet Girl.

I shoveled the food into my mouth, eating as fast as I could. My excitement was growing now. Is he going to kiss me? Wait...but how would I follow kisses? My eyes scan the kitchen, looking for another clue. There's a yellow star sitting on the counter, right in front of the coffee maker. Tiny silver things form a line on the counter leading to the pantry where Tristan keeps most of the canned and boxed foods. I hop down from my stool and pick up one of the silver things. Sticking out of the top of it is a white piece of paper with the word 'Kisses' written in blue. Is this what he means for me to follow?

I run to the pantry door, pulling it open quickly. Tristan is leaning against a shelf, hands in his pockets, one foot propped up. My breath leaves me at the sight of him. He is beyond handsome. Sandy hair is falling in his chocolate eyes that are looking right at me. His beautiful smile in place. He's wearing a red polo shirt with the collar flipped up, loose fitting light colored jeans and black boots. Mmmm. The fluttering in my belly goes crazy, my brain shutting down at the sight of him.

"Happy birthday, Kitten," Tristan whispers, his eyes darkening as he walks slowly to me. Oh God, he looks like he wants to eat me. And I think I might just let him. When he's close enough, I throw my arms around his shoulders and cling to him, koala style. My lips crash down on his, my legs wind around his hips and my fingers grip his amazing hair at the back of his neck.

Tristan is shocked at first but wastes no time parting

my lips with his tongue, turning and backing me against the shelf. The flutters in my stomach feel like a full on tornado. I feel his hand snake into my hair at the nape of my neck right before he pulls it. Hard. My head goes back with a gasp. Tristan's tongue traces up my throat, eliciting a whimper from me. The slight pain followed by the intimate pleasure is almost overwhelming. His lips press soft kisses to my chin and cheeks before he slides them back over my mouth. He releases the grip on my hair, smoothing it down.

With his face pressed into my neck, Tristan whispers. "We need to stop Kitten. Otherwise, I'll be taking something from you instead of giving you something." I don't know what he means, and really, I don't care at the moment.

"I'll give you anything you want as long as you don't stop," I tell him. My nails dig into his shoulders, making him grunt and thrust his hips at me.

Tristan places a soft kiss where my neck meets my face before pulling back and letting me down. My face falls and my lip pouts out involuntarily. Apparently that amuses him because he just grins back at me.

"You know, I thought you were a shy little thing at first. But I'm starting to see that with the right incentive, you go full blown hellcat." He smirks. I stick my tongue out at him, smoothing down my clothes in an attempt to calm my nerves. I wonder if he stopped because he doesn't want me like that. Maybe I should have asked before I jumped on him.

"Sorry, I couldn't help myself." I stare at my hand that's playing with a button on my pants. Suddenly I don't feel like I can look at him.

Tristan uses a finger under my chin to lift my gaze back to his. "I enjoyed every moment of what we did Sweetie. We just don't have the time right now. "His hand ghosts over my cheek." I also don't want our first time to be against a shelf in a pantry. You deserve so much better than this." He whispers.

My face flushes bright red. Is that where that was leading? Is my first time going to be with Tristan? I shake my head of those thoughts. I'll revisit that later when I don't feel like jumping him again. I look away and clear my throat.

"You said you had something for me?" Thankfully, Tristan accepts the subject change. He claps his hands, rubbing them together.

I'm led to a big red box with a blue bow. Tristan stands behind me with his hands on my shoulders. "Just lift the whole thing up. It doesn't have a bottom."

I do as he says, reaching out and lifting the pretty box quickly. I set it aside while I giggle uncontrollably. I clap and hop in place, staring at the pile of paintball gear that's stacked neatly in front of me. I see a gun with my name scrawled on the side and bring my hands to my chest. Tears threaten behind my lids. I can't believe they got me my own paintball stuff.

"I hope those are happy tears...?" Tristan questions. I turn to him and nod. "You haven't seen the best part," He says. He reaches for something in the back, hidden behind the pile. I gasp when I see it.

"Tristan..." I don't know what to say. He holds out the large picture frame that holds my flag. In the bottom corner is a picture of me, covered in paint splotches, looking up at Tristan with a dopey smile on my face. In the opposite corner is a silver piece of metal that reads, 'To my fierce Kitten, Conquering since 2015.'

"Logan took the picture and Reed got it off his phone. I hope that you don't mind that I took your flag from Logan's room. You like it don't you?" Tristan looks a little worried.

"I love it...I...I can't believe you did this for me." I lower the frame in his hands to the ground. Burying my face in his chest. "You're the sweetest boy in the world. Thank you." I kiss his cheek, and he wraps his long arms around my back.

"You say that now, but you don't know what the others got for you," He says playfully. I blink up at him, not understanding. "That's right Kitten, this is just from me. You have to hunt for the others now."

Tristan pulls an orange card from his back pocket, handing it to me. Without another word, he kisses my head and leaves the pantry. The card simply says, 'Follow my trail.' I wonder if I'm just supposed to follow Tristan, but that doesn't seem right. The card is orange, so I suppose that means I'm looking for Finn.

I leave the pantry and cross the kitchen. As soon as I reach the hallway, I understand what he meant. In the middle of the hardwood floor are paw prints. I walk next to them, excited to see where they lead me. After a while, I know where they're leading. The library room. I run the rest of the way there, keeping an eye on the floor to make sure I'm right. I throw the heavy door open wide.

A beautiful, sleek black wolf greets me. The mint green eyes tell me it's Finn and not Kellan. I walk to him and kneel. He drops the orange flower he had in his mouth in my lap, tail wagging, and nudges the side of my face with his nose. As Finn sniffs at my neck, I pick up the flower and examine it. It's a burnt orange color, his favorite color. He told me that it's a hard color to find in nature, but he's found this for me.

I break off the stem a little and tuck it in my hair behind my ear. Finn backs up and barks happily at me, licking my face. I giggle as I wipe away his drool. I watch as he trots away, wondering if I should follow him or not. Communication is hard when only one of us can speak. Before I can move though, he returns, sliding an orange box across the floor with his nose.

Inside the box is an assortment of books and a shiny black case. On top of it all is a note.

To the nicest, smartest, and loveliest girl I've ever known,

I chose to be in my wolf form not only because I know you like it, but because

I wanted to tell you things that are hard for me to say. I think I've fallen in love

with you Kitten. I know it's fast, and I realize we don't know everything about

each other yet. I'd like to spend the rest of our lives learning about you. No subject

has ever fascinated me as much as you do. Whether you are a wolf, a to-be wolf, or a

human, it matters not to me. You are simply you, and that is the girl I fell for. You don't

have to love me back, all I ask is that you let me love you.

Sincerely, Your Mr. Wolf

I think these men are trying to kill me with tears today. They fall freely as I hug Finn tightly. "I think I love you too Finn, that letter was better than any gift you could have given me." I don't know how long I sit there, my hands stroking his back, my face pressed into his neck. I think Finn is too smart to fall for someone like me, but I'll be damned if I ever tell him that. Selfish, but true.

Eventually, he breaks my hold on him, licking the tears from my cheeks. He hops up on the table with his front paws, picking up a card with his teeth. After bringing it to me, he lays his head in my lap. I laugh out loud when I read it. 'I don't know how these things work, I'm in my room, Ash.'

I show Finn the card after his head perks up at my giggling. He snorts and rolls his eyes, which I, of course, find adorable. I pat his head and get up. After waving to Finn one last time, I make my way to Ash's bedroom. I knock on the door, and he answers, pulling it open and taking a step back. When he does, I get a view of his bed.

I let out a girly squeal that I'm not proud of, and run to the end of the bed.

Ash chuckles. "Just the reaction I wanted from you." I rush back to him and hug him tightly. He strokes my hair with his large hand. "I love AJ so much that I thought he could use a few brothers." His voice is more gruff than normal, so I look up at him. He's staring at the assortment of stuffed wolves in the middle of his bed longingly.

"Are you okay Ash?" He isn't outwardly sad, but I think he might be on the inside. Why would seeing the stuffed animals make him sad?

"I'm fine Little One, go check them out," He tells me. "I had to get some girly hair shit to make Little

Logan have a blue streak. My fucking fingers are still blue. I wouldn't get that one wet." He shakes his head.

I run my hand over each one. The reddish colored one with gray eyes, the twin black ones with green eyes, the light brown one with brown eyes, yes, they're all here.

"You could take them each to their perspective rooms if you'd like...." Ash trails off as I shake my head no.

"They should stay together. They're a set."

"Yes they are, and they all belong to you," Ash says so quietly I'm not sure I was supposed to hear. Louder he says. "I would love to keep you here with me all day, but you should go. The others will be waiting for you."

I thank him, kissing each cute little wolf before kissing my giant Shadow properly. When we're both breathless, he hands me a small white card, folded in half. 'Meet me where the pure meets the chaotic.' Hmm...Now what could that mean? I run through a mental list of my boys that are left. I slowly walk the hallways, wondering who I'm supposed to search for now. Pure...Pure...Pure white! Reed! The chaos is his art room.

When I reach Reed's studio the door is open, and Reed is standing in front of one of the stands. His white button-up shirt has splotches and smears of color all over it, as do his light wash jeans, even his bare feet. Reed is simply stunning. I can't believe I get to be around these attractive boys. And this one loves me. My heart swells at that thought. I'm loved. By Reed, by Finn. I love all of them so much. I wasn't sure that what I was feeling was love, but I can't imagine feeling more strongly for another person than I do for them. It must be what this is.

"I love you," I whisper out. I don't think I meant to

say it out loud, but the smile my words create on his handsome face tells me they were welcomed.

"I love you too, Kitten. Are you having fun?" I feel the heat rise in my cheeks. Considering how I attacked Tristan, maybe a bit too much fun. I don't tell him that though, I just nod.

Reed extends his hand, wordlessly calling for me. I cross the room to him and he positions me in front of him to look at his work, his chin resting atop my head. "It's beautiful Reed. How did you manage so much detail with paint?" I ask stupidly.

I feel his laugh on my back. "Practice, Kitten. And the use of different brushes." He tells me. That makes sense. I had only used one. I study the painting, feeling lost in it. Reed made a perfect sunrise over a dark lake. It looks so real that I want to touch the dark blues and run my hand through the water.

"Come on," Reed says. "I have some things to show you. I think you'll like them." He takes my arm gently in his hand and pulls me to a table area in the corner. On it, is several framed pictures. Each of them is me with one of the guys, from the night we went to the restaurant. I'm so happy he took these, the boys look just as good here as they did then. I smile down at them, brushing my fingers over the silver frame.

"I got this for you too," Reed says as he holds out a box to me. I unwrap it quickly. There's a picture of someone holding a camera on the outside of the box. "I thought you might want to start taking your own pictures too. I'd love to see the world through your eyes, Kitten." He whispers the last part in my ear. I shiver.

"Thank you so much. I love it. I love all of it." I

refuse to cry again so I press my lips gently to his, finding a different emotion. Reed kisses me slowly, lovingly. His hand caressing the side of my face. When we pull apart to breath, his mysterious eyes are brimming with happiness. Reed is no longer my sad boy. That was gift enough.

After leaving Reed, the next card talked about puzzle pieces, and I knew that was Remy telling me to meet him in his bedroom. As soon as I had the door open, Remy spread his arms wide in invitation. Naturally, I ran and jumped on him.

Remy chuckled deeply. "Happy to see me, yes?"

"Oh yes! Today has been so exciting. I feel like it's been forever since I've seen you." I press my nose into his neck, inhaling him as he takes a seat on the bed with me in his arms. I snuggle in deeper.

"I have something for you as well, but I'm not ready to let you go just yet." His rumbly voice tells me. I'm not ready yet either. Eventually though, he does pull back. He reaches for two small boxes and places one by his side, bringing the other in front of me.

He flips the top of it open, revealing a pendant with eight shiny stones in different colors, or well, two of them are the same color. "This one I bought for you. It's Cartier, as you deserve the best. I had them add each of our birthstones, or as close to them as we know, into it. I wanted you to know that we are always with you."

I stroke my fingers over the delicate looking chain. It's so shiny and pretty. "I already have the best Rem. I have you guys." I tell him. I mean it too. I may not have had much interaction with guys before, but I know there can be no better out there. Not for me.

I lift my eyes to Remy's. His copper hair looks like

fire in this lighting. "I hope you know that you guys don't have to give me things. I love all of your gifts, I really do. But it's you I want. Just the eight of you. I wouldn't trade you guys for all the Cart-tee-ya necklaces and cameras in the world. You know that don't you?"

Remy leans down and presses a kiss to my temple. "We know that beautiful girl. We like spoiling you, just let us." He commands. I giggle at him, and his eyes darken. "I love that sound," He tells me.

He brings out the second box. "I had Ash make this for you, so really, it's from the both of us." He opens it and pulls out a copper circle. "In our time, women wore arm cuffs to show that they were taken, later women wore them to show that they were warriors, and even later, such in Tristan's time, they were a sign of status." Remy pulls at it and it opens a bit. It's then that I notice the head of a wolf engraved into it. It's beautifully crafted.

He lifts my arm and slides the band slowly up it. "You, dear Kitten, are all of those things. You are our Princess, our warrior, and most certainly taken." My breath hitches once he gets it closed. It fits perfectly. I look back to his serious eyes. He means every word.

I have no words for him. I don't think a simple 'thank you' will be enough. I crush my lips to his, trying to tell him with my lips what he means to me. I shift until I'm straddling his legs, my hands going straight for his fiery hair. Remy kisses me back, taking control of the kiss until I'm whimpering in his mouth. His hands grip mine, bringing them both behind my back. With one of his hands holding mine in place, he pulls away from the kiss, his other hand tracing my neck. I whine at the loss of his mouth.

"Ah ah young lady. You don't yet know what you are asking for." His voice is deeper than normal, and I swear his words are reverberating straight through me. I don't? I thought I was asking him to kiss me? Remy's fingers find the pulse point on my neck. It's beating erratically, I know. "So responsive....so delicate," He says lightly. He starts to lean forward but stops himself.

Before I know it, I've been released and am standing. Remy stands too, his tall frame towering over me. "Off you go." He turns me, swatting my behind harshly. I yelp in surprise, turning to see him smirking. "Logan will be in the basement, he's quite impatient, hurry along."

I walk on shaky legs through the house. I shake my head, trying to clear the fog that has taken up residence there. When I get to the bottom of the steps in the basement, Logan excitedly shows me all of the things he's gotten for me. I should have known if anyone was to go overboard, it would be Logan. His excitement infects me, and before I know it, I'm modeling all the clothes he's gotten for me. Most are made for skating, and some are just for fun, as Logan says. He even got me custom-made Leo's.

Once I'm in a black flirty skirt that flares out when I twirl and a tight pink t-shirt that's gathered on the sides and spiky boots, Logan sits me down and hands me two boxes. The paper is a shiny blue, like his hair. The bigger box contains a brand new pair of white ice skates. I squeal, and Logan mocks me, squealing too. We both laugh at that. He also got me a music player called an iPod. I've seen the advertisements for these before. He shows me how to turn it on and shows me how to get to playlist he already set up for me. Including the song he played for me at the rink.

I reluctantly leave Logan and go in search of Kellan. When I find him in the living room, he looks sleepy. I wonder if he nodded off while he was waiting for me. "Hi, Kellan," I say shyly as I take a seat next to him on the couch.

He scoots up, running a hand through his hair like he's trying to fix it. The shiny black locks look perfect to me. "Hey there. It's good to see you, Kitten."

"It's good to see you too. I feel like I barely to get to spend time with you."

Kellan sighs. "I know, the clinic has been busy lately," He tells me.

"I could always go with you. I mean, if you wanted me to. I'd like to see what you do." I bite my lip. I shouldn't have said that. I practically just invited myself to his work.

Kellan's grassy eyes light up. "You'd want to?" I nod excitedly.

"Well...I've always wanted a lovely little assistant," He says, grinning widely. He'd let me help? Yay! I wonder if he'd call me Dr. Kitten. How cool would that be?

"Ha! I can tell you really like the thought of that if the dreamy look on your face is any indication." He smirks at me. I blush at being caught.

Kellan reaches a hand into his pocket in the front of his black jeans. When he pulls it back, I see something that looks old and worn. "Since we don't get much time together, I wasn't sure what you would want. This necklace belonged to mine and Finn's mother. As the first born son, she gave it to me to give to the woman I wanted to spend my life with." He smiles sadly down at the necklace.

"It's not designer or fashionable or whatever, but if you would allow it, I'd like you to wear it. I've discussed it with Finn, and he agrees that you should have it." Kellan motions for me to turn around, so I do. He sweeps my hair to the side, placing the old leather band around my throat and tying it in the back. I pick up the pendant, the silver is bumpy, not smooth. It looks like a bunch of shapes locked together. I love it.

Kellan turns me back to him, his arm going around my shoulders as we cuddle together on the couch. "I know we haven't known you long Kitten, but you're a part of us now. I know my brother loves you wholeheartedly and I think you love him too, yes?" He quirks an eyebrow at me. I nod.

"Yes well, I don't know if I'm there yet, or if you are with me. But I know that I want to get there. I want to love you. I want to be loved by you. I never imagined sharing a girl with my brothers, but in a way, I think it will be better." He continues.

I peek up at him. "How will it be better?" I ask.

Kellan chews on his pouty bottom lip, thinking. "Because the others can be there for you when I can't. When I'm at work, or anytime I'm away...you won't be lonely, you'll always have someone there for you. When I'm too tired to play, you will have Tristan or Logan. When I'm not strong enough to protect you, you'll have Remington and Ash. I don't really get art, but you seem to enjoy it. Reed's here for that." I get what he's saying, but it still bothers me at how he is saying it.

"Kellan...I don't care if you are tired sometimes. I understand that, and there's nothing wrong with it. You work hard. You don't have to 'get' art for me to like you, or be as strong as Remy, or as playful as Logan. I like you the way you are. You know that right?" I ask him.

His green eyes lock on mine. I see no worry in them, just understanding. "I do know that Kitten. I just think it's better for all of us. We men can still have our work, and each other and you. While you get to do everything your little heart desires because the chances are, at least one of us will desire it as well."

As I'm about to respond, Jace bursts through the door. "There are officers here to collect Kitten." His face is clouded with worry, and I instantly panic. "Come on..." Jace takes my hand and the three of us run down the hall, away from the front door.

CHAPTER THIRTY

We enter a bedroom with bright purple carpet, neon pink walls, and an astonishingly large lime green bed. There are no windows, but an entire wall is made up of a fish tank. An open door reveals a bathroom with a huge tub. It's mostly white, but with purple accents and I see a stack of fluffy pink towels. I'm so shocked about the overly girly room that for the moment, all thoughts of cops flee my mind.

I look around the big room, now noticing that my stuff, including my gifts from today, are in here. Big Jace in the corner, my stuffed wolves placed on the bed with Noah, a bookcase with the books Finn gave me, a small table and two chairs with the shiny black case that I never opened. It's probably a chess set now that I think about it. There's a big mirror with a weird desk attached to it and a bench seat. I see the necklace Remy got for me in a wooden box sitting on top of it. My treasure chest is sitting at the foot of the bed. A painting of me hangs above the padded headboard; Reed must have done that. On shelves and the dresser are the pictures he gave me in the frames.

"What is this?" I whisper to no one in particular.

Jace walks towards me, clasping my hands in his. His face is pinched with worry. "This is my gift to you, Kitten. I wanted to give you a room. A space that is just for you. Your own bed, your stuff. You deserve to have that. This whole place is your home now, but here, this is just for you. For always." He tells me.

Tears stream down my face for the billionth time today. I tug his hands toward me, making him bend a bit. I reach up and kiss his lips. "Thank you so much, Jace, you can't even imagine what this means to me."

His long, elegant fingers find my chin, holding my head in place. "Pretty girl, don't you know we would give you the world?" His golden eyes are intense.

"Jace, I...." I'm cut off again when Kellan growls deep from his chest.

"No, he can't...." Kellan's face pales and his shocked and worried eyes turn to Jace, who gathers me in his arms and holds me tightly. I don't know what's going on, and it's scaring me.

───────●●●───────

REMY

"I still don't understand the whole scavenger hunt thing. If it means she wears outfits like she had on today, then we should have more of them though." Ash was telling me. I agree. Especially if she straddles me again. Fuck that was hot. I got her to submit nicely to me too. I wonder if she even realized she was exposing her neck to me so prettily. It took every ounce of my self-control not to bite her enticing flesh.

"Yo, you with me Rem?" Ash asks loudly.

"Yes, your words just brought something to mind is all," I reply smoothly. He smirks, letting me know I didn't fool him about the subject matter of said thoughts. Ash knows me well enough to see that my control slips quite often when it comes to our little Kitten. In return, I know him well enough to notice the changes she's brought about in him. Like how Ash talks much more often these days, and he actually smiles as well. Not his usual predatory smile meant to make you mess yourself, but real smiles. I admit, it's going to take some getting used to.

"We should shift and head out to..." I stop talking immediately, hearing cars coming up the drive. I look to Aeshlyn, his stormy expression telling me he hears it too. He takes a deep breath. I do the same. "Humans," I say aloud. It's safe to speak now, humans won't be able to hear us from this far.

"You better get back to the house. I'll shift and find out what I can." He tells me. That sounds good, so I gesture for him to turn as I race around the house to the back door.

I have time to enter the house, smooth down my clothing and peek out of a front window before the slow humans approach the door. They are police officers. I can't imagine they are here for anything other than

Kitten. What the fuck now? I spot Jace at the top of the stairs, he must have heard them as well.

"Hide Kitten. Now." I whisper, knowing he'll have heard me. I wait until he is well out of sight before I open the door and step outside.

"Good evening Gentleman. How can I help you?" The short, fat officer in front looks taken aback for a few moments. Either from my formal tone or the fact that he didn't have to knock, I'm unsure.

"We're looking for a missing girl." The guy behind him says, looking down at a folder in his hands. "A Mr. uh... Vanderson informed us that this is where she's been staying. Her paperwork at her workplace confirms it."

"What missing girl? Does she have a name?" I ask. If they give the last name, it might indicate who really wants her.

"A Katerina Ivaskov. Long blonde hair, four foot, eleven inches, ring any bells?" The second man's tone tells me that he knows for sure she's here.

"I know of her, yes. But she's not missing."

"According to her father, she is. Katerina seems to have ran away a couple weeks ago. He's been worried sick. The Vanderson boy came to our offices this morning, said something seemed fishy with her."

What. The. Fuck How in the hell am I supposed to keep her from them? I could kill them, No, Isigh. Too much attention. Shit! I hate looking so young at times like these. To them, I'm probably just hiding my runaway girlfriend. The second man isn't going to let this go. If I say she's simply not here, they'll obtain a search warrant and we can't have that.

"Are your parents home, son?" The first man says

kindly. He must see my inner struggle, but it's for different reasons than what he's thinking.

"No, sir. They're vacationing in Europe. I'm of age and chose to stay here."

The second man raises an eyebrow. "Of age huh? The girl in question is fifteen. You ever hear of statutory rape boy?" I curse myself for that one. He's purposely backing me into a corner. I know for a fact that she's older. Not that it matters.

"I haven't touched her." I glare at him. Maybe I should kill them. At least him.

The first man puts his hands up, taking a step toward me. "We're not saying you did," He says to me before looking back at the other guy. "We're just here to take the girl back to her father. He's not pressing any charges or anything; he just wants Katerina to come home."

"Not yet. He's not pressing charges *yet*." The other fucker says. I want to tell them that her 'father' left her in a trash bin, and he can go fuck himself. The best I can do here is make sure they take her back to the police station and not straight to the people who may want to kill her. I can get her out of there, it won't be a problem. I'll either hire someone to act as a caseworker or send in Miss Annie as the grandmother. I'm sure she'll be up for it.

"Look, she's here, you know that. I don't want any trouble with you. Did her father happen to mention how he beat the shit out of her? She showed up at my door with bruises all over her. Looked like the asshole took a belt to her." Now they have to investigate. They can't take her back to him without first questioning her.

The first man sighs, shaking his head. "I thought that might be the case. Usually is in these types of situations.

Go ahead and bring her out here. You can accompany us to the station and give a statement."

This is better than I thought. "My brother should come too then. I'll go get them." I don't wait for a response. Just turn and enter the house, slamming the door in the process.

Tristan, Logan, and Reed have all taken seats on the stairs, listening in. Good. As much as I'd like to take Ash with us, I know that's a bad idea. I need someone who looks younger than me. Ash is too big and scary and might send the wrong signals. Their expressions range from horror and shock to anger and disgust.

"Here's what's going to happen." I talk quickly and lowly. "Tristan and I are going to accompany Kitten to the police station. Logan, you and Finn find someone to pretend to be social services. I don't care if it's a bum from the street you have dress up in my suit. Make it happen. Get Jace to make travel plans for us all. Private jet, out of the country. As soon as we walk out of there, we're heading out. Understood?"

"What if they don't release her?" Reed asks.

"Then I'll pick her up and carry her to the car, I don't give a shit. We need to get her out of range." They nod, Logan and Reed racing off to do what they need.

Jace and Kellan bring a shaking Kitten with them down the hallway. I see in Jace's eyes that they heard me as well. "Kellan, make sure everyone has what they need from here. We'll come back eventually and pack up if we can't remain here, but for now, anything we don't want anyone finding, bring it with us. Get Ash to the plane early, he'll want to do his own maintenance checks, and we may not have time."

"Got it." Kellan whispers.

I turn to Kitten, gathering her to me. I kiss the crown of her head before whispering in her ear. "We will not leave you. Never. We have to do this and then we are taking you far away from here. Play along with what Tristan and I say. Okay?" I feel her nod. It usually bugs me when she doesn't speak, but in this case, it works in our favor that she keeps her thoughts to herself. The others briefly kiss her temples or squeeze her hand. We've probably taken too long already. Tristan joins us, and I pass Kitten off to him. The officers won't question if she clings to him.

I open the door, and we step out. The second guy looks smug as fuck, and I'd like nothing more than to smash his face in. The wolves last night had humans working for them, and it wouldn't surprise me one bit if this asshole worked for them. The first guy I highly doubt does. He seems more concerned for Kitten than anything. We're escorted to the back of one of the police cars. There were two more of them, but the officers never got out. The windows are down, so I know they are humans as well.

CHAPTER THIRTY-ONE

itten is shaking horribly next to me. I hear Tristan whispering to her, too low for the officers on the other side of the screen to hear. Probably too low for her to hear. It doesn't matter though, Tristan's voice seems to calm her. Good. I sit up straight and look out the window. I can't wait for this to be finished so we can get the hell out of here.

KITTEN

Tristan is whispering non-stop in my ear. I can't really hear what he's saying most of the time, but I catch phrases like 'It's going to be okay' and 'You're fine' every once in a while. I let his kind and soothing voice wash over me, soaking it in to try and stop my shaking. I know that everything is not okay though. I'm in the back of a cop car. I've avoided this for so long. I don't want to go into the system. I don't want to leave my new family, my new home. I trust Remy though. He said that he wouldn't let me go. I believe him. I have to. Maybe when they open the door, I can just run away. No....no I can't. Remy and Tristan would get into trouble. Even if they ran with me, the cops would just go back to the house, and the rest of the guys would get into trouble. That would be the first place they looked for me.

I look up into Tristan's face. He's looking out the window. I wish he would look at me. I want to stare into his chocolate eyes again. It might be the last time I get to see them for a while. I wonder if I'm taken away if they would still want me once the state deems me to be eighteen. That could be two years from now. Would they visit me? Tristan looks down at me, finally. His face is blurry through my stupid silent tears. His long fingers reach out and brush them away. I suppress a sob, not wanting the cops to hear me. The thin one in the passenger seat keeps looking back at me, and he has mean eyes. He's one of Davis' bad people. It's easy to spot.

Tristan mouths the words 'You're mine. You're okay' at me. The way his lips over exaggerate the words makes me giggle quietly. His face lights up with his smile. He shifts his arm a little, drawing my attention to it. I blink rapidly when I see the small amounts of blood on his arm from my fingernails digging into him. I release him immediately, looking back up at him. I mouth 'sorry' at him, but he just smiles and shakes his head. I grip his hand with both of mine instead, trying not to grip too tightly. Remy shifts his leg so it's pressed against mine. It's as reassuring as I'm sure he meant it to be.

The two cops start to talk quietly amongst

themselves. I can't hear them, but I'm sure my wolves can. I feel them both stiffen at the same time. That can't be good. The pudgy cop that's driving has a frown on his face when he looks back at me in the rearview mirror. He looks confused about something the mean one said. We slow down for a stop sign, and the mean one points out his window, making the pudgy one lean around him to look too. Tristan mirrors him, and a glance back tells me that Remy is looking as well.

"I don't see it." The driver says as the car rolls forward into the intersection. He's still looking out the right-hand window. And that's why he doesn't see the big bank truck barreling straight at us. Unfortunately for me...I'm looking right at it.

Before I can call out, it slams into the side of the police car. Time slows impossibly, every nanosecond seeming like an hour. I feel my body jerk at the same moment that glass floats at me from the closed windows. Tristan's body slams into mine and mine into Remy's. The sickening crunch of metal sounds and I watch in horror as the body of the car gives way and closes in on us. Shortly after that, I become disoriented as the car flips once, then twice....three times. The only reason I know it's doing that is because the view keeps changing from spotty white clouds in a darkening blue sky, to pavement.

I must have blacked out at some point because the next thing I know, I'm lying in a heap on the roof of the car. I look up and see the pudgy driver dangling from his seat. The blood and brain matter leaking from his head is enough to tell me he didn't make it. His seatbelt is keeping him in place. The other officer is groaning, so he might be okay.

Suddenly I'm being pulled backward, my body sliding over the glass that covers the floor, or hood I guess. My heart lurches, thinking it's Remy. He's made it, and he's okay. He's going to help me and Tristan. Tristan! My hand is still gripping his. As I'm being pulled, I'm pulling him with me. I cry out when I finally look at him. A piece of metal is stuck into his side, tiny glass pieces are embedded in his face, and his head is bleeding. He's not moving, other than my dragging him. Oh God, no. No! Tristan can't be dead. No way.

"Let go!" A voice I don't recognize keep repeating to me. I refuse to let go. If I'm going, Tristan is coming with me. We need to get him to Kellan. Kellan will fix him. He'll know what to do. Tristan isn't dead, he just needs Kellan. He'll make him perfect again, and I'll be his assistant. He'll call me Dr. Kitten and all three of us will laugh about it. No. All nine of us will.

A sharp blow lands on my elbow, making my whole arm go numb. I whimper, watching my fingers release Tristan. I try to use my other arm to brace myself. To stop me from moving backward, away from my sweet boy. Arms wrap around me once I'm free from the car. I don't recognize them. I now realize that it's not Remy pulling me out. As I'm swung around, I see him. I see Remy. He's sprawled on his front, his face to the blacktop. He's not moving either. I reach my hand out to him. I can't get my voice to work for some reason.

My brain finally catches up to my eyes, and I start kicking at the person carrying me. My body is too weak to fight though, and the person manages to get me in the back of the bank truck with little effort. There is a bunch of loud noises, but I can't process them. Two of my boys are badly hurt, possibly dead. I weakly beat on the doors, looking for a latch, but there isn't one.

As the truck lurches forward, I get knocked back. I curl into a ball and cry. I scream silently. I don't even care who has me now. Nothing they do could be worse than what's already happened. I've lost them. Tristan and Remy.... they're gone. My world goes black as I forget to breathe.

KELLAN

"Stop that!" I bark at Finn. I know he's nervous, we all are, but his leg is bouncing so hard it's shaking the whole truck. He crosses one foot over his knee and the shaking stops. For all of two minutes. I sigh.

I keep wondering if I missed anything at the house. I had planned on going room to room, grabbing anything we'd want or anything we didn't want others to find. That didn't work out though. Ash insisted on trailing Remy, Kitten, and Tristan in his wolf form. We had all tried to talk him out of it, but once Ash gets something in his head, well, he's unstoppable. I had raced through the house at that point, not wanting to be too far behind him. I spent the most time grabbing Kitten's things. I know she'll want them. I didn't bother with clothes or anything that's easily replaceable.

I'm not even sure where Jace arranged for us to go. I suppose it doesn't matter, we just need to get away. If only we would have done this earlier. Before the police showed up on our doorstep. I knew after last night that this was a serious situation but...I didn't think they'd risk exposing her to the authorities. It's a desperate move. Which means that whoever wants her, is desperate. And desperate people are the worst kind of people. I'd know, I see them every day.

The truck starts rocking from side to side again. I let out a frustrated breath of air. "Finn, seriously. Everything is going to be okay. She has two of us with her." I try to say reassuringly.

"I know." Long pause. "But what if they can't get her back out? What if..."

"They will." I cut him off. He needs to stop thinking so negatively. It's not helpful, and it's not healthy. "You know Tristan....he's not above whipping it out and shaking it around to draw attention to himself."

Finn cracks a small smile, probably thinking of the extra embarrassing moment in time when Tristan pulled his pants down in a crowded restaurant just because Logan said he wouldn't do it. I snort at the memory. It was a damn good place to eat too. That wasn't the only place we've gotten banned from. Secretly, I've always wondered if he did it because their chef's salmon was better than his. Tristan is a God in the kitchen but despises competition.

"Yeah, you're probably correct." Finn sighs out.

We continue to drive towards town. The trip seemingly taking days. Until we're stopped by a police barricade. It looks like an accident has taken place further up the street. The officer standing in front of his car in the middle of the road waves us to the left. As I straighten the truck out after the turn, I look in rearview, making sure Jace and the rest of them are staying right behind me. It doesn't appear to be, but it could be another trick for all I know. Logan must see me and waves like a loon. That's good, we need to stick together.

The road we end up on to avoid the car accident runs parallel to a wooded area. I tense, wondering if we're being followed or watched by the wolves that attacked. There's a loud 'thump' and the bed of the truck dips down. Before I know what's happening, Finn is out of the truck, snarling and wrestling someone in the back. I stop the truck quickly and jump out to investigate. Finn is now perched on the rail, and a naked Ash is laying in the back.

"What the hell?" I ask him. Ash's face is normally scary but the panic I see in his eyes stops me in my tracks.

"No time," Ash says, jumping back out. "We need to get Rem and Tristan." He dashes back into the woods and Logan and Reed follow him. I get back in the truck, positioning it right at the edge of the trees. Jace does the same with the white SUV.

When Finn gets back in, his face is sickly pale, and he's as stiff as a board. "He said Remington and Tristan." He turns his wide eyes to me. I frown at him. "Ash didn't mention anything about Kitten," He explains.

Oh God. He's right. Why would we need to get the guys and not her? Surely she's with them though? "He seemed in a hurry, maybe it doesn't mean anything." I don't know if I'm trying to convince myself or him.

"I told her I loved her today." Finn whispers. He swallows like he's about to throw up. "I was too chicken to actually say it though. I put it in a note."

"Hey, it's okay. It's going to be okay. And Kitten probably liked that better anyhow. Now she can keep it. She likes keeping things." I grip his shoulder, pulling him in for a one-armed hug.

"*Kellan*!" Ash's voice booms from the tree line. "Get your ass in the back!" He orders. He's got Remington's upper body in his grasp while Reed carries his legs. Behind them, I see Logan carrying Tristan, tears streaming down his face.

As soon as they are both loaded into the bed of the truck, I climb in between them. I assess the damage done to my brothers, holding my anger in check. When Ash jumps in the driver seat of the truck, panic takes hold of me.

"Where's Kitten?" I demand.

"Gone," He growls.

"*What*?! We need to go after her then!" Finn shouts at him.

Ash turns his big body to face him. "You think I don't know that! What was I supposed to do Finn? Leave Rem and Tristan on the side of the road? Let them be taken to a hospital where they'd see them recovering too quickly and they'd be given human blood?" He slams his palm on the dash, making it dent.

"Let's get them to the clinic," I interject. Tristan is barely breathing and Remy's smashed in face worries me. We can recover from a lot of things, but I need to clear away any and all debris in order for them to heal properly. I just hope that Remy's brain is still intact, if not..... No. I refuse to think that way.

The truck begins to move, and I duck down. I don't want anyone to see me back here and wonder what I'm up to. Police are still in the area. I have a million questions for Ash, but they'll have to wait. Obviously, my brothers were in that car crash we saw. I can't help think....If two strong as hell changed wolves look like this....then what happened to fragile little Kitten?

CHAPTER THIRTY-TWO

KITTEN

I wake up freezing cold. I don't know how much time has passed, but I'm no longer in the bank van. If I had to guess, I'd say I was in a basement of some sort. I push myself up till I'm sitting. I expected an assortment of pain but...I feel fine. More than fine actually. My clothes have been removed, which is scary as heck, but I'm able to see that I don't have so much as a scratch or bruise on me. "How...."

"Werewolf blood." Says a voice that sends ice down my spine. I jerk my head up, looking around for Adam. I don't see him. He sounded close though. I cover my exposed body with my arms and hair.

Adam laughs. "No need for that." I hear shuffling before I see him step out of the shadows in the corner. "You've been laying there for a long time. I've already seen everything." He leers at me while he circles around. I keep my eyes on him.

Adam clasps his hands behind his back, and he continues to circle me. "Did you know that born werewolf blood has curative properties? No? Well, it does. It can cure just about anything, broken bones, lacerations, disease."

I don't say anything. I don't want to talk to him. Adam continues. "I know you're just a street rat, and your werewolf lore is probably lacking, but did you know that the stupid humans invented vampires from wolves?" He laughs cruelly. "Funny how they pitted wolves against vampires when, in fact, we are the same. The longer life spans, the inhuman strength, the retractable fangs." As he says the last, he smiles, revealing his canine teeth sliding down from his gums.

I gasp. Adam is a wolf? How? He stops in front of me, stepping close enough that he's staring down at me. "I could never figure out why they said we were cold though. Wolves run hot." He shrugs. "Anyway, I've assumed that some idiot humans have seen us having sex before, as some of us like to bite during. We don't drink the blood though. That's just stupid, tasting it is amazing, but actually drinking all of it would be impossible. My guess is that they saw a wolf in human form fighting a wolf in wolf form, and that's why we're supposedly enemies."

Adam stares down at me. Does he want me to respond to that? "Look, Adam, that's interesting and all, but where are my clothes? Why am I here? Why are you here?"

He squats down in front of me, reaching out a hand and running his fingers over my shoulder. I flinch away.

His eyes narrow and he stands back up. "You're naked because you were tainted by those filthy changed wolves. You smelled like them. Don't worry though, I made sure you were nice and clean." His smile is predatory, and I shudder at the thought of him touching me.

"How...how did. I mean...the guys would have been able to smell you. They would have known you were a wolf." I ask. My heart clenches painfully thinking about them. Do they know about the accident yet? Did Kellan get there in time?

"There are ways around that. Pump enough human blood into any wolf and their scents will change." He shrugs again, looking bored.

There's a clanking noise and then a loud bang. Adam steps back away from me as a tall, wiry-looking man comes in. "Stop harassing my niece Vanderson, that's my job. Yours is to feed her. Go" He commands. Adam retreats from the room without another look my way as the man walks to the corner and drags a metal chair from the shadows to sit in front of me.

He stares at me for what seems like forever, one leg crossed over the other, shrewd blue eyes on me, his fingers rubbing at his chin. "Hello, Katerina." He finally speaks.

"That's not my name," I tell him. Maybe they've been after the wrong girl all along?

"Oh, but it is. You were born Katerina Ivaskov." I blink at him. Ivaskov? Like in the book?

I shake my head at him slowly. "Even if I was, even if that's the name I was given, it's not the name I've earned. I'm Kitten." I tell him.

The man laughs. "You are so right about that. You have not earned the Ivaskov name." That isn't what I meant, but whatever.

"Why am I here?" I ask again. Adam didn't tell me, but I'm hoping he will.

"To be honest with you Katerina, I wanted to kill you." He sighs, looking annoyed. "Fortunately for you, others have pointed out the benefits of keeping you alive. For now." He stands and walks away.

"Wait! Where are you going?" I call after him. Why did he even come in here? Why is he leaving me here? Tears of frustration leak onto my face. He doesn't answer me, just opens the heavy sounding door and slams it behind him.

I wipe the stupid tears away, standing up. I approach the door warily. It's completely smooth. No latch or handle, it's hard to even make out the lines where it's separate from the wall. I follow the wall around the room, looking for any means of escape. There is none. No windows or other doors. I push the panic threatening to overtake me back down. Grabbing the metal chair, I drag it over to a corner. I crawl underneath it, curling up. Eventually, I cry myself back to sleep.

ASH

I count the tiles on the ceiling yet again. There's one hundred and two. I already knew that. I've counted these fucking things a million times already. I shift uncomfortably in my hard as hell plastic chair, lifting my head from the wall in the process. It's been three days. Three days since I followed Kitten and my brothers. Three days since I saw an armored Brink's truck crash right into them. Three days since I saw my best friend in the whole damn world fly out the side of the spinning car and land face first on the pavement. Three days since I lost the most precious girl I've ever met. I had jumped the truck, but it took off, and I was torn. Remy and Tristan needed to be moved. I couldn't just leave them there. I've resented the beating in my chest ever since. My heart should not be allowed to beat if Kitten isn't here.

My brothers are worried about me. I can tell. I told them everything I saw, but since then, I haven't said a word. I don't feel like talking. I don't feel like doing anything except hurting things. Hurting people. Hurting wolves. Since the only people around me right now are my brothers, there isn't much for me to do. I took the time yesterday to go back to the house. I beat the piece of shit prisoner within an inch of his life. The asshole knew next to nothing. He told me that his pack leader wanted to get in the good graces of the Ivaskovs and sent them after Kitten. I killed their alpha the night they attacked us. The rest of them will split up now, seeking new packs. He told me about how they promised humans that they'd change them to get their help, I'll keep that in mind for later, but it wasn't useful right now. That's all. Shit we already knew for the most part.

"Dude, your constant growling is giving me a headache," Tristan whispers from the bed on my left. I stop growling, not even aware that I was doing it.

My inner wolf whines at the sight of him. The girls have always gone crazy for Tristan, and I'll admit, he's a handsome lad. Not right now though. His whole side was torn open by a sheet of metal. Kellan actually had to stitch him together so he didn't lose his insides before he could heal. It was rough shit to watch. He almost looks diseased right now as scabs from all the cuts the glass made heal over. It's a good thing but....damn he's ugly right now. With the broken blood vessels in his eyes, he could pass for a demon. If I believed in such things.

"I guess you're still not talking then." Tristan sighs. Or tries to. He coughs then groans at the pain that caused him. Kellan jerks awake at the sound and is on him in an instant.

"Still in pain?" Kellan asks him.

Tristan gives him a weak smirk. "It's a wonder you're really a doctor sometimes," Tristan responds playfully.

"No need to be a smartass." Kellan takes out a syringe and puts some kind of pain meds in the tube leading to his arm. "A few more days and you'll feel much better."

A few more days. I don't think I can hold back going after Kitten for that long. Even if she made it out of the accident okay, who knows what they are doing to her now? I don't know where to start. Figuring shit out is more Remington's thing, and he hasn't woken up yet. I've watched as his skull slowly knits itself back together. Finn tracked the bank truck from the plate number I gave him, but the cops found it abandoned a few miles away. According to the prick who survived the crash, there were no other passengers in the car. Just the dead driver. It was obviously planned because the two other cop cars had just driven away when it happened like they didn't see what just went down in front of them. I wonder how many of them the Ivaskovs had to pay off to make that happen.

Next to me, Tristan groans, calling out for Kitten again. He's been doing that every time he's been given the drugs. I wonder if he relives the crash or if he's having good dreams about her? I hope it's the latter. The few times I've drifted off I've seen the crash from my point of view. I can't imagine what it was like inside that car.

"You need to rest Ash. And you need to eat." Kellan tells me from across the room. I shake my head at him. He sighs in frustration. "We're going to need you, you know that. Once these two are healed up, we're going to be taking on the strongest pack in history. You can't afford to be weak, to be tired or starved. Kitten can't afford for you to be weak Ash." He pleads.

My anger bubbles to the surface. I stand up straight, glaring at him. "You think I'm weak!? Do you really think I'm just sitting here and moping around?" I shout at him. "I want to tear everything in this fucking room apart Kellan! I want to punch the walls until they are nothing but a pile of rubble. I want to find the bastards who did this and TEAR THEM LIMB FROM FUCKING LIMB!" I pace the room, trying to calm myself before I attack him. It's not his fault, I know that. But my wolf wants justice.

"Shut the fuck up." Comes a weak voice from behind me. I spin, seeing Remy raise his hand to his head.

"Remy," Kellan whispers in a shocked voice, pushing past me to get to him. I watch as he scrambles around for different instruments. Kellan asks him a series of questions, like his name and if he remembers what happened to him.

When Kellan's done doing his doctor shit, he shoots the drugs into the tube for Remy. He takes a seat across the room, rubbing a hand down his face. Up until now, Kellan's been very formal.

Every bit the doctor. It's now that I see the

exhaustion in him, and the relief. I take my seat again, waiting him out.

"I honestly didn't know if he'd make it," He says to the floor. "There was damage to his frontal lobe. Minor, yes. But still, the brain is too complicated a thing to mess with. A lesser wolf would not have pulled through." He tells me.

He thought Remy wasn't going to make it? What the fuck! He didn't say anything to me about it. His face looked like shit but...not make it? I don't even remember a time when Remy wasn't around. I can't picture one either. My depression lifts a bit now that he's woken up. Remy and Tristan are both going to be fine with time. I always believed it, but now it seems more real. They'll get better, we'll track down Kitten, I'll get to kill the people who did this, and then we'll all be happy and safe again. It sounds like a plan.

"I'm gonna go catch some sleep with Jace," I tell Kellan. He smiles at me and nods.

KITTEN

My insides freeze when I hear the clanking of the chains again. Strange how I now hope for Adam. He's the lesser evil around here. He brings me food, but he doesn't let me eat it unless I let him touch me. So I haven't eaten in what feels like forever. Little does he know that I've been here many times before. Only recently have I been spoiled with regular meals. My heart breaks every time I smell food anyway. It's not Tristan's food. Tristan will never again get to work his magic in the kitchen.

Adam takes a seat on the floor in front of me, crossing his legs and sitting the tray of food on his lap. "You going to be good today?" He asks. I shake my head, pressing myself further into the corner. "You know Kitty that at this point, you may as well be my twin. Any more of my blood and I'm going to call you Sis." He picks up the fork and takes a big bite of ham. My eyes track the juices that have escaped and run down his chin.

He sits so close that I know I can reach out and take the food from him. I know better now though. Every time I refuse to eat or drink, the man who called himself my uncle comes in and whips me with a belt on my back. After he leaves me in agony for a while, Adam shows up and gives me his blood to heal me. I think it was a day ago, I'm unsure of time in this dark basement, that I rushed the door as he was entering. I wasn't aware of the two guards standing outside of the room. Uncle hit me harder than ever then. I had blacked out from the pain alone. Later, I was angry and stole the tray from Adam, curled up in my corner and shoved the food in my mouth. Uncle had come in and shoved his fingers down my throat, making me throw it all up, then proceeded to whip my entire body. It was only the last meal that Adam came to give me his blood.

"I want the food. I don't want you to touch me." I tell him in a raspy voice. He takes another bite of food, licking his lips before he speaks.

"That's not the deal. You eat, I touch. Take it or leave it."

I shake my head, knowing that if I had any tears left, I'd be crying. I know what will happen next. I dread it, but I dread his hands on me even more. Adam grumbles as he stands and crosses to the door.

"It doesn't have to be like this Kitten," He tells me.
Oh yes, it really does.

COMING EARLY 2016

KEEPING MY PACK

BOOK TWO IN THE *MY PACK* SERIES

Made in the USA
San Bernardino, CA
04 November 2016